To perfectly imperfect families

Praise for the novels of Synithia Williams

The Secret to a Southern Wedding

An Amazon Best Romance Book of the Month!

"A pitch-perfect small-town romance focused on forgiveness, second chances, and new beginnings... Readers will eagerly look forward to revisiting this quaint community." —*Publishers Weekly* (starred review)

Foolish Hearts

"Full of drama among the beautiful and powerful, the series would make a fabulous soap opera." —*Philadelphia Inquirer*

"Williams's novel doesn't shy away from family dysfunction, and sometimes there are no easy answers, keeping readers guessing until the end." —*Library Journal*

"Fast-paced and balances drama with steamy scenes to keep you hooked." —*Women of Color Read Too*

Careless Whispers

"Williams' skill as a writer makes you believe in her protagonists' ability to overcome their differences and love deeply."

—*Frolic*, Book of the Week pick

Scandalous Secrets

A *Publishers Weekly* Buzz Book of 2020: Romance Selection!
An Amazon Best Romance Book of the Month!
A *Woman's World* Romance Book Club Selection!

"Fans of second chances, reconnecting friends, friends-to-lovers, and political romance stories will enjoy this book." —*Harlequin Junkie*

Forbidden Promises

"The perfect escape....a deeply felt, engrossing, soapy romance."
—*Entertainment Weekly*

"Fans of Elle Wright and Jamie Pope will be seduced by this charming and passionate family saga." —*Booklist*

"A deliciously soapy second-chance, brother's-best-friend romance. Readers of Alisha Rai's Forbidden Hearts series or Reese Ryan's *Engaging the Enemy* will be tantalized and surprised by the many twists and turns."
—*Library Journal*

Waiting *for* Friday Night

SYNITHIA WILLIAMS

CANARY STREET PRESS

CANARY
STREET
PRESS™

Recycling programs
for this product may
not exist in your area.

ISBN-13: 978-1-335-43054-0

Waiting for Friday Night

Canary Street Press
22 Adelaide St. West, 41st Floor
Toronto, Ontario M5H 4E3, Canada
CanaryStPress.com

Printed in U.S.A.

One

HALLE PARKER CHECKED HER WATCH AND CRINGED.
"I've got to get out of here soon." She looked up at her lunch
companion, cousin, and one of her two best friends, Dr. Imani
Kemp.

Imani's light brown eyes widened, and she pointed to the
half-eaten club sandwich in front of Halle. "You just got your
food. Why are you leaving already? Please don't tell me you're
going back up to that school again. It's summer vacation. If I
can make time to eat lunch, then surely you can."

Halle glanced down at her sandwich then back at Imani. Her
cousin was right. Imani worked with the hospital and was one
of two OB-GYNs in their small town of Peachtree Cove. Imani
was the poster child of busy with all the new patients she'd taken
on plus making rounds at the hospital, but she somehow managed to find the time to meet Halle for lunch once a month.

"You know I wouldn't typically try to get out of here so fast, but I need to go by the school and check a few things before I pick up Shania," Halle said, grabbing a sweet potato fry off her plate and taking a bite.

Imani arched a brow over bright brown eyes. Her dark hair was pulled back in a ponytail, and she wore a red fitted T-shirt with black slacks that fit her slim curves. "Why do you need to go by the school?"

Halle avoided eye contact and shrugged. "I just need to check on some stuff."

"Stuff like what? Just be real. There isn't anything for you to check up on. You just want to find an excuse to go into that building despite school being out for the summer," Imani teased.

"Well, can you blame me?" Halle admitted, not bothering to prove her friend wrong. "School will start in six weeks. I have a lot to get ready for. This is my first year as principal."

The former principal had retired at the end of the last school year, and Halle was quickly chosen to replace her. Even though Halle knew the school and its policies inside and out, she still wanted things to go smoothly her first year.

"Didn't you say you go back two weeks before the kids?" Imani asked. "You'll have plenty of time to prepare. Why don't you take this time to enjoy summer break?"

"I am enjoying summer break. We went on that weekend trip with Tracey last weekend. I'm planning a cousins' weekend with my family in a few weeks, and I've got several activities scheduled when Shania isn't busy with football practice." She held up her hand and lowered a finger with each activity. She quickly dropped her hand when two fingers remained standing.

Imani shook her head, not missing the remaining two fingers at all. "All of that is not the same as taking time to do something for you. When are you going to just sit still and enjoy a day of doing nothing? I swear you never slow down."

"When have I ever sat still?" Halle replied, pursing her lips.

Life was too short to sit still. Time was not promised. She hated when people used the excuse of being "too busy" to make time for the people or things they wanted to do. After losing her parents young, she always remembered that the person she blew off today may not be around tomorrow.

Imani opened her mouth and pointed up, paused, then sighed. "Girl, you're right. You were always on the go. Even in high school."

"Exactly," Halle replied with a vindicated laugh. "I'm team too much. Queen of doing the most. Quit acting surprised."

"That doesn't mean you really shouldn't try to slow down now." Imani leaned in closer. "Didn't you finally ask out Gregory Gaines? Please let me know when you're going to pencil him in."

Halle's heart flipped at the mention of her current crush. Though, at thirty-six, was it still normal to refer to liking a guy as a crush? The word didn't matter; Gregory Gaines was a guy who finally checked all of the boxes she wanted in a partner. The new English teacher at Peachtree Cove High School was perfect. Smart, well-read and articulate. After one conversation with him, she'd tumbled straight into crush mode. After years of focusing on being the best mother she could be to her daughter Shania, she hadn't been excited about dating someone for a long time until she'd met him.

"I asked him to coffee, but we haven't gone out on a *date* date," Halle said. When she'd found the potential man of her dreams, she'd had to tell her best friends. Ever since, they'd been encouraging her crush. They both believed it had been too long since Halle had spent any quality time with a man. Something Halle hadn't really focused on, until Gregory easily quoted Langston Hughes and her sex drive miraculously sputtered to life.

"Halle! If you can schedule coffee and go to this school then you can schedule an actual date. I know we came here so you can see him."

Halle glanced around but thankfully, no one else in the restaurant was listening to them. Still, she put a finger over her mouth. "Will you not announce it to the world? I don't need everyone in Peachtree Cove to know I'm trying to date him before he does. Besides, I really have to get back to the school today. The schedules are changing next year. I've got a few announcements to put together for the students and the families. Not to mention making sure maintenance fixed the leaking A/C unit dripping in the sixth-grade hall. I've got to check all that before picking Shania up from football practice."

Imani cocked her head to the side. "You've got six weeks to tell the parents about a new schedule, and with this modern device called a cellular phone—" Imani tapped her cell on the table "—you can probably call your maintenance people and ask them if the leak is fixed."

Halle shook her head. "Knowing the schedule is changing doesn't take away the nervousness related to the change. I'm making sure my parents and students are up to date on everything about the new schedule, and how it will affect them. That's my way of reducing their anxiety."

"You are not responsible for the anxiety of every person coming to the school," Imani lectured.

"No, but that doesn't mean I should contribute to it by not communicating," Halle countered and popped another fry into her mouth.

Imani just threw up her hands. "I don't know why I bother. I keep thinking that one day you'll realize you don't have to do everything yourself, that letting others help out isn't so bad. But I swear, if you didn't have something to do, then you'd start worrying about having too much free time on your hands."

Halle laughed and shrugged. "You might have a point."

Imani's words didn't hurt Halle's feelings. It wasn't the first time she'd been accused of trying to do too much. What could she say? She enjoyed being involved. She was an active part of the Peachtree Cove community and as the newly appointed middle school principal, she took her job as a community leader seriously. A lot of people depended on her, from the teachers, staff, students and their families. Involvement didn't mean sitting at home twiddling her thumbs hoping everyone understood what was happening.

"You know the school will still be there if you get hit by a bus."

Halle knocked three times on the wooden table to neutralize any bad luck attached to Imani's words. A superstition she'd inherited from her parents and kept going. "Or if I win the lottery and move to Tahiti," she countered. She hated the *hit by a bus* analogy. She much preferred to think of a positive reason to suddenly be gone.

Imani knocked on the table as well. "The result is the same. Peachtree Cove Middle School has been there since two thousand and ten and it'll be there long after you move on. You don't owe the school everything."

"Spoken like a reformed workaholic. Tell me again how you've mastered having it all. A wonderful career, loving relationship and time for yourself," Halle asked with feigned awe. Though, in truth, she was in awe of Imani. She'd managed the transition of moving to Peachtree Cove while also planning her wedding with her fiancé, Cyril Dash. Imani's life had been nothing but work before she'd come home to Peachtree Cove. Now her life was filled with spending time with her mom, her fiancé and her friends all while working.

Imani narrowed her eyes but grinned. "You're trying to be funny."

Halle shrugged innocently. "I'm just saying, Dr. Imani Kemp, please enlighten me. Oh wait, it was you who cut short the last ladies' night, am I right?"

Imani pointed a finger. "I had a patient giving birth. That doesn't count."

"I'm just making my point. Schedule changes at the school are the equivalent of someone giving birth at my job. Kinda. So, our lunch will be shortened today so I can handle it."

Imani sighed. "Point taken. Go on and check things out at the school. But you will set a date with Gregory."

"I will. The next time I see him."

"You said it, I didn't." Imani lifted a hand and waved. "Hey, Gregory, how are things getting settled?"

Halle gulped and spun around, hoping Imani was playing a prank on her. She was not. Gregory maneuvered through the tables as he made his way over to them. He was slightly under six feet tall, thick, with golden brown skin and kind, chocolate-brown eyes. Today he was dressed casually in a short-sleeved white three-button shirt and olive slacks.

"Hello, Dr. Kemp, Halle, good to see you." He spoke in a smooth, cultured voice.

"Gregory…hey!" Her voice squeaked. She cleared her throat and tried again. "How are you doing?" She smoothed her suddenly sweaty palms over her black pants.

"I'm doing well. Just came in to pick up my lunch." He held up a brown takeout bag.

"Oh, too bad you're getting it to go. You could have joined us," Imani said.

Halle blinked and kicked her friend's foot underneath the table. Imani didn't flinch as she smiled sweetly at Gregory.

"Oh, well, I'm not in a rush," he replied and glanced at Halle.

Halle's heart flipped. Did he want to join them? Was he saying he was willing to stay and have lunch with them?

"Unfortunately, Halle has to run," Imani said with exaggerated regret.

Disappointment flashed in Gregory's eyes. "You're leaving?"

A part of her was ready to say forget the new schedule and

water leak, then ask him to sit down. But a quick glance at her watch made her sense of responsibility kick in. "I do have to run. I've got to go by the school before picking Shania up from her first football practice."

He frowned. "Football?"

She nodded. "Yep. She played in middle school and is also trying out for the high school team." She waited for his reply. She understood girls playing football was still a new concept for some people. There were those in her own family who had snide comments about how Shania should be going out for the cheerleading squad instead of being on the field. She really hoped Gregory wasn't one of those people.

His frown cleared up. "Good for her. What position does she play?"

"She's played wide receiver in a recreational flag league and middle school. I think she wants to be the starting wide receiver."

"That's a big position. Especially in high school," Gregory said, not sounding discouraging. If anything, he sounded impressed by Shania's audacity. Further proof he was the man for her.

"Whatever she ends up doing I'll support her."

He nodded. "I hope she makes the team."

If fireworks would have gone off at that moment, she didn't think she could be any happier. Gregory was cute, smart and wanted her daughter to make the team. She'd been right to pick him out as the man to kick-start her dating life again. Maybe he'd turn out to be the perfect partner and father Shania needed.

"I'll be sure to tell her that."

"Did you also play sports?"

Halle cringed before shaking her head. "Not at all. Before Shania I didn't know the difference between a fourth down and a three-point shot."

Gregory laughed. "I'm about the same. I didn't play sports. Too busy with my nose in a book."

"I love a man that reads," she said with a sigh.

Imani made a small squeak of surprise. Halle pressed her lips together. That had come out a lot thirstier than she'd intended. Gregory, bless him, only smiled and rubbed the back of his head.

"Maybe we can meet up and talk about books sometime," he said hesitantly.

Imani kicked her under the table. Halle tried not to flinch, then grinned. No need to ask about progressing beyond coffee to a second date; they'd flowed right into that. She was one step closer to making this perfect man *her* man. "I'd like that."

"How about Friday?" Imani said.

Gregory and Halle broke eye contact and looked at her. "What?" Halle asked.

"Remember, I can't make our plans to have dinner at the new Italian place opening downtown. Maybe Gregory can sit in for me." She looked at Gregory. "You don't mind, do you?"

Halle would be forever grateful for a cousin like Imani. She nodded and played along. "We did just talk about that, didn't we?" She looked at Gregory and prayed she didn't look as eager as she felt for him to say yes.

Gregory hesitated for a second before looking at Halle and nodding. "I don't mind if you don't."

"I don't. Friday night sound good?"

"It does. I'll see you Friday." A small smile lifted the corners of Gregory's mouth. If she weren't being too confident, she'd be willing to say it was a satisfied smile.

She swallowed and grinned. "Friday."

"I'm looking forward to it. See you then."

Halle watched him walk out before turning back to her friend. "Did that just happen?"

Imani nodded then patted her own shoulder. "It did. Thanks to me."

"I could see myself marrying him."

Imani closed her eyes and shook her head. "Hold up before you start buying a dress and booking Tracey's bed-and-breakfast for the venue. Don't get ahead of yourself. You're going to dinner. It's only a second date."

"I know, I know, but I'm just saying. I haven't thought about getting serious with anyone in a long time. Gregory is sophisticated, smart and obviously open-minded. He's not only my dream man, but I could also imagine him as a good stepdad for Shania."

Halle had spent so much of her adult life taking care of Shania and being the best mom she could be that she hadn't focused on long-term relationships. Something she didn't regret at all. Although she'd dated, no one had ever made her think about inviting him into her life long enough to be a true part of her and Shania's life. Maybe it was watching Imani find her happily ever after, or maybe it was the realization that Shania would be graduating in four short years and she'd be left alone, but Halle was ready to fill the long empty spot she'd ignored for a long-term romantic partner.

"Stepdad? Weren't you the main one who said you could handle raising her all by yourself?"

Halle swiped away the familiar phrase with a flick of her wrist. "I did say that, and it's true. Shania keeps asking about her biological father. Maybe if I get serious about someone and he eventually turns into a stepdad, then she'll stop asking me about her biological father."

Imani narrowed her eyes and leaned in. "About her biological…"

Halle held up a finger. "Not today. Maybe one day, but not today. Today I'm going to be excited about dinner with Gregory." She glanced at her watch. "Crap, I really have to go. Are you leaving, too?" She pulled out some cash.

Imani looked like she wanted to push the topic of Shania's dad, but instead she waved her hand. "Nope, I'm going to sit here and enjoy my food in peace, and put away your money. You paid last time. I've got today."

Not one to argue when her friend offered to cover lunch, Halle put her money back. "Cool, but I've got next. Call me later? Y'all have to get me ready for my date with Gregory."

Imani nodded. "You know it. Tell Shania I said good luck."

"I will." Halle got up and hurried out of the restaurant. She was on cloud nine. She was one step closer to getting back out there in the dating scene. Maybe if this worked out Shania and everyone else would finally stop pestering Halle for the truth about Shania's biological father. Then she'd never have to admit she had no idea who he was.

Two

QUINTON EVANS BLEW HIS WHISTLE AND POINTED
to the practice equipment spread around the football field. The
fifty-plus kids on the field stopped chatting and horsing around
and looked his way. "Be sure to get this equipment put up before you leave for the day. And be careful. If we don't respect
our equipment, then no one else will."

His request was met with several nods, thumbs-up and "Got
it, Coach" before they immediately began gathering the cones
and practice balls. Quinton's lips twitched. If he was a grinning
man, that quick response might have resulted in a big one. The
fast movement by the players wouldn't have happened when he
first started coaching football at Peachtree Cove High School
four years ago. Back then, he'd inherited a team that was un-
disciplined and disorganized. Turning them to the organized,
focused team in front of him today had taken patience and

determination. The team still wasn't perfect, but they were a much better functioning group than before.

Zachariah Grooms, the defense coach, walked over to Quinton. The tall white guy was two years older than Quinton's thirty-six years and had been the defensive coordinator at Peachtree Cove High for ten years.

Zachariah stood next to Quinton, crossed his arms and watched the kids on the field. "What are you thinking?"

Quinton adjusted his Peachtree High baseball cap and squinted despite the aviator shades he wore to block the bright afternoon sun as he observed his team. "We've got some good players coming up from middle school. That should help the JV team. But it's still several weeks before the season starts. We'll see how they all shake out as we run drills."

Zachariah nodded. "What do you think of Octavius? He was wide receiver at the middle school over in Atlanta before moving to Peachtree Cove."

Quinton's eyes scanned the crowd until they landed on the young boy. Like other high school coaches, he paid attention to the kids making waves in middle school sports. He'd heard about Octavius and had been pleased when he'd learned the boy had moved to Peachtree Cove. But Quinton tried to avoid playing favorites. He'd been overlooked enough in high school and understood how demoralizing it was to be ignored because you didn't have enough "star power." He'd earned every starting position he had from school sports to the eight years he'd played professionally and expected the kids he coached to work just as hard to earn a position on his team.

"He'll have to try for the starting position like everyone else," Quinton said.

Zachariah laughed and shook his head. "You can play cool with me all you want, but I know you're excited to have him on our JV team. You know, when the district brought you in

I thought it was just because your time in the pros would help motivate kids to play."

"And now?" Quinton asked, raising a brow.

Though he already knew the answer. Winning Zachariah's respect had taken nearly as long as it had taken him to turn the team atmosphere around. Zachariah had wanted the head coach position and had made sure Quinton was aware he didn't appreciate being overlooked for some fancy former professional player. He'd proven his coaching abilities to Zachariah while also respecting the man's knowledge of the team's history.

"And now I'm glad to know I was right," Zachariah said, laughing. "Kids are ready to move here to play for a guy who was a professional. Not only that, you're winning games. If we keep this up, we'll get more kids like Octavius moving here."

Quinton shook his head. "I came here because I wanted to show these kids they can make it despite playing for a small rural school. Not just to draw star players."

After eight years of playing and working his way to being a starting receiver, Quinton made the decision to retire from playing professionally. Though he didn't have any championship rings, he'd made it to the Pro Bowl twice, and had been named as one of the best wide receivers in the league. More than what most people had expected of him when he'd been pushed aside and underestimated back in high school. When he turned thirty-two and his contract was up for renewal, he'd decided he had nothing else to prove. He'd walked away from playing, and his coaching career had begun.

"Giving back is cool and all, but I'm good with having you draw the top players," Zachariah said. "In another year or so, we'll be able to beat Peach Ridge."

Quinton grunted. "I don't give a damn about Peach Ridge. I care about winning our division."

Zachariah grinned and shook his head. "You can care about

our division, but the people in this town only care about our rival school."

"They aren't a real rival," Quinton said, irritated.

Peach Ridge High wasn't in their state much less the division. The decades-old rivalry between Peachtree Cove, Georgia, and Peach Ridge, South Carolina, wasn't something he understood or cared about. But the rivalry about which town produces the best peaches had spilled into almost everything. Including having a rivalry match between the two high school football teams that started twenty years ago and continued to this day. Quinton could win all the division games he liked, but until their high school beat Peach Ridge High, he was still considered a probationary coach.

"Real rival or not, now that we beat out Peach Ridge as a finalist for Best Small Town, everyone wants to cap it off with beating Peach Ridge High in football this year as well."

Quinton waved a hand. "Whatever, man. Let's wrap this up and get out of here. I see parents arriving to pick up their kids. I'm sure some of them want to talk about my plans for this year."

Zachariah clapped Quinton's shoulders. "Better you than me."

Quinton cocked his head to the side and pointed at Zachariah. "I thought you wanted to be head coach?"

Zachariah shook his head. "Nah, man, that's all you." He turned to the players and clapped his hands. "Alright, let's wrap this up."

Quinton chuckled to himself as Zachariah hurried away to help the rest of the team. He didn't blame him. Some parents made this job harder than it needed to be. Zachariah didn't want to be in the hot seat, but Quinton knew he and the rest of the coaches would back him up if any parent got out of line.

Quinton joined him, the rest of the coaching staff and kids getting the equipment put up and everyone ready to leave for the day. Even though he was tired after running a few laps with his team, the familiar thrill of excitement from the approach of a new football season kept his steps light. He *loved* the start of football season. He lived for this. The camaraderie and competition that seemed only to come when he was standing on a football field. His days of playing had ended, but this love of the sport never would. Now he got to lay the foundation for the next generation of potential professional players. Though he didn't like to get ahead of himself, he saw the same drive he'd had to prove himself in some of the players on his team. Those kids might one day walk in his footsteps.

There were a few parents waiting to talk to him. Thankfully, most were just wishing him well and asking how they could help. He directed the helpful ones to the booster club president, Cheryl Green, and accepted the well wishes of the others. After that, he made sure the gate to the field was locked and the locker rooms were clear before going to his Range Rover parked in the head coach's spot. He was ready to shower, rest and then meet up with his friend Brian later at their mutual friend Cyril's bar, A Couple of Beers.

"Excuse me, Coach Quinton, do you have a moment?" a woman's voice called from behind.

Quinton cursed underneath his breath. He'd thought he'd spoken to all the parents who'd waited around for him. Sliding his shades farther up the bridge of his nose, he pushed back any irritation at being delayed. He turned and was surprised to find Halle Parker power walking in his direction. He glanced over her shoulder and spotted her daughter, Shania, standing next to their car with a hand over her face.

Halle was the middle school principal and involved in almost every event that happened in Peachtree Cove. She was smart, enthusiastic about giving back, and could be considered overbearing or dedicated depending on which side of an issue you stood. Her dedication to making Peachtree Cove better and her daughter being the only girl on his team weren't the only reasons he'd noticed her. Halle was the kind of woman who made a man stop talking in the middle of a sentence to focus on her. She was little over average height, cocoa-brown skin with full breasts, hips and thighs that made his stomach drop. Quinton was a sucker for a full-figured woman.

"Ms. Parker? Is everything alright?" he asked hesitantly. Though he noticed Halle whenever she was in his vicinity, he rarely interacted with her. Outside of school district-wide trainings, they didn't hang with the same crowd. Her daughter played, but from what he knew, Halle hadn't been overly involved in the team when Shania played in middle school. She'd come to the initial parents' meeting before summer conditioning and practice began, but that was it. She wasn't a hovering football parent.

Halle stopped a few feet in front of him. She wore a black blazer over a white button-up blouse that revealed just enough of a V of brown skin above her cleavage to make his eyes want to linger, and fitted pants that weren't at all indecent but hugged her ass just enough to elicit thoughts of what it would be like to cup said ass. The idea of wearing a suit in this summer heat made him hot, but she somehow managed to look cool and sophisticated. Or maybe that was just Halle. Always in control and put together.

"Yes, I want to talk to you about Shania." Dark brown eyes stared directly at his, even though she would only see herself reflected in his shades.

He glanced over her shoulder again at Shania, then back at Halle. He relaxed a little but kept his guard up. Parents approached him for a variety of reasons. Some just wanted to know how they could help the team. Others approached to tell him why their kid was the best football player since Deion Sanders. Then there were those who approached to point out all the things he was doing wrong before making suggestions on what he should do instead. He could only imagine Halle approaching him for the first reason over the other two. Unless there was a problem.

"Is there something wrong?"

Halle held up a hand, palm out, and gave a quick shake of her head. "No problems. In fact, Shania is enjoying summer practice."

The tension in his shoulders eased a little more. Girls playing football in middle and high school wasn't as rare as it had been when he'd played in school, but it was still rare enough that they got challenged for daring to play with boys. Many of the freshman boys had played with Shania in middle school, but there weren't any other girls on the team. If any of the players had given her a hard time, he would deal with it personally. Bullying, of any kind, was a hard-line no for him and not just because of his own experiences being bullied when he was younger.

"That's good to hear."

"Don't worry. If there were any problems, she wouldn't hesitate to tell you. I made sure to raise Shania to speak up for herself."

The corner of his mouth twitched. He didn't doubt that any child of Halle Parker's would be afraid to speak up. In his few years in Peachtree Cove, he had yet to see Halle back down from anything. She was the one most likely to lead the charge.

"I've told all the players that they can come to me with any issues. I don't tolerate bad grades, bad attitudes, or bad decisions. If you're going to play for me, you're going to represent me and this team both on and off the field."

She blinked, and appreciation filled her eyes before she nodded. "I didn't know that about you. I thought most coaches only cared about winning."

The wind blew her curly hair into her face, and she pushed it aside. He'd noticed she typically wore her hair twisted up in a lot of fancy hairstyles. He liked it better like this, wild and curly.

His shoulders stiffened. Why was he thinking about her hair? She'd low-key insulted him. He tried not to take offense at her words. The previous coach had put up with almost any type of behavior as long as the team won. Unfortunately, they hadn't won much of anything and they hadn't cared about much either.

"Not all coaches are the same."

She nodded. "I'll remember that. My apologies if I offended you." Full lips lifted in a smile that made his stomach clench and almost got him to smile back.

"You didn't. If Shania is all good, then what can I help you with?" He took them back to the point. He could look at Halle's pretty face all day, but he was also ready to get in his car, get showered and get on with his day.

Halle crossed her arms and gave him a determined look. "It's about the position Shania will play."

"I haven't decided who will play what just yet," he jumped in before she could continue. He gave this same speech at the start of each season. "The first few weeks are conditioning, just to get them used to working out and introducing them to a few plays. When we get into running drills and plays, everyone will have a chance to try out for any position they like and then me and the coaching staff will decide who is best for what spot."

He kept his voice pleasant but firm. He liked and respected Halle as a teacher and was definitely attracted to her but wouldn't reveal his thoughts on team positions until he'd had a chance to evaluate everyone. He would give Shania a fair chance just as he would any other player, but he couldn't run the risk of favoritism toward Shania if he didn't give Halle the same story he gave every other parent.

"That's all well and good, but I want Shania to be wide receiver."

"Did you not hear what I just said about my process?"

"I did, and I'm telling you she wants to play wide receiver. And she wants to start." Halle lifted her chin. Her voice had gone from casual into a clipped and professional tone. He'd heard that before. Her Principal Parker voice.

"She will get a chance just like everyone else." He matched her Principal Knows Best tone with his own *this-isn't-up-for-debate* coach's tone.

Once again, her hand flew up in a stop position, cutting him off before he could say more. "I get it. You have to be fair. But I am going to do whatever I can to help Shania. If that means lessons or some sort of camp, let me know. You're a coach, so coach her. I'm sure we can work together to come up with a plan to make this happen."

Quinton blinked. Surprised and irritated that she spoke to him as if he didn't know what the job of coach meant. "I'm going to coach Shania just like I'd coach anyone else. I don't give preferential treatment."

"I'm not asking for preferential treatment. I'm saying you know my daughter's goals, so I expect you, as her coach, to help her meet her goals. That is your job, right?"

Quinton shifted his stance and crossed his arms. "My job is to do what's best for the team. All players, not just one or two."

"I understand. As a principal, I care about the well-being of all my students. My job is to help them. When there are students who come to me with a specific goal in mind, then it's also my job to help that student achieve that goal. I'm not asking you to automatically make her starting wide receiver. I am asking that you take her dream seriously and help her. If she needs to work on something, I want to know. If there is a way she can improve, tell me. Is that asking you to do anything extra or not in your job description?" She raised a brow and her chin with the question.

Quinton clenched his teeth. She wasn't asking for anything more. If a kid came to him and asked how to get better, he'd work with them. Halle's lecture put him on the defensive. And made him aware of just how sexy she looked when her eyes sparked with determination and challenge.

"Ms. Parker, I won't tell you how to be a principal if you don't tell me how to coach football. I've played football since I was four in the pee-wee leagues. I know how to instruct and help players improve. Your *advice* is heard, but not needed. Now, if you don't have anything else to say, I've got other places to be."

Her eyes narrowed slightly before she asked, "Are you like this because she's a girl?"

Quinton studied her for several long seconds before slowly pulling off his shades. He squinted at Halle and replied in a low, measured tone that barely hid the irritation crawling over him at her accusation. "I'm going to treat Shania like any other player on this team. If she wants to be a receiver, then she has to show me that she can run plays and catch the ball. Don't ever question my integrity like that again."

Halle unflinchingly returned his stare before the corner of her lip lifted in a smug smirk. "I'm glad to see that I haven't completely misjudged you. I hope that you'll take my words to heart. Have a great afternoon, Coach Evans."

She turned and strode away. Quinton frowned. What the hell had just happened? Had she been testing him?

"It's Coach Q," he shot back with the title the kids and everyone else used, thrown off by how quickly she'd switched and ended the conversation.

Halle threw up a hand but didn't turn around. She walked toward her car, curvy hips swaying with her confident steps. He felt like he'd just been released from a lecture in the principal's office, and unlike when he'd been called there as a kid, he wanted to go back and have another round. Grunting and scowling, he shoved his shades back on his face and got into his SUV.

Three

"WHAT WERE YOU TALKING TO COACH Q ABOUT?" Shania asked as soon as they got in the car.

Halle glanced over at her daughter. Shania was the complete opposite of her. Shania was going to be tall where Halle was lucky to be considered average height at five foot six. Sports had honed her daughter's athletic build whereas Halle had accepted no amount of CrossFit or cardio would do much to shrink her curvy figure. They both were passionate and cared deeply, but Shania was more likely to get into an argument defending a call in some game versus Halle who was willing to go to bat over a social injustice. If Halle hadn't delivered the eight-pound baby herself, she'd swear the hospital had mixed something up. But despite their different personalities, Halle loved her more than anything.

"I was talking to him about how things were going with practice," Halle said, pulling the car out of the parking lot. She turned up the air-conditioning and cracked the windows.

Shania's eyes narrowed and she stared back at Halle. "What about practice? I can tell you about practice."

"Nothing more than usual. How are things going? How did you do?"

Shania sighed and fell back in her seat. "You told him to make me starting wide receiver, didn't you?"

"Why would you say that?" Halle tried to sound innocent but failed. Shania knew her mother too well.

"I knew I shouldn't have told you. You can't just make me a starter."

"Don't you want to be a starter?"

"I do, but I've got to earn it. Coach Q says there are no favorites on his team. Only those who try hard."

"Do you believe that?" Halle asked.

He'd looked ready to explode when she'd asked him if he'd treat Shania any differently because she was a girl. She could feel the outrage radiating off him in waves. In that moment when he'd slid off those shades and hit her with the full extent of his intense, dark gaze, she understood what the women around town saw in Quinton Evans. The man exuded raw, masculine energy. If she were into brawn over brains, her heart might have fluttered. Her question had insulted him, but she didn't feel guilty for it. Her daughter was an anomaly on the team, and she needed to make sure her coach really supported her.

Shania sighed. "I do believe him, but there's this kid who just moved to our school. Octavius something or other. He's going to be starting wide receiver."

"How do you know that?"

"Because he was the starter at his last school. He's some kind of star and really good. Coach Quinton watched him all practice."

"That's favoritism," Halle said, lifting a finger. And he'd tried to be so smug with her with his *I evaluate all players* speech. The man's preference was already noticeable to the team.

"It's football," Shania countered.

"Well, you can't give up before you even get to the finish line. Coach Evans's one job is to coach that football team. I asked him to make sure he coaches you. Not just push you to the side."

"He teaches math," Shania said.

Halle frowned, confused by the comment. "Who teaches math?"

Shania raised her brows. "Coach Q. He teaches math."

"What does that have to do with anything?"

Shania chuckled and gave Halle that *my-silly-mom* look that let Halle know she was proving to be out of touch. "You said his one job was to coach, but he also has to teach math."

Halle considered. "I thought coaches always taught PE or something." At least in her years of working as a teacher the coaches at the middle school stuck to physical education or maybe social studies. She'd assumed the same thing took place with Coach Evans.

"They can teach other things. He teaches algebra and maybe an honors math class. I don't know for sure but that's what I've heard."

"Hmm," Halle said again.

She felt a little guilty for assuming he didn't teach a core class. But to her credit, she didn't spend a lot of time considering Quinton Evans. Yes, he was handsome. Tall, dark skin, with broad, muscled shoulders, piercing dark eyes and a chiseled chin his beard only enhanced. He'd gotten a lot of attention from the single female population of Peachtree Cove when he'd first moved to town. At that time, the rumor mill confirmed he was dating some model or actress that he'd been with during his time as a professional player. That had immediately put him off Halle's radar. She didn't want to say she was prejudiced against athletes, but she could say her ideal type wasn't someone who spent more time focusing on a sport than what she considered to be more serious matters affecting the world.

"He makes me think about my dad."

Halle slammed on the brakes at the stop sign. Her hands

tightened on the steering wheel and her heart jumped to her throat. She took a deep breath. Overreacting whenever Shania brought up her father only made her daughter dig deeper.

"Why in the world would *he* make you think about your dad?" Halle asked, trying to keep her voice even.

Shania watched Halle like a hawk. Halle realized too late she'd been set up. Shania understood Halle didn't like talking about her father. Lately, she'd taken to bringing up the topic randomly and throwing Halle off because she wasn't prepared. Like now, as they drove home from football practice.

"I was thinking he's someone like Coach Q, right?"

"What! No, he is not someone like your football coach," Halle said confidently.

"Think about it. He's into sports, I'm into sports. Coach Q is tall, I'm going to be tall. One kid even said we look alike. Be honest, my dad looked like him."

Halle visualized Quinton and then Shania and immediately pushed the thought aside. She refused to make any comparisons between Quinton Evans and her daughter's father. She'd made sure that Shania's father wasn't anyone like him.

Halle waved off her daughter's words. "Shania, stop asking me about your dad. You don't need to worry about him. And don't ever put your football coach and your potential dad in the same sentence. It takes a lot less than that to get gossip started in this town."

Shania crossed her arms and huffed. "Why can't I worry about my dad? It makes sense that I need to know who he is."

"Your dad isn't your dad in the traditional sense. Think of him as a donor and move on."

Shania scoffed. "Number one, that's nasty! Number two, that's not helping. Why won't you just tell me about him? I don't understand why this is a secret."

Halle didn't have the heart to tell Shania that her description was the closest Halle had ever come to the truth about her father. She couldn't tell Shania that she didn't know who her dad was because he *had* been a donor. A nameless, faceless man whose contribution to a private sperm bank had resulted in the greatest blessing of Halle's life.

"This isn't a secret," Halle said, focusing on the road instead of glancing over to meet Shania's gaze. "He just...isn't involved. I wouldn't know how to reach him if I tried."

Shania leaned over and peered at Halle. "Have you tried?"

She hadn't. Exchanging contact information hadn't been a part of the deal. Just the description of the type of donor she'd been interested in. A Black man, who was healthy and excelled in academics. Someone like Gregory. Not like Quinton.

"Shania, I get it—"

"No, you don't. You knew your dad. You had a family. I don't. You don't know how I feel." Shania didn't yell. Instead, she spoke quietly, in a small, disappointed voice. Yelling might have made it easier for Halle to get defensive. Instead, guilt fisted her heart.

The conversation had gone in a direction Halle didn't want it to go. "You're right, I don't. But trust me when I say this person isn't who you want in your life and he doesn't want to be in ours. I want you to have a father, too."

"What does that mean?"

"It means that I want to get married one day. Maybe even have another kid." She glanced from the road to Shania. Her daughter's eyes were wide, and her mouth had fallen open.

"Are you serious? I didn't know you wanted another kid."

Halle shrugged. "I'm not against it if the opportunity comes." She hadn't thought about kids much while she'd focused on raising Shania and progressing in her career. Now the fantasies of being in a relationship and settling down with the right guy had Halle thinking about having another child. She wasn't too old to start over.

"But when will the opportunity come? You don't date."

"I do date."

"You're not dating now."

"You don't know that." Halle hadn't told Shania about the coffee meetup with Gregory. Only because she wasn't sure if it would go anywhere.

She didn't date often after her last serious relationship ended when Shania was still in fifth grade. After they'd broken up Shania had asked about the guy constantly for weeks afterward. Although she hadn't made it a habit to introduce dates to Shania, she had thought that relationship might go somewhere. When she saw how hard the breakup had also been on Shania, Halle vowed to stop dating until Shania was old enough to understand that Halle going on a date didn't mean the guy would stick around.

Shania's eyes lit up. "You like someone?"

A vision of Gregory popped into Halle's mind. That and the promise for dinner with him on Friday. The corners of her lips lifted. She hadn't been excited about the possibility of dating in a long time.

"I do."

Shania gasped and placed a hand over her mouth. "Oh my God, who got you smiling like that? Do Aunt Tracey and Imani know? Are they hooking you up?"

Halle wiped the smile off her face. "How about you focus on football and let me focus on my dating life."

"You do have a crush. That's so cute! I can't wait to meet him."

Halle had to get through dinner first. She didn't want to get Shania's hopes up too soon. There were still so many things to settle on. First she'd get through her dinner with Gregory, and then, hopefully, another date. And then another.

"Trust me, when you meet him, you'll be happy," Halle said grinning. And she'll never have to worry about her daughter daydreaming about the possibility of Coach Quinton Evans being her dad ever again.

Four

"AND THEN SHE ACCUSED ME OF TREATING SHANIA differently because she's a girl." Quinton finished his story about his conversation with Halle to his friends.

Cyril, who stood behind the bar, stopped wiping down the smooth surface. He straightened and pushed back the brown fedora covering his bald head and rubbed his beard. Of similar height, with light brown skin and a love of graphic T-shirts, Cyril was an extension of the laid-back atmosphere of his bar.

His other friend, Brian, sat next to Quinton on the opposite side of the bar. He slowly lowered the glass he'd taken a sip from, pursed his lips and stared back at Quinton through narrowed dark eyes. The lights in the bar reflected off his friend's mahogany skin and the waves in the low fade of his stylish haircut.

Quinton looked from one to the other. The crowd was light for a Monday night, but steady enough for Cyril to have to walk away occasionally to fill an order while Quinton vented his frustration. He still couldn't believe she'd accused him of discriminating against Shania. In his career both on the field and as a coach, he'd never automatically made assumptions about a person's abilities. He may not be a perfect man, but he wasn't one who wouldn't give Shania a chance just because of her gender. He'd seen her play football. She was a decent receiver.

"Then what did you say?" Cyril asked. Thankfully sounding just as surprised by Halle's words as Quinton had been. He hadn't believed his friends would doubt him, but he felt vindicated that they hadn't made the same assumption.

"I was stunned at first, then I told her that Shania would get the same treatment as any other player. As long as she can run plays then she can be on the team. I told her to never question my integrity again."

Brian nodded. "Okay, then what did she say?"

"She just said *I'm glad you understand me* or some mess like that then walked off." Quinton took a quick sip of his beer. He let out a breath and shook his head. "She had me messed up."

Brian tapped his hand on the counter. "Wait, what? She just walked away. I swear, I'll never understand a woman's brain."

Cyril chuckled and went back to casually wiping the bar's surface. "I mean…the question may have pissed you off, but it shouldn't have surprised you too much. If Shania was my daughter playing football, I would have asked the coach the same thing."

"Even if it was me?" Quinton asked.

Cyril shrugged. "Look, I know you're not one of those *women need to know their place* kind of guys, but if it was my daughter in a sport dominated by young, hormone-fueled teenage boys, I'd be worried. I'd want to make sure the coach wasn't going to let her get hurt."

"I wouldn't let them do anything like that to her. If anything, I'm going to make sure no one treats her like she doesn't belong. Shania loves football. Hell, from what the middle school coach told me, she knew the plays better than some of the guys on the team."

"You know that, and I know that's all you care about in a ball player. But Halle doesn't know you like that," Cyril said. "She's just protecting her daughter."

"If that was her only concern, then I wouldn't be so upset. My problem is what if she tries to use that as an excuse if I don't make Shania a starting receiver? I can't promise her that." He scowled and took another sip of his beer.

"Look, I've known Halle since we were kids," Brian said. "She was always like that. She put her mind on something and fought like hell to get it. She was always raising money for some cause or getting in trouble because she'd skip school to go to some rally. If she thinks her daughter is going to be treated unfairly, then be ready for her to fight."

Unlike Cyril and Quinton, Brian had grown up in Peachtree Cove. Cyril had grown up in Baltimore and Quinton had grown up in a small town on the outskirts of the Atlanta area. They'd both moved to Peachtree Cove around the same time. Quinton had originally connected with Brian through an intramural football league in town and they'd recently become friends with Cyril. During his years of playing professionally, Quinton was used to only having friends that were connected to him through playing. When he'd retired and chosen to coach in a small town, some of those relationships had fallen off. He liked having Brian and Cyril in this new chapter of his life.

"I'm not trying to fight with Halle Parker," Quinton said. "There are a lot of things I'd like to do with her but fighting ain't one of them."

Cyril and Brian exchanged looks before Brian grinned and leaned in. "What do you want to do with her?"

Quinton shook his head. He wasn't getting caught up in that trap. They knew he thought Halle was attractive. He'd mentioned it before, but he wasn't about to let them sidetrack the conversation with thoughts of something that wasn't going to happen.

"All I want to do with her is find a way to get through the football season without any trouble."

Cyril grinned and gave Quinton a sly look. "I don't think that's what you meant."

He did mean it, but that didn't mean there weren't other things that he wanted to do with Halle. There were a lot of things he'd rather do with Halle. He'd love to pull her curves against his body. Taste her lush lips. Palm her firm breasts and watch the fire flash in her eyes from passion versus the need to challenge him. The old him would have gone after her just to see if he could change the spark in her eye. He'd give his second Pro Bowl ring to take his time and prove to Halle just how good things could be between them. Had even considered pursuing her once. That was until he'd once overheard her give an offhand comment about not being into jocks. He was out of the business of trying to prove himself to anyone.

"Regardless of what you *think* I meant," he said, "that's what I'm saying right now."

"You can be real with us," Brian said. "If you like her, you like her." Spoken like the friend who always had a new woman on his arm.

"If I like her then that doesn't mean anything. I can't mess around with the parent of one of my players. I'm already trying to convince everyone I don't play favorites. I've got kids transferring to Peachtree Cove to play for me. If I start messing around with one of their mommas..." Quinton shook his head. "You think there's gossip in this town now? Wait until that happens."

"Gossip in this town will start up either way," Brian said with a grin. "You might as well give the people something worth gossiping about."

"Spoken like someone that doesn't give a fuck," Cyril said with a laugh.

Brian shrugged. "I don't. Half this town is full of hypocrites. If they're going to talk about me, I might as well be doing half of the crazy stuff they're accusing me of doing."

"I'd rather be off their radar," Cyril said. A patron across the bar got his attention and he walked away.

"And I'd rather not get entangled with a player's mom," Quinton said. "If things don't work out, then that makes it harder to deal with the player. No matter how much I might be interested in…showing Halle what I'm all about, I think it's best to keep well enough alone."

"Show Halle all that you're about?" Brian said with a laugh. "Is that your way of being cute? Just say it, man. We're all adults. You want to fu—"

"Nah, man," he cut off his friend. "Besides, she's too uptight. Sleeping with her probably wouldn't be any fun anyway."

A sound of surprise came from behind before a woman's voice said, "Oh really?"

Quinton froze as Halle's voice fell on him like a ton of bricks.

Halle wished she would have had her phone out so she could capture the picture of shock on Quinton's face. She didn't typically come out on a Monday night, but Tracey had texted her and Imani, saying she needed to talk and that her bed-and-breakfast wasn't the place. Halle and Imani had immediately gone into friend mode and shuffled their evening so they could get with Tracey. Thankfully, Halle's cousin Kayla was okay with Shania coming over. Kayla's daughters Maya and Michelle were close in age with Shania and the three were almost inseparable.

She hadn't expected to find Quinton at A Couple of Beers and she sure hadn't expected to find him sitting around the bar talking to his friend Brian about all the *things he wanted to show her.* As if he'd ever get the chance.

"Hey, Halle, what are you doing here?" Quinton said, not sounding the least bit embarrassed to have been caught talking about wanting to sleep with her. Why she was surprised, she didn't know. As a former professional player, he probably believed half the women he met wanted to sleep with him.

"I'm allowed to be here," she said, crossing her arms. "Now, tell me again what exactly you would like to show me?"

Quinton held up a hand. "It wasn't like that."

"Then what was it like?" she asked, cocking her head to the side.

"I was just telling them that even *if* I were interested, which I'm not, I wouldn't show you anything because you're the parent of a player."

"You wouldn't have to worry about being interested, because even if you were it never would happen."

He raised a brow. "Oh really?" His voice dipped to a low tenor and his gaze sharpened before it traveled over her face.

Prickles of heat danced across Halle's cheeks. She sucked in a breath and narrowed her eyes. She fought not to shift as the awareness in his gaze tapped on something long dormant inside her. "Really. Nothing would ever happen between us."

He let out a breath before the corners of his lips twitched in the barest hint of a smile. "Okay."

The tone of his voice, as if he agreed with her, went against the challenge in his eyes. Was he calling her bluff? The man was handsome, and yes, she could see the sex appeal when he looked at her like that, but she wouldn't give him the satisfaction.

"I'm serious," she said. "I wouldn't give you the time of day."

He lifted a shoulder in a nonchalant shrug. "Whatever you say. That's cool."

Her eyes narrowed. Did he think she was joking? "You're not my type."

"And you're not mine."

She uncrossed her arms and put her hands on her hips. "What's that supposed to mean?"

"It means the same thing as what you said," he replied easily. "You aren't my type and I'm not yours. So, neither one of us will be showing the other anything."

Halle narrowed her eyes at him. "I'm glad we're on the same page."

"Yes, we are. The exact same page." He nodded his head as if the words were official.

"Hey, Halle!" Imani's voice came through the crowd.

Halle glanced over her shoulder at her friend. Imani and Tracey had both arrived and were heading their way. Imani went straight to the end of the bar, where her fiancé, Cyril, had finished helping a patron. She leaned over and kissed him. Tracey stood next to Halle. Her body stiff, her arms crossed over her chest and her lips pressed together.

Brian frowned at Tracey. "Why are you scowling?"

Tracey narrowed her eyes and flipped her long, knotless box braids over her shoulder. She wore a yellow polo shirt with her bed-and-breakfast's name, Fresh Place Inn, on the breast and dark jeans hugged her curvy hips. "There you go, minding my business again," she said pursing her lips.

Brian shook his head and held up a hand. "You know what? Never mind. What's up, Imani?"

Imani smiled at Brian. "Hey, Brian, Coach."

Quinton nodded before giving Halle a quick glance and turning back to face the bar. Halle had the urge to tap his shoulder and finish their conversation, but for what? His saying she wasn't his type shouldn't bother her anyway. He wasn't her type either. But the words burrowed in her head like a worm. She wasn't conceited by any means, but she also had enough self-esteem to know there was nothing wrong with her. He'd be lucky to consider her his type.

"I didn't know you all were coming tonight," Cyril said, joining Imani back on their end.

"It was a last-minute thing," Imani replied. "We're going to the table over in the corner. Will you bring something over?"

"You know I will." Cyril smiled at her.

Pushing aside the need to say one more thing to Quinton, Halle followed her friends to the table Imani mentioned. After they were settled, Imani eyed Halle.

"What's going on with you and Coach Q?"

Halle scoffed and shifted in the seat. "Not a damn thing. Why?"

"Because I could have sworn I saw sparks flying between you two," Imani said.

Tracey nodded; some of the stiffness had left her posture as she eyed Imani curiously. "I mean, she's not lying."

"Please. I was just making sure he understood that he'll never get a chance with me. I only need him to help make Shania a starter."

"Why would you worry about him thinking he has a chance?" Tracey asked.

She held up a hand, palm out toward her friend. "I'm not worried. I just want him to understand."

Imani eyed her curiously. "That's all?"

"What else would it be? You know I'm only interested in Gregory."

"Before you put all your hopes in Gregory, you can consider other options."

Halle firmly shook her head. "Not that option. He's got too many strikes against him. One being he's Shania's coach. I've seen too much messiness in school when a teacher and a student's parent get involved. No way."

Halle glanced at Tracey. She'd pulled out her cell phone and was frowning at the screen.

"What's wrong?" she asked.

Tracey put her phone back on the table facedown. "Bernard is acting weird."

Bernard and Tracey had been married for years. She'd known Bernard in high school. He'd been quiet, smart and the complete opposite of Tracey, who was always loud, brash and ready to defend herself against anyone who dared insult her or her family. When the two got together after Bernard moved home after college, Halle had been surprised but happy for her friend. They'd always seemed happy, if not still the odd couple with Bernard's quiet reserve and Tracey's take-life-by-the-horns attitude.

"Weird how?" she asked.

"I think he wants a divorce." Tracey spoke the words bluntly with no hint of emotion. Yet, her fingers toyed with the end of one of her braids. Halle's heart rate picked up. When Tracey didn't show emotion that usually meant she was swimming in them.

"Why would you say that?" Imani asked.

Tracey lifted a shoulder. "He's been talking a lot about how we got married young. That neither of us really got the chance to go out and explore. And that we've wasted years." Tracey spoke quickly, as if the words weren't that big of a deal.

Which made Halle's concern grow. Tracey was good at playing off things that bothered her, but after years of friendship Halle saw through it. She glanced at Imani and the worry in her friend's eyes meant Imani felt the same.

"He really said all that?" Halle asked, trying, and failing, to picture sweet and solemn Bernard saying he wanted to go out and explore.

Tracey nodded. "He did. That, and today he said I was boring." Her eyes flashed and she slapped her chest. "Me? Boring?"

Imani shook her head. "You're the least boring person I've ever known. You're always fun."

"I'm hot-tempered," Tracey said. "That doesn't make me fun."

Halle wrapped an arm around Tracey's shoulders and squeezed. "You are fun. Don't listen to him. Bernard's probably going through some midlife crisis and speaking dumb. He'll snap out of it."

Tracey gave her a half smile before shrugging. "Maybe so. I just needed to get out of the house. He walked out after saying that, and I didn't want to just sit at home like a *boring* wife waiting on him to decide to come back. Thanks for hanging with me."

"That's what we're here for," Halle said. "Don't worry, if Bernard keeps acting up then we'll come over there and get him straight."

Imani nodded. "Yep. Just say the word and we've got you."

Finally a true smile creased Tracey's lips. "I appreciate that. We'll see. We've gone through stuff before so this time may not be different." Tracey sighed and pushed her braids back. "I don't want to spend the entire night talking about Bernard being dumb. Let's talk about something more fun."

Halle quirked a brow. "Like what?"

"Like your date with Gregory on Friday, or the happenings at the hospital, anything other than my husband trying to call me boring."

"I'm good with that," Halle said. She hated hearing the doubt in her friend's voice. Tracey put on a brave front, but Halle and Imani both knew how easily she could be hurt. She sent up a quick prayer for Bernard to come back to his senses.

Cyril brought over their drinks and the three women clinked their glasses together in a toast before Imani went into a story about the latest update on the dating life from her friend Andrea in Texas. Halle glanced over to the bar when Quinton got up to leave. Their eyes met and a jolt made her suck in a breath. She was only irritated with him; that was all. She looked away quickly and asked her friends for advice on the best way to impress Gregory on their upcoming date.

Five

QUINTON ENTERED THE PEACHTREE COVE ELEMEN-
tary School gym and scanned the room. A dozen round tables
with six chairs were scattered around the space. Other teachers, administrators and support staff from within the district
milled about the room, searching for a place to sit. He typically
received district information from the high school principal,
but since there were going to be some district-wide changes,
the superintendent had insisted all teachers attend one of two
information sessions.

He didn't mind attending district-wide training, but hated
that this one happened right when he was in the heat of getting ready for the football season. He, Zachariah, and the other
coaches agreed to split up attendance between the two meetings so that football practice wouldn't have to be canceled. Even
missing one day of practice was crucial while they tried to get
the team ready for the season.

Deciding that he wasn't eager enough to sit in the row of tables closest to the podium or disengaged enough to be one of the teachers filling up the back row of tables, he opted for a table near the middle. He peeled off the sticker name tag that he'd scribbled his name on and slapped it on his chest before heading toward his chosen section. He nodded and greeted some of the other teachers from the high school. He recognized many of the other people filling the space but there were also a lot of new faces.

Teachers rotated in and out of the district. Some coming to give back in a small town, or because they were more likely to have received college scholarships if they opted to work in a small district after graduation. After four years in the district, Quinton had to admit that Peachtree Cove felt like home. If he continued to have a successful season, he could see himself settling in Peachtree Cove for good.

"Hey, there he is!"

Quinton looked up from where he'd settled in his seat. No one looked his way, so they weren't talking about him. The two women sitting at the next table pointed toward the door. Teachers at the middle school. He'd seen them at previous district-wide trainings. Curious about who'd made them so excited, he glanced in the direction they indicated. The guy standing in the doorway didn't ring a bell. He must be a new teacher to the district. Which explained the excitement. Heaven help the guy if he was single. The single teachers would be all over him if he were. Quinton knew from experience.

"He is cute," one of the women, Rachel he believed her name was, said.

"Yes, he is," said the other woman, Gayle. He knew her from the spring break learning program they both volunteered for the previous year. "I wish he'd come to teach English at the middle school instead of the high school."

Quinton shook his head and pulled out his cell phone to

scroll through plays while he waited. Definitely a new teacher who'd gained the attention of the single population. Quinton would feel bad for the guy, but instead he was relieved. Even though Quinton couldn't consider himself a new teacher anymore, once word got out last year that he'd broken things off with his girlfriend, he'd once again gotten on the radar of the women in town looking for a man. After ending the long-term relationship, he wasn't in the mood to try to start something else. He didn't envy the guy for what would come his way, but he couldn't say he was sad about the distraction the guy would provide.

"Me too, but it doesn't matter," Rachel said on a sigh. "I heard he's already hooking up with Halle."

Quinton's finger stopped midscroll and his head popped up. Halle? Halle Parker?

"Ms. Parker? For real?" Gayle asked, gleefully soaking up the potential gossip.

Rachel nodded. "Yep. They had dinner together at the Italian place a few weeks ago."

Gayle scoffed and pushed Rachel's shoulder. "Dinner doesn't mean hooking up."

"No, listen," Rachel said and leaned closer to Gayle. Quinton leaned toward them, too. "It's not just dinner. They've both been popping up at the same place for lunch every week. Not only did they have dinner, but they were seen together having coffee *early* the other morning. They're hooking up."

Gayle gasped before grinning. "You think so?"

Rachel nodded as if she had all of the latest information anyone needed to know on Halle and the new teacher. "Early in the morning. Why they having coffee that early, if you know what I mean?"

Quinton frowned and looked back at the man in question. Was that guy Halle's type? Quinton studied him more closely. He looked like an English teacher with his fitted polo shirt, khakis and square-framed glasses. The guy reminded Quinton of his high school English teacher. The man who'd told Quinton he might as well quit after the first week of Honors English. That he'd be better off switching to the regular English class to avoid failing. Quinton had stayed and proved the man wrong by passing.

"Look, look, look," Gayle said, tapping Rachel on the arm and pointing.

Quinton's eyes narrowed as Halle came to the door. English teacher turned and smiled at her. Halle returned his smile with a bright one of her own. Her hair was twisted up in an intricate style with the top a mass of thick curls. English teacher motioned for her to go ahead of him and followed Halle farther into the room.

"See, he was waiting on her." The smugness in Rachel's voice was all Quinton needed to hear to know she felt vindicated in her assumption that they were hooking up.

Had the guy been waiting on Halle? Quinton shook his head. Wait—why was he worried about this guy waiting on Halle? This wasn't his business. Who she did or didn't hook up with didn't matter to him.

Halle glanced around the room for a seat. Their eyes met. Quinton sucked in a breath. She *was* fine. The corners of her mouth tipped up in a tight smile before she quickly looked away. His breath came out in a quick rush. The hell? What was that about? He looked back down at his phone.

"And they're sitting together," Gayle practically squealed.

"What did I say? Hooking. Up," Rachel replied knowingly.

Quinton focused on the plays on his phone. Halle wasn't his type. She and the English teacher probably belonged together. Two judgmental people who could look at him and say he isn't up to standard. Quinton shifted in his seat as decades-old insecurity crawled across his spine.

Damn, he'd really let Halle get under his skin that day in

the bar. That had to be why he was overthinking this. Her adamant refusal that he wasn't her type of guy had poked and prodded at not just his pride, but also an insecurity he hadn't felt since graduating high school. If the woman could put him in knots with just a few words, he was better off not pursuing her. Which he couldn't. Even if he wanted to.

"Coach, what's up?"

Quinton looked up and nodded at Blake, the middle school's soccer coach. "Nothing much."

"Mind if I join you?"

"Cool with me."

Quinton forced Halle out of his mind and focused on the conversation with Blake about their expectations for the upcoming football season.

Halle clutched her information packet tight and sent up a silent prayer. They'd gotten through the introduction part of the district meeting and the superintendent had given the major updates related to the district. Now it was time for the group exercise. Halle loved group exercises. She enjoyed pulling a team together and completing whatever task they were assigned. Her team usually won or had the best presentation no matter who was in her group. She could usually find a way to work with anyone.

This time was different. This time she hoped, wished and prayed that the stars would align and put her in the same group as Gregory. Their dinner date had gone great; he'd even called her later that night with the title of the book he couldn't remember the name of. They'd since met up for coffee and lunch a few times. Everything was going great with him. So much so, she was considering telling Shania that she was dating him. Otherwise, the town's rumor mill would get it back to her daughter before she got the chance. She hadn't missed the way a few nosey folks paid attention to them hanging together.

"Okay, everyone," the superintendent, Dr. Stann Watts, said. He was a tall, heavy-set guy, with dark skin and a deep, booming voice. Instead of the suit he usually wore to district meetings he'd opted for casual with a pair of slacks and a gray button-up shirt. "Open your packets and see what color you have. Each color will split up into groups where we'll pass out the instructions."

Halle tore her packet open and snatched out the orange square. She quickly turned to Gregory sitting next to her, hoping he'd also have an orange square. He held a green square. Her heart sank.

"Dang, I'd hoped we'd be in the same group," she said.

"It's no big deal. I still got to sit with you today." He smiled as he spoke the words and Halle returned the gesture.

Gregory was so nice and sweet. Even though they hadn't kissed, she had a feeling when they did it would be amazing. Usually, she wasn't overly eager to rush the physical side of a relationship, but she liked spending time with him and talking to him. His ability to have an conversation about literature had only stoked a fire beneath her long ignored libido. She wasn't typically one to lose herself in daydreams of fairytales. Losing her parents taught her that life could be heartbreaking, but for the first time in a long time, she felt hopeful. She'd wanted more than one child, but after having Shania right before graduating college, she'd realized being a single parent was a lot of work. If things worked out with Gregory, her dreams of having more children wouldn't be too late to realize.

"I guess we should find our groups," she said.

They got up and made their way to the tables around the room with the various colors. Halle walked up to the orange table at the same time Quinton walked up holding an orange square. He was dressed like he did for football practice, in a pair of fitted joggers and a Peachtree Cove High School athletic shirt. The aviator glasses he liked were folded into the collar of his shirt. Of course, she'd end up in a group with him.

"Orange, huh?" she said, trying to hide her disappointment. She was able to work with anyone in a group. Even guys who insisted she was not their type.

He nodded. "Yep." He sounded just as enthusiastic about being in a group with her as she did.

"Guess we'll see how many others join our group."

"Yep," he agreed.

Halle fought not to roll her eyes. Was he only capable of one-word responses? They looked around and waited for others to come over. The crowd split up and people joined the other tables. No one else came to the orange table. Halle crossed her arms. There had to be someone else joining them.

Dr. Watts headed their way. He grinned and held out his arms. "We only had two orange tabs. We tried to break everyone up into groups of five but didn't have enough. Instead of making an uneven group we decided to just have one group of two."

"Wouldn't we need more people in our group for the exercise?" Halle asked.

Dr. Watts shook his head. "Not at all. In fact, this exercise is about brainstorming ways to handle the biggest challenges you see in the upcoming year. We're looking for ideas of ways the school and the district can support overcoming those obstacles. You two work together on that and then you can report back out to the larger group. Sound good?"

Quinton grunted then nodded. Dr. Watts beamed before looking at Halle. If Halle was anything she was a team player. She nodded and smiled.

"Great! I'll let you two get to it." Dr. Watts turned and walked away.

Halle glanced around the room at the various tables. Gregory was on the other side of the room. The one lone man at a table full of women. She sighed. Why couldn't he have picked the other orange square?

"Are you two dating?"

Halle blinked and focused on Quinton. "Huh?"

He raised a brow and then nodded in the direction of Gregory. "You and the English teacher. Are you two dating?"

Halle lifted her chin. "That's none of your business."

Quinton pulled a chair out and sat down at the table. "According to the teachers in the middle school you two are hooking up."

Halle gasped before sliding out the chair next to him and plopping down into the seat. "We're not hooking up."

"I just thought you should know. That's what they're saying."

She crossed her arms on the table. "And you care about the gossip."

He held up a hand. "I don't care what you do."

"Then why ask if we're dating?"

He shrugged and then slid the papers with the instructions for the exercise over to him. "Forget I asked." He scanned the first page and started reading. "Think about the upcoming school year and list what may prove challenging with the upcoming changes."

Halle's eyes narrowed on him. "We're not dating."

"Okay," Quinton said before continuing to read. "Identify ways to overcome the challenges."

"Not yet anyway."

Quinton stopped reading. He lowered the paper to the table. "So, you want to date him?"

"I thought you didn't care."

"I don't, but you're talking about it, so I guess you want me to care."

"I don't want you to care. You brought up the conversation and I'm finishing it."

She reached for the instructions he'd put down and a pen.

She read where he'd stopped. "One big challenge is making sure everyone understands the schedule change."

"I guess he's your type, huh?"

Halle sighed and met his gaze. His eyes were dark, piercing even, and they didn't waver as they met hers. That was something she appreciated about him; he didn't break eye contact when he spoke. He watched, listened. She'd at least give him that. Quinton Evans gave you his full attention when you spoke to him. Which could be considered attractive.

"If you must know, yes. He is my type."

"Hmm." He watched her for a second; she expected him to say more, but instead he slid over the legal pad on the table and a pen. "The new schedule is going to cause some problems. Parents who have to get to work early may drop off kids at the front door of the middle school now that middle school is starting at eight thirty instead of eight. For kids with special needs who will need to have someone at the school when they're dropped off, this could cause some conflicts."

Halle nodded. "That's a good point."

"You sound surprised that I'd make a good point?"

"Not surprised, just glad to see that you're thinking outside of your box."

He leaned an elbow on the table and met her eyes again. "It's not outside of my box. My younger sister is a paraplegic and in a wheelchair. Back home our middle school started at eight and kids couldn't be dropped off until seven fifteen. But my mom had to be at work at five and my dad didn't get off work from his shift job until ten. So, she'd drop me off at the school with my sister and I waited with her until the teachers arrived."

Halle's face heated and her stomach twisted in knots. She was an asshole. "I'm sorry for assuming."

He shrugged. "No need to be sorry for the facts of my life. I just know the change in schedule can have consequences others may not have considered."

He looked down at the paper and wrote: have someone at the school to meet kids with special needs. His handwriting was bold and messy. Completely opposite of his neat and controlled appearance.

"What is your type?" she blurted out.

The words landed like a brick on the table between them. Heavy and awkward. She had no idea why she asked. She didn't care about his type. Except, she would assume he was into supermodels and actresses because he was a former professional athlete. Just like she'd assumed he'd have neat handwriting or wouldn't think of the school schedule outside of how it affected his football team. She might be wrong, and suddenly, she was curious to know more about Coach Quinton Evans.

He stared at her, a line between his brows and confusion in his dark eyes. Halle held up a hand to stop him from answering. "Forget I asked."

"I don't have a type," he said right after.

Halle cocked a brow. "Does that mean you're a man who dates all types of women?"

"I am someone who doesn't limit his possibilities to a person that meets certain criteria. You never know what makes a person tick until you get to know them. Why would I say I only date women with X type of personality or who look a certain type of way, when someone who is completely different is the right person for me?"

She was once again surprised by his answer. "Are you serious?"

"I am. I've been underestimated my entire life. Why would I underestimate someone's potential?"

Again, his gaze didn't waver as he spoke to her. His deep voice resonated with truth and confidence. "You think I'm limiting myself by having a type?"

He lifted one broad shoulder. "Only you can answer that.

But I mean if you rule out a guy simply because of some arbitrary trait then…yeah. Maybe you are."

"Or, maybe I just know what I like and who I'm compatible with."

"If that's what you want to go with."

"It is what I'm going with." Damn, did she sound defensive? She did sound defensive.

He shifted forward in his seat. "Cool with me."

"Good." She pointed to the paper. "Let's finish this."

They worked through the exercises. When they were done, Quinton got up and went to the side table where snacks and bottles of water were placed while Halle finished writing up their comments. She watched him walk away and admitted she'd misjudged him. One bad situation with a football player and uncaring coach in high school and she'd been judging athletes ever since. Quinton continued to have good insights about the way the district wide changes would affect students and parents in the upcoming school year. Not only that, he'd had thoughtful ideas about ways to overcome them. She'd assumed that he wouldn't take this seriously or be interested in working on the project. She'd painted Quinton with the wrong brush and that was on her.

Quinton came back to the table and put a bottle of water in front of her. Halle glanced at it and raised a brow. "For me?"

He nodded. "We talked a lot while working on this. My throat is dry so I figured yours may be, too. I got you these." He slid a package of fruit snacks her way.

"Snacks, too?" She was thirsty, and she did need a sugar pick-me-up.

He slid back into his seat with a grace she wouldn't have expected from a guy so big. "You eyed them when someone passed by with them while we worked."

Heat filled her cheeks. He'd been paying that much attention to her? "I was going to get some."

"Well, now you don't have to. You want me to present our ideas?"

She shook her head. "Nah, I can do it. I don't mind."

"Suit yourself." He opened a pack of peanut butter crackers and took a bite.

"I'm sorry."

He frowned. "For what?"

"For assuming that you wouldn't judge Shania fairly. She says you're not like that."

He finished chewing then took a sip from his bottled water. "I'm not like that. I remember what it was like to be overlooked in high school just because I wasn't what the coach or teacher expected I should be. Because I remember that, I don't want the kids I come in contact with to feel that way. I want them to know that I judge them for what they do, not what they look like or where they come from."

"You were judged about where you came from?"

Quinton met her eyes. For the briefest moment he appeared uncomfortable, vulnerable. The timer went off, indicating the group exercise was done. In that quick second his calm, confident demeanor returned, and he focused his attention back to Dr. Watts, who'd stood.

Halle hated the interruption. She wanted to finish their conversation. To learn more about Quinton Evans. She had to add *thoughtful* to the things she'd learned about him. He didn't have to bring her water and fruit snacks. He was also insightful. He was turning out to be an interesting person, and, heaven help her, Halle was always drawn to learn more about interesting people.

Six

QUINTON SIGHED AND SHOOK HIS HEAD AS HIS MOTHER asked the same question she always asked before they ended a phone call. "When are you going to settle down and give me some grandchildren?"

He'd heard that question consistently since he signed his contract to play professionally. Before that, throughout high school and college, all he'd heard from Laura and Willie Evans was *"You better not get anyone pregnant"* followed by *"We can't afford to take care of any kids you bring around"* and wrapped up with *"You know what will land you in jail faster than robbing a bank? Child support!"*

After spending most of his life hearing about all the reasons why he couldn't afford to have a kid and how he better not bring around any babies, you'd think they'd understand his hesitancy to have kids before he was ready. Quinton didn't have any kids.

That you know of.

The thought crept into his mind as it always did when his mom asked. Thoughts of that one time he'd been desperate for money and had rushed into a decision that may have resulted in him having a child.

"Mom, when I'm ready to settle down you'll be the first to know."

"You don't have to settle down to have kids," his mom said.

Quinton still couldn't believe she was uttering those words. She would have slapped him upside the head if he'd even thought those words in high school.

"She's right, you know," his dad chimed in.

Quinton scoffed. "Dad, you in on this, too?"

"I'm just saying," his dad said. "Having some young'uns around would be kind of nice. You and your sister are grown. I missed all the fun stuff when you were kids because we were struggling to make ends meet. It would be nice to spoil a grandbaby."

"If I do have a kid, I'm not spoiling it," Quinton said firmly. "My kids will understand that you've got to earn things in life."

His mom sucked her teeth. "Just because you struggled doesn't mean my grandkids have to struggle. What's the point of making all that money if you aren't going to spend it on something worthwhile? Kids deserve to be spoiled."

Quinton sat up from where he'd been lounging on the couch and pressed his free hand to his temple. "Excuse me, have you been invaded by a body snatcher? You are not the same person who raised me," Quinton teased.

"Ain't nobody snatch me. I'm ready for grandchildren. Is that so hard to believe?"

"Can you wait until I find someone I'd like to have kids with? I swear, the way you're pressing you might be okay with me just having a kid with anybody."

"You sure you don't have any kids out there?" his dad asked. "I mean, you were in the league for eight years."

Quinton shook his head. "Dad, stop it. You both know I wasn't out there like that. I didn't call for this. I called to check on how things were going. Did you get the pump on the well fixed?"

After he'd started playing professional football the first thing Quinton had done was get his parents out of the cheap apartment they'd struggled to keep and into a house of their own. They'd been worried he would tear or break something in the first year and be broke again. Knowing firsthand how easily an injury could end his career, Quinton made sure to take care of his body and quickly addressed any bumps and bruises. They'd finally agreed to move into a house in the country when he'd made it three years without any serious injuries. After years of being cramped in an apartment his parents wanted nothing but space and privacy. Living in a rural area meant they also had to deal with using a well for water, and the pump on the well had broken recently.

"I can fix the pump myself." Stubbornness filled his dad's voice.

Quinton rubbed his temples. He was tired of having this same conversation. "Dad, you don't have to fix the well yourself. We can afford to have someone come check it out."

"Why pay someone for something I can do myself? It's a waste of money. Just let me handle it. We'll be good."

"No, you won't. How is not having running water going to be good?"

"You remember all the times the water got cut off when you were younger. We survived then and we'll survive now."

"That was different. The water was cut off because we couldn't pay the bill. Now I can afford to take care of things. I'm sending someone tomorrow."

"I don't need someone to—"

"I don't care about what you need," he cut off his dad. "I care about making sure you have water in the house."

"Quinton!"

"Dad, I'm not arguing about this. Someone will be there first thing in the morning."

His mom jumped in. "If you want to send someone then go ahead."

"Laura!" his dad exclaimed. Clearly upset that his wife was accepting their son's help.

"Let it go, Willie. Quinton wants to do this for us so let him."

His dad grumbled a little longer then finally agreed. Quinton understood his dad's hesitancy. For so many years his parents had done everything they could to keep the family afloat. They'd worked multiple jobs, went without eating so their kids could eat, and found ways to make a dollar stretch for thirty days. All while never asking for help and always finding a way to make ends meet. Their refusal to ask for help was part of the reason why Quinton had made the decision in college to get money by any means possible instead of asking his parents to help him when he needed shoes, books or his partial scholarship only made a small dent in his tuition. He'd done what needed to be done to make it to the pros so that he could make their lives better. He wouldn't let his parents suffer because of pride.

Halle sat at the kitchen table looking up activities for cousins' weekend later that month. Cousins' weekend was an idea she'd come up with to stay connected with her extended family. Once her great aunt who used to plan family reunions passed away and the get-togethers stopped, she'd missed hanging out with her cousins who were like siblings to her. So, she'd started planning the yearly get-together. She and her cousins got together and played games, competed in little activities and grilled out. Even though it was Halle's idea, her cousin, Kayla, had helped her plan each one.

Shania came into the kitchen and came toward Halle.

"Hey, sweetie," Halle said, not looking up from the laptop.

"Mom, can I ask you something?"

Halle turned away from her laptop and gave Shania her full attention. "Sure, but first tell me what you think. Tug-of-war or a spades tournament?"

Shania pursed her lips. "Tug-of-war. You know Mick gets real crazy when y'all play spades."

Halle laughed when she thought of how serious her first cousin got whenever they played spades. "That's part of the fun. Watching him act a fool."

"Let's just put him on the grill and not have him act up."

Halle nodded. "You're right. We don't need anyone acting a fool. Our family has enough foolishness as it is."

Shania grabbed the back of the chair next to Halle and raised her brows. "Soooo, about my question."

"What is it?"

Shania squirmed for a second before blurting out. "My dad."

The smile on Halle's face fell away. "Shania…"

"Are you really not going to tell me who he is?" Shania asked, her eyes narrowed.

"Why are you dragging this out? I told you not to worry about him."

"I just don't believe that you'd keep this a secret from me. Why?"

"Because you're better off not knowing him, that's why." Halle stood and went to the fridge.

"I don't believe you. Are you ashamed? Did you do something you weren't supposed to? Did you keep me a secret from him?"

"You've been watching too many television shows."

Halle opened the fridge and pulled out a soda. The movement allowed her to avoid meeting her daughter's eyes. She wasn't ashamed of what she'd done, but she also didn't want to face the judgment of her family, friends and possibly her daughter if they knew the truth.

"I want to know."

She turned back to her daughter and held up a hand. "No, Shania. Stop it. I'm not going to get into this with you. Not tonight and not ever. Your dad is not a part of our life. Haven't I given you enough? Why won't you trust me on this?"

Shania crossed her arms. "Because you won't tell me anything. Nothing about him. Even if he was a deadbeat who hated you that would be better than you telling me nothing."

"Are you bringing this up because you want a dad?"

"It's not about wanting a dad. It's about knowing who I am. Where I come from."

"You know where you come from. Me. I gave birth to you. I raised you. I gave you everything you needed. Now you want to throw all that away just to find some random guy?"

Shania scowled. "Random guy?"

Halle sighed and pinched the bridge of her nose. She'd said too much. Gone too far. "That's it. Stop asking me. I'm not going to talk about this anymore." Her voice tightened as frustration squeezed her.

Shania uncrossed her arms and placed her hands on her hips. Her eyes flashed defiantly as she stared back at Halle. "I'm not giving up on this."

Halle pointed at her. "Yes, you are. This is over and done with. If you want a dad, then I'll find you one."

Her daughter scoffed and rolled her eyes. "I don't want you to find me one. I'd rather you stay single forever than try to be with some guy just because you think it'll make me stop asking about my real dad."

Halle flinched as Shania's words stoked the fire of her guilt. That was what this was about. Halle had told Shania that she was dating Gregory and now Shania thought she was just trying to distract her from her questions about her dad. The situation would be laughable if the thought hadn't crossed her own mind. Halle liked Gregory and wanted to make their relationship work, but the more she'd hoped things would work out with Gregory, the more she'd wondered if Shania would stop asking questions if they became a real family.

She hated that the thought had even slipped into her head. She'd thought that she was enough for Shania. When she'd made the decision to have a child on her own, she'd been young and hadn't thought about the eventual questions she'd be faced with. She didn't want to be with Gregory just to make Shania stop asking questions about her dad, and she didn't want Shania to think she was with Gregory for that reason.

"This conversation is over."

"But, Mom—"

She held up her hand for Shania to stop. "Don't *but Mom* me. This is done. I'm serious, Shania. Don't bring this topic up to me again. It's over, you hear me? Let it go."

Shania stared back. Rebelliousness in her eyes. The same rebelliousness that had burned in Halle whenever she'd argued with her parents about why she should be allowed to attend a protest or rally. Halle met her daughter's gaze unwavering. They were both just as stubborn, just as tenacious, when they wanted to know something.

After a few tense seconds, Shania shook her head before turning and rushing out of the room. Halle let out a sigh. She went back to the kitchen table and sat in her chair. She took a long sip of the soda and wished she'd chosen something stronger. Shania was getting more and more insistent about this. Halle had been able to deflect and change the subject easily for years, but now her daughter was persistent in knowing the truth. She didn't know what to do. Halle didn't believe for a moment that this was done. Anxiety clawed at her throat, and she squeezed her hands into fists. What would she do if Shania found out the truth behind her birth? How would her daughter feel to learn that her dad really and truly was some anonymous donor? It might break her heart even more to know there really was no way to find him.

Seven

QUINTON BLEW HIS WHISTLE. THE KIDS ON THE FOOT-
ball field stopped running the drills they'd been practicing and
glanced his way. "That's it for today. Let's clean up."

A mixture of groans and claps met his response. Some kids
would practice all night if he let them. Others were just as ready
to get home and get showered as he was. He didn't fault either
side. As long as they did what he asked and kept their heads on
straight off the field, he was good.

He glanced at the group of wide receivers practicing with
one of the assistant coaches, Clyde Tucker. Shania hung on the
outskirts of the group. That was unusual. She was always ready
to jump in and be front and center when it came to practices.
She'd seemed distracted all day.

As the players started toward the locker room, Quinton called
over Clyde. "Everything went well today?" he asked.

Clyde shook his head. He was average height, thin, with a

bald head and dark brown skin. "Yeah, pretty good. I tell you, that kid Octavius really knows how to run the routes. I think he's going to make a big difference this year."

"That's good to hear. What about the rest of the receivers? They're doing well?" Quinton wasn't surprised about Octavius; he'd also noticed the boy had picked up on the plays quickly and tried to motivate the rest of the receivers to learn their routes.

"Yeah, they're learning the plays and understanding where they need to be to catch the ball."

"How is Shania doing?"

Clyde lifted a shoulder. "She's doing alright, I guess."

Quinton shifted his stance, focusing on Clyde instead of continuing to watch the kids gather equipment and head to the locker rooms. "You guess? What does that mean?"

"You know, she's good at learning plays, but let's be honest." Clyde leaned closer to Quinton. "If we want to win this year then we can't put her in the game."

"Why not?"

Clyde glanced around before meeting his eyes. "I mean… because she can't keep up."

Quinton removed his aviator shades and crossed his arms. "I've watched her practice and she doesn't seem to have a problem keeping up."

Clyde let out an uneasy laugh. "You know what I'm saying."

Quinton didn't laugh or smile. "I don't. Tell me what you're saying."

The fake smile on Clyde's face disappeared. "She's a girl. If we put her in the game, then she'll be a liability."

Quinton didn't move, but disappointment settled around him. He'd expected this from some of the parents and a few of the players, but he'd hoped to avoid it on his coaching staff. He'd assumed they would follow his lead and support Shania on the team.

"We don't know that until she plays in a game." Quinton

held back his displeasure with what Clyde said and spoke evenly, giving Clyde the opportunity to correct himself. "And from the way she practices I don't see her as a potential liability."

"As soon as one of those boys tackles her on the field, you'll see that."

"She's been playing tackle football for a few years. She knows the risks and she's good at what she does. Don't skimp on giving her attention because you don't think girls should play football."

Clyde's eyes widened. "I didn't say that."

"You don't have to. What you said before—prove it."

"I'm just stating facts. She is a girl and, yeah, right now she's as big as some of the boys, but that's because it's JV. As the year goes on and if she keeps playing, she's going to get hurt."

Quinton understood the risks. He knew Shania ever playing professionally was unlikely, but there were other opportunities she could have if she wanted to continue playing football. He wasn't going to be the person to kill her dream and he wasn't going to let someone on his coaching staff do the same.

"If she continues to play with us, there are other positions she can switch to. Girls have gone on to play college football, not just as kicker but even as a defensive back. She'll also have opportunities to coach if she continues to learn the game. If I ever hear you underestimate her contribution to this team because she's a girl, then you may as well find another team to coach for. You understand?"

Clyde leaned back. "Coach Q, don't be like that. I'm good with her on the team. I'm just looking out for you. The district wants us to win. We can't be putting her in the game for clout."

"I won't put her in the game for clout. But I'm also not going to keep her out of the game unless I know for sure she can't keep up. Keep working with her. We'll go from there."

Clyde held up a hand and sighed. "Aight, I hear you. I've got you."

Quinton slid his shades back on. "Good."

He turned away from Clyde and headed toward the locker rooms. Clyde's comments irritated him the entire way back. He'd made a big deal of telling Halle that he wouldn't treat Shania any differently than the other players, but he hadn't considered that some of his coaching staff may be treating her differently. He'd bring up player progression at his next coaching meeting and check to see if anyone else was intentionally not looking at Shania's talents and only focusing on her gender. She wasn't quite as good as Octavius physically, but her tenacity and knowledge of the game put her close to his level. He understood the coaches' need to win, he felt the same urge, but the need to win didn't mean they couldn't give Shania a chance.

He checked in with the kids coming in and out of the locker room to make sure they were good and give suggestions to keep them motivated. He kept an eye out for Shania, but didn't see her. Maybe she'd taken off early. Hopefully, not because Clyde had given her any problems during practice.

He rounded the hall to his office and stopped short. Shania stood outside his office door, arms crossed and a frown on her face.

He walked toward her. "Everything okay?"

"Yeah." She shook her head. "No. Not really."

"Do you want to talk about it?"

She nodded. "I do."

"Come on inside." He opened his office door and motioned for Shania to sit in the chair across from his desk. He left the door open and sat in his chair. "Is this about playing? I spoke with Coach Tucker and he says you're doing a good job learning the plays."

"I am, but he still only wants to focus on Octavius. He doesn't think I can keep up." She stated the words as a fact, not like someone who was jealous of the attention Octavius got, but aware that she wasn't on the radar.

"Did he say that?" If so, Clyde was going to be off the team sooner rather than later.

She shook her head. "He didn't have to. He shows it in other ways."

"Like what?"

"Like telling me to keep up all the time. Saying I'm not running fast enough, even when I beat the other kids getting into position. He even says that I have to be faster to avoid taking a hit. Like I haven't been hit before," she mumbled, irritation finally entering her voice at the questioning of her abilities.

"I'll have a talk with him. I know you playing for the high school is something new for everyone, but I meant it when I said that all kids were going to get the same opportunity. If you prove that you can do what we ask, then you'll get a chance to play."

The corners of her mouth lifted a little. "That's cool."

Quinton relaxed. He felt good about solving her problem. She could go back and tell Halle that he was really doing what he said about giving all kids a fair shot.

"Good." He moved to stand. "Now, your mom should be here."

"Are you my dad?"

Quinton froze; his eyes went from Shania to the door and the empty hall beyond, and back to her. "Excuse me?" He couldn't have heard her right.

She stared back at him, her gaze steady as she watched his reaction closely. "Are you my dad?"

Quinton shook his head and lowered back into his seat. "I'm not your father. Why would you ask that?"

He'd never met Halle before moving to Peachtree Cove. In that time he'd barely had the chance to speak with her before Shania joined his team, much less date or make a baby with her. He knew rumors in this town grew like weeds, but this was one he couldn't comprehend ever starting.

Shania reached into her gym bag and pulled out a folded sheet of paper. She unfolded the paper and slid it across his desk. "This says you are."

Quinton scowled at the paper on the table. He looked from it to Shania. Was this a prank? A joke the kids on the team wanted to play. "What's this?"

She held his gaze. No twitch of the lip. No flash of humor in her eye. Just dogged determination and a stubborn set to her jaw. For a second, she reminded him of himself. A thought he quickly swept from his head.

"It's something that says there's a 99.9 percent chance you're my dad."

Quinton stared at the paper. At the top was the familiar logo for a popular genealogy website. The same website he'd signed up for and used that one Christmas two years ago when he'd been caught up between sentiment and heartbreak.

Quinton's heart fell to the bottom of his stomach. If he hadn't been sitting down, he probably would have sunk to the floor. There was no way this could be happening. No way one of his worst fears, and biggest hopes, would come through in this fashion. His hands shook as he took the paper. "Where did you get this?" he asked, his voice tight.

"I did one of those online DNA things. Mom didn't want me to, but I did it anyway. I checked the option to find any relatives. It says you're a match as my dad."

Quinton lifted the paper. Confirmed it was the same company he'd used. That night came back clearly. When he'd confessed to his sister about what he'd done in college. About being broke, needing books, their parents almost being kicked out of their apartment and not being enough of a superstar in college to get the big money deals or full ride. How he'd listened to a friend.

"They pay big money for our sperm. Women want babies by strong men. I donate all the time."

It had all sounded so easy. So simple. He'd donated, gotten paid and his parents hadn't been put out of their apartment. He'd tried to put out of his mind the idea of there being a kid out there who belonged to him, but never quite could. Thoughts of who'd gotten his sperm. Had that person had a boy or a girl? Thoughts he'd kept to himself until that Christmas when he'd been in his feelings after breaking up with Megan and he'd drunk too much of his aunt's Christmas punch.

"Take a DNA test and list yourself to be connected to relatives. If you have a kid out there, maybe they can find you." His sister's Christmas punch–induced advice.

He'd done it. Never in his life thinking a decision made in desperation would come back to him like this. Quinton looked up from the paper that linked him to Shania. Her brows were risen, and she watched him with intense, focused eyes. His eyes.

"So, are you my dad?"

Halle scanned the school parking lot for Shania. Other players got into either their cars or the cars of their waiting parents. A few of the coaches lingered or walked up from the field with kids, but none of them were Shania. She checked her watch and waited. Maybe Shania had gotten caught up with something and would be out soon, but as the players thinned with still no sign of Shania, Halle began to worry.

Had she left already? Why would she do that without talking to her first? Had she wandered off? Some kids walked from the school to the McDonald's across the street, but Shania should know not to do that without permission. Halle pulled out her cell phone and called.

Shania answered after the third ring. "Hello?"

"Where are you? I'm in the parking lot," Halle asked in a rush, the rising anxiety subsiding knowing that her daughter wasn't missing.

"I'm inside talking to Coach Q." Shania spoke easily enough, but something in her voice put Halle on edge.

"Is everything okay?"

"Not really," was Shania's cryptic answer.

Halle turned off the car and reached for her purse. "What does that mean? Are you hurt? Did something happen during practice?"

"This isn't really about football. Can you come in here?"

"Here where?" Halle opened the car door and got out. What was going on? Why did Shania sound so...off? What could have happened not related to football that made her talk to Quinton about it? She was supposed to come to Halle with any problems. Not her football coach.

"Come in the back door by the parking lot. I'm in his office at the end of the hall near the gym. Last door on the right."

Halle spotted the door that the kids and coaches typically came out of after practice. "I'm on my way."

She hurried inside the building. All types of scenarios played in her mind. Had one of the boys on the team said or done something to her? Had Shania gotten fed up with something and decided to get Quinton's advice? Had he pulled her aside for some random reason, and if so, why would he single out Shania?

Halle pressed a hand to her chest and took a deep breath, stopping her mind from going all over the place before she walked down the hall. There was no need in making up all kinds of stories. Whatever was going on she'd find out in a matter of minutes anyway, and she'd deal with it then.

The last door on the right was open. Halle quickly walked down the hall and entered. Shania sat in a chair on one side of the desk, Quinton on the other. Shania's face was stony. Her jaw clenched and her eyes burning with accusation as she stared at Halle. Quinton leaned back in his chair. His jaw slack and his eyes slightly unfocused as if he'd been stunned.

"What the hell happened?" Halle asked. The tension in the room was thick as molasses.

Quinton's head slowly turned to her. His gaze focused and his brows drew together. "Umm... Shania just asked..." He cleared his throat.

Halle raised her brows. "Asked what?" She looked at her daughter. "What did you ask?"

"Is he my dad?" Shania asked bluntly. Accusation steel in her unexpected question.

Halle's heart flipped. Pressing a hand to her temple, she closed her eyes and sighed. "Not this again. Coach Evans, I'm sorry. This is a conversation between me and my daughter. She never should have brought you into this."

"You're still going to pretend, huh," Shania said, disappointment and frustration thick in her voice.

"Pretend about what? Coach Evans is not your father. Just because some kid said you look like him doesn't make him your dad."

Quinton cleared his throat again. "There's just one problem."

Halle's attention jerked to him. "What problem?"

"This paper says something different." He picked up the sheet of paper in front of him and held it up.

Halle blinked, her heart racing and the hairs on the back of her neck stood. She crossed the room and snatched the paper. "I don't care what this paper says..." Her gaze landed on the top of the page and her voice trailed off. She frowned and turned to Shania. "I told you not to do the online DNA test."

"Why, so I wouldn't figure out that you and Coach Q are pretending as if you didn't know each other?"

"We don't know each other," she replied.

"We didn't know each other like that." Quinton spoke right after.

Shania crossed her arms and glared at them both. "Then why would he pop up as my biological father on this DNA test?

Don't even try to say immaculate conception. I'm young, but I'm not dumb. I know how babies are made."

"There's no way." Halle scanned the paper again, reading over the words and seeing the connection. The results that said Quinton Evans had a 99.9 percent chance of being Shania's father. Her heart rate sped up. The words on the page blurred and swam together as her world imploded. "It can't be," she whispered.

"Are you saying you don't remember?" Shania asked. "Mom?" She looked at Quinton. "Coach Q? What's going on? You don't have to pretend anymore. Just tell the truth."

Halle looked from the paper to Quinton. Tall, Black man who was smart and healthy. That was all she knew. But could it really be? Could fate be this much of a bitch?

Quinton's eyes reflected the same shock as hers. After a few tense seconds he spoke slowly. "One time in college. I donated—"

Halle held up a hand. "No. Stop. Not right now. Not like this."

Quinton's thick brows drew together. "You're saying you received my—"

"Come on, Shania. It's time to go." Halle spun away from Quinton. She hurried over to Shania and pulled on her daughter's arm until she stood.

"Wait, Mom. What's going on? Donated what? Received what?"

"We can talk about this somewhere else. Not here." She pulled Shania toward the door.

Shania jerked her arm away. "No, I want to understand this now. You can't keep pushing this aside. Mom, please, tell me what's going on?" Shania didn't yell, but the quaver in her voice broke Halle's heart.

"I can't…" Halle's voice trailed off.

Couldn't what? Tell her the truth of her birth? Tell her daughter the one thing she'd always wanted to know, but Halle had always been too afraid to admit? Afraid of what her family would say? How her aunts, uncles and cousins would have judged her for the decision? How they would have viewed Shania? The gossip that would have surrounded them in a small town full of people with even smaller views of what was acceptable in the world?

"Mom, please," Shania whispered. "Tell me what's going on."

Halle looked at Quinton. She didn't know what to say. She was never supposed to meet the man. Never supposed to know. Damn online DNA tests and the havoc they caused on people's lives.

Quinton slowly stood and walked to them in the small space. Shania turned to him. He straightened his shoulders and met her gaze. "One time in college, I, uh, donated my sperm."

Shania's brows drew together. Confusion clouded her face before she sucked in a breath and looked back at Halle. "Mom?"

For once, Halle couldn't ignore the plea in her daughter's voice. "And, if your paper is right, I'm the person who received his donation."

Eight

"WHY DIDN'T YOU TELL ME?"

Halle looked up from the cup of tea in front of her at Shania sitting across from her at their kitchen table. After the revelations in Quinton's office one of the other coaches came to the door to talk with Quinton. Halle had used the interruption to quickly leave with Shania.

Too much was happening. Too many things coming to light at such an awkward time. Her mind still reeled from the revelation. Quinton was Shania's father! Out of all possibilities, how in the world had *he* turned out to be the donor?

"Mom," Shania called her name.

Halle blinked and focused on her daughter's confused face. "We need to verify the results."

"That's what you're thinking? What happened? Is it true? Did you go to a sperm bank or something?" Shania leaned forward with each question until she was nearly folded over the table.

Halle gently pushed Shania's shoulder so she would sit back up. "It wasn't a sperm bank. It wasn't like that."

"Then what was it like? You're still not telling me what happened and why. I think I deserve to know now."

Sighing, Halle took a sip of tea, hoping the chamomile worked and soothed her nerves, but her fluttering pulse and sweaty palms proved she wasn't getting any relaxation.

"You know I lost your grandma when I was around your age." Shania nodded. "After your grandpa died, I was alone." She remembered those days. The crushing pain of knowing she'd never hear their voices again. That she was the only one left. She took a shaky breath before continuing.

"I'd just finished undergrad and was working part-time at a private school. The principal there understood how I felt. Her parents passed away three years before and she was alone. She'd given birth to a son the year before. She didn't say much about the father and no one asked, but she told me about a company she used. One that matched people who wanted kids with private donors. I had the money from my parents' estate and I had the will so I did it."

At the time the idea of having a kid had seemed like the perfect answer. A way to keep her parents legacy going. A chance to have someone she could love unconditionally. A chance to rebuild her family.

Shania glanced around the room. Her shoulders rising and falling in a manner that was controlled enough to tell Halle she was trying to remain calm. "Who else knows?"

Halle shook her head. "No one. I kept what I did to myself."

"Why didn't you say anything?"

"I didn't want anyone to treat you differently."

"Who would treat me differently?"

Halle sat back in her chair. She tightly held on to the cup of tea in her hand. The warmth of the liquid had gone away. "This is a small town. People here would speculate or have something sly to say. Our family wouldn't understand. They'd think I'd been rash in my decision."

"So you'd rather they think my dad was some deadbeat who didn't want anything to do with you or me?"

"Honestly, yes. I'd rather they think that." Her aunts and uncles wouldn't have understood. They were great, but they weren't open-minded. A distant cousin had adopted a child when she was younger, and she remembered her dad's sister asking why they would do that not knowing if the kid would grow up to have any problems from their parents. She'd spoken the words with a casual callousness that let Halle know she would accept the child in the family, but that she would also never see the child as a real part of the family. Halle hadn't wanted that for Shania.

"Were you ashamed?" Shania asked quietly. "Did you regret what you did?"

Halle sat forward and spoke confidently. "I never regretted what I did. Having you was a blessing."

"A blessing you were ashamed to let people know about."

"That's not true."

"What about me? Why couldn't you even tell me?"

"I know how much you want a father. I didn't know a good way of saying you'll never meet him."

"But I did meet him. I found him through a simple DNA test. I could've found him years ago. What if he had other kids? What if his sperm was given to a lot of women? I could've gone off to college and married my brother or something." Shania shivered and gave Halle a look of horror.

Halle held up a hand. "No, that wouldn't happen. The point of this private donation meant no one else received the same donation."

"But what if he donated somewhere else?"

The simple question was one Halle hadn't allowed herself to consider before. She'd gone the private route because she hadn't wanted her kid to end up with forty other siblings spread across the US. She'd assumed the person on the other end felt the same way and hadn't given multiple donations, but there was no way to prove that.

And why had Quinton donated in the first place? It wasn't as if he was the type of guy who would have trouble starting a family. He'd mentioned needing money. Had he struggled that much to go that far? If so, why wouldn't he have considered making an additional donation?

"We'll ask him," Halle said. "After we verify these results. They may be wrong."

Shania's look said that she thought Halle was being delusional, but to her credit she didn't say it out loud. "But if they're right, it means he's my dad. That changes so much."

"It changes nothing," she said automatically. She didn't want this to change anything even though she knew this information was a grenade that would blow up her entire life.

"Yes, it does. He's my dad. We can't ignore it."

Shania's dad. Would he make demands now? Would he expect her to listen to him when it came to decisions about Shania? Would he fight with her for joint custody? Quinton seemed reasonable, but that was before he found out he had a kid. Halle didn't know what he would want or expect from this. She only had one thing to cling to.

"Don't forget he made an anonymous donation," she reminded them both. "He may not have wanted you to find him. We can't assume he'll want to be a part of your life."

The flash of hurt on Shania's face made Halle wish she could take the words back, but she couldn't. It was true. That thought quelled the anxiety rising in her chest. Quinton may not want to be involved. And Halle wasn't sure if she wanted him involved. Her life plans didn't include him. She was dating Gregory; they were finally making headway. Now this? How would he react to the news? How would her family and the rest of the people in town? The thought of the gossip made her stomach clench.

Halle's cell phone rang. Her cousin Kayla's number flashed on the screen. Probably calling to ask about the cousins' weekend. She sent the call to voice mail, not wanting to deal with that right now.

"Go shower and get some rest. We can talk more later."

She expected Shania to argue or push for more. Instead, she nodded and stood. Shania turned and walked toward the door, her shoulders slumped. Halle's heart broke.

"Shania," she called. When Shania turned around, she tried to smile. "We'll figure this out, okay? No matter what it is, don't we always make a way? We will this time, too."

Shania's lips lifted in a weak smile before she left. Halle's phone rang. Kayla again. She answered instead of sending her cousin to voice mail.

"What's up, Kayla?"

"Umm… Halle, I'm gonna ask you something and I need you to not get mad, okay?" Kayla spoke quickly, her tone already telling Halle she was about to have to deal with some foolishness.

Halle frowned. "Are you changing the plans for cousins' weekend again? I already told you we don't need a spades tournament. Mick will act the fool."

"Nah, it's something else."

"What is it?" Halle sipped her cold tea and wondered what new game her cousin had discovered and wanted to include in the weekend.

"Look, there's no easy way to say this so I'm just gonna ask. Is Quinton Shania's daddy?"

Halle spit the tea across the table. "What? Why would you ask that?"

"See, that's why I said you can't get mad, alright. Look, Zach said he overheard y'all talking in Quinton's office and that's what he heard. I told him that can't be true because ain't no way you wouldn't have told me that Quinton was her daddy."

Halle pinched the bridge of her nose. "Shit, you've got to be kidding me." Zachariah and Kayla had been dating for years. Halle hadn't considered they'd be overheard. Or that if they were overheard that Zachariah would go back and tell her cousin immediately. This day was getting even worse.

"See, that's what I thought. I told you you heard wrong," Kayla yelled, obviously talking to Zachariah. "You can't be just saying stuff without being sure. You know how rumors go in this town. You gonna have everyone talking about Halle and Shania."

"That's why I asked," Zachariah said in the background. "I wasn't trying to spread rumors."

"He didn't hear wrong," Halle mumbled.

"Wait, what?" Kayla nearly screeched. "Zach, hush. Halle, what you say?"

Halle looked at the ceiling and wished that the light fixture over the table would fall, hit her on the head and she'd wake up tomorrow realizing this was just a really bad dream. The light remained in place. Which meant she had to deal with this immediately.

"He didn't hear wrong. Did anyone else hear?"

"Hold up! Quinton's her daddy for real. How could you not tell me?" The accusation in Kayla's voice made Halle's stomach twist. She was going to have everyone asking her the same question. From her family to her friends, and even the people who worked at the school district.

"It's a long story, but I don't want to get into that right now. Ask Zachariah if anyone else overheard."

Kayla asked. "Nah, no one else that he knows."

Halle let out a breath. The last thing they needed was for this to be on the Peachtree Cove gossip circle before she and Shania had a chance to figure out what this meant.

"Well… I don't think no one else heard," Zachariah said a second before she could feel any relief.

Halle groaned. Her life was about to get out of hand.

"I never should have listened to you," Quinton said later that night when he was on the phone with his baby sister, Dawn.

Dawn scoffed before replying. "About what? I always give you good advice." The sound of her fingers tapping on her keyboard were in the background. Dawn worked remotely as a training coordinator for an insurance company. She'd said she was chatting with her colleagues in India when he'd called to tell her just how much her advice had thrown his life for a loop.

"Not this time. My life is about to turn upside down."

The typing stopped. "Ooh, you may need your life turned upside down. Your life is way too boring considering you were a professional athlete."

Quinton paced back and forth in his living room. He'd come home, showered and changed into joggers and a T-shirt, and hoped to spend the evening watching a fantasy football show on the sports network. He would not be able to focus on anything football related for the night or foreseeable future.

"I like it boring," he said. "That kept me out of trouble and my name out of the headlines."

"Are you about to be in the headlines?" He could visualize the delighted smile on his sister's face with those words. She loved it whenever he got attention.

"Lord, I hope not," he sighed and shook his head.

"What's going on?" The teasing had left her voice and concern crept in.

He stopped pacing and stared at the family picture of him, his sister and their parents on the wall. His mom had insisted they take the picture for holiday cards the year before. "Remember that time we were hanging out at Christmas and I told you about the donation I made in college?"

"Donation?" A heartbeat later she sucked in a breath. "Oh, *that* donation."

"Yeah. That one. I wondered if I had a kid out there and you told me to do an online DNA test just to see if I got any hits."

"Uh-huh, I remember. You didn't get any hits."

Quinton stared at the picture and tried to imagine Shania in it. If Shania was there, then Halle would be there, too. His heart rate sped up. What the hell was happening to his life?

"Back then I didn't."

There was a long pause and Quinton could imagine his sister's brows drawing together as the meaning of his words worked their way through her brain. She gasped after several seconds. "Nooooo!"

"Yeah." He turned from the picture and started pacing again.

"You found your kid?"

Your kid. The words hit him like a freight train. He had a kid. A kid! Biologically, but did that make Shania *his* kid? Did he have any right to claim her as his daughter considering how she was conceived?

"More like she found me."

"Aww… I have a niece!"

Quinton stopped pacing. His sister sounded delighted. She wasn't supposed to be delighted. She was supposed to be stunned, like he was. "Okay, stop it right there. Don't go calling her your niece or anything. I don't know what any of this means."

"How did she find you? Did she call you or message you through the website where you took the test? Or maybe she hunted you down via social media. You know, she would see that you played professional football. I hope she didn't come to you with some sob story. I don't care if she is your kid. She can't just try and milk you for every dime you've got."

Quinton shook his head. That was like Dawn; she could go from zero to a hundred in less than ten seconds. Which meant she'd see the bright side in a situation and before you could think things were great, she'd also hit you with the worst-case scenario.

"She didn't come to me with a sob story. And she didn't come to me via social media or the website. She came up to me after football practice."

"She hunted you down in person? Oh no, that's the sign of a stalker."

"Hold up, before you go left, let me explain. It's not that bad, but kind of worse. She lives in Peachtree Cove."

"What!"

Quinton jerked the phone away. When Dawn didn't continue yelling, he put it back to his ear. "Not only that, she plays football."

"Wait! The girl on your football team is also your daughter? Quinton, how in the world did that happen?"

He sank down on the couch. "I wish I knew."

"Oh my God, it's meant to be. We always wondered why you took that job in that small town instead of coming back here. Now I know. It was fate."

"It's not fate. It's messed up. Dawn, don't you know how messed up this is? My kid is one of my players. I don't even know if I can call her that. What does this mean? What does this make me to her? Am I supposed to step in and try to be a father now?"

"Do you want to be a father?"

He thought about raising a kid. He was a coach because he wanted to give back. To pour into the younger generation some of the support and respect that hadn't been poured into him. He felt responsible for every kid on that team and wanted them to all feel like they were a part of a family. Now one of them really was his family. He didn't know how to handle that.

He jumped up and started pacing again. "I don't know. I

don't know how knowing this is supposed to change anything. Halle wanted—"

"Who's Halle? Your daughter?"

"No, Halle is her mother."

"Ahh, gotcha."

"Halle wanted an anonymous donation. She didn't want her child's father to be a part of her kid's life. I should have thought of that when I did the DNA test."

"Well, your daughter found you, so obviously she wants to know who her dad is."

He thought about Shania's eyes as she'd confronted him. Straightforward and insistent. He looked back at the family picture. His eyes. She wasn't going anywhere.

Then he remembered the horror on Halle's face with the revelation. "Her mom can still say that I'm not allowed to be involved."

He wouldn't be surprised if that was what Halle wanted. They were barely on each other's radar. Both distant employees in the Peachtree Cove school district. He'd noticed her because she was a good-looking woman. She'd only noticed him because she'd wanted to make sure he wouldn't treat her daughter unfairly. Otherwise, she never would have looked twice at him.

"Can't you fight for rights?"

"What rights? Come on, I didn't exactly make the donation because I wanted kids or because I wanted to be involved. I made that donation so Mom and Dad wouldn't get kicked out of their apartment. I made the donation and moved on with my life. I never thought about it again."

"I don't believe that. Otherwise you wouldn't have spilled your guts that day after Christmas," Dawn said, slapping away his bullshit of an answer. "You admitted then that you always wondered what had happened. Who'd gotten your donation and if you had a kid out there. Admit it, Q, you wanted to find your child. Now that you have, you can't just turn your back and pretend as if you don't know."

"But that doesn't mean I can force my way into their life. Or that I'll be welcome." That Halle would welcome him.

"I mean…true, but you never know. Things are kind of messy right now. It's going to take some time for things to settle down. Just take it one day at a time. You've found her. That's the good thing." Dawn's voice was filled with optimism.

"Maybe you're right. I'll get with Halle, and we can figure out what the next steps should be."

Even though he had a pretty good idea based on her reaction that she wouldn't want any next steps. The way she grabbed Shania and rushed out of his office made him think she didn't want him to have anything to do with her or Shania.

"I needed to tell someone, but can you keep this just between us?" Quinton wasn't ready for his parents and their *give me grandchildren* request right now. Figuring this out with Halle, the school, the team, was going to be hard enough.

"You're not going to tell Mom and Dad?"

"Not right now. Not while I'm still trying to figure out what all this will mean. You know how Mom and Dad are. They want a grandkid more than anything. If they get even a hint of this, they'll be down here making things worse. Promise me, Dawn, that you won't say anything."

His sister sighed. "Fine. I won't say anything until you tell me to."

"I mean it. Don't let it slip out or anything like that. They can't know until I say they need to know."

"What if your daughter finds them?" she said smugly.

"Dawn," Quinton said in a serious voice. Shania had looked for him. Now that she found him there was no need for her to look for his parents.

"I'm just saying. What if she does?"

"I'll worry about that if it happens," he countered. "But unless that happens, then we won't bring it up until I say it's time."

"What if you never say it's time?"

"Dawn, please." His voice snapped with exasperation. His sister was like a dog with a bone on some things. She was decent at keeping a secret, but she would eventually spill. He knew he couldn't hide this from his parents forever, but he needed a window before involving them.

"Fine. You're right. I won't say anything."

"Good. The last thing I need is for them to just show up here and make this situation worse."

Nine

QUINTON WASN'T SURE WHAT HE EXPECTED TO HAP-pen next, but it wasn't for Halle to call him later that night insisting they needed to speak. From the way Halle had dragged Shania out of his office and deflected during the conversation, he half expected her to ignore the issue for as long as possible. He shouldn't have been surprised she'd taken the initiative. Halle wasn't one to ignore a problem when it popped up.

When she'd called him, she'd already had a plan in place. "We need to talk, and it has to be someplace where we won't be overheard. I don't want Shania to get involved and, knowing her, she will insert herself. Do you mind if I come by your place in the morning before football practice?"

She'd spoken to him in her clipped principal voice and he'd said yes before he could think about offering a different option. He hadn't had the time or felt the inclination to say no. Afterward, he'd chastised himself for agreeing so quickly. With a few words Halle had him following her lead. He felt like he had the first time he'd stepped on the football field in college and the coach blew the whistle. Halle was not going to be blowing his whistle.

The doorbell rang right on time at seven in the morning. Quinton ran a hand over his shirt to straighten out any wrinkles, realized what he was doing and shook out what he'd smoothed. He opened the door. Halle stood on the other side, dressed in a blue dress that clung to her full breasts and hips. Something he noticed even with the beige blazer she wore over it. She looked sexy and put together as she always did. He wished she were at his place just to see him and not because of these circumstances.

He stepped back to let her in. "Do you want something to drink? Coffee or anything?"

She shook her head. "No, this isn't a social visit."

"It doesn't have to be a social visit for this to be a cordial visit."

Halle watched for a second before nodding. "I'll take some coffee."

"Come on in the kitchen."

She followed him into the kitchen. She looked around his place, which was stylishly decorated thanks to the interior decorator he'd hired, and full of mementos from his days playing football as well as pictures of his family. He liked his house and wondered what she thought of it.

In the kitchen, he went to the coffeepot and poured her a cup of coffee. He drank multiple cups in the morning, black, and didn't bother with the single-serve machines that were popular now. He brought the coffee over to her with the sugar bowl.

"No cream, right?" he asked.

Her brows lifted. "Right. How did you know that?"

"I noticed you didn't put cream in your coffee at one of the district trainings."

She blinked several times. Quinton was a master at keeping his emotions off his face. Being bullied in high school followed by years of proving himself on the field trained him to keep emotions hidden, but that didn't stop the embarrassment of admitting that he paid attention to her from churning his stomach.

She looked away and added sugar to her coffee. Two teaspoons. He made a mental note of that and then brushed the back of his neck. "So, what did you want to talk about?"

Halle took a tentative sip before looking up and meeting his eyes. "We need to have another test."

"Another test?"

She nodded. "Yes, to verify what Shania found out."

"You don't believe I'm her father." Even though he couldn't believe it, this couldn't be a coincidence.

Halle held up a hand. "I don't know if the test is correct or not. But before we shake things up, I think we should verify. It could be a fluke."

"It could be." He hesitated a beat. "But did you really get artificially inseminated?"

Her lips pressed together before she nodded. "I did."

"Where did you go for the donation?" Could it be possible they'd gone to different locations?

"I used a private donation company. Fertile Grounds in Atlanta?" Her voice rose at the end, making the sentence a question.

Quinton closed his eyes and sighed. "That's where I went." He'd never forget walking into that office. The pictures of fruit orchards and vegetable fields all over the walls. They'd taken the fertile grounds name and worn it into the ground.

"What made you donate?"

He shrugged. "I needed money. A friend on the team told me that women would pay a lot of money for the sperm of an athlete."

"And you thought donating sperm was your best option?"

"I did what I had to do to keep my parents in their apartment at the time. I was told my sperm wouldn't be split between multiple women. I didn't like the idea of having…dozens or more kids out there. Not when I was aiming to play professionally."

He'd made sure of that before donating. That was the only reason why he'd gone with his friend's idea. He could donate as much as he wanted, but his sample would only go to one person. After one donation he'd had enough. The idea of lots of kids tied to him that he had no clue existed had made him uncomfortable.

He studied Halle before asking, "Why did you get inseminated?"

She lifted her chin. Her lips pressed together and he worried she wouldn't answer. After a few tense seconds she spoke. "I lost my mom in high school and my dad when I was in college. I have aunts and uncles, but I still felt alone. So, I decided to have a child and have my own family."

Quinton didn't know what to say. He wasn't surprised that Halle would take fate into her own hands and decide to have a child on her own terms. But there was also an ache in his chest imagining her feeling so alone that she would make that decision. She was smart, strong, and always helping others, but who was there to help her?

"I'm sorry. I didn't know about your parents," he said quietly.

She swallowed hard before nodding. "Thank you." After a pause she continued. "We still should verify the results."

The coincidence was too much to deny, but he could understand her reasoning. They could have just ended up at the same place. An online DNA test could be wrong. Unlikely, but stranger things had happened. "I agree."

"Regardless of the outcome, Shania wants this. You don't."

Quinton frowned, thrown off by the comment. "What do you mean?"

"You made an anonymous donation. I understand that you don't want to be involved."

He'd made the anonymous donation then because he hadn't wanted the word to get out about what he'd done to keep his parents housed. That didn't mean that he was against ever being found. Otherwise, he wouldn't have taken the online DNA test, no matter what his sister said.

"You want me to pretend as if I don't know?"

She gave him a questioning look. "I'm just saying that I don't expect anything from you. Would I like for Shania to have a father figure in her life? Yes, but someone that I also want to be with. Not someone forced into the role."

"You mean someone like Gregory?" The words came out before his thought finished forming. Was she really trying to get him to step aside to avoid causing problems with that guy? Would she just brush this under the rug if he agreed so she could stay with the English teacher?

"I'm not dating Gregory just so he could be a father to Shania, but, yes, he is someone I would want."

Quinton studied her through narrowed eyes. "You don't want me?"

She swallowed hard. "If the test is positive, we'll go from there. If you don't want to be involved, I won't blame you. You literally were a sperm donor. I won't force you to do anything."

"What if I want you?" he asked. He'd been pushed aside in his life before, but this time, he wasn't willing to be disregarded. Not by Halle. He ignored the part of him that wanted her to want him even if Shania wasn't their kid.

Halle's dark eyes widened. Full lips parted as she inhaled sharply. "What?"

Quinton's eyes remained fixed on her face. On the doubt in her eyes about him wanting to be involved in Shania's life. The thinly veiled expectation that he was going to disappoint her and Shania. Just like that, he had the answer to the question he'd been unable to give when he spoke with his sister.

He moved to stand next to her at the kitchen island and asked again, his voice direct and low. "What if I want to be a part of your life?"

Halle clutched the coffee mug with both hands. The heat radiating through the ceramic container overpowered the spark she'd felt when Quinton asked if she wanted him. She blamed it on the shock of an unexpected question. That was all it could be. His words were getting scrambled up in her brain.

Verifying the test results would make him a part of her life. Not just Shania's, but Halle's as well. His wanting to be involved only meant that he wanted to be there for Shania. No matter how much her heart rate had picked up or how her cheeks prickled with heat, his words weren't directed at her specifically.

"Do you want to be a part of Shania's life?"

"If the results are true. Yes." He raised a brow. "You look surprised."

"I am, a little. You donated and didn't look back."

"I donated because I had to. I went with that company because they promised me they wouldn't spread a word about my donation to the school or the media."

"You didn't make other donations?" she asked hopefully.

He shook his head. "Other teammates made multiple donations. I didn't. The thought of having multiple kids out there wasn't something I wanted. Afterward, I always wondered what had happened. If there was a kid out there."

The slight wistfulness in his voice told more than his stoic expression had. He hadn't donated and walked away. He had wondered what happened with his kid. "You want to be a father?"

He glanced away quickly and shrugged before meeting her gaze again. "I've thought about it. I don't want to have kids with just anyone. I want to be in a relationship. I want to give my kid stability. Something I didn't have a lot of growing up."

"Weren't you dating someone when you first moved to town?"

His face shuttered before he spoke. "I was."

"No kids?"

He shook his head. "Not with her or anyone else."

"Well, if the results are right, you've got one with me."

The idea shook the foundation of everything in her life. Shania had a father. A father who might want to be a part of their life. Not some mystery person behind a profile she'd chosen, but this man in front of her. A man who was more interesting with each conversation they had.

"I don't have any kids through the traditional sense with anyone else," he said with a half smile.

Halle's lips quirked at the nice way he'd cleaned that up. Then she thought about him creating a child in a traditional way. Thought about him creating a child with *her* in the traditional sense. Then she wasn't thinking about kids at all as her curiosity did what it always did: took an idea and clung to it. What kind of lover would Quinton be? Would he listen or was he like a bull in a china shop, just going for his own pleasure?

She blinked and took a sip of her coffee. She was not going to think about Quinton that way. If she was going to think about sex, then she was going to think about sex with Gregory. Quinton may be Shania's biological father, but he was not about to be the father of any new brothers or sisters she may have.

"I just wanted to talk with you about what we do next. Now that we've gotten that straightened out, I guess I should go."

"Are you going by the middle school today?" he asked. His dark eyes traveled down her body and back up. Not long enough to be considered a leer, but still intense enough to make heat flash in her chest. "Or do you have other plans?"

"I am going to the school. I've got a lot to do to get ready for the upcoming year. Other than practice, are you getting ready for the year?"

"I do manage to drag myself away from the football field and get caught up on the lesson plan before the year starts." The light in his eye told her he was teasing even though his face was serious. He would be cute if he smiled. It was time for her to go.

She pushed away her barely touched coffee. "Good to know. I'll call you when I set up the time for the test."

"We can purchase a DNA kit."

"I'd rather go to a professional and be sure."

Quinton held up a hand. "Whatever you want."

Why did he have to say it like that? In a deep, rumbling voice that sent little earthquakes off in her body. He was not agreeing to *whatever* she wanted. Just agreeing to her wishes related to Shania, who was the most important person in her life and the reason why Halle was here in the first place.

She straightened her shoulders. "Good. I'll give you a call when I have the appointment scheduled."

He nodded. "Just say when." He led her back through his home to the front door.

"Halle," Quinton said just as they reached the front door.

She turned to face him. He stood close enough for her to smell the fresh scent of his body wash but not close enough for her to feel the heat of his body. Yet, in the small area of his entryway, he sucked up the space. All she saw was broad shoulders and a wide, muscled chest. His dark eyes met and clung to hers.

"Yes?" she asked, her response coming out breathier than she intended.

"I don't want to make this difficult for you or Shania. Despite my reason for donating, I'm willing to be as involved as you want me to be. I may not have created her in the traditional sense, but she's still mine. I take care of my responsibilities."

His eyes and voice were steady and strong. The tremors from her earlier emotional earthquake started again. If she wasn't careful, she'd begin to fall for him. Quinton was handsome, and, she had to admit, nice. He hadn't been someone she'd considered dating before. She didn't want to fall for him just because he was a decent guy offering to be responsible. Then there was Gregory, the man she'd considered perfect for her, the man she'd already fantasized about building a life with. Was she really going to throw that away because Quinton happened to be the guy who donated sperm fourteen years ago? This coincidence didn't mean they belonged together.

"Thank you for that, but if the results turn out to be true, I don't mind you becoming a part of Shania's life, but there will be clear boundaries. We won't be a family or anything like that. Just co-parents."

He raised a brow. "Co-parents?"

She nodded. "Exactly."

His jaw twitched as if he was going to say something before he shook his head. "If that's what you want."

"It is."

"Fine," he said easily.

"Fine," she shot back. Once again, she felt as if there was more to be said. That even though he'd agreed with her, he still thought she was going to regret her words later.

Halle spun around and reached for the door. The bell rang just as she was swinging it open. Her gaze collided with Gregory's, and she sucked in a breath.

Gregory's eyes widened in surprise. He looked from Halle to Quinton standing behind her and back again. "Halle?"

She scrambled for words. "G… Gregory. What are you doing here?"

He held up a package. "Quinton's mail was delivered to my place yesterday by mistake."

"His package?"

Quinton stepped forward. His chest nearly brushed Halle's back. She shivered as the heat of him seeped into her and scooted out of the way. He reached for the package. "Thanks. I appreciate it."

Halle frowned. "Why are you getting his packages?"

"I live at three fourteen and he's three forty-one. Last week they mixed up our mailing addresses and we found out we were neighbors." Gregory frowned. "What are you doing here? First thing in the morning?"

"She came about Shania," Quinton spoke quickly.

Gregory's frown deepened before a heartbeat later his face cleared up. "Something with football, right?"

Quinton opened his mouth, but Halle jumped in. "Yeah, something with football. Shania had a rough day yesterday and I wanted to talk to Coach Evans without everyone around. You know how I am about Shania."

Gregory's smile creased his face. "I do. If you're done, I'd love to take you out for coffee."

"She just had coffee," Quinton said matter-of-factly.

Halle glared at him. "I didn't finish it." She turned back to Gregory. "I'd love to have coffee with you. And I was just leaving."

"Good," Gregory said. He reached out and took her hand. "Quinton, see you later."

Quinton made some type of noise of agreement. He gave Halle one last look before turning and going into the house. Gregory squeezed her hand and led her off the porch. Halle didn't look back as she fought of a weird feeling that she'd somehow wronged Quinton. Her life wasn't going to change just because of this. Until she proved he really was Shania's father, she wasn't about to upend the good thing she had going for her.

Ten

A KNOCK ON HIS OFFICE DOOR INTERRUPTED QUIN-
ton as he reviewed the drills he planned to run the kids through
before their first scrimmage of the season. Zachariah stood at
his door. "Umm, you got a second?"

Quinton pushed aside the three-ring binder that contained
the outline of the drills he liked to run, some of them familiar
ones, some plays he'd come up with over the years, and nodded. "Yeah, what's going on?"

Zachariah looked over his shoulder before coming into the
office and shutting the door. "I need to ask you something."

Quinton frowned. Typically, Zachariah would come straight
in, plop down in a chair and get straight to whatever was on his
mind. He didn't typically close Quinton's door. Which meant
his question couldn't be good.

"What's wrong?"

Zachariah shifted in his chair and wrung his hands. "Nothing, I hope. It's just... I kind of overheard your conversation with Shania and Halle the other day."

Quinton's body stilled. "What part?"

"The part where you and her told Halle that she was your daughter." Zachariah raised one bushy brow. "Is it true?"

Quinton swallowed and considered his words. Halle didn't want this information out there already. Hell, he didn't want the information out just yet. He didn't doubt the online DNA results Shania showed him, but a part of him still didn't feel like the situation was real. He was good with focusing on the ramifications of this after Halle got her second test.

"Did anyone else overhear that?" That was the most important thing. If this had already gotten out, he needed to know how much damage control he'd have to do.

Zachariah shook his head. "I don't think so."

Quinton's eyes narrowed. "You don't think so or you know for sure?"

"No one else was in the hall when I heard. I was coming down looking for you to make sure things were good when I overheard. I wasn't trying to eavesdrop."

"But you did."

Zachariah held up his hands in defense. "Aye, I was just coming down the hall when Shania blurted it out. I wasn't eavesdropping like that. Besides, that's a conversation you have behind a *closed door*." He pointed to the shut office door.

Quinton sighed. He had a point. "Alright, I'll give you that."

"So you and Halle..."

"It's not what you think. In fact, I don't really want to get into it. For now, please, just keep what you heard to yourself. We're still trying to figure this entire situation out."

"What's there to figure out? Either you're her dad or you're not."

"It's complicated," Quinton said. Two words that were the biggest understatement he'd ever heard.

Things were more than complicated. They were tangled and twisted and could spiral out of control. He wanted to be a part of Shania's life. Being a part of her life was also being a part of Halle's life. But from the way she'd rushed off his porch with her hand in Gregory's reminded him that he was not Halle's type. He may be clocking for her, but she most definitely wasn't thinking about giving him the time of day. Gregory was whom she wanted for Shania's father. Not Quinton.

"Damn right it's complicated," Zachariah said, scattering Quinton's thoughts.

"Huh?"

Zachariah scooted forward to the edge of his chair. His eyes intent as they met Quinton's. "I know you're not going to act like you don't know how this changes things."

He had a good idea that this would change a lot. His life. His relationship with Shania. Everything was changing, but he wasn't sure how that was Zachariah's concern.

"Changes what things?"

"The team," Zachariah said as if that was the obvious answer. "Its dynamics. The way the rest of the school and the district is going to view things."

Quinton wanted to play dumb, but he immediately understood. "I don't play favorites."

"It doesn't matter if you don't play favorites or not. When you have a kid on the team it'll look that way. You've already gotten into Clyde's ass about not including Shania enough."

"I did that because he wasn't. He doesn't want a girl on the team." In the practices since then he'd done a better job of including Shania, but only marginally.

"You think he's going to care about the reasons after this gets out? He's already a borderline crybaby. He's going to assume that anything you say to him about the way he coaches her is because she's your daughter. Then there's the district."

Quinton scowled. "Why would the district care?"

"They've let us make concessions for Shania playing ball with us. But they also want to see us win. No matter how you frame it, Shania being on the team is already something they weren't sure we'd be able to accommodate. We have, but any other requests might be viewed the same way. Then there are the parents who'll get mad that she'll get play time and their kids don't."

"She'll get play time because she's a good receiver."

Zachariah placed a hand on his chest. "I know she's good. You know she's good. But all they'll see is a parent letting his kid get play time instead of putting their kid on the field."

Quinton held up a hand, realized he was mimicking Halle, and dropped it. "Look, I get it."

"Nah, you don't get it. It was easy for you to ignore some of the taunts before because they were just directed at you. Now they'll be at you and your kid, and you can't pop off."

Quinton blinked and drew back. "I don't pop off."

"Wait until someone talks about your kid. I almost got into it with another parent at my kid's soccer game when they were eleven. It's why I'm glad he stuck with that over football. It hits different when it's your kid."

"I'll be able to handle it," Quinton said confidently. "No matter what they throw at me."

It couldn't be worse than what he'd heard from angry fans in the stands in high school and college. Not to mention the people who criticized everything he did from sports reporters to couch coaches online. Quinton had formed a thick skin.

"You say that now, but I'm telling you. Shania being your kid is going to be a problem."

"Shania being my kid is *my* problem. Not the team's, not the school, not the district and damn sure not any of the other parents. I'm not the kind of person to let this change the way I coach. I'm still the same Quinton Evans."

Zachariah sighed and shook his head. "I'm just trying to look out for you."

"And I appreciate that." He really didn't. He wanted to tell Zachariah to kiss his ass and get out of his office, but he wouldn't. Zachariah really was trying to be a good assistant coach and colleague. "Trust me. I've got this."

"Quinton is Shania's what!" Tracey's yelp echoed across the lake.

Halle placed a hand over her face. She, Tracey and Imani sat on their boulder close to the banks of Ridgeview Lake. Their high school hangout spot that they'd turned into their adult hangout spot after Imani moved back to Peachtree Cove. When they were teens the boulder at Ridgeview Lake was a place where they could talk without being overheard by their parents. As adults, the lake was a place where they could slip away to and forget their responsibilities for a little while. Today, Halle suggested the lake because she needed to slip away and the privacy to tell her friends what happened.

They were in their typical setup. A blanket spread out, with Solo cups filled with cheap wine instead of soda and homemade charcuterie spreads on paper plates versus eating whatever junk food they'd get from a convenience store.

"Can you not yell it so everyone in Peachtree Cove can hear you?" Halle said from behind her hands.

There was a tug on her arm. She dropped her hands from her face. Imani gave her arm a gentle squeeze before raising a brow.

"Are you for real?" Concern filled her friend's eyes and voice.

Halle slowly nodded. Tracey's eyes narrowed and she leaned in closer. "How? Not once since he moved here have you said anything about you two hooking up."

"Because we never hooked up."

Tracey shifted and waved a hand as she shook her head. "Nah, that's what I don't understand. You got to explain to me like I'm in kindergarten. Simple words because this ain't making sense."

Sighing, Halle held up her cup. "Pour me some wine before I tell you this story."

Tracey quickly lifted the bottle and poured rosé into Halle's cup. Halle took a fortifying sip before spilling the truth she'd kept to herself for nearly fourteen years. She was barely able to get the story out; Tracey and Imani kept interrupting her for clarification.

"Why would you do that?" Tracey.

"Why didn't you tell us?" Imani.

"Where did you go?" Tracey.

"How did you get this idea?" Imani.

Halle threw up her hands. "Can you give me a chance to get the story out?"

Tracey pursed her lips. "You're not talking fast enough."

Imani patted Tracey's arm. "Okay, let her talk." She looked back at Halle. "Just talk quickly."

Halle uncrossed her legs to fold them and rest her chin on her knees. "I told you why I did it. I felt so alone after losing my dad. Suddenly, I realized I was all that was left of them. No one would talk about or remember them once I was gone."

Imani frowned. "That's not true. I remember them. What happened to your mom is the reason I became a doctor."

Halle gave her cousin a small smile. When Halle's mom had died after complications with her pregnancy and the poor medical care she'd received, Imani had decided to become a doctor. She was a dedicated and great OB-GYN.

"A part of me understood that, but having my aunts and cousins remember or tell me things were going to be okay didn't feel like enough. I wanted my own family. I wanted to share the love they'd given me with someone else. I was interning at that private school and when the principal mentioned that's how she'd had her child… I thought it was a good idea."

"Why on Earth would anyone artificially inseminate a twenty-two-year-old?" Tracey asked. She pointed to Imani and Halle. "I clearly remember both of you saying I was too young to get married, but you can have a whole baby on your own?"

Halle sat up straight. "For the record, that was Imani who said you were too young."

"Hey!" Imani slapped Halle's calf.

"It's true. And they inseminated me because I had the money. They didn't care about my reasons why. It was a private donation company. I didn't need anyone's permission but my own."

"Why didn't you tell us?" Imani sounded not just surprised but hurt about being left out.

"I didn't want anyone to judge me or Shania. You've met my dad's side of the family. My aunt Lydia? Do you really think she wouldn't have thrown the words *test tube baby* in Shania's face?"

Imani cringed but Tracey shook her head and pointed a finger. "That's your mean-ass aunt. I'm talking about *us*. We wouldn't have judged you."

"Yes, you would. You're judging me now."

"No, we're not!" Tracey and Imani spoke in unison.

Halle finished drinking the wine in her cup. "Yes, you are. You're asking why I did it? You would have done the same thing then. I knew that I was walking into a hard situation. I was just out of college. I was starting graduate school and starting out as a teacher. Throw in having a kid with no father on purpose, I knew people would tell me that I was making a mistake. So, instead of dealing with that—"

"You made up a story about some nameless guy on some random night," Imani said.

Halle shrugged. "Would I make a different decision about telling the truth now? Probably, but I don't regret what I did. I know that side of my family. She was going to have a hard enough time not having a father around, but if they knew that

I really had no idea who he was, then that would be just another thing for her to overcome."

"And to think the guy is Coach Q. You two were meant to meet up," Tracey declared.

Halle unfolded her legs and leaned forward, one hand raised to stop that train of thought. "This was a fluke. It's not fate, or anything meant to be."

"Yes, it is. Shania has been bugging you about who her dad is. Then she ends up playing football for him." Imani shrugged. "I don't know, Halle. Maybe you two will end up—"

Halle pushed forward her already raised hand. "Nope. Don't go there. We are not ending up together. I'm making things work with Gregory."

Imani cringed. Her short, manicured nails tapped the cup in her hand. "Have you told him yet?"

"Not yet. I need to get the results verified before I say anything to him."

Halle didn't know how to break the news to him. He'd easily bought her explanation for being at Quinton's place as something to do with football. He was sweet and genuinely seemed to want to see where things would go with their relationship. She was afraid of hurting him, even though she knew she couldn't keep this a secret.

"How do you think he'll take it?" Imani asked.

"He's a reasonable guy. I think he'll understand that even though Quinton is Shania's biological father, it doesn't mean that we can't be together. If things work out with him we'll be a different kind of family."

"So, you're giving Shania two daddies?" Imani asked, sounding skeptical.

Halle opened her mouth to give a smart reply, but stopped. She perked up. "I didn't think about it like that, but I guess so."

"Oh, Lord," Tracey said. "Don't tell her that, Imani. You

know she's an overachiever. Now she's going to try and get Quinton and Gregory to really co-parent."

Halle waved a finger. "Now that you say that it's not a bad idea. Quinton already has a bond with her through football. She gets along well with Gregory. We could make this work."

The more she thought about it the more the idea took hold. Shania could see Quinton and talk to him whenever she wanted. Halle could keep Gregory and still have the relationship she wanted. Shania would have two positive role models and father figures.

"This doesn't sound like it's going to work out the way you want it to work out," Tracey said skeptically. She tugged on her braids with one hand before sipping from her cup.

Undaunted, Halle straightened her shoulders. "Maybe it will. You know me. I can make anything work if I stick my mind to it. If this is the hand I've been dealt, then I'm about to win this game. Just wait and see."

Eleven

"WELL, QUINTON, YOU ARE SHANIA'S FATHER."

Halle expected the answer but hearing the words coming out of Imani's mouth still made her feel as if she was going to fall over. And she was sitting down!

The three of them: she, Shania and Quinton sat in the exam room in the doctor's office connected to the town's hospital. Imani saw her OB-GYN patients there and had agreed to order the DNA test for Halle. Imani gave her a smile that Halle assumed she also used when trying to soften the effect of delivering bad news to a patient.

"I told you," Shania said, sounding triumphant.

Halle pressed a hand to her temple and closed her eyes. "Shania, please."

"Please what? I told you he was my dad. I don't know why we had to do this, but now that we have, we know it's true and I was right. So, what happens now?"

Halle dropped her hand and looked from her daughter's expectant face to Quinton's unreadable one. "What happens is we figure this out."

"What's there to figure out? He's my dad. Which means he's going to be around a lot more and we can do stuff." She turned toward Quinton. "Right?"

Halle shifted forward in her seat. She shot a *help me* glance at Imani, but her friend seemed just as surprised as she was. "Shania—"

"I'll be around as much as you and your mother want," Quinton said evenly. He sounded just as unfazed as he looked. Did anything ruffle this guy's feathers?

Shania grinned. "Really?"

"Yes, but…"

Shania's face fell. "But what?"

"It's going to be an adjustment." He glanced at Halle. "For all of us."

"I'm okay with adjustments," Shania said.

"I'm sure you are, but everyone isn't."

"You're worried about what people will think?" Shania said, being her usual observant self.

"I don't care what people think about me. I just don't want you to be hurt as the word gets out."

Halle appreciated his words. He didn't have to comfort Shania. He didn't have to even promise to be there for her. He could have turned his back on them both and said his initial donation was the only involvement he wanted. She hoped he genuinely meant what he was saying because if he hurt Shania, Halle would find a way to make his life miserable.

"If anyone tries to say or do anything out of line then they'll have to deal with me," Quinton continued. "Plus, it's none of their business."

Imani grunted before clasping her hands on her desk. "As if that stopped people in this town from commenting."

"Let them comment," Halle said, her hand balling into a fist. "They just better do it behind my back because if I hear any kind of talk I'm going to shut it down."

Shania grinned. "You sound like Aunt Tracey."

"I've known her most of my life so that's not a surprise."

Shania's expression turned curious. "So, you're not mad at me for doing this?"

"Being mad won't change anything. We're here now." She looked at Quinton. "We've got to figure this thing out."

"Are you going to invite him to cousins' day?" Shania asked.

"Cousins' day?" Quinton asked, frowning.

Halle looked to Imani for help, but Imani only watched her with barely hidden amusement. "I don't think I should."

The look of affront on Shania's face almost made Halle feel guilty. "Why not?"

"Because Quinton has his own life and he doesn't have to come. Plus, I'm already bringing Gregory."

"What's cousins' day?" Quinton asked.

Shania turned in her chair to face him. "It's a thing Mom and her cousins do. They all get together at the park and do games and stuff. It's the first time Imani will be able to come. And she's bringing Cyril, right?" Imani nodded and Shania grinned. "He's a friend of yours so you'll get to have fun."

"I don't think that will be a good idea," Halle spoke up.

"Why, because of Gregory? He's gotta find out eventually," Shania said, not sounding the least bit concerned about how awkward it would be to have Quinton and Gregory there. "Besides, he's cool. He'll understand."

Halle threw Imani another *help me* look. Thankfully, this time her friend nodded. "Shania, how about we go grab a soda out of the vending machine and let your mom and Coach Q talk."

Halle threw her friend a grateful look before waving toward the door. "Yes, please go get a soda."

Shania's eyes narrowed. "I'm not thirsty."

"Yes, you are," Halle said. "Go and give us a moment."

Shania stared defiantly. Quinton shifted forward and got her attention. "I do need a moment to talk with your mom."

Shania's defiance immediately went away. "Fine."

Halle watched, both amazed and frustrated by how quickly she'd given in to Quinton. She'd been ready to demand Shania leave the room, soda or not. He gives a few evenly spoken words and she agreed. Had to be a fluke. Shania was being nice but her rebellious side would show up with Quinton eventually.

They didn't speak again until after Imani and Shania were out of the room.

"You don't want me at cousins' day?" His voice was calm, but despite the lack of emotion she still felt as if she'd somehow hurt his feelings.

Halle shook her head. "I don't think that's the best time."

"Best time for what?"

"To announce this news to the rest of my family." She had no idea how to tell her family, but was pretty sure introducing him at the pseudo-family reunion would be a recipe for disaster.

"When will be the best time?"

A few weeks. Several years. Never. She couldn't imagine what her family was going to say, much less how they would react when they got the entire story. Her aunts, uncles and cousins had been so supportive of her as she'd raised Shania. They'd wrapped Halle up in their love and care after she'd lost her parents. Even more so when she'd returned to Peachtree Cove with a baby, "abandoned by the child's father." Now, *ta-da*, the dad was back, and not only had he not abandoned her, but he hadn't known who she was to start with. They were going to say she lied to them. She *had* lied to them. She'd never admitted the truth and they'd come up with their own story, and she'd never bothered to correct anyone.

She sighed and shook her head. "I don't know when the best time will be."

"We won't be able to ignore this. The word is going to get out and the people of Peachtree Cove will have things to say, but I meant what I said. I'll be there to protect Shania. And you."

"I don't need you to protect me."

"You may not need me to, but that doesn't mean I won't try."

His words stirred something in her chest. The warmth of comfort, a hope that his words were true and a belief that they were based on the sincerity in his eyes. An unwanted thrill went across her skin. She cut it off before it could settle in and get comfortable. She was not going to start this. She had Gregory. She liked Gregory. She'd fantasized about possibly *marrying* Gregory if things worked out. Now, because handsome, dependable and considerate Quinton Evans was thrust into her life, she was supposed to change her plans?

She stood. "Gregory can protect me. You worry about Shania. There's no need to come to cousins' day."

She walked to the door, done with the conversation, but Quinton stood and blocked her path. "I don't care about what Gregory can or can't do. I'm telling you what I'm going to do."

"I didn't ask you to do anything."

He took a step forward. "You don't have to always ask. My help is freely given."

"I don't need your help."

"Then what do you need?" He quirked a brow before his eyes dipped to her lips.

Heat flashed through her body. He was standing too close. She could smell the spice of his cologne. His dark eyes were hypnotic as the honesty in his question started that thrill up in her again.

"I need—"

He took another half step forward. "Because if you tell me

what you need from me, I promise I'll do whatever I can to give it to you."

She squeezed her thighs as heat turned into the burn of desire. She hadn't felt like this in a long time. She was attracted to Gregory. But this, this thing Quinton just stirred in her, was wild and hot and raw and completely unexpected.

"I have everything I need," she blurted out. Embarrassed by how she felt and the train of her thoughts.

"Do you?" The quiet question wrapped around her like red silk and pulled tight.

She swallowed hard. "I do."

His eyes dropped to her mouth. She licked her lips. His gaze rose back to hers. He didn't come closer, but she saw that he wanted to. That he was thinking what she was thinking. Saw it, and her heart impersonated a jackrabbit in her chest.

Then he took a step back. His expression cleared and he nodded. "Fine."

She blinked. Waited for him to say more. He didn't. Just watched her. She lifted her chin. This was good. He understood what she was saying. "So we're clear."

"Very clear. Let's go find Shania." He turned and walked out.

Halle watched him saunter away and frowned. This was not fine.

He shouldn't have come. He wasn't supposed to come. But damn his competitive spirit. Halle wasn't his. She made it very clear that she wanted Gregory. He was not the man she would have picked for Shania's father, but damn if he didn't want to prove that since he was her father that fate hadn't made a mistake. He wasn't going to be pushed out.

Feeling unwanted or underestimated wasn't new to him. He'd battled against that most of his life and had proven his worthiness ten times over. He'd considered himself over the need to prove himself to anyone again, but Halle hit his buttons. One thing he knew was that he didn't back down from a challenge. He'd known he was going to show up the minute Halle insisted Gregory was coming so he wasn't needed.

He spotted his friend Cyril talking with Imani and a few other people beneath one of the picnic shelters. Sliding on his aviator sunglasses and Peachtree Cove High School baseball cap, Quinton took a deep breath and crossed the grassy field toward the shelter. Cyril noticed him first. His friend grinned and waved him over. Imani turned toward him; her eyes widened and her jaw dropped. She turned back to Cyril and said something. Quinton was too far away to hear but didn't need to. The *what's he doing here* look followed by Cyril's quick shrug told him everything.

"Q, you decided to come," Cyril said when he got close.

"I did. You said you needed a little help with the flag football, so here I am."

Imani raised a brow. "Flag football, huh? That's what you're here for?"

Quinton turned to her. "Yep."

She shook her head. "Alright," she said in a *this is going to be interesting* tone of voice. "Quinton, these are my cousins and their spouses." Imani introduced the three men and two women, who then turned and pointed out their kids either sitting beneath the shelter on their phones or enjoying the playground equipment nearby.

Some Quinton recognized from around town. Others he learned were from out of town and here for their cousins' day.

"What is cousins' day, exactly?" Quinton asked.

Imani's cousin Mick answered. He looked to be in his late thirties, with dreadlocks that hung down his back and a broad smile. "After our grandmother passed a few years back, the family didn't get together for holidays like they used to. This is our way to keep the family together."

Quinton nodded and tried to think about the last time he

hung out with his cousins. His mom was one of five and his dad the youngest of three. His aunts and uncles had struggled to get by just as much as his parents had. Each of them scattered to different parts of the country and rarely came together without a wedding or funeral involved. He was cool with a good many of his cousins, but honestly, they didn't call him unless they needed something.

"Does everyone come?" he asked.

Mick shrugged. "Most everyone. If they can't, no big deal. We'll catch 'em the next time."

"You came up with the idea?"

Mick shook his head. "Nah, it was Halle's idea."

Quinton wasn't surprised. If Halle spotted a problem, she would find a way to solve it. The family drifting apart would be the kind of thing that would spur her to pull everyone back together.

Imani's eyes lit up and she pointed. "There's Halle."

Even though his heart rate picked up and his stomach clenched, Quinton turned slowly in the direction she indicated. He was glad he wore shades, so any hint of his uncertainty was hidden behind the reflective lenses. When he spotted her, he was happy the shades blocked his expression for another reason. His eyes widened at the sight of Halle in a pair of short basketball shorts, which left her thick thighs and long legs out for his viewing pleasure. Her smooth shoulders were bare in a sleeveless sports top that she'd tied into a knot at the front, revealing an enticing sliver of cinnamon-brown skin. Quinton licked his lips. She looked damn good dressed like this.

Shania walked to Halle's right and waved. Gregory stood on Halle's left. Quinton's brows knitted together. She had brought him. When her eyes landed on Quinton they narrowed and her lips pressed into a line.

"Right on time," Mick said before frowning. "Did you bring the coolers?"

Halle nodded. "They're in the back of my SUV. I wasn't carrying all that by myself."

"Doesn't look like you're by yourself," Mick said with a grin. "You must be Gregory." Mick held out a hand.

Gregory smiled and shook Mick's hand. "I am. Has Halle been talking about me?"

Mick's wife, Beverly, grinned. "Maybe just a little bit."

"Coach Q, you came," Shania said, beaming. She quickly moved to stand next to Quinton.

Quinton couldn't help but return her smile. She, at least, was happy to see him. "Yeah, when Cyril mentioned flag football, I said I'd come and referee."

Halle raised a brow and looked at Quinton. "Oh really."

Cyril looked to Mick. "Want to grab those coolers? It's going to be a long, hot day."

"Sure," Mick said. "Where are your keys?"

Halle handed them over. "It's two back there."

"Do you need any help?" Gregory asked.

"Nah, we've got this," Cyril said.

Mick and Cyril walked toward the parking lot. Halle eyed him warily while Gregory gave Quinton a quizzical look.

"I didn't know you referee as well as coach," Gregory said. He sounded pleasant enough, but Quinton saw the question in his eye.

"I don't. Just helping out my boy, Cyril."

"Hmm," Gregory said, eyeing him. A second later he slid closer to Halle. "What do you need me to do? You know I'm here to help."

Halle clasped her hands together and nodded. When she spoke, it was in her efficient, principal's voice. "Mick and I usually set up before everyone gets here. Cards and board games over here under the picnic shelter. We can set up the badminton net next to it, and Zachariah said he's bringing the flags for the football game. My cousin Robbie is going to fire up the grill."

"Zachariah?" Quinton asked. "My coach?"

Halle nodded stiffly. "Yeah, he's dating my cousin, Kayla. You didn't know that?"

He shook his head. "I didn't realize she was your cousin."

"Yep. Small world."

They exchanged a glance. Did she know that Zachariah already knew? Zachariah had approached him about overhearing his conversation with Halle, but that didn't mean her cousin had said anything. It was one thing for Imani to know; she was closest to Halle and wouldn't say anything. With two other people who knew what was up, he wondered if they could keep the secret during the entire day. He knew they had to tell everyone eventually, but he didn't think Halle wanted it blurted out at cousins' day. He'd be sure to pull Zachariah to the side when they got there and ask him to keep things quiet.

"Ooh, Halle, look at you! Got your boyfriend and your baby daddy here," a woman's voice called from behind them. "Girl, you're really trying to shake up cousins' day, huh."

Halle's eyes bugged. Quinton sucked in a breath. Shania's jaw dropped. The three of them turned just as Zachariah strolled up with a woman with bright, inquisitive eyes, a short, cropped haircut and a similar stature to Halle. With the arrival of Halle's cousin Kayla, Quinton understood why he should have stayed his ass at home.

Twelve

"WHAT IS SHE TALKING ABOUT?" GREGORY ASKED, CON-fusion clouding his voice.

Heat engulfed Halle like a ball of flames straight out of hell. Why in the world would Kayla come out here and tell the whole world everything? Because Kayla was the world's messiest gossip, that was why.

Halle hurried over to Kayla's side and elbowed her cousin. "If you don't stop playing, you're going to start something."

Kayla frowned. "Huh?"

"Oh look, there's Robbie with the grill." She pointed in that direction. "Gregory, can you help him with that? Quinton, will you go with Zachariah to set up for flag football?"

Thankfully, Quinton didn't hesitate a beat. "Yeah, come on, Zachariah." He walked over and grabbed Zachariah by the elbow and pulled him away.

Gregory looked ready to ask another question, but Robbie, as loud and impatient as usual, was already hollering for someone to help him pull the grill. Gregory gave her one last glance before hurrying to help. Once the guys were clear, Halle pinched Kayla's arm.

"Ouch! What was that for?" Kayla rubbed her arm.

"Because you're messy and starting stuff," Halle shot back, not feeling an ounce of guilt for the pinch. "Please keep your mouth shut."

"Why, isn't that why he's here, for everyone to know what's up?"

"He's here because he's helping Cyril," Imani jumped in. "That's it."

Shania crossed her arms. "I don't know why we can't just tell everyone. He's here because he said he wants to be in my life."

Halle took a long breath. "And he can be, but the cousins' day cookout is *not* the day to tell the story."

"Then when is the day?" Shania asked.

"Yeah, when?" Kayla followed up. "Because I can't keep this secret forever."

Halle barely stopped herself from rolling her eyes. "It's not a secret forever. It's just not the topic of conversation for today, okay? Now, keep this quiet or else I'll tell Zachariah about all the boxes you ship to my house." Kayla loved trying out new sex toys, but Zachariah hated when she used them, which Halle thought was dumb, but when Kayla asked if she could ship them to her place, Halle had agreed.

Kayla's eyes narrowed. "You wrong for that."

"And you're wrong for blurting out my business like that. Now zip it." Halle ran a finger across her mouth and twisted as if zipping her lips and locking them.

Sighing, Kayla threw up a hand. "Fine. Just for today."

"Thank you. Now, will you go help your sister with her bags? She just showed up with her kids."

Kayla pursed her lips but turned and walked away. Shania

immediately came up to her. "Mom, are you going to keep this a secret from everyone?"

Halle placed a hand on Shania's shoulder. "No, baby, but today, like this, isn't the time or the place. Let's enjoy the day and I'll let everyone know soon."

"I can't pretend as if I'm not happy that he's here."

"I'm not asking you to. Just let everyone think it's because he's your coach. We'll figure this out, okay?"

Shania sighed. "I don't get it, but fine. I'll go help him and Mr. Cyril set up."

Halle watched her daughter jog over to Zachariah and Quinton. Imani wrapped an arm around her shoulder. "Are you going to make it?"

"No. Did you know Quinton was coming?"

She'd hoped he wouldn't show up. Prayed even, but she'd seen the look in his eye. The look that said she wasn't going to ignore him. He wanted to be involved in Shania's life, and honestly, she wanted him to get to know Shania. But she wasn't sure if she was ready to have Quinton in *her* life.

Imani tilted her head to the side. "I didn't, but I'm not surprised. I saw the look in his face yesterday when you said you wanted to keep things quiet."

"What look?"

"It's hard to describe it, but I think he likes you."

Halle scoffed. "Quinton? Nah, he dates Instagram models and pop stars."

"The man dated one R and B singer and they broke up. Why would that mean he doesn't like you?"

"Because. I'm not his type. He told me." Numerous times. The look in his eye the day before—that was just a challenge. Not because he really was into her. He'd lose interest in a day once he realized she didn't give a damn about football that didn't involve Shania, and that she was just as boring as people expected high school principals to be.

Imani bumped Halle's hip with hers. "Yeah, well, the way he looked at you the other day said otherwise."

"You're seeing things because you're in love now. Quinton is just being nice to Shania and me. That's it."

"I don't know. I think the man is going to try and lay claim to you."

A weird shiver went through her at the thought of him laying claim. She shook her head and moved out of Imani's embrace. "Stop it. You're just as messy as Kayla. Besides, I'm with Gregory."

"Gregory isn't the father of your kid."

"Girl, stop! Quinton was a donor, that's all. There's nothing between us. Just mutual interest in doing what's right. Now, will you please stop being messy? It's cousins' day and I need to set up the board games."

"Who you calling messy? Miss *got my man and baby daddy at the same event*," Imani said with a grin and a laugh.

Halle swatted at Imani, who easily evaded the hit. "Go find something to do and leave me alone."

Imani continued to chuckle as she blew Halle a kiss and hurried over to help grab the food from Kayla and her sister. Halle shook her head. Quinton liking her? No way. She looked in the direction he'd gone with Zachariah. He was looking her way. She couldn't read his expression, not with the aviator glasses and the hat he wore shadowing his face. Still, heat spread through her body. Tightening her nipples and sending a shiver down her spine. She spun away before she began to believe the foolishness Imani was spouting.

"The man is going to try and lay claim to you."

Halle sucked in a breath and looked up from the cards in her hand to the field where the flag football game was about to start. Quinton wore those damn aviator glasses, but she swore he looked her way. She could feel the pressure of his stare just as surely as she could feel the cards in her hands. She quickly focused on the game. Now Imani was in her head with that foolishness.

But what if it isn't foolishness?

She looked up from the cards again. Quinton's attention was focused on Shania instead. What if Imani was right and Quinton was interested? She wasn't interested in him. Not seriously. Sure, he was attractive, confident and good with Shania, but she'd never considered him as a potential dating partner before. She wasn't going to mess up things with Gregory because Quinton may be attracted to her. She also couldn't let Quinton get the wrong idea.

"Halle!"

Halle blinked as her cousin Cassidy's voice broke into her thoughts. "Huh? What?"

"It's your turn?" Cassidy said, raising a brow.

"Oh, my bad." She was being a horrible spades partner. Imani quickly grabbed a card and threw it down.

Cassidy groaned while Kayla and her partner, their cousin Mick's wife, Beverly, cackled with glee. Halle looked down at the table and cringed. She could have easily won that hand if she'd been paying attention.

"We might as well call this game because you're too distracted to play," Kayla said, sliding the cards on the table her way.

"No, I'm not."

Kayla continued to smirk. "We'll see."

Kalya turned out to be right. Halle was distracted and they lost the game. She was going to get Imani for putting ridiculous thoughts in her head. The flag football game was ready to start. Kayla set her folding chair next to Halle's on the side of the makeshift field where those not playing watched and cheered on the teams.

Gregory had joined the five-on-five setup. Halle hoped Shania would end up playing with Gregory but as the teams were chosen, she ended up on the opposite team with her cousin Mick and Cyril. Quinton served as the referee for the game.

Imani pulled up a folding chair on the other side of Halle. "Which team are you pulling for?"

"Shania's, of course," Halle said.

"Not going to cheer for your boyfriend?" Kayla asked with a smirk.

Halle rolled her eyes. She was not following up Kayla's foolishness. "You can cheer for his team since Zachariah is on his side."

"You know I will," Kayla said, grinning.

Gregory ran over to Halle. "A kiss for good luck," he said with a grin.

Halle's eyes darted past him to where Quinton watched, and she immediately hated that she'd made the movement. She looked back at Gregory. A shadow crossed his features. Halle jumped up, lifted on her toes and brushed her lips over his.

"Good luck."

His smile returned. "I'm going to need it. I told you I'm not athletically inclined."

"Then why did you agree to play?"

"Why do you think? I did it for you."

"Why me?"

"Because I like you, Halle. I like your family. Maybe one day, I'll be considered a part of your family."

Her heart squished and she remembered why she'd chosen him in the first place. He was nice. He said sweet things. He was the guy she wanted, and she wouldn't get distracted.

"You've got this."

He leaned in and kissed her quickly again before running back to his team. She hated the urge to look back at Quinton. To see if he'd watched and wonder what he was thinking. She ignored the urge and sat back down. Thankfully, Quinton blew his whistle to get everyone's attention. He went over the rules and the game started.

The competition was all in good fun, and everyone had a good time watching the teams compete. Shania's team had the lead and with each score on their part and fumble on Gregory's part, Halle noticed that Gregory got more agitated. He didn't like Quinton's calls. Claimed everything was a foul against him, and grew increasingly upset as the game ended. Shania scored the final game-winning touchdown. Gregory's smile was tight and drawn as the two teams slapped hands afterward.

Shania ran over to Quinton. "Did you see the way I blocked the pass before last?"

Quinton gave her a high five. A grin creased his face. A rare sight but she'd been right; he was cute when he smiled. More than cute. The guy was fine.

"You did a good job with that."

"You think it'll work in a regular game?"

Quinton shook his head. "The block worked because we were in flag, but you'll have to go for the tackle in a regular game."

"Wasn't I in position for that?"

"Nah, you were reaching. That's a way to get hurt."

"Shania," Gregory called, his voice sharp.

Shania and Quinton both looked up. Halle blinked and her mouth fell open as the rest of the family hushed.

Gregory cleared his throat and softened his tone. "You played well. Why don't we pack up and then me, you and your mom can go celebrate with ice cream."

Shania's brows drew together. "Um… I'm going to spend the night with my cousins."

Halle walked closer to the three. "We can do ice cream another day."

"Oh, that's fine," Gregory said, sounding disappointed.

"Yeah, another day." Shania looked back at Quinton. "What

are you doing tomorrow? Can you come by and show me some passes?"

"I'm sure your coach has other things to do," Gregory cut in. "He can't just come by the house and practice with you."

"He's not just my coach," Shania said.

Gregory frowned. "He's not your friend either. He's a teacher and an adult." He looked at Halle. "Isn't that right, Halle?"

Halle opened her mouth, but the words stuck in her throat. She didn't want to admit to everything here in front of her family on cousins' day.

"He is her coach...and..."

Gregory's brows drew together. "And what?"

Kayla leaned forward and eyed Halle. "Yeah...and what?"

Halle glared at her messy-ass cousin. "Kayla, hush."

Imani started laughing, but the sound was thin and forced. "Oh man, look at the time. We better get things cleaned up. We only rented the park until four."

Before the relief could settle in, Gregory held up a hand and looked back at Halle. "No, I want to hear this. And what, Halle?"

"Gregory, we can talk about this later, okay? Quinton is a good guy and there's nothing to get worked up about."

"Who's worked up? I'm not worked up. I'm just asking a simple question."

By now everyone was quiet and watching them. Damn Quinton for showing up and making cousins' day awkward.

"He's my dad," Shania said. Loud and proud.

Gregory's eyes widened and he spun toward Shania. "Your what?"

Quinton's shoulders squared and he looked back at Gregory. "You heard her. My daughter."

Kayla slapped her hands and cackled. "Finally. I couldn't hold that in for much longer."

Thirteen

"WHAT'S THIS I HEAR ABOUT A GRANDCHILD?"

Quinton closed his eyes and barely suppressed his groan. When he'd received the text from his mom saying he needed to call her back immediately because it was important, he'd thought there was an emergency. He did not want to deal with breaking the news to his parents after the fiasco that just went down at the park.

All manner of hell broke loose after Shania announced to the rest of her family that he was her father. Halle's cousins demanded answers. Halle had tried to defend herself. Shania had tried to defend him. He'd tried to defend them both. In the end, he'd been told by Mick that this wasn't the end of things after Halle finally shut things down and said this was her life, her business and they could stay out of it.

What stuck with him out of everything was Gregory's response. The way he'd looked at Halle as if she'd cheated on him with Quinton and given birth to Shania two days ago, not fourteen years ago. He didn't like the way he'd looked at her and wanted to step in. Instead, he reminded himself that her relationship with Gregory wasn't his business.

"Quinton! Do you hear me?" His mom's voice sliced through his thoughts. "What's this about a grandchild?"

"What grandchild?" He reverted back to his old high school tactic of playing dumb before admitting to any wrongdoing.

His mom sucked her teeth. "Boy, don't you play with me. Do you or don't you have a kid?"

"Don't you lie to your momma. Give her a straight answer now," his dad's voice chimed in.

He must be on speakerphone. "Where did you hear that I had a kid?" He knew the answer. Dawn couldn't keep a secret to save her life. As long as he could delay the inevitable, he would.

"Don't worry about where I heard it," his mom said, sounding exasperated. "Just tell me if it's true."

"Nah, I need to know where you heard it. If you're calling me about a kid, then I want to know who told you."

"Aha! So it's true," his mom exclaimed. "Why would you keep this from us? Thank goodness your sister is loyal."

"You mean she can't hold water," Quinton mumbled.

"Hey!" his sister's voice chimed in. "They forced it out of me."

Quinton glared at his phone before putting it back to his ear. "I don't even believe that. I'm surprised you made it this long."

"Wait? How long have you known about this?" his mom asked.

His sister grunted. "This is his secret. Don't get on me."

"She's right." His dad's voice. "Why are you keeping this a secret from us in the first place? Who is this woman and who is this child?"

Quinton sighed and sat on the couch. He leaned back into the cushions and swirled the whiskey he had in a highball glass with ice. "I didn't keep it a secret from you on purpose. I just found out about her a few weeks ago."

"Is your sister right? Did you…donate your semen?" His mom said the word *semen* as if it was a bad word. He felt like it was a bad word; he never planned to have a discussion with his mom about his semen.

He took a sip of the whiskey. The smoky flavor and warmth of the liquor spread through his chest. "It's a long story, but yes. I don't want to get into all the reasons why."

"You better get into the reasons," his dad said. "Why would you give away a piece of yourself like that? It don't make no sense. Didn't I tell you not to be spreading your stuff around like that?"

"I wasn't spreading anything. I needed the money, and I did what I had to do. It was one time. I never thought I'd even find out who got it, but fate had other things in store."

"What did you need money for?" his mom asked.

Quinton cringed; he hadn't meant to let that slip. Proof that the day had lowered his defenses. "That's beside the point."

"Was it to take care of us?" The concern in his mom's voice was like a kick in the gut. This was exactly why he didn't want to tell them.

"Look, I did what needed to be done at the time."

"It was when we were losing the apartment," his mom continued. "You suddenly had the money and claimed one of the donors to the school gave it to you. But I knew you wouldn't take it because you didn't want to ruin your chances to get drafted with a scandal. I knew we shouldn't have laid that burden at your door."

"Again, it doesn't matter," he said firmly. He wasn't about to have this argument with his parents over something that happened over a decade ago. "It's done, and now I have a kid to show for it."

"What's she like?" his mom asked, curiosity about a possible grandchild outweighing her earlier concern about his decision. "Does she really play football?"

"She does. Like I said, fate had to step in on this one."

"What about the mother?" his dad asked. "Is she going to try and keep you away from our grandchild?"

"We're figuring out how to work this out. And will you stop saying *our grandchild*?"

"Why?" his dad asked. "She is our grandchild, isn't she?" He spoke as if he'd known Shania from the moment she was born. With a certainty that let Quinton know his parents weren't going to easily stay out of this.

"Yes, technically, but Halle and I need to figure this out first. We're still getting used to the idea."

"But she said you can be a part of her life, right?" his mom asked hopefully.

"She did."

"Then that means we can be a part of her life." The excitement in his mom's voice made him sit up.

"Mom, don't get overly excited. I need you to please give me a chance to work this thing out before I get you all involved."

"What's there to work out?" his dad asked. "She's your kid. You're going to be a part of her life. We're all family now."

This was exactly what he'd been worried about. He did not want his parents to swoop in and take over before he had the chance to get used to the idea of being a father. Shania wasn't a newborn; she was a teenager. He and Halle weren't together. This situation was going to be challenging enough to maneuver without adding his eager parents.

"We're not all family," he said slowly but surely. "Let us figure this out first before you start planning family dinners, please."

"Are you keeping us from our grandchild?" His mom.

Quinton looked to the ceiling and let out a silent scream, then he took a deep breath before answering. "No. I'm just asking for some time. We just found out a few weeks ago. Please, trust me. When the time is right, I'll introduce you to her and her mom."

His mom sighed and so did his dad. Thankfully, Dawn finally chimed in and helped him out. "We'll give you some time. Won't we?"

His parents grumbled but agreed. Quinton released a sigh of relief. That would give him some time to get things straight with Halle before they moved forward. He ended the call with his family with the promise that they wouldn't just pop up and try to insert themselves in this situation right now. He got in the shower and washed off the sweat and irritation from the afternoon.

After the shower, he slipped on a pair of basketball shorts and went into the kitchen to grab some water. The doorbell rang just as he filled his glass. Frowning because he wasn't expecting anyone, he went to the door and opened it. His breath caught at the sight of Halle standing on the other side of the threshold. She'd changed from the athletic clothing she'd worn earlier at the park into a pair of loose-fitting pants and a T-shirt. The material looked soft and comfortable and brushed across her curves with the skill of an expert artist, drawing his eye to her full breasts, wide hips and supple behind.

Her eyes lowered to his bare chest and then down to his shorts. They widened before jumping back to his face. He swallowed as heat filled his face. He wasn't wearing underwear beneath the shorts, and the thin material of his worn, "around the house" shorts had to make that obvious. He warred with embarrassment and the satisfaction with seeing the flash of awareness in her eyes.

"Is this a bad time?"

He shook his head. "Nah, I just got out of the shower. Do you want to come in?"

She looked over her shoulder then back at him. "Just for a second. We need to talk."

He stepped back and she crossed the threshold. She followed him into the living area. When they faced each other, her eyes dropped to his bare chest. Her lips pressed together before her eyes met his.

"Um...could you put on a shirt?"

"Give me a second." He went into the bedroom, grabbed a T-shirt out of the drawer and came back.

Her eyes scanned his bare arms. "You didn't have anything with sleeves?"

"I grabbed the first thing I saw." He ran a hand over the front of the faded red sleeveless Georgia Bulldogs T-shirt. It was one of his favorites that he'd worn when he'd played professionally. A go-to, and he hadn't even thought about the lack of sleeves when he'd grabbed it.

"Do my arms bother you as much as my chest?" he asked, raising a brow.

Halle crossed her arms over her chest. "No part of your body bothers me," she replied in a tight voice. "It's just a little inappropriate of us to talk with you...like that."

"That's why I put on a shirt. The last time I checked, having my arms out isn't scandalous." The corner of his mouth quirked with a thought. "Unless any sight of bared body makes you *uncomfortable*."

Anything between Halle and him would be too complicated and too tangled to even try to work out. But some part of him, that primitive part that was attracted to her, couldn't stand the idea that she was willing to dismiss him as someone unworthy of her attention. He wanted her to acknowledge that, despite the reasons they shouldn't be together, if they could make things work, they would be fucking fantastic.

Halle cleared her throat and raised her chin. When she spoke, she was back in the crisp school principal tone that only made her sexier. "No part of you makes me feel any type of way, Coach Evans. I didn't come here to talk about your body parts or anything else. I came here to talk about our daughter."

Our. Daughter.

The words hit him straight in the chest, knocking the wind out of his lungs and the smugness out of his thoughts. Damn, they did have a daughter. The situation between them was convoluted, unorthodox and could easily result in Shania being hurt if they didn't proceed with extreme caution.

"Is Shania okay?" He motioned toward the couch for Halle to sit.

For a second she hesitated, and he thought she would remain standing. But she eventually took a deep breath and sat on the edge of the couch. Not trusting his thoughts to stay on topic if he sat close to her, Quinton sat on the love seat.

"Shania is fine. In fact, she's over the moon."

"I thought the outburst this afternoon might have upset her."

"No, she's wanted to know who her dad was for a long time. Now that she knows, I think she wants the world to know as well. I knew it was hard on her, not knowing who her father was. But after she burst out and insisted everyone know, I think I have a bigger appreciation for how much not knowing has affected her. She doesn't want to be the kid who was abandoned."

"I won't abandon her," he said quickly, meaning the words. "I meant what I said about being a part of her life. I'm willing to take responsibility."

"I know, and even though I was hesitant to let you in, I realize that it's best for Shania, but…"

"But what?"

"But we need some ground rules or something. A way to make our lives coincide without interfering with the others."

"Okay," he said slowly. "I don't know how we coincide without interfering."

"I stay out of your business, and you stay out of mine. Unless it concerns Shania, we don't get involved."

"Involved how?"

She gave him an exasperated look. "Like today. You showed up and made things uncomfortable for Gregory. That was unnecessary."

He blinked. "Uncomfortable for Gregory. Are you that worried about his feelings?"

Halle swallowed the "no" that threatened to burst from her lips. She was not that concerned about Gregory's feelings. She'd think about that later, but his showing up had interfered with her life. Shania had been happy, and Quinton had gotten along with her cousins easily. He'd fit in with her family with no problems. While Gregory had seemed uncomfortable and irritated from the moment he'd seen Quinton there.

Afterward, when Gregory had driven her home, he'd asked her the real reason why she'd been at Quinton's house that day. Halle admitted the truth. They'd argued and then he'd suggested they take a break while she "figures this thing out." Gregory believed Quinton was going to try to work his way into her life and that Halle needed to "set him straight" so he understood exactly what his place would be in her life.

The frustration she'd felt in that moment and the rush to take back control of her life returned in a surge. She lifted her chin and crossed her arms. "I just want to make sure we're all clear. That we have boundaries."

Quinton's eyes narrowed. "Is this really about boundaries or is it about Gregory's feelings?"

"It is coming from me. Don't you think we need to come up with boundaries? Some type of schedule or rules about ways to make this work?"

He shook his head. "I think we're going to have to feel each other out. See what does and doesn't work. I've never been a parent, but I promised myself that if I ever had kids I would be there for them. I don't have a game plan for co-parenting, but I'm ready to come up with our own rules."

"I don't have a game plan either. I may have had help from my cousins and friends with Shania, but I'm the only parent. My word is the last word. You showing up unannounced today undermined my wishes. Is that what you're going to do with Shania? If I say no, you're going to say yes?"

The challenge left his eyes and his shoulders relaxed. The look he gave her was apologetic. "Look, I'm sorry I showed up like that today. I felt pushed aside when you told me you didn't want me around your family. I'm not good with that."

His words stopped any quick retort she had. She'd expected him to argue or say he had a right to just show up, not open up a part of himself and admit he was wrong. "And, you're right, I may have been pushing you aside, but it's only because I've been on my own. I don't know how to share. My life, Shania, any of that. I wanted this to come out on my own terms."

"It felt like you were trying to keep it a secret, but sorry, that won't happen. Not in this town. I'm a deal-with-it-head-on type of guy."

"So am I." She didn't usually back down from a challenge or push back uncomfortable situations. Life had taught her that bad things didn't wait to happen when you were ready for them.

"Then we'll tackle this head-on. Together," he said. "And as for Shania, your word is still the last word. At least until you trust me. I'm not trying to butt in and change the way you raise Shania. I just want to get to know her. See how I fit into her life. Which means I'm going to have to fit into your life."

He was going to have to fit into her life. He wasn't going anywhere. Which meant if she wanted the break to end with Gregory, she'd have to find a way to include both of them. "Fitting into my life means respecting the people in my life."

"People like Gregory?" He didn't sound impressed.

"Yes, Gregory."

"Is it serious between you two?"

"It's serious enough." Once she convinced him that Quinton's being in her life wouldn't affect her ability to start a relationship with him. She'd have to convince herself of that, too.

"If it was serious enough then you wouldn't be over here handling his insecurities for him."

"He's not insecure. He just notices a threat when he sees it." Halle pressed her lips together as soon as the words were out of her mouth.

Quinton tilted his head. "A threat? How am I a threat?"

"He wants to build a relationship with Shania. Now it'll be harder. That's all I mean." The words were true, but they both knew that his standing with Shania wasn't what she meant.

"Is that all you mean?" The words may have been a question, but his unflinching gaze dared her to admit the truth.

Halle could ignore his meaning, but she wasn't the backdown type. If she really was going to put up a boundary between them then she couldn't ignore the sparks between them. She had to put them out. "I thought we already dealt with this that day at the bar. I'm not your type and you're not mine."

"I believe having a type is limiting," he reminded her.

"Maybe so, but you were very clear that even with your lack of a type, that I'm not someone you're interested in."

"I said that because you insisted you weren't attracted to me." The evenly spoken words threw her off course. The words in Halle's brain scrambled and then came back together in a picture she didn't recognize. This was supposed to be an easy boundary because he wasn't interested in her. "Wait. What?"

"You said you weren't interested in me, so I did the same. What was I supposed to do?"

"Tell the truth," she blurted out and stood.

Quinton rose slowly and stepped toward her. "Do you really want the truth?"

Halle's heart rate picked up. *Did* she want the truth? *Yes!* a daring voice screamed. *No!* caution yelled back. She was supposed to be over here putting space between them, not making it worse.

She held up a hand. "About the rules."

"However you want me to deal with Shania, I'll do it. I'm her biological father, but I understand that I've got to build a relationship with her. You've got to trust my judgment with her as well. That's no problem at all."

Her body stiffened and she felt like she was standing on a tightrope. She could feel there was more after that statement. "And the rules when it comes to your relationship with me."

"Again, do you want the truth, or do you want me to say what you want to hear? What Gregory wants me to say?"

Halle's breathing shallowed. The look in his eye, challenging and bold, pushed right up against what she needed to say. He was challenging her. Daring her to ignore the spark between them and hide what she really felt and thought. She could either go against herself and resist the challenge, or risk things by allowing him to take the lid off a box that needed to stay closed.

"Say what you need to say," she replied in a calm voice. Even though her heart beat quickly and she fought the urge to hold her breath.

The satisfaction in his eye both irritated and thrilled her. He slid a few inches closer. "Am I attracted to you? Yes. I've always been attracted to you. First, I kept my attraction to myself because I know you don't like athletes. Then I kept it to myself when Shania came to play for me because I don't get involved with the parents of my players. Do I give a damn about Gregory's feelings? Not one bit. If this situation wasn't already confusing enough, I would say you being the mother of my child means my interest in pursuing you is fate, but I won't. Not while you're with Gregory and not if you don't want to go there. So, I'll keep the way I feel about you in check. We'll figure this out with Shania and be there for her. But believe me when I say this. When you end things with Gregory, and if you give me the go-ahead, I'm not going to hesitate to try and be the man in your life."

Fourteen

"THAT'S NOT GOING TO HAPPEN."

The words Halle had thrown out after his confession played in his head like a radio jingle. She'd shut him down so fast he hadn't known how to react. After all of the rejections he'd experienced in life: the English teacher who thought he wasn't good enough; the high school coach who thought he wasn't important enough; the college coach who'd assumed he wasn't strong enough; the teammates after he'd been drafted who expected a seventh-round pick to struggle to keep up. No matter how much he thought he was used to rejection, Halle's rejection had hit differently.

He understood. She was still with Gregory. They were getting to know each other because of Shania. There were a lot of complications. He'd put himself out there and she'd rejected him. He would have to focus on Shania and building a relationship with her. There would be no relationship building with Halle outside of being mutual parents.

Which was what he reminded himself as he entered Books and Vibes later that week to get a book for Shania. He'd seen her flipping through the first book in the series after practice while she'd waited on Halle to pick her up and mentioned the second book was releasing this week. He'd decided to get it for her as a surprise before visiting her and Halle later that day.

Instead of going out in public to meet with Shania, he and Halle agreed that he should come to her house, or they come to his. News had spread like wildfire through Peachtree Cove after cousins' day at the park. The players on the team asked if it was true. Instead of ignoring their question he'd answered them straight on. Yes, it was true. No, it didn't make a difference in how he coached. If they had a problem then come to him and give him and Shania privacy regarding their relationship.

A request that was a hope and a prayer if he ever asked for one. He knew he couldn't deny the gossips from discussing the situation. But on his football field, his personal life was off-limits.

"Well, well, well, if it isn't Coach Q," Patricia Norris said from behind the counter. She and her husband, Van, owned the bookstore that was also a coffee shop. "What can I help you with?"

"I'm looking for a book." He pulled a slip of paper out of his pocket and read off the title.

Her eyes sparkled with knowing. "Oh, that must be for Shania, huh? She loves that series. We got a few copies in this week. They're in back on the romance shelf."

Quinton didn't bother to ask how Patricia knew the book was for Shania. He wasn't a frequent customer of Books and Vibes. He may have come in once to pick up coffee, but he wasn't the *hang out in a bookstore and coffee house* kind of guy.

"Thanks." He nodded and headed in the direction she pointed toward the back of the store.

Two steps in that direction and he stopped. Gregory came his way. The book Quinton was there for already in his hand. He raised a brow when he saw Quinton.

"Fancy seeing you here," Gregory said in a voice that was pleasant enough to anyone listening, but irked Quinton. What, was he not allowed in bookstores?

"I came to buy a book."

Gregory raised a brow. "Which one?"

Quinton pointed to the book in Gregory's hand. "That one. I was getting it for Shania."

Gregory nodded slowly. "Ah...trying to get on her good side."

Quinton pressed his lips together. "Just trying to build a relationship with my daughter."

The congenial expression melted away as irritation flared in Gregory's face. He adjusted his glasses. "I understand. You made a donation and thought you were done. Now you've got to step up. Must be challenging."

"Being a decent father may be challenging for some, but not me." And he didn't appreciate Gregory implying that it might be.

Gregory tilted his head to the side. "I guess that is part of the DNA of an athlete. You all can't wait to prove yourself."

Time to end this conversation before he got ready to pop off. "Get to your point, Gregory."

If Gregory had a problem with him then he needed to get it out of his system. Quinton meant what he said; he wouldn't step to Halle as long as they were dating. He wasn't one to break up others' relationships, but he also wasn't going anywhere. He was a part of Halle's life, and if Gregory was going to remain a part of her life, then they had to figure out how to get along.

"No point. Just making conversation. We're going to be

seeing each other more. We'll have to get to know each other. Won't we?"

"I guess. But seeing as how you and Halle aren't engaged or married then who knows how much we'll need to get to know each other."

Gregory's eyes narrowed. Quinton kept his expression neutral. He'd dealt with smug assholes since high school. People who thought they had some type of leg up on him for whatever reason. He hadn't let that intimidate him then and he wouldn't let it intimidate him now.

"Mr. Gaines, I thought that was you." A woman's voice interrupted them.

They both turned as Miriam Parker, the town's mayor, came up. She grinned her usual welcoming smile as she came over to the two. Miriam was a tall, statuesque woman, with a can-do attitude that resulted in her having over 70 percent of the votes in town for the past two elections.

"Coach Q, good seeing you as well. I'm looking forward to another great year of Peachtree Cove football."

"I'm hoping to give you one."

She pumped her fist. "Just what I like to hear. Mr. Gaines, I'm glad I ran into you."

Quinton spotted his exit. "I'll let you two talk."

She shook her head. "No, it's good to catch you both. Now that we've completed the renovations on the old high school and turned it into a community and arts center, I'd like to do something great for the editors of *Travel Magazine*. We made the finals in Best Small Town, and they'll be here for a visit soon after school starts. We're hosting a welcome dinner and we'd like to schedule a tour of not just the renovated center, but of the community college's campus." She looked at Gregory. "I'd like to bring them to your literature class. Halle said your poetry is fantastic and you're really bringing out the best in your students. Would that be okay to bring them by when you're teaching?"

Gregory immediately nodded and beamed with pride. "Of course. I'm happy to help."

"Fantastic." She turned to Quinton. "They'll be here during the second week of school. I know it's hectic, but I'd like to have them attend the football game. They'll sit with the boosters and get recognized at half time, but I'd like to introduce them to our local celebrity. Would that be fine with you?"

Quinton had two Pro Bowl rings, but he was far from being one of the most popular people in the league. "I'm not really a celebrity," Quinton said.

"You're close enough, and you've turned our team around. This will be a good boost to get us that final recognition. I want to show them the best of Peachtree Cove."

Quinton shook his head. "I appreciate that, but I'm just a part of Peachtree Cove. Besides, I'm not good at interviews or anything like that."

"Oh, don't worry. In fact, the editor for the magazine was particularly interested when he learned you were the football coach. He said you two were old friends and he looks forward to learning more about what you're doing in Peachtree Cove."

Quinton frowned. He was pretty sure none of his friends worked for *Travel Magazine*. He only had a handful of good friends—a few from college, one or two from his days playing professionally and Brian and Cyril here in Peachtree Cove.

"Who is he?"

"Wait, let me check my email." Miriam dug into her purse, pulled out her phone. "I've been dealing with one of the writers, but the editor reached out after we made the finals. Here it is. His name is Khris Simmons, with a K. He says you all went to high school together. Typically, the editor doesn't come to town for this, but he's coming to catch up with you. So, we definitely need you for this. Not only will it give the town a leg up, but you get to catch up with an old friend. Isn't it great?"

Quinton's stomach soured at the mention of the name. There was no way in hell he was going to play nice to the guy who'd made high school a living hell for him. Khris Simmons wasn't his friend. He'd been Quinton's bully.

"Why did he give me this?" Shania asked, confusion knitting her brows together.

Halle looked at the book on the table and smiled. "He knows you like the series and wanted to be nice."

"Gregory doesn't have to be nice to me," Shania said.

"Do you want him to be mean?"

Shania sighed and plopped down in the chair. She frowned at the book. "No. It's just… You two just started dating and that's cool, because he wasn't trying hard to get on my good side." She poked the book. "This feels like trying to get on my good side."

Halle hadn't expected Gregory to show up today with Shania's favorite book. Not after he'd said they needed to take a break. But he'd apologized for overreacting. Said he should have been more supportive of her and hoped she would give him another chance. She'd been surprised by how much she'd considered saying no, before reminding herself that this was good. This was what she wanted.

"Again, why is that a problem?"

Shania looked at Halle as if she should already know the answer. "He's not my dad. He doesn't need to be on my good side."

"But he is the guy I'm dating. What's wrong with him wanting to get on the good side of my daughter?"

"I don't know. It just feels weird and sudden. I think it's because of Coach Q."

Halle hated how observant her daughter was sometimes. "What do you mean?"

"Well, now I have a dad and everyone knows. So he's doing all this extra stuff he didn't do before." She motioned to the book on the table.

"Quinton being your father doesn't mean Gregory shouldn't do nice things. Wouldn't you want the man I date to be nice to you?"

"Are you going to marry him?" Shania asked pointedly.

"I don't know," Halle answered quickly. "Maybe." A few weeks ago, before this revelation, she would have said she wasn't against the idea. She would have said Gregory was the perfect guy for her and she could see this growing into something serious. But a few weeks ago she'd looked at Gregory as the right guy for her and a good father figure candidate for Shania. Now she was having doubts. She hadn't liked the way he'd acted during and after cousins' day, but she could also see why he would have been confused and upset after learning about Shania's relationship with Quinton.

Quinton's filling the role of father didn't mean he was going to fill any other role in her life. She'd gravitated toward Gregory, not Quinton before. Then he'd gone and thrown down the gauntlet with his "when you break up with him I'm stepping in" statement. She'd been shocked at his admission and surprised at how easily he assumed she and Gregory wouldn't work out. Even if she now had to figure out what was going on with her and Gregory, she didn't want Quinton's words to influence her decision.

"Mom!" Shania's voice broke into her thoughts.

Halle blinked and focused on her daughter. "Huh, sorry, what did you say?"

"I said you can't be thinking about marriage right now."

"Why not?"

Shania's brows rose and she gave Halle a bewildered look. "Because of Coach Q."

"What does he have to do with my decision to get married or not? I'm not marrying him."

Shania waved a hand and scrunched up her face. "Eww... I'm not telling you to marry him either. I'm just saying. This is a lot. Can we get through one transition before we add another?"

Halle frowned. "I thought you wanted me to get married."

Shania shrugged. "Yeah, one day. If you find the right guy, but not because you're trying to find me a dad."

"Who says I'm trying to find you a dad?"

Shania gave her a *you can't be serious* look. "Mom, I know part of the reason why you're interested in Gregory is because you want me to have a dad. But I don't want any dad. I want my dad. Plus, you've shown me that it's okay to be single. I'm not expecting you to just get with a guy out of obligation or something. You just started dating Gregory and my dad has popped up out of nowhere. Face it, Mom, your life is kind of jacked up."

Halle shook her head and laughed. Shania's straightforward way of thinking was more proof that she was her and Quinton's child. "My life is not jacked up."

"I'm just saying. Let's figure out this thing with Coach Q before you let Gregory put a ring on it. I don't think they like each other. And I kind of would like to get to know my dad without a potential stepdad making things worse."

Shania's request made sense, but it still surprised Halle. She would have expected her daughter to be into the idea of her and Quinton possibly dating. Except, she'd raised Shania to be self-sufficient and happy. She shouldn't be surprised that this was her daughter's response.

"How about you let me figure out my love life, but I promise to let you know if things get anywhere near serious enough to discuss marriage between me and Gregory."

Shania nodded. "Cool."

The doorbell rang and Shania's face lit up. "That's Coach Q." She jumped up from the table, then stopped and turned around. "And…about Coach Q."

"What about him?"

"I know you kind of wanted to be with Gregory because I asked about my dad a lot, well, now I know. I don't expect you to marry Coach to try and make us a family either."

Halle sucked in a breath. "Who said I'm going to marry him?"

"That's what I'm saying. I don't want you to. Not because of me. I'm good with just having him as my dad. Besides, he's my coach. I don't want to imagine you and him…" Shania shuddered. "You know."

Heat filled Halle's face. She pointed toward the front of the house. "Go answer the door."

She followed slowly behind Shania as she considered her words. If Shania was so direct when it came to Gregory, of course she'd be the same with Quinton. Shania had never pushed her to find her a father; she'd just wanted answers about who her father was. Shania was right; Halle needed to get to know Quinton and see how he fit into their life, not rush into any situation.

She walked up just as Quinton came through the front door. His dark eyes met hers and he lifted his chin in acknowledgment. The words he'd spoken, the way he'd looked at her as if he couldn't wait for her to say she was free of Gregory so he could pursue her, flashed through her mind and heated the blood in her veins. Halle tugged on the front of her shirt in a weak attempt to cool herself off.

"Thank you for coming by." She said the first words that popped into her head.

"No need to thank me."

Shania grinned. "Do you want to watch the University of Michigan game?" Shania asked.

Quinton frowned. "Why Michigan? I thought you'd want to watch Georgia."

She shrugged. "We can switch to that one, too, but Michigan has a female graduate assistant coach. I started following them, too."

"I heard about that. Yeah, we can watch the game. Whatever you want to do."

Halle stepped forward. "I was thinking we could talk. Maybe discuss how this all works out and the ground rules." This was their first official meeting as a family. They should lay out some rules.

Shania groaned and shook her head. "Mom, come on. Let's just hang out. We've got time for that. Besides, the game is about to come on."

Halle wanted to argue. She didn't want Quinton here just *hanging out*. That made him more like family, and he wasn't family. Not really. Not if she was establishing boundaries. Boundaries required a game plan and rules for how all of this would work.

She met Quinton's eyes. His expression was neutral, yet she felt the judgment. The *she can't go with the flow and let things happen*. She looked to Shania, whose eyes pleaded with her not to be Principal Mom as she sometimes called her.

Sighing, Halle nodded. "Fine, we can talk after the game."

Fifteen

WHY WERE COLLEGE FOOTBALL GAMES SO DAMN long? The thought went through Halle's mind for the umpteenth time that afternoon. Shania and Quinton didn't seem to mind. They were having a ball discussing the plays on the field and debating if the right calls were made. The two of them laughed, cheered and groaned together. Halle knew enough about football to get the gist of the game: the team with the ball had four times to move the football ten yards. But when Shania or Quinton talked about a blitz or an I formation, she was lost.

The get-to-know-you meeting she'd planned was not happening the way she wanted. She'd imagined them sitting down and talking. To maybe order food. Discuss visitation schedules and the rules to follow when Shania was with him. Watching the two of them cheer and grin and bond over football, she realized her vision was not going to happen.

"Mom, can you get some more chips?" Shania held up the

empty green plastic bowl that had once held an entire bag of potato chips.

Halle looked away from the television to the empty bowl in Shania's hand. "Why can't you get more?"

"Because this game is good. I don't want to miss a play."

Sighing, Halle stood and grabbed the bowl. Quinton reached for the bowl at the same time. "I can get the chips."

Halle pulled the bowl out of his reach. "No, you're a guest. I've got it."

"You sure?"

She gave him a tight smile. "I'm sure."

She turned and went into the kitchen. She grabbed the bag of chips off the counter and poured the remainder of them into the bowl. Was this how things were going to be? She'd be the third wheel when they were together. She was happy that Shania and Quinton got along. She could have found her biological father and he could have turned out to be a jerk. Halle just wasn't used to being left out when it came to Shania. She was trying not to feel like she was being pushed out in her own house.

"Hey, where do you keep the sodas?" Quinton's voice came from the door of the kitchen.

Halle straightened and tried to smile. She hoped her earlier thoughts hadn't shown on her face. "Why didn't you ask me? I'd bring it."

He came farther into the kitchen. "I don't mind getting things for myself."

"What about potentially missing a great play?"

The corner of his lips lifted. Not quite a smile but she'd noticed it was how he expressed amusement. "Shania's phone rang and she had to run to her room and take the call."

Halle tilted her head to the side. "Wait, she said she couldn't miss a play for chips, but the phone is another story?"

Quinton shrugged his wide shoulders. "I guess whoever was on the other side is more important."

She shook her head. "Kids." She pointed to the fridge. "I've got soda in the bottom drawer."

"Thanks." He walked over toward the fridge, but stopped by the table. "Gregory brought that over?"

She glanced at the book Gregory had dropped off. Considering her daughter's feelings about the situation, Halle wasn't even sure if Shania would read the book since Gregory had gifted it to her. "How did you know?"

"I ran into him in the bookstore. I was going to get it for Shania."

"Really? How did you know she wanted it?"

"I noticed she'd sometimes read the first book in the series while she waited on you to pick her up after practice. Last week she mentioned being excited about the next book releasing. I thought I'd do something nice."

Halle held up a hand and smiled. "You actually lucked out not buying it. She thought Gregory was being weird and trying too hard by getting it."

Quinton cringed. "Would she have said the same thing about me?"

"Who knows, but I don't think you have to worry about bringing her gifts or anything. Just come watch football with her and she'll be good."

Quinton had nothing to worry about. Shania had already looked up to him. Halle would bet money that if Shania had a list of men she wished could be her father that Quinton would have been somewhere on the list.

"I'll do that." He went to the fridge and opened the door.

He bent over to open the bottom drawer. Halle's eyes dropped to his ass. Then she jerked her gaze back up when she realized what she was doing.

She cleared her throat and rubbed the back of her neck. "Do what?"

He pulled out two cans of soda and straightened. "I can come over on Saturdays or Sundays and watch football with her."

"Wait. What?" He wanted to do this every weekend?

He stood next to her and put the sodas on the table. "It's a good way to spend time with her and do something we both enjoy. Do you mind?"

"Uh...no, but what about you? You don't hang out with your guy friends to watch the games?"

The corner of his mouth quirked. "My guy friends will be okay. This is about building a relationship with Shania. I'm good to do this. If you are?"

She tried to think of a reason to say no. A reason why she didn't want him in her house once a week, bonding with her daughter over a sport that she only knew enough about to be dangerous. But what else was she going to offer? To say that he could only come over and do activities that interested her? That they could read together, watch documentaries and discuss current events? That wasn't helping him get to know Shania; it was getting to know her.

"That's fine," she said lightly.

Quinton's eyes narrowed. "We can do other stuff, too."

"No, you both like football. It's football season. That's fine with me."

"I don't want to leave you out. How about we switch things up. One weekend we'll watch football, another weekend we'll do something you pick. Deal?"

She waved a hand. "That's not necessary."

Quinton took her hand in his to stop her dismissive wave. "It is. I'm not here to butt in. I'm here because I want to be around if Shania wants me around."

His hand was large and still cool from when he'd held the

sodas from the fridge. Despite that, warmth spread up her arm. Halle pulled back and he let her go. His touch lingered.

"I thought you wanted this, too."

He flexed his fingers before settling his hand on the back of one of the kitchen chairs. "I do, but I'm still finding this entire situation surreal."

"Tell me about it."

"I know what I did. And I knew what they were going to use my sperm for, but still. I never expected to meet her."

"Do you wish it had stayed hidden?" Yeah, he'd accepted the situation and was willing to have Shania in his life, but that was because Quinton was a decent person. He wouldn't have pushed Shania away. That didn't mean he'd wished to ever be revealed.

His brows drew together before he shook his head. "I wouldn't have taken the online DNA test if that were the case."

"Why did you take it?"

He lifted one shoulder. "It was on a whim. I told my sister what I did in college. I mentioned that I wondered if I had a kid out there. She said I should register through the online testing site and maybe one day I'd find my kid."

"You went looking for her?"

He shook his head. "I took the test, got the results with my ancestral background, turned on the part that allows family to find me and then never logged on again. I figured, if I had a kid out there and if the kid took a test and wanted to know me, it would be on them. I wasn't going to search them out."

"Why not?"

"Because whoever the mother was had chosen to go that route. The mother didn't want to know me. They just wanted that part of me. So, why push into their life?"

The way he said it, as if he had nothing else to offer at the time, made her want to reach out and comfort him. It also made her evaluate what she'd considered when she'd chosen a donor. She hadn't cared about the person, just their attributes. Who could give her a beautiful child with no involvement.

"Yet, here you are, in our life."

"Do you regret that it's me?" His expression revealed nothing, but she could feel the weight of the question. Was she going to push him away? Did she still only want his donation and not him?

She shook her head. "No. I mean, this isn't going to be easy. Navigating this and having to tell the truth to everyone. People are going to talk. When school starts, rumors will get to Shania even faster. I don't want her to be hurt."

He stepped closer. "I won't let anyone hurt her. Or you."

"I told you we don't need your protection."

"I know you don't, but I still want to give it to you. You're part of my family now."

The warmth that spread through her chest and wrapped around her heart brought a smile to her face. "What an unorthodox family we have."

"Unorthodox doesn't mean bad. We'll make it work. Don't you think so?"

"I hope so," she whispered.

Their eyes met. The memory of his words, the promise to step in if Gregory and she broke up. The way he'd admitted to being attracted to her. She wanted to lean closer, breathe in the spicy scent of his cologne.

He leaned closer, or maybe she imagined that. Maybe she wanted that. She sucked in a shallow breath. Did she want that?

Shania came into the room, halting any wayward thoughts or unnecessary feelings. "Mom, you got the chips?"

Halle stepped back from Quinton. From a dream she wasn't even sure she wanted to complete. She looked away from Quinton, from the look in his eye that wanted to hold her captive, and focused on her daughter. "Yeah, baby, let's go watch the game."

Sixteen

QUINTON WAS SETTING UP HIS CLASSROOM FOR THE first day of school when someone knocked on the door. He turned away from hanging a poster of famous mathematicians and nodded when he saw Principal Heyward.

"Jeremiah, what's up?" Quinton turned back to his poster.

Jeremiah came into the classroom. "Nothing much, just checking in to see how things are going."

Quinton pressed the corners of the poster into the wall, before stepping back to make sure it wasn't crooked. Nodding, he turned back to Jeremiah. The older man had been principal at Peachtree Cove High School for the past seven years. He was shorter than Quinton, with pale skin, thinning red hair and clear brown eyes. He always dressed professionally in a button-up shirt, tie and slacks, and today was no different.

"Things are good with me." Quinton crossed over and sat on the edge of his desk. "Just getting the classroom set up."

Jeremiah nodded and grinned. He ran a hand over his head. A familiar move he made when he was nervous. "I remember when you first started coaching," Jeremiah said. "I didn't believe you really wanted to teach."

He'd known. They'd hired him to turn the football program around. When they'd learned he also wanted to help educate the kids off the field he'd been met with skepticism. "No need to waste the education degree I worked hard to get."

Quinton hadn't made it to college on a football scholarship like many assumed. He'd known he wanted to give back, and that football shouldn't be his only plan for his future. He'd majored in childhood education and minored in math, a subject he'd loved in school.

"I understand but you know it was hard for people to believe. You are a Pro Bowl player. You could coach anywhere. Without the hassle of lesson plans and setting up classrooms." Jeremiah indicated the organized classroom.

"I could, but doing that isn't what I want. I enjoy teaching. It's just another form of coaching."

Jeremiah nodded and gave Quinton an appreciative look. "That's admirable. You know, a lot of people thought you had an ulterior motive to come here. When you had the choice of so many other places."

"I have no other motive. Football and helping kids. That's it." He crossed his arms and waited. He liked Jeremiah. They got along well and rarely bumped heads, but Jeremiah didn't ever come and hang out in Quinton's office. They'd gotten the reasons why Quinton was here out of the way in his first year and he'd proven that he meant what he said. This conversation was about something else.

Jeremiah shifted his stance. He glanced around the room before focusing on Quinton with a concerned gaze. "I know you said that. I even believed you."

Quinton's chin lifted and he crossed his arms. "What changed?"

"I wanted to believe you were just here to give back and teach." A hint of disappointment drifted into Jeremiah's voice.

Quinton scowled. "That is the only reasons I'm here."

Jeremiah pursed his lips before asking. "Is it?"

"You've beat around the bush long enough. Say what you need to say." Though Quinton was starting to get an idea of what Jeremiah was getting at. Though he hoped this was not about Shania.

"Your daughter playing on your team. You came to Peachtree Cove because of her."

Quinton took a long, steadying breath. He waited three seconds to let the initial frustration that jumped on his back from taking control of this conversation. Getting frustrated and defensive wasn't going to help him with this situation.

"That's not the reason I came to Peachtree Cove. I told you that I wanted to start over. To get away from professional football and the expectations of my hometown. That's why I came here."

Jeremiah's brows lifted and his expression turned doubtful. "But you have to admit that your daughter also being one of your players is quite a coincidence."

"It is a coincidence."

"You know I don't try to get into the personal lives of my teachers."

Quinton uncrossed his arms and leaned forward. "Then don't start getting into mine."

Jeremiah lifted a hand but he didn't back down. "But I do step in if I think that a teacher's…personal issues may affect the way they do their work."

"How is this going to affect my work? This is between me, Shania and her mom."

Jeremiah waved a finger. "See, that's where you're wrong.

You're our football coach and your success at this school is important. We were okay with letting Shania continue to play football, but—"

"But what?"

"But if your relationship is going to make it harder for you to focus on what you need to do to help the team win, then that's a problem."

"This isn't going to change the way I coach the team." Quinton heard the defensiveness in his voice and didn't care.

"Don't get upset with me. Some of the other coaches have expressed concern about your favoritism with Shania."

Quinton scowled. "Favoritism? What favoritism?"

"I understand that there would need to be some changes to accommodate a female on the team."

Quinton snapped his finger. "It was Clyde Tucker, wasn't it?"

Jeremiah paused long enough to confirm Quinton's suspicions. "Despite the accommodations we still want to win. I hope that you don't force Shania into a starting position just because you want to make up for the years you lost."

Quinton shook his head and scoffed. He should have known Clyde would be the first one to run to the administration and complain once he found out about Shania and his relationship. The guy hadn't wanted her on the team in the first place. He'd deal with him later today at practice; right now he had to get Jeremiah straight.

Quinton didn't stand. He didn't like to use his height to try and tower over and intimidate his principal. But he did stare Jeremiah straight in the eye and kept his voice firm. "First of all, never once have I given you a reason to question my integrity, so you and anyone else who thinks I'm showing favoritism instead of just asking everyone on the team to treat a player like the rest of the players on the team can kiss my—"

"But she's not like every other player on the team," Jeremiah cut in with a raised finger. "She's a female and therefore she's going to need adjustments made in order to accommodate her. Now, the district is okay with that, but you need to remember that these parents and the rest of the community already are judging you and every move you make with this team. I want you to remain our football coach. Doing so means you can't stick your head in the sand and pretend like you don't know what you and Shania will be facing. You can get mad all you want, but it's reality. If I didn't warn you, then I wouldn't be a good principal or a good friend."

"You call this being my friend?"

"I call it not being your enemy," Jeremiah said. "Just think about what I said. Your situation is unique to say the least. I support you, but don't give me a reason not to."

Quinton glowered but nodded stiffly. Jeremiah patted him on the shoulder. The supposedly reassuring move he used after having any type of course-correcting conversation with a teacher. Quinton frowned as he watched Jeremiah leave the classroom. As much as he wanted to finish his sentence and tell Jeremiah, Coach Clyde and anyone else in town who questioned his coaching ability to kiss his ass and mind their business, Jeremiah had made a point. Quinton couldn't pretend as if every move he made wouldn't be scrutinized even more. He was already being scrutinized and was just beginning to earn the respect and trust of the people in this small town. Of course, people would judge him and his abilities more as word got out about Shania being his biological daughter. Even worse, Shania would be under the microscope. Judged. Possibly bullied.

The situation gave him flashbacks of his high school days. When he was judged on where he came from and what he had to offer instead of what he could accomplish. He thought about the mayor's request. Not only would he have to deal with this, but he'd be dealing with it when Khris Simmons showed up with *Travel Magazine* to judge the town. All of the stuff Quinton had walked away from would be back in his face. How could he pretend as if he had everything together when the person who'd tormented him the most was going to be in town with the sole purpose of judging him and his involvement?

The shadow of an ache started in his shin. Quinton closed his eyes and took a deep breath. The break had happened years ago and no longer bothered him. But when he thought about how it happened, he could still feel the pain of that moment.

He shook his head and opened his eyes, letting go of the past before it overwhelmed him. Football practice would start soon. He could focus on that. He stood and shook out his shoulders. He needed to let go of the irritation coursing through him like a raging river before he dealt with his coaches and the rest of the team.

He left the classroom and headed for the gym. He could go through the equipment and make sure everything looked good before the kids started arriving for practice. He entered the hallway leading to the locker room just in time to overhear, "My mom said she's a test tube baby."

Quinton stopped in his tracks. At the end of the hall Deandre, one of the players on the team, spoke to another player, Malachiah.

Malachiah let out a surprised laugh. "What?"

"Something they used to say back in the day," Deandre continued. "Kids not born the regular way."

"Test tube baby." Malachiah laughed harder. "That's crazy."

Quinton cleared his throat. The two jumped and faced him. Their eyes widened as they exchanged worried glances. "Um… Coach, hey," Deandre said, waving stiffly.

"What was that you were saying?" Quinton pointed between the two.

Deandre shook his head. "Nothing."

Quinton came farther down the hall. "Nah, sounded like you two were having a fun time. I like laughing. Go ahead. Tell me what you were saying."

Malachiah held up a hand. "My bad, Coach. I shouldn't have said anything."

Quinton placed his hands on his hips and eyed both boys. "That's right. You shouldn't have. Shania is a member of this team. My business and how she got here doesn't have anything to do with how she plays or how I coach. But I never have and never will stand for bullying and talking about each other. You got me?"

"Yes, sir," they both said.

"Now leave, and don't let me hear you saying anything like this again."

They nodded and then scrambled down the hall into the locker room. Quinton watched them go. His stomach twisted in knots. He'd caught them, but how was he going to stop this from creating problems on his team?

Halle looked at the pile of decorations in front of her on the table in Tracey's kitchen. "Tell me why we're doing this again?"

Tracey sighed and pointed at the mountain of artificial flowers, tulle and rhinestones. "We have to make a good impression when *Travel Magazine* is in town. Homemade decorations give my place a spot over others."

"But you aren't craftsy," Halle said, not to be insulting, but because it was true. Tracey was not into the arts-and-crafts life.

"They don't have to know that I learned recently." Tracey tapped the screen of her phone and a video about ways to make a wreath for the door played. Her braids were piled on top of her head in a bun and she wore black leggings with a green Fresh Place Inn T-shirt.

Halle fingered the tulle. She was just as bad at crafts as her friend. "You really can just have someone make these for you. They'll still be homemade."

"But I want it made from my hands. The Fresh Place Inn is

about the down-home touches. That's what makes it *the* place to stay in Peachtree Cove."

"It's *the* place to stay because you have great food, and your service is impeccable. You making the wreath on the door has nothing to do with it."

"I just feel like I need something else. Some sort of umph to make it stand out. It's not just about Peachtree Cove being named Best Small Town, but about me getting named best place to stay in Peachtree Cove. Maybe even my own separate feature."

"Then why am I helping?"

Tracey gave her an isn't-it-obvious look. "So I don't have to make them all myself."

Halle narrowed her eyes and Tracey laughed. "You are not funny."

Tracey shrugged. "What? I need help learning this. Imani is working and let's admit it, you're fantastic at everything you touch. So, you can help me figure this out."

Halle snorted even though the compliment warmed her heart. "Hardly fantastic at everything."

"Well, you're fantastic enough to help me get this win. I need a win."

The defeated tone in her friend's voice made Halle stop watching the instruction on how to twist the vines of the flower into a wreath. "Hey, what's going on? Are things still weird between you and Bernard?"

She glanced around the kitchen. They were alone, but Bernard was upstairs in his man cave. He hadn't even come down to greet Halle when she arrived.

Tracey shrugged. "Weird doesn't describe it. He won't say it, but I think he might be cheating."

Halle dropped the flowers in her hand and leaned toward Tracey. "What?" she hissed. "Are you serious?" And how could she sound so matter-of-fact about it? Halle couldn't understand why Tracey didn't sound more upset.

"I don't have proof, but I watched my mom cheat on my dad enough to know the signs."

"Are you sure you aren't projecting?"

Tracey's parents had an unusual relationship. Her dad was an alcoholic and her mom frequently stepped out on him with other men. Though the family had their issues, Tracey always stood up to anyone who had anything to say about her parents. She defended her family, even though the rumors and the situation had wounded her.

Tracey shook her head. "No. I know the signs, and he's giving the signs."

"What are you going to do? Do we need to bust the windows out in his car?"

Tracey laughed but Halle was dead serious. No way could she sit back and watch her friend be mistreated. Tracey was as close to her as any of her cousins. Closer, in fact. If her friend was ready to ride out, then Halle would be right there with her.

Tracey raised a brow. "Bust a window? Girl, we're too old to be doing that mess."

"I never would have thought I'd hear you say we were too old for anything."

Tracey sighed and twisted one of the plastic vines into a circle. "Well, I'm too old for this. If he is, and if I find out, then he's gone. I'm not sticking around to be embarrassed."

"Have you asked him?"

Tracey cocked her head to the side. "For him to lie about it? No. He's slipping up because I haven't been on his ass about things. If he is, the truth will come to light."

"Wouldn't you rather know than wait and see? What if he doesn't mess up and you never know?"

Tracey sighed and looked back at the video. "I don't think that'll happen. He's going to slip up. Just wait and see."

Halle's cell phone rang. Shania's number showed on screen. Frowning, she picked up the phone. "Shania, is practice over already?"

"Yeah, but Kayla is here to pick up Nadia for band and she's done. Can they bring me home?" The question was innocent enough, but Shania sounded eager for Halle to agree.

Halle checked her watch and then the pile of decorations on the table. It would take her a while to finish this. "I'm at Tracey's house helping her out. Go on to Kayla's house and I'll pick you up from there."

"Great, thanks, Mom." Shania's relief from Halle's answer was clear in her voice. "See you later."

"Shania done?" Tracey asked.

Halle put her phone down and nodded. "Yeah, practice usually doesn't end this early, but I guess since school starts next week they're wrapping up."

"You don't sound convinced."

She looked at the phone. "Because she sounds... I don't know. Like she didn't want me to pick her up. I hope everything is good."

"Don't go borrowing trouble."

Halle gave her friend a pointed look. "I'd say the same to you."

Bernard came down the stairs before Tracey could reply. Bernard was tall with chestnut-brown skin and a slim build. He and Halle had been cool in high school. He'd been the high school salutatorian; Halle had been valedictorian. He'd been quiet, and studious and a tad bit judgmental about kids who weren't on the same academic standing as him. She'd been surprised when he and Tracey had hooked up. Tracey was brash, bold and more toward the middle of the class standings. She'd assumed opposites attracted because they'd stayed together this long.

Halle couldn't believe he would cheat. Even now he was dressed in a pressed button-up shirt and slacks that weren't particularly fashionable or stylish. He didn't look the part of cheating husband.

Tracey frowned at him. "Where are you going?"

He ran a hand over his low-cut fade before he pointed over his shoulder. "My cousin needs me to go with him to check on something."

Tracey's eyes narrowed. "Oh really?"

Bernard sighed and threw up his hands. "Come on, Tracey, why you got to say it like that?"

Tracey pointed to his outfit. "Because of this. That's how you're going out? Come on, Bernard. Really?"

He pressed a hand to his chest. "What? Are you accusing me of lying?"

"I'm saying you don't look like you're going to help your cousin. Does he, Halle?"

Halle looked Bernard up and down. She tended to stay out of other people's business, but this was her best friend. "Help him with what?"

Bernard shook his head. "You two are ganging up on me, and I'm not doing this."

He walked toward the door. Tracey jumped up and followed him. "Hold up one second."

Tracey followed him out the door. Halle heard them arguing on the porch. Tracey would be better off confronting him than playing this game of back-and-forth. Halle's cell phone chimed. A text message from Shania.

What does test tube baby mean?

Halle's insides sank to the floor. Where the hell did that come from? If someone at that school had used those words, then Halle was going on a rampage.

Who said that?

Calm down. Eye roll emoji.

Halle rolled her eyes in response.

No, tell me now.

It's cool. Coach Q handled it. I just want to know.

Coach Q handled it? What was that supposed to mean? She
called Shania while also keeping an ear out for Tracey's argument with Bernard to make sure neither of them got out of
hand.

"Mom, you didn't have to call. I'm with Kayla and Nadia."
She could hear the *please don't do this in front of family* plea in her
daughter's voice.

Halle took a deep breath and placed a hand over her racing
heart. Shania was right. This didn't need to play out in front of
her cousin. "Just say yes or no. Did someone say that to you?"

"No."

"Did someone say it in reference to you?"

A pause. "Maybe."

"And Coach Q heard it and handled it."

"Yes. Now, can we please go over this later? It's not a big
deal," Shania pleaded.

"If it wasn't a big deal, you wouldn't have texted me."

"Mom," Shania said, almost in a whine.

"Fine, we'll talk about it when we get home. In fact, tell
Kayla to take you home."

"Why?"

"Tracey has some stuff she's taking care of here. I'll meet
you at home and we can talk about it."

The argument ended with Bernard storming out and Tracey

cursing at the door. Halle sighed. She'd make sure her friend was okay and then she'd find out who she had to go off on for daring to insult her daughter.

Seventeen

SHANIA WAS ALREADY AT HOME WHEN HALLE FINALLY
made it there. Getting Tracey to calm down after Bernard left
hadn't taken that long. Her friend was already convinced he was
doing something he wasn't supposed to and that she was going
to wait for him to out himself. Halle had again tried to convince her to just go ahead and confront him, but for some reason Tracey hesitated. They had been married for twelve years;
she supposed she could understand why Tracey wasn't ready to
just pull the plug on her marriage. Still, if Halle got proof before Tracey did, she wasn't going to hesitate to give Bernard a
piece of her mind and a foot to the ass.

Shania was in the shower when Halle got home, so she went
into the kitchen and made a bag of popcorn and poured two
cups of grape soda, Shania's favorite, even though Halle hated
the flavor, and sat on the couch in the living room. She pulled
up her streaming service and clicked on *Living Single*. Halle's

mom had loved that show and she still felt connected to her whenever she watched it.

Shania came out a few minutes after Halle was settled. She wore a pair of gray joggers and an oversized white T-shirt. Her hair was pulled back tight in a ponytail and her face was freshly scrubbed. She fell onto the couch next to Halle smelling like the rose-scented body wash they shared in the house's one bathroom. She grabbed a handful of popcorn and pointed at the television.

"Season one again?"

Halle nodded. "Yep, I thought I'd start from the beginning."

"Even though you like season two the best."

"Sometimes you've got to go back to where it all started."

Shania nodded and reached for the cup of soda. Halle watched her for a few seconds before reaching over and running her hand over Shania's hair. Shania smiled before pulling away.

"I'm fine."

"Tell me what happened?"

Shania sighed and took another handful of popcorn. Halle let her munch and get her thoughts together versus pushing. After she'd finished the handful and washed it down with the soda, she spoke.

"Some boys on the team were talking about test tube babies. One of them said their mom called me that. They'd never heard that before, but once they understood the meaning, they thought it was funny."

Halle clenched her hands into fists. "Did they say that to you?" She tried to keep her voice calm even though she was ready to find the kids in question and give them a lecture on feelings and what wasn't appropriate.

"Nah, they were talking in the hallway. I overheard them."

"What did you do?"

"Nothing. I didn't know what to do. I mean, they aren't like my best friends, but I thought we were cool. Me and Deandre played together in middle school."

Deandre Brown. Halle knew him and his mother. She was definitely going to have something to say the next time she saw Natasha Brown.

"I'm sorry that you had to hear that. Especially from kids you thought you could trust."

"I was upset, but then Coach Q came out of nowhere. He heard them and was all *what did you say?* And *don't ever let me hear you say that.*" Her voice filled with admiration as she spoke, and a smile broke out across her face. "He said he wouldn't stand for bullying on the team. He said we were all supposed to stick together and that he wouldn't accept anyone getting in his business or gossiping about one another on his watch. It was really cool."

It sounded pretty cool. She was impressed that he'd taken up for Shania. "What did the boys say?"

"Nothing really. They straightened up and apologized. I thought maybe it would come up at practice, but it didn't."

"Why are you frowning?"

"I don't know. Coach Q was different. He's never been overly nice to me, but he's always been helpful. He seemed kind of… I don't now…like he was avoiding me today." Shania's eyes met Halle's. The concern in her daughter's expression made her heart twist. "Do you think he's regretting finding out that I'm his daughter?"

"I wouldn't say that, baby. I mean, he did step in and defend you. Maybe he was just distracted today."

Shania reached for more popcorn. "I hope so. It was fun hanging out with him at cousins' day and having him come over to watch football. I mean, I just found my dad. I don't want to lose him already."

"You won't lose him. He said that he wanted to be there for you, and I believe him."

Shania nodded and gave a small smile. "You're right. I hope so."

"I know so. And if he isn't telling the truth, don't worry. I'll deal with him."

Shania laughed. "I know you will, but I think you're right. Coach Q isn't one to quit."

"I agree."

They watched three episodes before Shania disappeared into her room after getting a text from one of her friends. Halle got her phone and went into her bedroom. She called Quinton before she could stop herself.

"Halle?" his voice, deep and rumbly, came through the phone.

Halle's stomach quivered. Damn, he sounded good over the phone. *Focus, Halle!* "Hey, Quinton, I wanted to talk to you about today."

"What about today?" he asked in his easy, no-worries voice.

"Shania overheard what the kids in the hallway said. About her being a...test tube baby." She whispered the last words and her hand tightened on the phone. She wished she could give those kids a piece of her mind.

"She overheard that? I didn't know. Damn, I would have said something to her if I'd known."

"It's okay, she heard you handle it, and she appreciated it. A lot. That's why I'm calling. To say thank you."

"There's no need to thank me. I told you I'd protect her as much as I could."

"I know you did. I just didn't think I'd need you to have to defend her so soon." School hadn't even started. For the first time, Halle dreaded the first day.

"The word is getting out," Quinton's voice was determined. "I have to nip it in the bud before school starts."

"Did anyone else say anything?"

"Jeremiah wants to make sure I don't give her preferential treatment. Said the parents will watch me more."

Halle rolled her eyes and sat on the edge of her bed. Jeremiah was a good principal, but he was also a worrier. Warning Quinton about preferential treatment was just his style. "Is that why you were distant with her today?"

Quinton was quiet for a second. She expected him to deny it, but he sighed. "Yes. Some of the coaches, no one in particular, already thought I was going easy on her. After Jeremiah's warning and the talk with the boys, I thought stepping back would take off some of the heat."

"She was worried you changed your mind about being in her life."

"No. Never that. I didn't realize I'd hurt her feelings. My bad. I'll do better tomorrow. Is she okay?" He sounded regretful and worried.

"She's okay. Don't feel bad. I understand what you're doing. We're both still figuring this out. If we talk about what we're thinking and feeling, then that's better than assuming."

"Call me anytime. If you have something you want to know I won't hide it."

"Thanks, Quinton. I'll do the same." They were quiet. She'd said what she needed to say, so she didn't have to stay on the phone, yet she didn't want the conversation to end. "Are you going to the Business Guild meeting tomorrow?"

"Yeah," he said, not sounding excited at all.

"Why say it like that?" she asked with a laugh. "What's wrong?"

"The mayor roped me into meeting with the editor of *Travel Magazine*. Talk about the football team and why I relocated here. She thinks it'll help us win Best Small Town."

Halle leaned back against her bed frame and nodded. "She has a point. Why the problem, though? Don't you want us to win?"

"It's not that. It's the editor. I knew him in high school. We weren't friends."

"Oh, well, you're adults now. Maybe things will be different."

Quinton grunted. "Doubtful. But anyway, I said I'd help so I will."

"I'm glad you're helping." She meant it. As high school football coach, Quinton was an important member of the community. "I'll get to see you tomorrow at the meeting."

"I'd like to see you," he said in a low, easy tone.

Her stomach clenched. Heat blossomed in her cheeks. "Gregory will be there, too." Not with her, but he'd mentioned he would be there to represent the community college where he also taught literacy classes. He'd hoped to see her. For them to try starting up again. She hadn't told Quinton about their break. She was afraid. Not of Quinton, but afraid of her ability to pretend as if she wasn't attracted to him if he knew she was free.

"I don't care about Gregory. I'll be happy to see you." He spoke with a confidence that made her body tremble.

She cleared her throat. "Well, I guess I should go. I don't want to keep you."

A pause before he replied in a knowing tone. "Have a good night, Halle."

Eighteen

QUINTON WALKED INTO THE PEACHTREE COVE BUSI-
ness Guild meeting the following night. He'd barely had time
to go home and change after football practice ended, but he'd
made it. Just as he heard the president call the meeting to order.
He scanned the room. He didn't even pretend like he wasn't
looking for Halle. He'd thought about their phone conversation over and over. Though he couldn't prove it, he didn't think
she'd wanted to get off the phone with him the night before.

A hand waved and he spotted Cyril sitting near the front.
His friend also served as the Business Guild's secretary. Quinton threw up a hand in response. Cyril then pointed toward the
side of the room. Quinton glanced in that direction and spotted Halle sitting in the third row on the far side. He glanced
back at his friend and lifted his chin in thanks. Cyril grinned
and nodded. Quinton made his way to the side of the room
where Halle was.

"Anyone sitting here?" he asked quietly because the president was once again asking everyone to settle down for the meeting.

Halle looked up at him, her dark brown eyes widening. She glanced toward the door then looked back at him. "No. No one is sitting there."

"Cool." He slid into the seat next to her.

"I was beginning to think you weren't coming," she whispered. She shifted in her seat before straightening the material of her skirt. It was a bright, orange flower pattern and she wore a beige, fitted shirt tucked into the waistband. Even sitting with the matching orange blazer she wore he could tell the outfit accentuated her curvy figure.

"Would you have been disappointed to miss me?" he asked in a low voice.

Her lips pressed together before her back straightened. "No. The thought just happened to cross my mind."

His lips twitched with the need to grin. She was sexy as hell when she got all buttoned up. Prim and proper. But then there was the spark in her eye when she was passionate about something. Made him wonder about getting the fire in her eye for other reasons.

"Where's Gregory?" he asked. "I thought he was coming." He really didn't give a damn about Gregory, but he wanted to know if the guy was going to show up and put his sensitive ego between him and Halle.

"He had to work at the technical college and fill in. He said he might make it if he could."

"Hmm," was his only response.

Halle turned his way. "What's that supposed to mean?"

He shook his head. "Nothing. I didn't say anything."

Her eyes narrowed. "You're glad he's not here, aren't you?"

"Am I sad that Gregory didn't make it? No."

"Why are you like that?" Her tone was exasperated but her full lips twitched.

"Like what?" he asked, raising a brow. "I already told you why I don't care about him." That he was more than willing to step in as the man in her life if she gave him a chance.

She sucked in a breath. Her lips parted and something flashed in her eyes. Something that made him wish they were anywhere else but in the middle of a damn Business Guild meeting. Because if they'd been anywhere else, alone, with no chance of interruption, he would slide closer to her. Slip his arm around her waist. Lower his lips and taste hers. What would she do if he kissed her? Pull back or melt into him?

His eyes lowered to her mouth. He licked his lips then raised his gaze back to hers. There was that spark he wanted to see. No, more than a spark. This was a fire that lingered and teased and sent a rush of blood straight to his dick.

"Coach Q," a voice interrupted them.

Quinton blinked and looked around. Who had called him? Someone pointed toward the front of the room. He looked that way and noticed Emily, the guild president, watching him expectantly.

"Can you tell us about your plans when the editors come to town?" Emily asked.

His brain replayed the words she'd spoken. Plans? He was supposed to have plans? "What do you mean?"

She smiled as if he was a kid in class who needed a little extra attention. "I mean, what are your plans related to showing off how you've improved the football team? Have you put together a schedule? He'll be with you all day."

Quinton scowled. "All day? Why will he be with me all day?"

The president shrugged. "It could turn into a day. He'll be visiting the school and checking out the education and athletic accomplishments."

"Then the principal can handle the schedule," Quinton said. "I'll just give him the basics of what we're doing at the team."

The less time he spent with Khris Simmons, the better. Halle may be right, and that people grew up and got better, but that didn't mean he could easily forget how much Khris had made his teenage years a living hell. He was the reason Quinton had lost a scholarship to play football and had to work his way onto the team as a walk-on candidate and then prove himself even more every day to get drafted professionally.

A hand rose and a throat cleared. Jeremiah stood and gave Quinton a tight smile. "It's all good. We've planned a day for the editor and included not only Coach Q but other members of our staff. Don't worry, we'll be sure to highlight the strides we've made with the football team."

Emily's worried expression changed into a grateful smile. "Great. Now, Carolyn, I've heard the bakery has some sweet treats planned. Tell us about it."

The conversation moved on to what Sweet Treats was putting together. Quinton's body remained stiff. It was one thing to have to talk to the guy and give him an interview. A few minutes pretending as if he could get along with him was one thing. But an entire day? There was no way in hell he was spending an entire day with Khris.

Halle's hand brushed his arm. "Hey, are you okay?"

He glanced at her and nodded stiffly. "I'm good."

"You sure?" Concern filled her eyes.

"I'm good."

She frowned and gave him a look that said she knew he wasn't *good* but thankfully she didn't push. The remainder of the meeting revolved around the talk of the upcoming visit and how the different Business Guild members would work to decorate their storefronts and have specials or sales to entice the magazine's crew when they arrived.

As soon as the meeting ended, he jumped up. He was ready to get home. He turned to Halle.

"I'll see you this weekend?"

Halle nodded as she stood. "Yes. Shania is looking forward to it."

He relaxed a little. "So am I. She doesn't mind that it's not football?"

Halle grinned and shook her head. Damn, she was fine when she smiled. "She's good. She enjoys going out to the lake."

"Then I'll see you both then."

"Oh, are you having a date?" came an intrusive voice.

Quinton suppressed a sigh, but didn't soften his features as he turned from Halle to Mattie. The mayor's sister and biggest troublemaker in Peachtree Cove.

Halle spoke first. "Hello, Mattie. Can I help you?"

Mattie gave them a false smile. When she spoke, it was loud enough for people mingling about to hear. "I was just wondering if you two were dating now that the cat's out of the bag."

"What cat?" Quinton asked, his voice hard.

Mattie gasped as if she couldn't believe he didn't know what she was talking about. "I mean that you're Shania's father. That has been the talk of the town. Is it true? You donated your sperm and you—" she looked at Halle "—were artificially inseminated?"

"The business between me, Shania and Halle is our own. So why don't you go find someone else to bother," Quinton said, not caring about being rude. He was not going to stand for anyone trying to make an issue out of his situation.

Mattie pressed a hand to her heart. "Well, I was just asking. I didn't realize you would be so testy about it."

"Now you know. Come on, Halle. Let's go." He put his hand on her elbow and walked toward the door. He glanced in Cyril's direction. His friend gave him a thumbs-up and a grin. The crowd parted and let them pass.

Once they were outside, he let her go. "I'm sorry."

"For what?"

"For being rude. I just don't like to pretend when people are obviously up to no good."

She grunted and glared at the door. "You don't have to apologize. Mattie loves to stir up stuff. If you hadn't put her in her place I would have."

The corner of his mouth lifted. Halle was sexy when she smiled and when she was ready to defend. "I guess I had your back again."

Her eyes met his. A second passed before she nodded. "I guess so. I know I said I don't need it, but I have to admit that I kind of like it."

His eyes widened. "Do you?"

"I do. I've fought against the gossips in this town by myself for a long time."

He reached out and gently tapped her arm. "Now you've got me to fight with you. I mean it, Halle, whatever you need from me just ask."

The flare from earlier returned. This time they were alone. The members of the guild were still inside talking about the event and enjoying the snacks. He had one maybe two minutes before someone followed them out. Was that long enough?

He slid closer to her and placed his hand on her elbow. "Halle," he whispered her name. Did she feel this? This energy and vibe humming between them. The feeling that this was much more than just finding out they were connected through Shania. She had to feel this.

"Quinton... I..." She paused, but didn't pull away.

His heart soared. She felt this. His fingers firmed on her elbow, and he drew her half an inch closer.

"Halle." Gregory's voice broke the moment.

Quinton closed his eyes and groaned. Halle pulled away from him toward the street. "Gregory? You still came?"

"I did. I thought we could talk."

Halle glanced at Quinton. He wanted to ask her to stay, but this was her decision. He stepped back.

Halle threw him a grateful look before walking away from him to Gregory.

Gregory walked Halle to her car. Halle pressed her lips together and tried to calm herself down. She didn't know what had her heart racing more: Quinton coming close as if he was going to kiss her; annoyance from being interrupted; frustration with the way Gregory called her name as if she were a kid acting out.

Definitely the last one. That was what had her so upset. They weren't going to be able to find a way to make things work. Not with Quinton in her life now.

Once they reached her car he asked her, "What was that all about?"

Halle crossed her arms. "I was standing outside of the guild meeting talking to Quinton about Shania. You're the one who came up and called my name as if I was doing something wrong."

"Because you two were standing too close to each other."

Her gaze drifted away. "No, we weren't." Not yet, at least.

He scoffed and rolled his eyes. "Don't lie to me or to yourself. Just be honest. Is there something going on with you two?"

"Nothing except for trying to figure out how this relationship with Shania is going to work out. We were talking about him spending time with her this weekend."

"Her or both of you?"

"I'm going to be there as well. I just found out he's her dad. I'm not going to just leave Shania alone with him."

She didn't think Quinton would do anything to harm Shania. In fact, she was comfortable with them being alone, but she wasn't ready to give up control completely.

"I thought you were setting boundaries?"

Halle uncrossed her arms and sighed. She didn't know how to tell him that they were, but her idea of a boundary didn't include never being alone with or talking to Quinton. "We are, but to be fair it would be almost impossible to do that and never come in contact with him."

"How do I know you won't also start getting feelings for him?"

She didn't know. She'd thought one thing about Quinton, only to discover he was interesting, considerate and straightforward. She understood all the reasons why they shouldn't jump into anything, but she couldn't promise that she would never feel anything. "Gregory, he's going to be a part of my family."

"You're attracted to him. Admit it." His eyes were hurt and accusing.

The denial was on the tip of her tongue, but she couldn't do it. Why lie? Yes, she was attracted to him. Attraction didn't mean she would act on it.

"I'm attracted to Idris Elba, but that doesn't mean I'm going to do anything with him."

Gregory narrowed his eyes at her. "That's not the same and you know it. You don't know Idris Elba. He isn't your kid's father. How can you be around him if you're attracted to him?"

"Because Shania doesn't want us together. We both are trying to learn how to co-parent. There are a lot of things more important right now than our attraction."

"You say that now, but how do I know that nothing will ever happen?"

The pain in his voice prodded at her guilt, but the other emotion lingering there kept guilt at bay. She frowned. "You don't trust me."

"Would you trust me in this situation?" he shot back versus denying.

"I would try. If I really wanted to be with you. Do you really want to be with me?"

"Do you?" he asked.

"I did—"

Her words cut off. That was just it. She had. Past tense. Now her life was all out of control and confusing. She didn't know what she wanted or what was going to happen next.

Gregory took two steps back. "You did?"

She sighed and realized the break he'd asked for was going to be more than that. She was going to have to let her dreams about her and Gregory go. "There's just a lot going on right now. I've got to figure things out. Figure out how to make things work out between me and Quinton and this co-parenting thing."

"You want to break up?"

She frowned, stunned by the surprise in his voice. "You asked me for a break. What do you want me to do, Gregory? You don't trust me around Quinton. I've got to be around him because of Shania. Whether I like it or not, he's in my life now. It's going to take some time for things to settle down. Maybe I need to get this part of my life settled before focusing on a relationship."

"You know what? Maybe you do need to do that." He turned to walk away.

Halle watched him leave and considered calling him back. She didn't. What was she calling him back for? To prove to Quinton that she and Gregory would make it? To try to avoid Quinton at all costs just to make Gregory feel more comfortable? Because she didn't want to fail at the first relationship she'd actively pursued having?

She got into her car and drove home. She replayed her night over and over. Everything was in chaos, and she didn't know how to get things back on track.

Shania came out of her room to greet Halle when she got home. "How was the guild meeting?"

Halle gave her a small smile as she dropped her purse on the sofa. "It was pretty good. They're ready for the visit from the magazine."

"Was Gregory there?"

"He got there late. Um, we broke up," she blurted out. Shania hadn't known about Gregory asking for a break. Halle hadn't wanted her to feel like she was responsible. Now that they were officially through, she couldn't keep her daughter in the dark.

Shania's eyes widened. She crossed the room and sat on the couch. "Oh no! Mom, really?"

Halle sat on the arm of the sofa. She ran her hand over Shania's curly hair. "Yes, but it's okay. Nothing for you to worry about."

"Was it because of me and Coach Q?" Shania asked in a small voice.

Halle held her daughter's face between her hands and stared her in the eye. "No, it's because we both realized we have a lot going on and we just need to focus on that."

Shania didn't look convinced. "It is because of me. I'm sorry, Mom. I didn't think about this breaking up you and Gregory."

Halle kissed Shania's forehead and pulled her in for a hug. "You don't need to worry about me and Gregory." She let her go and gave her a smile. "Right now, let's worry about navigating this new normal that we have. That's all."

"Are you sure you're okay? I know you liked him."

Halle had liked him. She expected to be more upset about things not working out. But she wasn't. She didn't want to cry, or eat a tub of ice cream, or call Imani and Tracey and ask them to help her curse his name. She felt relief that she wouldn't have to navigate his feelings while also navigating hers.

"I'll be okay," she said honestly. "I did like him, but I can't force something that isn't working. I've survived being single before. I can survive it again."

Shania nodded. "I know you can. You're the strongest person I know."

Halle's heart warmed at her daughter's praise. She leaned in and gave Shania another big hug. "Seriously, don't worry about me. I'm going to be okay and so are you. Things will work out the way they're supposed to."

Shania nodded and pulled back. "If it makes you feel better, I liked Gregory, but I wasn't crazy about him. So, don't feel as if you're letting me down with this either. I know you thought about making us a family."

"Why didn't you tell me how you felt about him before?"

Shania shrugged. "Because you liked him. It was the first time you'd told me about a guy in a long time. I didn't want to mess that up."

"You can always tell me how you feel. Regardless of who I'm dating."

"As long as he makes you happy then I'm happy. And, as long as it's not Coach Q. I really don't want to make things weirder than they have to be."

Halle's smile froze on her face. Memories of the way Quinton had looked at her today. How he'd pulled her close. She'd swear he'd almost kissed her. Gregory had taken one look at them and known there was something there. She didn't know what would happen with Quinton. If they were really attracted to each other or just drawn together because of the unusual circumstances. Until they worked through that, she wouldn't upset Shania switching from Gregory to Quinton.

"I'm not trying to date anyone right now," Halle said.

Shania seemed satisfied with that answer. "How about I make some popcorn and we watch a movie?"

Halle smiled. "Let me go take a shower and then I'll be ready."

She went into her room and began to undress. Her cell phone rang before she could go into the bathroom to shower. Quinton's number was on the screen. She sucked in a breath and quickly swiped to answer.

"Hello?"

"You good?" he asked in a concerned voice.

Halle couldn't hold back her smile. How long had it been since someone called to make sure she'd made it home okay? "I'm good. Were you worried?"

"I was worried about you. Gregory didn't look happy when you two left."

She sighed and sat on the edge of her bed. "That's because he wasn't happy."

"Is he demanding that you put space between us again?"

"He did."

"And what did you say?"

"I told him that was impossible. You're Shania's dad. We can't ignore that and I can't pretend as if you won't be around. That won't work for anyone involved."

"How did he take it?"

She let out a long breath. "We broke up."

There was silence on the other end of the phone. Halle swallowed hard as she waited. She wished she could see him. See the look on his face.

"Are you telling me you're free?" His voice was intense and direct.

Halle pressed a hand to her chest. Her heart fluttered wildly beneath her palm. She had to calm down. She was only telling him because they'd promised to communicate. Shania had just made it very clear that she didn't want them together. "I'm telling you that Gregory and I broke up, but that doesn't change anything between us."

"It changes a lot between us."

Did he have to sound so confident? So sexy? Heat blossomed between her thighs. She jumped up from the bed and started pacing. "No, it doesn't, and it can't. Shania doesn't want us to be together."

"What? Why would she talk to you about that?"

"Because this entire situation is weird enough for her. She was only supporting me with Gregory because she thought he made me happy, but she told me weeks ago that she didn't want us together because it would be weird and the two of us would only be together because of her."

"That's not the reason why I'm attracted to you. I told you that."

"Maybe, but it doesn't change that we weren't likely to become an item if fate hadn't put you as the donor who helped me have Shania. She's right in a way. I don't want to force anything. Let's just focus on her and see how things go."

"Is that really what you want?"

No. She wanted him to get in his car. Drive to her house and kiss her the way she'd thought he would earlier. How long had it been since she'd had an orgasm that wasn't self-induced?

Halle shook her head. Horniness could not rule the conversation. "It's really what I want. I don't want to make things harder for Shania. You know what happened at school and even tonight at the guild meeting. One day at a time. If this thing between us means anything, then time will tell."

"You really like to plan ahead and think things through." She was sure he meant the words, but he'd softened them with humor in his tone. "Do you ever not think like a teacher and just go with the flow?"

Halle smiled but it faded quickly. "I can't. I learned early on that life comes at you hard. After my parents died, I had to figure everything out. They didn't have a will or any type of plans in place. It was unsettling and left me feeling even worse about their death. I don't want to make things more difficult for Shania than they have to be. If she doesn't want us together, then I'd rather let her get used to the idea of you being her dad than anything else. Understand?"

He was quiet for a second before sighing. "You're calling the shots. I said I'd go along with it, so that's what we'll do. But remember, Halle, I'm willing to wait. When you're ready, I'd like for you to give us a chance."

Nineteen

HALLE USUALLY LIKED THE FIRST DAY OF SCHOOL.
Seeing all the kids' faces, some enthusiastic and others not quite
so excited, typically brought a smile to her face. The rush of
helping the teachers get settled and calming the nerves of the
kids new to middle school all brought her a sense of accomplishment. She felt in control in the middle of the chaos.

She was not enjoying this first day of school. Nothing went as
planned. Everything was out of order. Despite emailing the parents constantly about the change in the schedule, there were kids
who showed up either super early or very late. Parents blamed
her because they didn't read the fifty-eleven emails, texts and
phone calls she sent about the changes. The power went out
right after the homeroom bell rang and took everything offline
for nearly forty minutes. Teachers struggled to keep kids excited
about being back in school under control, while the district's IT
staff tried to get everything back online. Once the systems were

back up and running, a pipe burst in the lunchroom, meaning the cafeteria staff couldn't make lunch for everyone, and they'd had to rush in food to feed the rest of the kids. She'd prayed for the day to just end and get a do-over tomorrow, but a fender bender in the car rider line turned into an altercation between parents that she had to help defuse.

By the time she got away from the school and headed to pick up Shania from football practice, she wanted to cry. And Halle wasn't a crier. Crying solved nothing. She learned that after crying uncontrollably after the loss of her parents. She'd cried, but they hadn't come back, and that hadn't made figuring out life without them any easier. So instead of crying she pushed aside the frustration and sat in her car, making a list of all the things to do tonight when she got home to make sure things went better tomorrow morning.

She was busy scribbling when someone knocked on the passenger-side window. Halle startled at the interruption and looked up from the pen and pad in her hand. Shania waved; Quinton stood behind her. Halle's heart jumped into her throat. She'd tried not to think about what Quinton said. Tried not to picture him as the man in her life and just view him as Shania's father. It didn't help that every time she saw the man he looked better than chocolate ice cream in a freshly baked waffle cone covered in sprinkles and syrup on a hot summer day.

Halle licked her lips as she quickly got out of the car and tried to control her facial features. "You ready?"

Shania frowned. "Bad day?"

"No, it was a good day," Halle lied.

Shania tilted her head to the side. "You're making a list. Whenever you're upset you make a list."

"No, I don't."

"Yes, you do. Your way of getting the world to do what you want it to do."

Halle crossed her arms and looked from Shania to Quinton. "What's going on? Did something happen at practice?"

Quinton shook his head. "No, I was talking to Shania after practice and just walked with her over to the car. How did things go today? I heard about the power outage at the middle school."

Of course he had. News traveled fast in Peachtree Cove. "That was the least of our worries," Halle said. "But we got through. Turns out squirrels in the ceiling got to some wires. The IT team created a work-around and they're getting in a contractor to work on the lines."

"Hopefully, tomorrow will be better. Let me know if you need anything."

He wore those aviator sunglasses he seemed to favor. She hated that she couldn't see his eyes but could feel his stare from behind the lenses. She felt open to his scrutiny and didn't like it.

"I'm good," she said in a tight voice. "Let's go, Shania. I've got a lot to do to prepare for tomorrow, so we'll go eat at the Fresh Place Inn. I've already emailed Tracey and she says it's cool. Shirley made enough for us to have seconds."

Shania's face lit up. "Sounds good. I've got some homework that I need to do, even though it's the first day of school."

"Then we'll get the food to go and head home. Quinton, we'll see you this weekend?"

He nodded. "You will."

She nodded. "Until then." She looked away and got into the car. Shania talked to him for a few seconds before getting in the backseat of the car.

"Are you mad at Coach Q?" Shania asked as she put on her seat belt.

Halle didn't look at Quinton as she drove away. "No, why would I be mad at him? I just had a long day and we've got a lot of stuff to do. School is back in session, and we'll be busy."

"I know, but I think he wanted to talk to you about something."

She glanced at Shania. "About what?"

"I don't know. You know he doesn't usually walk me to your car to keep people from making things weird."

"Are the kids on the team making things weird still? Did anyone say anything else?"

Shania sat back in the seat. Her fingers tugged on her shorts. "There were some whispers at school today, but nothing too bad."

Halle placed her hand over Shania's. "I'm sorry. Who said anything? You know you can go to the principal."

"I know, but there's no need. No one said anything to me. Besides, there's some girl drama happening online that is more interesting than me right now."

"What type of girl drama?" Halle asked, concerned. She knew how quickly online disputes could spill over into a fight at the school.

"I don't know. It doesn't involve me and I'm staying out of it. I keep to my cousins and stay out of the drama. So, no need to worry."

"Still, if you hear anything let me know."

Halle would call Jeremiah and give him a heads-up. No need to have him blindsided if anything did blow up at his school. They went by the Fresh Place Inn. Tracey was busy getting a new tenant set up in their room, so she grabbed the food from Shirley and headed home. They ate dinner and then Shania showered and went to her room to do homework. Halle spread out her paperwork on the kitchen table and went over the list of things she needed to prepare before the next morning. The people to call and the maintenance items to follow up on. She'd hoped the district could cover the cost of repairs. Otherwise, the school's maintenance budget would go over.

Her cell phone rang around eight that night. Quinton's number. Frowning, she answered. "Is everything okay?"

"It is, but I wanted to run something by you. You got a second?"

She looked at the papers on the table, but suddenly the issues didn't seem as important. Quinton didn't call her unless it was important. "I do."

"I'm in the neighborhood. Can I stop by?"

Halle glanced around the room. She'd changed and was in her after-work, no-bra outfit. A pair of pajama pants that might have a hole in the crotch and an old T-shirt. "Um...give me about ten minutes or so."

"That's fine. See you in a bit."

Halle hurried to her room and put on a sports bra. She peeped in on Shania, but her daughter was already in the bed, out like a light. Between first day of school and football practice she wasn't surprised to find her already knocked out.

She went on the porch to wait for Quinton. She didn't want the doorbell to wake up Shania. Quinton's truck pulled into her driveway soon after she went out. He got out of the car and walked toward her. The shades from earlier were gone but his expression still wasn't easily readable. He looked good in the basketball shorts and sports shirt that clung to his shoulders.

"Everything okay?"

"Yeah." He held out a bag. "I brought these for you."

She looked at the bag from the Sweet Treats bakery. "What is it?"

"Open it up and see."

She took the bag and checked inside. Her mouth watered. "A lemon blueberry cupcake!"

"The last one they had. I figured you could use it after your day. I went by the grocery store after practice and heard about the issue with lunch and the car rider fight. You had a rough day."

"The life of a principal. I'm going to eat this now."

"Go ahead."

She sat on the stoop and Quinton sat beside her. She pulled out the cupcake and took a bite. The sweetness burst on her taste buds, and she groaned. "This is so good."

"Good." He sounded satisfied.

Halle glanced at him out of the corner of her eye. "Did you really come here just to bring me a cupcake?"

"No, I do need to talk to you."

So Shania had been right. "What's going on?"

"It's about my parents. They're coming to visit me next weekend. They want to meet Shania."

The cupcake nearly stuck in Halle's throat. "Your parents? You've got parents?"

Quinton laughed. "Most people have someone who brought them into the world."

"I'm sorry, I know that. It's just, I never really thought about your parents." Or his family. She'd just thought about getting to know him and making him a part of her life. She hadn't considered what it would be like to include the rest of his family.

"I know. I asked them for more time, but they're excited." He sounded apologetic. "They've always wanted a grandchild. My sister isn't having any kids so they're looking at me."

"They aren't upset about Shania?"

He shook his head. "Nah, they're upset that I donated in college, but they aren't upset that she's here."

"I guess I can understand that."

He sighed and stretched his legs out in front of him. "The money I got helped them keep the apartment. I didn't have a lot growing up. My parents worked, but it wasn't enough to really make ends meet. Then they had to legally separate because my dad's income kept my mom from getting assistance. They said her income combined with his pushed them out of the assistance program."

Halle put the rest of the cupcake in the bag. Her stomach soured by the reality she saw play out in her school each year. "I hate that. I see it with so many kids. Their parents are barely making it and if you do better you lose assistance. Without the assistance you can barely get by."

He nodded. "Getting out and getting a decent job was my only goal. I knew football could make me a lot, but it's no guarantee. Anything can derail a career. So, I also majored in education. Schools always need teachers."

"Were you the star of the team?" She'd assumed he'd been one of those great kids destined to play professionally. Catered to and obstacles blocked so that he could succeed on the field.

He shook his head. "Hardly. I grew up in a decent enough school district. Not rich, but fancy enough that the football team was run by boosters who could donate and get their kids to play. My parents weren't part of that. I had to fight just to get noticed or taken seriously. When I proved I could make plays, they didn't have a reason to keep me off the team."

"Then you got a scholarship for college?"

"Nope."

"Really?"

"I was injured my senior year. I lost the scholarship I was offered. I had to be a walk-on at another school."

"Injured how?"

His body tensed. "Accident with some kids at school. It was bad enough to ruin my season, but not bad enough to keep me from playing. Thankfully, I recovered and was able to walk on at Clark Atlanta. But paying for school while trying to prove I deserved a scholarship was tough. So, I did what I could to make extra money. I qualified for work study, so that helped. I gave a lot of blood. I knew some guys on the team donated sperm. There was a doctor affiliated with the team who worked at the donor place. He convinced some players that there were people who'd pay extra to have 'prime quality sperm.' His words.

I held off, but when my family was about to get kicked out of the apartment, I did it."

"I'm sorry."

"Don't be. I don't regret what I did. Even though I didn't do it again. You got Shania and here we are."

"With your parents wanting to meet her." Everything about Quinton was different from what she'd imagined. He wasn't just kind, considerate and straightforward, he was also a hard worker. She liked him. Something she hadn't expected when she'd first met him, but was glad to be proven wrong about.

"Do you have a problem with them meeting her?"

Halle considered it and shook her head. "No. Not really. My mom died when I was in high school. Dad my junior year of college. Losing them is the reason why I wanted to have Shania. I felt so alone and I wanted someone I could love who would also love me. Having Shania alone was hard, but I made it work. It also means I haven't had to think about parents in a long time."

"You never thought about having in-laws?"

She glanced at him. "They aren't my in-laws."

He grinned and her stomach flipped. "Not right now."

Her eyes widened. "Don't even play."

He reached out and wiped the corner of her mouth. "I'm just talking. You've got icing on your lips."

His fingers lingered on her lips. His eyes, dark and alluring, stared back at hers. The background sounds in the neighborhood faded away. Her breath stuck in her chest.

"We can't."

"I want to kiss you. I thought about kissing you before I knew Shania was my daughter. Maybe we shouldn't, but we damn sure can give it a try." He brought his finger to his lips and licked the icing off his finger. "Can I kiss you?"

She couldn't for the life of her think of a reason why not. She nodded. Quinton leaned forward and his lips pressed against hers. His kiss was perfect. His lips firm but gentle as they played against hers. He gently sucked on her lower lip and fire spread through her. It invaded her bloodstream, her lungs, her heart. She leaned in closer to him, wanting to get more. Quinton met her intensity with his own. One hand cupped the back of her head; the other pressed into her thigh.

She was lost in the sensation. She wanted more. Wished that she could take him in the house and feel the heat of his skin against hers. His hand squeezed her thigh before sliding up to her side, then slowly up to cup the side of her breast. She pushed her chest forward and his thumb brushed across her hardened nipple.

Halle gasped and his tongue slid past her parted lips. She was one minute away from forgetting all the things she said about not getting together with him. His thumb circled her nipple. Scratch that: she was two seconds away.

Quinton slowly pulled back. His eyes were bright with desire and his breathing just as choppy as hers. "I didn't mean to go so far."

"Neither did I." Without his intoxicating kisses she could think clearly. "We shouldn't do this here."

He nodded. "I'll go." He pulled back.

"Quinton, we—"

"I know. There's a lot to work out before we do this." He leaned in and kissed her softly. "I'm still waiting for you to say the time is right." He pulled back and stood.

Halle's eyes dropped to the bulge in the front of his shorts. She pressed her thighs together and desire blossomed even more raw and potent. Quinton adjusted his shorts, but the move didn't help.

"I'll call you about next weekend."

The reminder cooled the arousal in her body. His parents. Their complicated situation. Cooled but didn't douse. "I'll wait to hear from you."

He nodded, stared at her for several tense seconds. Would he kiss her again? He blinked then turned and went back to his car. Halle sat there after he pulled away. She reached into the bag and pulled out the rest of the lemon blueberry cupcake. She took a bite, enjoyed the sweetness and smiled.

Twenty

THE FIRST WEEK OF SCHOOL FLEW BY AND BEFORE he knew it, Quinton was standing on the sidelines for the first JV home game of the year. By halftime Peachtree Cove was up twenty-one to seven and from the outstanding way the defense was holding up, he was confident that they could maintain the lead. The rhythmic chants from the cheerleaders and cheers of the fans pushed his team to try even harder. By the end of the third quarter, they'd stopped the other team at the one-yard line and he grew even more confident in the victory.

He watched as the offense ran a play that would put the ball in Shania's hands. He held his breath as the quarterback snapped the ball and the players all jumped into action. The ball flew through the air. Shania's hands lifted. Quinton swore time stopped. He watched anxiously to see if she would catch the ball. Every time they ran this route in practice she caught the ball. He'd noticed the other team ignored her side of the field. Their mistake. She was wide open and well matched with the defensive player. When the ball landed comfortably in her hands and she took off, running the necessary ten yards to get the first down, he pumped his fist.

That was his girl! The thought rushed through his mind as pride swelled in his chest. The rest of the team cheered, but this wasn't time to celebrate. He motioned with his hands for them to line up again and run the same play, this time to the other side. They ended the game twenty-eight to seven.

He walked over to Zachariah and patted him on the back. "Good game, huh."

"Hell, yes. The kids did good."

The rest of the team jumped up and down and cheered. Quinton waved a hand. "Alright now, settle down. Save that until after we've shaken the hands of the other team."

The kids settled but their grins were wide and eager as they formed a line and shook hands with the other team after the game. Quinton shook the hands of the other coach.

"You got me with the girl receiver," he said. "I didn't expect that play."

"Never underestimate any player on the field," Quinton said, unapologetic. If the other coach chose to assume Shania didn't have any abilities, then that was his fault. A fault Quinton would happily take advantage of with any other team that chose to underestimate her.

The other coach laughed. "True that. Good game."

"Good game." Quinton slapped him on the back and then went to join the team.

As he ran toward the locker rooms located behind the goalpost on the field, he looked toward the stands. Halle stood there, her friends Imani and Tracey on either side of her. They all wore bright smiles and chatted excitedly. Halle threw her head back and laughed. Her shoulders trembling with her happiness. Her body had shaken when he'd kissed her, touched her, the other night.

Quinton stumbled and barely caught himself from falling. Damn him and the thoughts that came into his head. The other good thing about the game was the distraction. He hadn't been able to get the feel of Halle in his arms out of his mind. The taste of her lips and the way her fingers had clenched his shoulders; the softness of her thighs and the heavy weight of her breast in his hand.

"You okay, Coach?" one of the players asked.

Quinton cleared his throat and looked around the field. "Must've been an uneven patch of grass or something."

The kid, Paul, cocked a brow as if confused. There were no uneven patches on the field, but thankfully, he didn't mention it and hurried on to join the rest of the team.

After the post-game pep talk, Quinton and the other coaches helped the kids gather up their items for the end of the night. Shania found him as he was leaving the locker room.

"What did you think?" Her eyes were bright with excitement.

He patted her on the shoulder. "What do you mean *what did I think*? I think you did a great job out there."

Her face split with a bright smile. "I could've run it in for a touchdown."

"Going out of bounds wasn't bad. You got the first down, that's what matters." They walked together toward the stadium where her mom would be waiting.

"I knew we were getting close to the end of the quarter with no timeouts," Shania said. "I tried to help stop the clock."

He nodded, proud that she'd paid attention to the time and chosen to be strategic. "Smart. It worked and gave us more time to set up for the next play."

"I was worried I wouldn't catch it."

"If you think about it too hard, then you won't. Just let things happen. That's the best thing about football."

Octavius ran up to them. "Good catch, Shania." He held out his hand.

Shania slapped hands with him. "Thanks."

"Not as many yards as me, but still good," Octavius said with a confident grin.

Shania rolled her eyes. "Whatever, if Jabari knew how to scan the field he would have thrown to me sooner and I'd have just as many yards."

Octavius shrugged but nodded. "You right. They were straight up ignoring you over there. Wanna run routes this weekend?"

Shania looked surprised. "Sure. Give me a call."

"What's your number?" He pulled out his cell phone.

Shania rattled off her number when a young girl ran up. "Octavius, what are you doing?"

"Getting Shania's number. We're going to practice this weekend."

The girl glared at Shania. "Practice?"

Quinton easily saw where this was about to go. "I'm going to be there. Working with my two receivers."

Some of the animosity in her gaze disappeared, but her lip was still twisted. "All you care about is football," she said to Octavius. She slid her arm through his and tugged. "Come on, let's go."

Quinton and Shania watched the two walk away. "What was that about?"

"Octavius's girlfriend?" he asked. When she nodded he sighed. "Maybe she's jealous."

Shania scrunched up her nose. "Of what? I am not interested in him like that."

"Yeah, focus on studying and football. Not boys."

Shania rolled her eyes. "What if I'm into girls?"

He held up a hand. "That's cool, but still focus on studying instead."

She laughed and shook her head. "You sound like Mom."

They walked toward the parking lot. "Are you...interested in girls?"

Shania laughed and slapped him on the shoulder. "Not particularly, but if I find out later that I am, I'll let you know."

He shook his head. "Make it a while out. I haven't gotten to the dating chapter in the how-to-raise-kids manual."

They were still laughing when Halle walked over. "What's so funny?"

"Coach Q thinks Octavius's girlfriend is jealous."

Halle's eyes widened. "What? Did she say something to you? What did she say?"

Quinton held up a hand. "Hold up, Warrior Mother. It's not that bad. I'm probably off base anyway."

The fire left Halle's eyes. "Well, let me know if she starts any girl drama."

Shania groaned before rolling her eyes. "There isn't any girl drama. I'm hungry. Can we eat?"

Halle nodded. "Yes. And to celebrate your play, you get a victory dinner of anything you want."

"McDonald's?" Shania said.

Halle frowned. "That's what you want?"

"You said anything. Their Sprite be hitting," Shania said, rubbing her stomach.

Halle chuckled. "McDonald's it is." She looked at Quinton.

A moment passed as the memory of what they'd done jumped between them. How the hell was he supposed to be around her and not let everyone in the world know that he wanted to kiss her again? For Shania's sake he understood. Her world was turned upside down as it was. No need to make it even more complicated with her parents dating. What if they broke up?

Would you really want to let Halle go?

No. He knew that. But he also knew life had a funny way of kicking you in the balls. Anything could happen that would tear them apart.

"Well, I'll let you all have your victory dinner," he said.

"You're not joining us?" Shania looked expectantly at him.

"You want me to?" Honestly, he wanted to celebrate with her.

"Yeah, plus, half the team goes to McDonald's after the game. You've gotta come. Please."

He looked at Halle. "As long as your mom doesn't mind?"

He could see the no in her eyes. But she looked at Shania and relented. "Sure."

That Saturday, as Halle watched Quinton squeeze avocados in the middle of Walmart's produce section, and her mind jumped back to the way he'd squeezed her breast on the front porch, she realized her life had truly gotten out of control. Avocado shopping shouldn't arouse her. Walmart shopping with Quinton and Shania shouldn't feel so normal. They weren't supposed to click like this. Were they?

Quinton held up an avocado. "What about this one? It seems good."

Halle blinked and tore her eyes away from his long fingers wrapped around the small fruit. "Yes, it does look good."

He frowned. "You alright?"

She nodded quickly. "Yep. Shania!" She called her daughter's name louder than she'd planned. Shania stood a few feet away near the bananas.

Shania's brows drew together as embarrassment spread over her face. "Right here."

"Did you get the seasoning mix for the guacamole?"

Shania held up the packet of seasoning mix. "Got it."

"Good. Bring it back over here and don't stray too far."

Shania fanned herself with the small seasoning packet as she came over. "I'm fourteen, not four. I know how to find you if we get separated in Walmart."

"Hush up and put the seasoning in the buggy." Halle didn't care if she sounded foolish. When Shania was close it was easier to remember why she didn't need to have a repeat of what happened between her and Quinton. Shania didn't want them getting together and making a complicated situation more complicated. Shania just wanted to get to know her dad. Halle didn't know what she was feeling for Quinton other than a deep primal urge to have the man plant his face between her thighs.

She suppressed a groan. Damn, now that thought was in her head. "What's next on the list?"

Quinton looked at the sheet of notebook paper she'd used to scribble up a quick list. "Looks like we need to get chicken and ground beef for the tacos."

Halle nodded. "Good. Let's head to the meat section."

Quinton came into step next to her. "You really don't have to cook anything. Knowing my mom, she's going to bring half of the groceries we'll need anyway and insist on taking over my kitchen as if it's her own."

His parents were coming into town the next day. When they'd had the celebration dinner at McDonald's after the JV game, Halle came up with the idea of putting together a nice dinner for everyone to get to know each other. They'd agreed to have it at Quinton's house. His was larger and could hold everything and was already accessible for his sister's wheelchair.

"If they're coming all this way then they shouldn't have to make dinner for us."

Quinton put his hand on the cart handle next to hers. "Believe me, my mom is going to insist. She loves to cook."

Their hands brushed against each other. Halle lifted hers to wave off his concerns. "She can cook the next meal. Besides, tacos are Shania's favorite."

Shania walked on Halle's other side. "We don't have to cook my favorite meal."

"They're getting to know you, so this is a way for them to get to know you."

Shania gave Halle a knowing look. "You're using the meal as a distraction. If we're eating we can't talk much. Plus, you get to control the atmosphere."

Halle eyed her daughter, who grinned back. "Quit acting like you know me."

Shania just laughed. She looked over Shania's shoulder and grinned. "Hey, it's Carmen."

Before Halle could process what she'd said, Shania was already around the buggy and heading in the direction of one of her friends. Halle stopped and watched her daughter.

"Who's that?" Quinton asked.

Halle glanced that way. She recognized the girl. "Ah, that's Carmen. She and Shania were close in middle school, but she switched to a different high school this year." Halle held up her hand and waved. Carmen waved back before she and Shania continued to chat.

"They don't see each other anymore?" Quinton asked.

"They talk to each other all the time. Switching schools doesn't mean the end of a friendship anymore. They've got social media and texts. They just don't see each other daily."

Halle continued to the meat section and scanned the selection of meat.

Quinton looked over his shoulder at Shania then back at Halle with a questioning glance. "Um…is that her girlfriend?"

Halle looked up at him. "Like friend who's a girl or girlfriend?"

"The latter? The other night she said something about letting me know if she likes girls and I wasn't sure if she was serious."

"Would it bother you if she were?"

He shook his head. "It wouldn't. I just want to know for

sure. I don't want to make a mistake and put my foot in my mouth by assuming."

Halle relaxed, once again pleased to find another way that he was considerate of getting to know Shania. "I don't think she likes girls. She's never told me that she has."

"I think Octavius on the team likes her."

Halle blinked. "The other receiver?"

"Yeah, when we were throwing the ball earlier today, he had the look on his face of a guy in love. I'm curious how this may go."

Halle looked at Shania and her friend and then frowned. "I'd be happy if she didn't start dating someone on the team. I didn't play sports, but I was in the band and I remember what happened on the band bus."

Quinton's eyes narrowed and the corner of his mouth lifted. "What happened on the band bus?"

Heat spread through Halle's cheeks. She rolled her eyes and looked away. "Just keep an eye on them. No making out on the way back from a game, please."

Quinton continued to smirk but nodded. "I'll keep an eye on the Octavius situation. If things look like he's getting serious, I'll try to keep them apart."

"You will?"

"I may not know what happened on the band bus, but I know what can happen when romance develops on a football team. I need my team working together, not dealing with love drama. Especially when Octavius is already dating a cheerleader."

"You want to avoid any potential of drama with Octavius's girlfriend?"

He nodded. "Exactly."

"Well, if it helps any, I don't think she likes Octavius. I think she's into the boy who lives across the street. He's a theater kid and isn't intimidated by her playing football. She said he was *interesting.* Which is the most I've heard her say about anyone. Boy or girl."

"Then maybe the Octavius thing will work itself out."

"I hope so." Halle focused on the ground beef offerings.

"Just like the things between the two of us can work out." Quinton's softly spoken statement made Halle stop as she reached for a package.

Halle's eyes widened and she looked around. Shania was still chatting happily with her friend and had drifted farther away. "We aren't going to talk about that."

"Why not?"

"Because Shania is with us and we're in the middle of Walmart." She motioned to the other shoppers around them.

He shrugged. "She's not here now. And I'm pretty sure worse conversations have gone down in this store."

Halle fought not to grin at his observation. She pointed at him. "That's not the point. Your parents will be here tomorrow. We need to focus on that."

Desire still lit his dark eyes, but he nodded. "We'll do that. I just want you to know that I can't stop thinking about you. The feel of you." His voice lowered and he leaned in close. "The taste of you."

If her body got any hotter, she'd roast the meat in the deli section. "You're not helping."

He leaned back and held up a hand. "Then I'll keep my thoughts to myself."

She meant what she said, but she also liked knowing he felt the same as her. She needed to sort out exactly what she wanted from Quinton. A relationship? Sex? A one-night stand to get it out of her system?

His cell phone rang. He pulled out the phone and frowned at the screen.

Halle rose on her toes and tried to see his phone, but couldn't. "Who is it?"

"I don't recognize the number." He slid his finger across to answer.

"Then why answer?"

He shrugged. "Could be important. Hello?" He listened for a second before a scowl covered his face. "How did you get this number?" A pause. "Yeah. No." Another pause. "There's no need for that. I'll talk with you when the school hosts you and that's it. Goodbye." He hung up the phone.

Halle frowned. "Who was that?"

"The editor for the magazine."

"The guy you went to school with?"

He nodded before walking away from the ground beef section to the chicken. Halle followed. No way was he going to clam up and not give her more details.

"What did he want?"

"To hang out when he gets in town." He pointed to the case. "Breasts or thighs?"

"Breasts. Why don't you want to hang out?"

He looked at her as if she'd grown a third eye. "We didn't get along in high school."

"And again, maybe he changed. You're adults now."

His face hardened. "I don't care how much he changed. We're not hanging out."

"Well, you can't be rude to him. Not when he's judging the town."

"I have my reasons." He picked up a family pack of chicken breasts.

"What are they? Maybe hanging out with him will help us win Best Small Town. Don't you want to help the town?"

He leaned a hand against the shopping cart. "Help the town, yes, but if it means hanging out with that asshole, then hell no."

This was the first time she'd seen Quinton close to being angry. For someone who was so in control, the response surprised her. Quinton holding a grudge back to high school seemed out of character.

"The mayor asked you to help. You can't back out now. What happened? I'm sure you two can work it out now."

Quinton watched her with flat, angry eyes. "Remember when I told you about the accident that kept me from getting a scholarship? Well, he's the reason why. He bullied me throughout high school and when a scout noticed me and not him, he and his friends beat me up and broke my leg. Hell will freeze over before I ever hang out with him."

Twenty-One

QUINTON STOOD ON HIS FRONT PORCH AND WAVED as his parents' van pulled into the driveway. He sent up a quick prayer that they wouldn't be too over-the-top with this meeting. He hurried down the steps and went to the passenger side to open the door for his mom.

She got out and immediately wrapped him up in a bear hug. "It's my baby! Oh, it's been too long since I've seen you. Let me take a look at you." She leaned back to eye him. His mom was tall and thick with dark eyes that missed nothing. Her hair was styled in an intricate twist in the back with curls in the front and she wore a flower-printed flowy top with wide leg pants.

"I haven't changed since the last time you saw me," he said after pulling back.

His dad was already out of the car and heading toward him and his mom. "Yep, still ugly," his dad said with a laugh. Willie Evans was shorter than his mom and Quinton. With a friendly face, dark skin and a joke always ready. He wore a light blue T-shirt and jeans belted tight.

Quinton only grinned and pointed. "Everyone says I look like you, so…"

His mom slapped down his hand. "Shut up. Both of you are my handsome men."

"Hey, don't forget me back here." His sister's voice came from the inside of the van. "Quinton's ugly and looks like Dad, now open the door."

Quinton moved and went to the sliding door that automatically opened. His sister grinned at him. She reminded him of his mom, with her sharp gaze and eager smile. She had their dad's darker complexion and wore her natural hair in a short, stylish cut. "Lord, they forget all about me whenever they see you."

"That's not true," his mom said, not sounding convincing.

His dad brought his sister's wheelchair from the back of the van and Quinton helped Dawn get out. Once she was settled, she grabbed his hand.

"Where is she?" She eyed the house eagerly.

Three sets of eyes zeroed in on him. "She's in the house. She came over with Halle, who made dinner."

"Why did she cook?" his mom asked indignantly. "I was going to make your favorite. I got all the stuff in the back of the van."

"Make it tomorrow. Tacos are Shania's favorite. Halle thought it would make things easier if we have Shania's favorite meal."

"Tacos?" his dad said with a scowl. "Who eats tacos on Sunday? Tacos are for Tuesday. Pot roast or fried chicken is for Sunday."

Quinton shook his head. "You can eat whatever you want on any day. Please, just let things go and be cool with tacos today."

His dad nodded but grumbled. "I just like tacos on Tuesday."

His mom pointed at the house. "Is she living here?"

Quinton frowned. "Who? Shania?"

"Well, both of them. Why is she cooking in your kitchen? Don't tell me you two are hooking up or anything."

"No, we're not hooking up." Not yet anyway. Quinton hoped that one day they would get to that point. "Why would you say that?"

"Because she's in your kitchen. When a woman cooks in your kitchen that means she's laying the foundation to be your wife," his mom said as if that were the gospel truth.

Quinton frowned, not familiar with that saying. "Says who?"

"Everyone says that." His mom spoke confidently.

Quinton looked at his sister, who usually gave him the same *whatever* look whenever their mom came up with some new superstition they'd never heard of. Instead of rolling her eyes, his sister gave him an interested look and eyebrow wiggle.

"Not you, too?"

"I'm just saying, it is odd that she's cooking over here." Dawn continued going along with his mom's newfound saying.

Quinton swallowed his frustration. He loved his family, but they were exasperating. "She's only cooking here because I'm hosting at my house. She was worried about her house not being easily accessible for you. That's it."

Dawn pressed a hand to her heart. "Aww, she was worried about me?"

"She's a planner and doesn't leave anything out." He didn't focus on the way his heart warmed at his sister's appreciation. "Come on, let's go in so you can meet Shania."

They headed toward the house. When Quinton purchased the place, he'd installed a ramp that led up to the front door. Even if his sister didn't visit him often, he wanted her to feel welcome in his home.

Worry still creased his mom's face as they got closer to the door. "Well, if it's just for that then I'll let it slide. Just don't start messing around with her."

"Why would you say that?" Was everyone against him and Halle getting together?

"Because, she had a baby on her own and obviously didn't want or need a man if she's still single. Don't go falling in love with someone who won't love you back."

"No one's falling in love," he said automatically. He was used to his mom trying to plan a wedding whenever he was remotely interested in any woman. For her to be against Halle, though, surprised him. He'd expect her to have already put him and Halle together.

"I'm just saying. Focus on my grandbaby and not the momma."

They reached the front door before Quinton could say anything else. His mom rushed toward the kitchen.

"Where is my grandbaby?"

Quinton hurried behind her, and his dad and sister came up the rear. They entered the kitchen in a rush. Halle froze at the stove and turned to face them. Shania looked up from where she was cutting tomatoes at the island. Her eyes were wide as she looked at his family.

"Um…here?" she said, raising a hand.

His mom threw up her hands. "Oh my God, you look just like Quinton." She hurried to Shania's side and reached for her. Shania thankfully had time to put down the knife before his mom impaled herself on it as she pulled her into a huge bear hug. His mom squeezed Shania before pulling back and cupping her face. "Oh, look at you. You're so beautiful. I knew you would be. And so tall. Oh my goodness, Willie, do you see how tall my grandbaby is?"

"I see," his dad said, coming around to stand next to his wife. "She definitely got the height from our side."

"Isn't she pretty? And smart," his mom continued. "Your dad told me you were smart, too. I knew you would be. Oh my goodness. Just look at her."

Shania's eyes remained wide as she watched them. A wobbly smile on her face as she looked at his mom and then his dad. "You think I'm pretty?"

"Of course you are," his mom exclaimed. "Oh, listen to her. Doesn't she sound smart?"

His dad nodded. "Sure does. But of course, she would be. We ain't no dummies."

Halle slid forward and gently pulled Shania back. "Hello, I'm Halle. It's nice to meet you."

His mom frowned at having Shania taken out of her reach. But thankfully she didn't jerk her back. "You're the mother?"

"I am. And I'm guessing you're the grandparents." She looked at Quinton and his sister. "And you're the aunt?"

His sister beamed. "I am. Dawn Evans. It's nice to meet you, too. Sorry for my parents. They're Willie and Laura. They've wanted a grandkid for a long time. They'll calm down soon enough."

He met Halle's eyes and suppressed a smile, because he could read her thoughts on her face. His parents calming down couldn't come soon enough.

Quinton sat on his back porch with his sister. His backyard butted against a wooded area. He'd also purchased the lot behind him so that in a few years he wouldn't have to worry about anyone moving in and ruining his view. His sister loved herbal tea and always brought her favorites with her, so he'd made a pot and brought it out back to drink with her. Even though he wasn't a big tea drinker, he always enjoyed drinking tea with his sister. Their parents were upstairs getting the room ready.

"Do you think Mom is rewashing the sheets on the guest bed?" he asked.

His sister laughed. "Only if she didn't pack her own sheets."

He shook his head. "I don't remember her being like this when we were younger."

"That's because we didn't travel when we were younger. Plus, remember that stint she worked at the motel on the outskirts of town? Mom is convinced all hotels are dirty."

"But my house isn't a hotel."

Dawn laughed. "She's also convinced you're a man who doesn't know to change the sheets in the guest bedroom. She probably thinks they've been there since her last visit."

"Give me some credit. I know to change the sheets." He'd made a point of putting new sheets on the bed for her and his dad before they'd arrived. "She's going to drive Halle crazy."

"Probably so." Dawn looked at him. "Does that bother you?"

"A little. I'm trying to convince Halle that I'm not trying to intrude on her life. I want this to be a smooth transition."

Dawn grunted and took a sip of her tea. "Nothing about this is smooth. This entire situation is straight out of the headlines. I don't know how you can blend your families without any bumps. Is she giving you a hard time? Have you found out if she's a gold digger?"

He glared at his sister, but thankfully, the smile on her face let him know she wasn't serious. "She isn't a gold digger. She doesn't want anything from me."

"You sound like that bothers you." His sister gasped and pointed. "You like her!"

He shook his head and poured more tea into his cup. "Stop."

Dawn wagged her finger. "Yes, you do, I can tell by the way your nose it twitching. You like her."

He rubbed his nose. "Shouldn't I like her? We've got to figure out how to raise a kid together."

"I'm not talking about liking her in general as a person. I'm talking about *like* liking her. You want to get with her. Does she want to get with you?"

Quinton knew she was attracted to him, but he didn't think she wanted to be with him. "I don't know. I think she does."

"Why do you think so?"

He wasn't about to tell her about the kiss. His sister would broadcast that to his parents before the night was over. "We vibe. That's all. But she just broke up with the guy she liked. And Shania doesn't want us together. She thinks it'll be weird."

"That's because it's new. She's getting used to you being a family." They were silent for a few seconds before Dawn said, "I like her. She did well with Mom and Dad today, and they can be a lot."

Quinton thought about how Halle let his mom's comments about not needing to cook anymore and his dad's insistence that tacos are for Tuesday roll off her. Although his parents were much, he'd also noticed the way she'd smiled as they'd gushed over every accomplishment Shania had. They may have been their usually overbearing selves, but they'd been sincere in their delight with Shania, and Halle had noticed that.

"A part of me wants to pursue this thing with Halle," he admitted. "I worry that I'm going to mess things up with Shania. She's the most important thing right now."

Dawn poked his elbow. "I hear a but?"

"But I was interested in Halle before this. I overheard her say something about not dating athletes and then she was with that English teacher, so I never approached her. Now I've got a chance, but it'll piss off my kid. What am I supposed to do?"

"Damn if I know." Dawn sighed and sipped her tea.

Quinton chuckled. "Thanks a lot."

"I know, I'm no help. Again, your situation is awkward as fuck. I don't know how you navigate."

"I hear a but?" he countered.

"But you know me and you know I love love. I'm rooting for you and Halle to get together. Mom is worried that's why she said not to do anything. She doesn't want you to get hurt like you did with Catherine."

Quinton scowled at the mention of his ex-girlfriend. "We broke up two years ago. I'm over her."

He and Catherine had tried long distance and it hadn't worked out. He'd been hurt about the breakup but not heartbroken.

"Still, Mom wants you to settle down."

He stared down at the tea in his cup and admitted softly, "I can see myself with Halle."

Dawn turned to study him. "Is that because you really want to see yourself with her, or because she's a ready-made family?"

"Huh?"

"Huh!" his sister repeated with a grin. "Whenever you answer a question with that it's because you don't know the answer or you're afraid to answer. You heard what I said. Figure that shit out first. Either you really want to be with Halle or you're seeing a family because the kid you always wondered about appeared with a woman you're attracted to. They're right here, in the town you moved to. I say it's fate, but I'm a realist enough to know that you don't believe in fate. You believe in hard work and effort. So, put in the work and figure out if this is really fate that brought you together."

Twenty-Two

HALLE WAS GOING THROUGH THE ITEMS SHE'D NEED for the next week at school when the doorbell rang. That would be Quinton to visit Shania. She glanced at the clock then cringed. Shania wasn't back yet. She quickly got up from the kitchen table and went to the door. Quinton stood on the other side, looking delicious in a black T-shirt, dark pants and those aviator glasses he loved.

"Hey, Halle," he said. "Shania ready?"

Halle focused on his face and not how good his legs looked in the athletic pants. "She spent the night at my cousin's last night. Give me a second to check and see when they'll be back. Come on in." She stepped back, and he crossed the threshold.

Halle went back to the kitchen and grabbed her cell phone before meeting him back in the living room. A quick call and she learned Shania was eating at the local breakfast place with her cousin. She turned back to Quinton after ending the call.

"They're waiting on the check and will be here soon. Do you want to wait?"

"Do you mind if I do?"

She didn't, but the idea of being alone with him made her giddy. They rarely had time to be together without Shania or his family around. His phone calls to make plans for how he and Shania would spend time together was their only alone time.

"I don't mind." She motioned for him to sit on the couch. "Good job on the varsity game last night."

He sat and stretched his long legs out in front of him. "Thanks. I was worried we wouldn't be able to get the win, but it worked out. Were you there? I didn't see you?"

Halle sat on the far end of the couch. "No, Shania went to the game with her cousin and then they had a sleepover afterwards. She told me about the win."

The edge of his mouth lifted up in a slight smile. "You don't like football, do you?"

"Why do you say that?"

"I remember overhearing you talk about how you wish you could get rid of the football program at the middle school."

Her eyes widened. "When did I say that?"

"It was an offhand comment. It was at my first district meeting. You were upset that they focused on me joining the high school coaching staff and said you wished they'd focused on academics as much as they focused on football. That if you could, you'd get rid of the program all together."

She pressed a hand to her temple. She remembered that comment. She had been annoyed about the district training being all about the high school's newest celebrity coach. "I'm sorry. I had to have sounded terrible."

"You sounded honest. I was surprised when I found out your daughter was playing at the middle school."

"I was surprised when she went for the team. She played flag at summer camp and was always into basketball, but I thought it would end with middle school. She proved me and everyone else in town wrong."

"But you still don't like football." There was no judgment in his tone.

Halle decided to be honest. "I've grown to appreciate it. Shania's confidence has grown, and I know she's talented. My issue is growing up in this town when they cared more about football than anything else. In college, I also noticed the school cared more about the teams winning than the other programs. So, I'm a little jaded."

"A lot of schools put more emphasis on sports than they do on academics. I'm not saying it's right, but it's not uncommon. What specifically jaded you?"

Her answer usually satisfied most people; she was surprised he'd realized there was more to her story than an overall disdain of sports. Then again, she shouldn't be surprised. He was observant.

"I was a student tutor. I didn't mind helping, so when the former Peachtree Cove High principal made me tutor the star football player, Darren Jeter, so that he could get the team in the playoffs, I didn't like it but I tried. The problem was that he kept blowing me off. When I confronted him, he said it didn't matter and that he would be able to play anyway. I went and complained. The principal listened to me, but ultimately blew me off. Not only that, Darren miraculously got an A in English and a B in math. Something I know he couldn't do and later realized that his grades had been changed. They let him play, patted me on the head and told me that's the way the world works, and that was that."

She still was upset when she thought back on that. It was one of the reasons she went into education and later became a principal. To give all students a fair advantage. Academics was her main focus; she wanted all the kids to succeed. If they played a sport or not shouldn't be a ticket to passing.

"I'm sorry that happened to you." His eyes were sincere along with his tone. "But you can't put all athletes under the same umbrella because of that."

"I don't, but I don't have to like the way they're coddled either."

He cocked his head to the side. "All athletes aren't coddled."

"What about you? You were good in high school before your accident, right? Did the teachers cater to you?"

He snorted. "Hardly. In my hometown, the kids whose parents were able to contribute to the booster club were the ones who got preferential treatment. The poor kids like me, we were lucky to even make the team."

"But you're a good player?"

The look he gave said being a good player wasn't enough. "I was, but if someone else's kid's dad gave enough to the booster club then that kid was the starter. I fought for my position, but I also did what I needed to do to keep my grades up because I knew that football may not be my way out of poverty. The accident proved that. I got into college on an academic scholarship. From there, I walked on to the team and earned an athletic scholarship later. It wasn't easy."

"I'm sorry for misjudging you. Tracey and Imani tease me about having it out for athletes. I guess I did let what happened in high school cloud my judgment."

He reached over and squeezed her hand. "No harm was done. I just hope that you're willing to give this athlete a chance."

Warmth from his touch traveled up her arm, across her chest and neck and down through her midsection. She wanted to give him a chance. The thought made her take in a shaky breath and her heart rate increased. She did want to. She liked Quinton, not the idea of him, but him as a person. But there were so many things they needed to fix before she could do that.

She pulled her hand away before her newfound revelation sent her across the couch and into his arms. "You said the *Travel Magazine* editor caused your accident. How did it happen?"

Quinton's jaw tightened. She thought he wasn't going to answer but he spoke after a tense second. "According to my principal, boys just playing around."

Halle's hand balled into a fist. "What? He didn't take it seriously?"

"Khris's family contributed to the booster club, the school giveaways, and was a donor to the mayor's election campaign. Most people in town ignored any wrongdoing on their part."

"Did your parents do anything?"

He shrugged. "What could they do? Khris's dad owns half of the rental property in my hometown. Hell, the apartment my parents could barely keep was owned by him. They covered up being slumlords by giving a lot to the community and the school. When they argued that their son was just horsing around and 'accidents happen,' there wasn't any way for my parents to fight. They didn't even bother to pay my hospital bills. It's part of the reason why my family struggled when I was in college. My dad was trying to make enough money to pay for what the scholarship didn't cover, but there was too much debt and too much to take care of."

Halle understood why he didn't want anything to do with Khris Simmons. The more she learned, the more she didn't want anything to do with him either. "What are you going to do when he gets here?"

"What do you think? Should I beat him up?" he asked with a half smile.

Halle reached over and poked his arm. "I don't condone violence. I don't know how you can avoid him, but I know you don't want to be around him. Do you need me to talk to your principal?"

"Are you offering to take care of me?"

The question was innocent enough, but the spark in his eye and the sexy tone of his voice made her stomach flip. "I'm offering to step in and help. You said you'll look out for me. I can at least do the same."

"I appreciate that, but don't worry. I can deal with talking to him. Years have passed and I've more than proved that I can survive. I'll tell him about the football team and avoid him after the interview is over."

He wrapped his fingers around her wrist and gently tugged. Even though she shouldn't, Halle slid closer. "Are you sure? You shouldn't have to put yourself in an uncomfortable situation just for the town."

"Coming from the woman who will bend herself into all kinds of contortions to make other people happy." He let go of her wrist and spread his fingers.

Halle mirrored the movement and pressed her palm against his. "That's just for special people."

His fingers threaded with hers. "Am I a special person?" he asked in a low, sensual voice.

"You're a certain type of special, but not getting any contortions from me."

His lips quirked and he gently squeezed her hand. Tingles flashed from her arm down her spine. Quinton's dark eyes met hers as he slid closer on the couch. "I might like contortions from you, Halle."

Images filled her mind. Her body bent with pleasure. Her legs twisted around his waist. Delicious spasms as she clenched around his length. "Don't tease me like that."

"It's not teasing." His thumb brushed over the racing pulse in her wrist.

Her nipples hardened and desire slid between her thighs. "Shania should be here soon."

His hand rested on her thigh. His gaze was questioning, asking if the touch was okay. Halle scooted even closer, until their bodies touched. His palm slid up her thigh to her waist. He leaned in and murmured in her ear. "I want to see you."

"You see me now." She tried to tease, but her voice was breathless.

His nose nuzzled against her hairline. "Not like this. The two of us. Without Shania, or your cousins or my family. Just us."

Halle closed her eyes. She savored the way his lips lingered over her temple. "We can't be together right now."

His lips brushed across her ear. "We can find a way to make this work."

"Shania doesn't want us together." Her hands went to his chest, but she didn't push him away. His heart was a heavy drumbeat beneath her palm. Her fingers trailed down to his stomach.

"Because she's afraid we won't make it, but what if we can make it? What if this is real?"

"Quinton, I—" His lips brushed against her neck, cutting off her words. Her body shuddered as he pressed sweet, hot kisses across her neck. She needed to pull away, but instead she leaned into him. Her head fell to the side and he gently sucked on her neck. His hand came around and slid beneath her shirt, cupping her breast. His fingers played with her nipple, and she gasped. Her hand lowered from his stomach to the hard ridge of his dick. Quinton sucked in a breath as she palmed his length.

Quinton's hand left her breast and lowered to the waistband of her loose-fitting pants. She should stop him. This was getting out of hand. But by now, desire had taken over her brain. Her legs spread. One agonizingly slow beat later, Quinton's hand slid past the elastic waistband. The seconds it took for his hand to reach her center felt like an eternity before his long fingers finally brushed against her panties.

He let out a hiss. "Damn, you're so hot. Can I touch—"

"Yes," she said quickly. If he didn't touch her, she was going to scream.

Quinton's fingers pushed past her underwear and slid across

the slick heat of her sex. Halle cried out. God, it had been too long since someone touched her like this.

The sound of voices and laughter came from the front porch. Halle's eyes flew open and she pushed on Quinton's chest. "It's Shania."

Quinton cursed but quickly pulled away. Halle eyed his bulging erection. "She'll see that."

"Bathroom?"

She pointed. "Down the hall."

He jumped up and moved with lightning speed. The front door opened just as he reached the bathroom door. Halle stood and hoped she didn't look too ruffled. She felt as if her world had been knocked off-kilter.

"Mom, Coach Q, are you here?" Shania called.

"I'm here," she called back. "He's in the bathroom."

Shania came into the living area. Kayla and Nadia right behind her. Halle went through the motions of thanking Kayla for letting Shania spend the night. Shania and Nadia went into a story about what they'd seen at the diner, which kept Kayla from being nosey and asking questions. Questions she knew her cousin had from the way she eyed Halle.

Quinton came out of the bathroom just as the story ended. "Shania, you ready?" They were going back to his place to spend time with him and his family.

Shania nodded. "Yep. Let's go."

Quinton glanced at her. Their eyes met and she was back on the couch. She quickly looked away. They didn't get a chance to talk about what happened or make plans for what would happen next as everyone shuffled to get out of the house and Kayla watched them like hawks. Quinton was the last one out the door and he turned to her when Shania walked off the porch with Nadia.

"Let me see you. Away from everyone. Just us."

She didn't hesitate to answer. "Just say when."

Twenty-Three

QUINTON WATCHED AS THE OTHER TEAM SNATCHED the ball before Octavius could catch it. The kid didn't hesitate and immediately headed for his end zone. Quinton cursed and balled his hand into a fist. The rest of the coaches yelled for the players to stop him, but it was too late. The boy had reached the goal line and scored a touchdown. The buzzer sounded the end of the fourth quarter.

Groans of disappointment went through the home crowd and were echoed by the coaches and players on the sideline. They'd had a good run so far in the season, but that didn't make losing any easier. Quinton walked down the sideline and patted each player on the shoulder.

"It's okay. Go shake hands and then huddle up in the locker room."

They nodded and formed a line. Quinton hoped the varsity team had a better showing the next night, but the team they'd played was good. They'd outmaneuvered them and played a little harder. He'd take what he'd learned today watching the JV team play and see what he could use for the game tomorrow.

"Coach Q, do you have a second?" a voice called from the stands.

Quinton turned to see the players on the field to where superintendent Watts and Jeremiah stood against the railing. Quinton walked over. "I'm going to congratulate the other team."

Jeremiah nodded. "That's fine, but when you're done stop by the booth."

Dr. Watts grinned down at Quinton from next to Jeremiah. "We want you to meet someone."

"Who?"

Zachariah called his name before Jeremiah could answer. Quinton turned in that direction. He needed to join them to shake hands with the other coach. He turned back to them both. "Alright, let me finish this and talk to the team then I'll head that way."

Jeremiah gave him a thumbs-up. "Good. Thank you!"

Quinton went back to console his team. A loss was never easy. They had several more games to play. Sometimes, the other team just played better. Which was exactly what he said to them after they'd huddled up in the end zone for the post-game talk. Once he released the team to go back to the locker rooms to change, he turned to Zachariah.

"I need to go talk to Jeremiah and the superintendent. You make sure they're good?"

Zachariah's brows drew together. "I got you, but what does he want?"

"Wants me to meet someone."

Zachariah laughed. "Still using you to get clout for the school."

"I guess so. As long as he lets me do my job with no problems, then I'll go shake the hands of his friends to make them feel special."

Quinton made his way back to the stadium to meet the principal and superintendent. He spotted Halle talking to one of the teachers from the high school just inside the stadium. His steps faltered as a familiar warmth spread through his body. She'd told him to say when they could see each other again, but school, football season and his visiting family made that next to impossible. He was going to have to make the time. Not just so they could finish what they started, but because he wanted to spend more time just getting to know what made Halle tick.

"Here he is, our own celebrity coach." Jeremiah's voice came from Quinton's left.

Quinton tore his gaze away from Halle laughing to focus on whichever relative, friend or church member Jeremiah wanted him to meet. His practiced smile he used when signing autographs froze on his face when he saw who stood between Jeremiah and Dr. Watts.

Dr. Watts beamed as he made the introductions. "Coach Q, this is the editor for *Travel Magazine*. Khris Simmons. Khris, this is our star football coach and your old friend, if I'm not mistaken."

Khris grinned and held out a hand. "You're not mistaken. Quinton, long time, no see."

Quinton's stomach twisted into a knot. He hadn't laid eyes on Khris since high school graduation. He didn't go back to his hometown because he never wanted to run into Khris or his family. Even though he'd known he would have to meet him eventually for the Best Small Town designation, and had prepared himself for the meeting, queasiness rolled through his stomach. The same queasiness he used to feel whenever Khris and his friends had waited outside the locker room to torment him.

But they weren't in high school anymore. He wasn't the poor

kid with no one to back him up or believe it when he said the town's prodigal son was making his life a living hell. He was a grown man who'd proven to himself and the rest of the world what he was capable of.

Khris's smile didn't fade as he pulled back his unshaken hand. "You look good. Guess all those years of getting beat up in the NFL didn't do you too bad."

"I was used to getting beat up," Quinton said, not breaking eye contact.

Khris's smile flickered. He leaned back on his heels. Like Quinton, Khris was older but he looked like he took care of himself. The tall, lean figure he'd had in high school was thicker but still defined; lines spanned out from his gray eyes, and creased his tan skin. He dressed in a light gray shirt and slacks, which appeared casual, but the logo stitched into the front said it was expensive.

"You're not still holding a grudge about us playing around back then." Khris spoke easily, with a hint of a chuckle as if they really had been *playing around* when his friends held Quinton down so Khris could stomp on his legs.

"Playing around?" Quinton said flatly and raised a brow.

"Yeah, you know how kids play around. It was all in good fun. Besides, you made it to the pros. I'm just sitting behind a desk working on a magazine."

Quinton scoffed and shook his head. "Whatever, man."

Jeremiah noticed the tension in the air and chimed in. "Quinton, even though we'll get to spend more time with Khris when he visits the school later, he came into town early. Said he wanted to see you. Maybe we can go to A Couple of Beers and all catch up."

"I'm busy," Quinton said.

Khris's slick smile returned. "Come on. Show me around town. I'd like to catch up."

No way in hell. He'd agreed to show him the school and talk

about football. Not pretend as if they were friends and share a beer together. "I need to get ready for school tomorrow."

Khris watched him for a second before nodding slowly. "Maybe another day, then. I really want to catch up with you before I go out of town."

"Maybe," Quinton said noncommittally.

The sound of his parents' voices came from behind as they noticed first Halle and then him. They walked over with Halle.

"Quinton, I'm so sorry about the loss, but I tell you what, Shania did a great job." His mom's voice rang with pride.

Grinning, his dad continued. "Yes, she did."

They focused on who stood with Quinton. The smile on his mom's face melted into a scowl when she noticed Khris in the group. "Khris, what are you doing here?"

"Mrs. Evans, I didn't know you were in town." Khris spoke as if he'd made a pleasant surprise. Maybe he was happy. He could try to torment Quinton's family as well as him.

Dr. Watts answered. "Khris is here to judge Peachtree Cove for *Travel Magazine*'s Best Small Town feature. We're all ready to show him the best of Peachtree Cove."

His mom's lips pressed together before she looked at Quinton. "It's getting chilly out here and you know the weather is bad on my joints. You ready to go?"

There was nothing wrong with his mom's joints, but he took the hint. "As soon as Shania comes out."

"Shania?" Khris looked at Quinton with renewed interest. "That's the girl playing on the team, right? I hear she's your daughter?"

Quinton glared at Khris. "Shania stays out of your story."

"It's a great thing to feature. A young girl playing high school football."

Halle stepped closer to Quinton. "I'm her mother and you'll have to get my permission to put her picture in your magazine or say her name."

Khris took in Halle's stubborn expression and let out an easy chuckle. "Just a thought. I don't want to make anyone uncomfortable."

His dad coughed, "Bullshit."

Khris frowned and Quinton knew it was time to end this conversation. "Shania should be coming out soon. Let's head that way. Jeremiah, Dr. Watts, see you tomorrow."

When they were out of earshot his mom asked, "Is he really here with some magazine?"

Quinton scanned the crowd for Shania. "He is. Don't worry. I'm good." He spotted Shania and pointed. "There she is."

His parents were distracted as Shania ran over. Halle's hand brushed his arm. "You okay?"

He relaxed. "I'm good. I promise."

"Just let me know if I need to hit him upside the head or something," she said with a teasing grin.

Damn, he wished he could kiss her. Instead, her brushed his hand over her arm and nodded. "I'll let you know. Thank you."

"I've got you," she said before turning to console Shania, who was still down about the loss.

Quinton watched them and the corner of his mouth lifted. With Halle by his side, he was going to be okay.

Twenty-Four

THE NEXT NIGHT, HALLE SAT WITH QUINTON'S FAMILY and watched the varsity team try to get a win. Shania had started the game hanging with them, basking in the adoration of her new grandparents, but she'd ditched them during the third quarter to go stand along the railing with her friends. Unlike the JV team the night before, the varsity team was holding their own and might win the game.

Jeremiah walked up the stairs toward the top of the stadium. He spotted them and waved. "Ms. Parker, good to see you."

"Likewise." She looked from him to Khris coming up. Halle nodded but didn't speak.

Quinton's family stiffened next to her and looked pointedly away from Jeremiah and Khris down to the field.

Jeremiah glanced at Quinton's parents, noticed they weren't going to acknowledge either of them and looked back at Halle. "Are you enjoying the game?"

"I am." Halle pointed to the scoreboard. "Looks like we'll win tonight."

Jeremiah pumped his fist. "Let's hope so. A win tonight means they'll be more likely to beat Peach Ridge in a few weeks."

"And we all know that's the most important game."

Jeremiah grinned, oblivious to the sarcasm in Halle's voice. "It is. Well, we'll head back up to the box. We're sitting with the mayor."

"Tell Miriam I said hello."

"I'll do that." He walked away. Khris gave Quinton's family one more look, but they pointedly kept their eyes averted. After a beat he followed Jeremiah.

As soon as he was gone Laura sucked her teeth and rolled her eyes. "I still can't believe he has the audacity to pretend like he's Quinton's friend."

Dawn shook her head. She scowled in the direction they'd gone. "I believe it. He always wanted to act like what happened wasn't a big deal."

Halle leaned forward to look at Dawn, whose chair was on the opposite side of Laura. "Quinton told me a little about it. That he was the reason he broke his leg and missed out on a scholarship."

Laura looked at Halle, clearly surprised she knew the story. "Yes, he did."

Dawn crossed her arms and sneered. "And his family only tried to brush the incident under the rug."

Laura waved a hand. "That's typical of his dad." Resentment filled her voice.

"Khris's dad was the same?" Halle asked.

Laura nodded. "Exactly the same."

Willie abruptly stood. "I'm going to the concession stand. Anyone want anything?" he asked in a stiff voice.

Halle shook her head. "I'm good."

He nodded then walked toward the concessions. A worried

expression crossed Laura's face. "I'll get something, too." She jumped up and followed.

Halle looked back to Quinton's sister, who shook her head. "My parents don't like Khris's parents."

That much was clear. The sight of the man made the typically happy and outspoken duo clam up. "Because of what happened with Quinton?"

Dawn tilted her head to the side. "No, it started before that. But the accident didn't help. Khris's dad always had it out for our family. Always had something negative to say or found ways to talk about us in the community. I think because he looked down on us it made it easier for Khris to do the same thing."

She understood that a kid would mimic what he saw his parents do, but why would Khris's dad be so rude to Quinton's parents? Was it just because they didn't have the money he had? Quinton said his family couldn't donate to the school or booster club and those who could were treated differently. Was Khris an elitist asshole like his dad?

"Why do you think he wants to talk to Quinton?" Halle wondered out loud.

Dawn let out a heavy breath. The nights were getting cooler and she had a red blanket with the Peachtree Cove mascot stitched into the side. When Halle asked where she'd gotten it, she'd admitted she'd had it made specifically to support her brother.

"Who knows," Dawn said. "Probably because Quinton did something with his life and he wants to pretend like they're friends so he can use that for clout. Maybe he wants to make Quinton's life a living hell. It could be anything with Khris."

Halle looked toward the box where the announcer called the plays and Khris sat with Jeremiah and the mayor. She shouldn't have asked Quinton to work with him to help their town get a leg up on winning. Now that she knew more, she understood why he didn't want anything to do with Khris. Because he was a part of the community, he'd put his own hurt to the side to try to get through it. That was the type of guy Quinton was. He looked out for people who were a part of his team, and the town of Peachtree Cove was a part of his team. She wanted to prevent him from being hurt with all of this. Wanted to protect him, but protecting Quinton wasn't her place, was it? But they were a family, weren't they? Imperfect, messy and unorthodox, but still a family. Not the perfect family she'd envisioned creating one day, and the scary thing about it was she wasn't sure if she wanted that perfect family anymore.

Peachtree Cove's varsity team did bring home the win. And although everyone wanted to celebrate afterward, Halle insisted that she and Shania go home. She needed some space to digest the feelings growing inside her. The need to protect and care for Quinton. The need to pretend like they were a family. A need she wasn't sure she wanted to feel. Not when she wasn't sure if she and he could have a future if Shania didn't want them together.

As a compromise, they all agreed that Shania would come visit Quinton and his family the next day. She and Shania rang the bell at Quinton's house early that Saturday afternoon. Quinton came to the door wearing a pair of gray joggers and a dark T-shirt. The soft material of the outfit hugged his thick thighs and broad shoulders. The taste of his lips on hers, the feel of those thighs beneath her hands, the stiff thickness of his erection, flooded her memory. The air thinned and the sun became ten times hotter as desire wrapped around her neck and chest and squeezed. She'd agreed to see him alone but they hadn't found the time to be alone.

Maybe that was a good thing. The man made her want him with just a look. How was she supposed to be alone with him and think rationally? To not slide her hands beneath the thin material of his T-shirt, feel the soft heat of his skin and kiss his perfect lips?

Shania bounced beside Halle, unaware of her mom's struggle. "We're early, but it's my fault. I was ready to get here."

Quinton grinned. The pride whenever he looked at Shania, a bright star in his eye. "Come as early as you want. Everyone is sitting in the living room watching television."

"Is that Shania?" Laura's voice came from inside the house. "Come here, girl!"

That was all the encouragement Shania needed. She hurried inside toward the living room. Her gaze locked with Quinton's. Desire burned away the pride in his eyes. Her stomach clenched. Did he feel this, too?

He motioned for her to come inside, and she crossed the threshold. "How are you?"

"Better, now that you're here." His voice was low and deep. He stood close enough for her to smell the rich scent of whatever cologne or body wash he used.

Halle didn't move to put any distance between them. She craved his nearness. "Shania was eager to get over here. She loves hanging out with your parents and sister."

"They love hanging out with her. I didn't lie when I said they've been harassing me about having a kid. Now they've got a grandchild and she's smart, beautiful and takes after me and my love for football. They're thrilled."

"Is it okay for me to stay? I can leave and come back to pick her up." They wanted to see Shania, not Halle.

Quinton's brows drew together. "Don't go. Shania will want you here."

She tilted her head to the side. "Just Shania?" There was a note of flirtation in her voice.

"I want you here." His fingertips brushed across her elbow. Down her forearm until they wrapped around her fingers.

The air between them became electric. Pricks of awareness crackled across her skin as she sucked in a shallow breath.

"Do you?" The question wasn't necessary. She saw the longing in his eyes. Felt the same pull deep in her midsection. They shouldn't be doing this. Not here and not like this, but she also couldn't pull herself away.

"Quinton!" His mom's voice broke the spell. "What are y'all doing over there?"

He stepped back and sighed. Halle's lips lifted in a half smile. "Here we come!" he yelled back. His eyes remained fixed on her face. The promise that this wasn't over clear as the tension pulled tight between them.

She followed him into the living room. His mom and dad were on the couch. Shania sat between them while his sister was in her chair next to the couch. ESPN played on the television.

"Oh, Halle, I didn't know you were here, too," Laura said as if she hadn't just asked what she and Quinton were up to.

Halle gave a stiff smile. "I am."

She didn't think Quinton's parents disliked her, but she also hadn't gotten the hurry-up-and-join-our-family vibe from them either. Another reason why this thing between her and Quinton was so tricky.

"You don't trust her with us or something?"

Quinton made a sound of disagreement. "Mom, Halle is welcome to stay."

"I want her to stay," Dawn chimed in. She reached out a hand toward Halle. "Sit over here next to me."

Halle relaxed and sat in the love seat next to Dawn. Quinton's hand brushed against hers as they both moved in that direction. She glanced at him. His fingers stretched her way as if to touch her again but pulled back at the last second. Heat flashed across her cheeks. She tried to ignore the need to reach for his hand in turn. She could not get lost in these feelings. Not in front of Shania and his parents.

She settled in the love seat next to Quinton's sister. Quinton sat next to her. The love seat was big enough that they didn't have to touch each other, but small enough that if they moved they were bound to brush against the other. The conversation flowed easily around football and the games that would come on during the day. Halle tried to follow along, but she was not interested. She couldn't focus with Quinton next to her.

He shifted and his leg brushed against hers. When he got excited as he spoke with his family, their arms touched. As he settled back into the seat, their hands touched. Each brief touch only made her want to touch him more. For her body to remember how good he'd felt as they'd kissed. How much she wanted to feel his skin against hers.

The touches weren't the only torture. The glances between each accidental caress. The moment when their gazes caught, held. Each second drove the air from her lungs. She wished she could find a moment to be alone with him. To cash the check of desire in his eyes.

"I want some wings," Willie said when it was nearly half time of the first game.

"Me too," Dawn agreed, looking at Halle and Quinton. "Where's the best place to get some?"

Shania answered. "There's a wing and deli place out near Walmart. Their wings are really good. We can order some and get them delivered."

"They deliver?" Willie asked.

"I use the app on my phone." Shania pulled out her phone.

Willie twisted his lips and shook his head. "Ain't no way I'm going to pay those fees. We can order and pick the food up."

Dawn slapped her hands together. "That sounds like a good idea. We can go get the food and bring it back."

Quinton sat forward. "All of us don't need to get the food."

"Well, I need to go to Walmart," Dawn said. She looked at

her mom. "Didn't you say you needed to pick up something from Walmart?"

Laura's eyes lit up. "I do. I can go in there while you pick up the food."

Dawn gave a quick nod before looking to Shania. "You want to ride?"

Shania looked at Halle. "Can I?"

The quick decision to take a trip to Walmart was surprising, but she didn't have a good reason to say no. "That's fine."

Shania pumped her fist. "Cool."

Halle and Quinton walked them to the door. Dawn had conveniently left out Quinton and Halle on this outing. Halle wasn't sure if that was on purpose or not, but she wasn't about to volunteer to go. After the hustle and bustle of getting everyone out of the house ended, she and Quinton stood in the quiet of the entryway. Their eyes met. Quinton took a step toward her. Halle slid closer to him. Then they were in each other's arms.

The kiss was rough and fervent. Fueled by longing they'd had for each other and the pressure behind each touch and glance during the afternoon. His hands were all over her body. Her back, breasts, sides and ass. It still wasn't enough.

"Touch me," she breathed against his lips.

His reply was rough and eager. "Yes, ma'am."

His large hands slid beneath her shirt and cupped her breast. Shock waves rippled across her skin. She had to touch him. Her hand slid down the tight muscles of his chest and abs to cup the thick press of his erection against the front of his pants.

"Keep that up and we're going to my bedroom," Quinton said against her lips.

She didn't release her hold on him. "Do you have condoms in there?"

His head pulled back and his eyes met hers. "Are you serious or was that just a rhetorical question?"

Her brows drew together. Didn't he want to do this, too? "Serious, but maybe we shouldn—"

His mouth covered hers, cutting off her words. Thoughts about what they shouldn't do fled. He grabbed her hand and hurried toward the stairs. Halle pressed a hand to her cheek, unable to believe that she was doing this. She waited for common sense to kick in and tell her to stop. Shania and his family could come back at any moment, but the short amount of time they had alone together only made her feet move faster.

They crossed the threshold into a bedroom and she was back in his arms. She didn't take in the decoration. All she noticed was that the room was warm, the smell of his cologne was stronger and his bed was large. She couldn't think of anything else as his lips swept over hers.

Quinton took her to the bed where he wasted no time. He pushed down the waistband of her leggings. Shoving down the thin material along with her underwear. She gasped, then grinned at his urgency. His fingers slid between the juncture of her thighs, and a low moan echoed in the room. Her moan. He kissed her lips, neck and lowered to take one plump nipple into his mouth. Halle hissed and clutched his shoulders. She let the wave of sensation wash over her and take away all her inhibitions. Quinton's warm lips eased away from her breast as he lowered to his knees.

"Wait," she said at the same time his tongue slid across the crease of her sex.

He stopped and looked up at her. His dark eyes serious and brimming with passion. "Do you want me to stop?"

Her heart hammered. She didn't know what she was doing. How they'd gotten here. If this was going to complicate things or make them easier.

Quinton licked his lips. He could do that to her. Halle's brain short-circuited. "Don't stop."

With the same determination she saw him use on the football

field, he went back to pleasuring her body. Halle's knees gave way as he kissed and licked her. Just like a coach, he encouraged her as if she was doing the work. Whispering in a low, commanding voice, "Yes, Halle," "spread a little wider," "keep moaning like that" between each decadent press of his lips against her sex. Her legs shook. Her knees weakened and Quinton gently laid her back on the bed. His soft lips pressed sweet kisses over her abdomen before he pulled away and grabbed a condom from the nightstand.

Halle watched as he put on the condom. Her sex clenched in anticipation. Quinton gave her another long look. The question in his eyes clear. Was she still okay with this? Halle nodded and parted her thighs.

"Give it to me," she whispered.

He settled between her thighs. "You can have all of me."

He pushed inside her. Halle's eyes fluttered closed. The emotion squeezing her heart was like a vise. Stealing her breath, her ability to think. Quinton shoved away all her sensibilities and made love to her with a quick, steady pace that made her toes curl and her moans of pleasure fill the room. He shifted his position. His body pressed down onto her clit just as he thrust, and her body shattered into a thousand droplets of pleasure. Every ounce of good sense she may have thought she had when it came to Quinton was irrevocably compromised.

Twenty-Five

HALLE WALKED THROUGH THE HALLS OF PEACHTREE
Cove Middle School with her fingers mentally crossed and doz-
ens of silent prayers that everything had gone according to plan.
It was the day that Khris Simmons toured the school with the
superintendent and mayor. All a part of their plan to show him
just why Peachtree Cove was the best small town.

She didn't understand why the school needed to be featured
in a travel magazine, but wouldn't complain about bringing attention to the work they did at the school. The mayor wanted
to present everything that was good about Peachtree Cove,
and Halle was more than ready to show them how the staff
at Peachtree Cove Middle School was an essential part of this
community.

"And that's pretty much everything about the middle school,"
Halle said when they were back at the front office. Thankfully,
the HVAC system hadn't rattled, the leak in hall three had been

repaired and no kids loitered in the hallway. It was as if the stars had aligned and understood the school's best foot needed to be put forward today.

"Thank you, Halle," Miriam said, clasping her hands. Delight about the smooth visit visible in her eyes. "I told Mr. Simmons that you were one of our best principals and that you've done a lot to improve things at the school."

Halle beamed; she always enjoyed praise for the work they did at the school. "I want to see every child succeed. High school is important, but you start laying a foundation for a kid's future here in middle school."

Khris scribbled notes in a small notepad and nodded. "I remember middle school being rough for me. Always a trying time. It's a good thing these kids have such an understanding principal."

Halle raised a brow. "You struggled in middle school?"

"I did, puberty and whatnot. Trying to figure out my way," he said with a grin that would appear charming if Halle hadn't known how he treated Quinton in school.

"We deal with a lot of bullying here," Halle said. "Kids struggling to find their way often take out their problems on other kids who are less fortunate. Our goal is to show each child that they are important. Find out why the bully is picking on others and provide the kid who's being bullied with whatever support they need."

His eyes met hers and his smile curved even more. "Hurt people hurt people, am I right?"

Halle hated the condescension in his voice. "Unfortunately, yes."

Miriam checked her watch. "You're about to have lunch, right? I added lunch here at the school on the itinerary before we head to the high school. Then tonight Khris will attend the Business Guild meeting and some of our local businesses tomorrow."

Halle was more than ready to be rid of Khris and his fake smiles, but she nodded. "Sure, let's go to the cafeteria."

They arrived just as sixth grade was finishing lunch and seventh was preparing to come in. They went through the line where Khris was nothing but charm and graciousness as he talked with the cafeteria staff and made everyone laugh about how he'd traded French fries for extra pizza at lunch in middle school. Based on the way he acted, Halle couldn't imagine him bullying anyone enough to break their leg. She didn't doubt Quinton, which only made her more leery of Khris.

They were settled around a table when the seventh grade students began to pile in. Halle noticed one of the teachers she needed to talk with and excused herself. When she returned several minutes later, she hoped they were closer to being done and she could end this meal.

Khris turned to her when she sat down. He spoke so that only she could hear. "Are you and Quinton dating?"

She frowned, thrown off by the unexpected question. "What?"

He pressed a hand to his chest. His face a mask of congeniality. "I'm sorry, we're old friends and when I found out that you two had a kid, I was curious."

Halle kept her expression neutral even though she wanted to roll her eyes. "Have you had the chance to catch up with him since you've been in town?"

"No, apparently he's very busy. Almost as if he's avoiding me." He let out a self-deprecating chuckle.

She raised a brow. "Based on the way he described your friendship, I can understand why."

Khris paused then nodded slowly. The not-quite-charming smile back on his face. "Remember what you said about bullies earlier?"

"I do."

"Well, it's true. I found out something in middle school and I didn't know how to handle it."

"And you took it out on Quinton?"

He looked her in the eye. "I did."

His admission surprised her. She waited for him to pair the admission with an excuse or justification. "Why?"

"Because I didn't have anyone else I could take it out on." He shrugged. "I'm older now. There are things we need to talk about. Things that he needs to know. Will you ask him to talk to me?"

She didn't want to do any type of favor for Khris, but she also was caught off guard by his candidness. Quinton didn't owe Khris his forgiveness, but did he need to hear the full story? "He won't listen to me."

"I think he will."

Dr. Watts interrupted them. "Khris, are you ready for the next stop?"

Khris nodded. "I am." He looked back at Halle with a pleading look. "Principal Parker has been very helpful. I hope she continues to be."

Quinton accepted the beer from Cyril. He sat at the corner seat in A Couple of Beers and despite the hum of conversation in the bar, the noise still seemed quieter than his house.

"Your parents still in town?" Cyril asked.

"Yeah, still here." He took a sip of the beer.

"How long are they here for?"

Quinton shrugged. "I don't know. They're retired and don't have any reason to rush back home. My sister can work remotely so she's good."

Cyril cocked a brow. "Wait, they didn't tell you how long they plan to visit?"

Quinton shook his head. "They usually show up, stay a few days and then leave. I don't ever ask how long because I'm always happy to see them." Because they were enamored with Shania, he didn't expect them to leave anytime soon.

"You not happy this time?"

"I am, but I damn sure miss having the house to myself. I'm used to living alone. I miss my privacy."

Cyril chuckled and leaned a hip on the bar. "After living with my dad when we moved to Peachtree Cove, I can understand. I'm just glad he stayed out of my business."

The door of the bar opened and Brian entered. He spotted the two of them and came over. "What's up, fellas?"

"Nothing much," Cyril answered, slapping Brian's hand over the counter. "Just talking about privacy."

Brian raised his brows. "Who needs privacy?" He looked at Quinton and realization dawned. "Your parents still here?"

Quinton responded, "Yep." He sipped his beer.

Brian sat at the stool next to Quinton. "You live like a monk. What you need privacy for?"

"I just need to hear my thoughts," Quinton said. He wasn't ready to admit that he'd slept with Halle. That quick stolen moment in his bed that Saturday made him want his privacy even more. The way he could have turned that into an afternoon of lovemaking if his parents weren't there. Instead, they'd had to dress quickly and then pretend as if nothing happened when everyone returned not long after they'd ended.

Brian frowned. "What thoughts you need to hear? Spill 'em. That's what we're here for."

Cyril nodded. "Everything good with you, Halle and Shania?" He poured Brian's usual into a glass.

Quinton lifted one shoulder. "We're figuring this thing out. Shania is great."

Brian accepted the beer from Cyril. "How are things on the team now that everyone knows?" he asked.

"They've mellowed out. I don't do favorites and even with

her as my daughter I've kept it that way. Some coaches are still watching me and waiting, but we both know that."

Brian gave him a questioning stare. "Halle letting you have any say so in Shania's life?"

"She's getting there. I'm worried my parents are going to give her a heart attack. They want to spend so much time with Shania to make up for the lost years. That's going to be hard for Halle."

"I can see that," Cyril said. "Halle likes to be in control and that's Imani's words not just mine. But from what Imani has said, I think she's learning to handle it."

"As long as I keep my parents in check then that will be good."

"What about you and Halle?" Brian asked slyly. "You two getting along?"

The memory of sliding deep inside Halle. The way her heat squeezed around him. Watching her eyes roll to the back of her head as she'd said his name on a sigh before climaxing, filled his brain. "Yeah, we're getting along."

Brian cocked his head to the side. "Hold up. You smiling a little hard there."

"Yes, he is," Cyril said, grinning.

Quinton quickly wiped the smile off his face. He was not the kind of guy to act love-struck. "I'm just saying. We're getting along."

"Man, you've been into Halle since before you found out about Shania. Admit it. You taking your chance now?" Cyril asked.

"I'm not against seeing what happens," he said casually.

"What about Shania?" Brian asked. "I thought you said she wasn't into you all getting together."

"Which is why we're just waiting to see what happens before we make a big deal out of it," Quinton said. "No need to upset Shania if we don't work out."

"But you two are trying to see if you can make something work?"

"Yeah, if we can get some time together. Getting her alone is the hard part." Quinton realized he was grumbling.

"Aaah, now the privacy thing makes more sense. Can't be alone with her if your family is all up in your space."

"Exactly. Outside of seeing Shania I don't have a reason to be alone with her without tipping off everyone that we're seeing each other."

Brian halted mid sip. He and Cyril exchanged glances before he looked at Quinton with wide, curious eyes. "Wait, you are seeing each other?"

"We're just chilling right now. One day at a time, but damn, can I get a day?"

The three laughed and the conversation moved to the woman Brian was seeing. Brian didn't date women in Peachtree Cove because he didn't want the entire town in his business. He also didn't date seriously. Just a fling here or there.

"I'm not looking for anything serious," he'd said once. "I did the marriage thing and that didn't work out. Not going down that road again."

They were wrapping up their drinks and getting ready to call it a night when Khris entered the bar. Quinton's stomach clenched. He hated that he still had a visceral reaction whenever he saw Khris. Life would be easier if he could push the trauma of the years under Khris's bullying out the window and ignore it for the rest of his life.

Quinton stood. "Time for me to go, fellas."

"Let me finish this and we can leave together," Brian said, pointing to the beer in front of him.

He wanted to say no, but he also hated the urge to flee the building. He was not going to give Khris that kind of power over him. "I'll wait."

Khris spotted him and quickly made a beeline to Quinton and his friends. "Quinton, I was hoping to run into you."

"I'm just about to leave," Quinton said. He gave Brian and his beer a pointed look. His friend, thankfully, didn't play dumb and lifted the glass to his mouth.

"You still don't want to sit down and chat with an old friend?" Khris said, trying to sound wounded.

"We're not old friends," Quinton said firmly. "The mayor isn't here or anyone else that I need to play nice in front of. Let's stop playing around."

The smile left Khris's face. Good, he needed to drop the act, too. "Look, Quinton, I was an asshole as a kid. I get that. I've worked through my issues. You know, therapy is beneficial."

"Good for you." Quinton did not care at all about Khris's journey to enlightenment.

"But part of my growth is to face what I did in the past. I want to apologize for the way I treated you back in school."

Quinton looked back at Khris. Not feeling an ounce of forgiveness inside him for the guy who'd made his life a living hell, but also not wanting to drag this out longer than it needed to be. "Apology accepted. Now we can both move on."

"Can't we talk?"

"About what? You apologized, I accepted. End of story. We're never going to be friends, Khris."

"Why not? I said I'm sorry. That was a long time ago."

"You broke my damn leg." Quinton scowled. "Your friends held me down and you stomped on me until my leg broke. I can accept your apology, but it doesn't mean we have to be friends."

Brian and Cyril both stiffened with Quinton's words. He hadn't spoken loud enough for the rest of the bar to hear. He understood Khris was there to give the town something it wanted, but he wasn't going to pretend in front of his friends. Khris had been more than an asshole; he'd been a bully and an abuser. Quinton wasn't going to act like that never happened.

"Look, I was jealous. I had a lot going on."

"Jealous? That's your excuse?" Quinton shook his head and waved off his words.

"My dad kept comparing me to you," Khris said quickly. "I didn't know how to take it. Especially after—"

Quinton held up a hand. "Look, I don't care about whatever you got going on with your dad. That was your issue. You decided to take it out on me. Now we're adults. I'm not going to bother you about that because you're here to judge the town. Not to reconcile or bury your demons with me. Let's just keep it at that."

"But—"

Quinton looked at Brian. "You ready?"

His friend hadn't finished his beer, but he stood. "Yeah. Let's go."

Quinton nodded and brushed past Khris. Brian walked out with him. Once they were outside, Brian stopped Quinton.

"What you said in there? Was it true?"

"I wish it wasn't." Quinton shifted from foot to foot. Frustration and anger coursed through him. He'd let Khris get to him. He stopped moving and took a deep breath.

"He broke your leg?"

"He tormented me since eighth grade."

"And no one did anything?" Brian looked ready to go back in the bar and confront Khris.

Quinton put a hand on Brian's shoulder before he could move. "My family didn't have money and his did. Story of kids all over this damn world."

Brian pointed over his shoulder. "What are you going to do about him?"

"Nothing. He's only here for a short time. After tonight, he shouldn't have anything else to do with me. I'm good."

"You sure?" Brian's tone and questioning expression said he was ready to handle Khris if Quinton wanted him to.

Quinton was human enough to admit he was tempted to go off on Khris with the backing of his two best friends, but he wouldn't. He'd gotten what he needed to say off his chest. He just hadn't expected to feel so exposed. Raw. His leg ached with the phantom pain of the break years ago, and his heart felt stomped on just as it had when the school said they were just "playing around" and hadn't pressed charges against Khris. He appreciated his friend's concern, but right now he needed a moment to regroup.

So he gave his friend a confident smile and lied. "I'm good."

Twenty-Six

THE HOUSE WAS QUIET WHEN QUINTON GOT HOME. Thankfully. His parents went to bed early and his sister typically went into her room to log on and finish off work.

He went into the kitchen and immediately saw the homemade carrot cake sitting on the counter. He smiled, some of the pain from earlier easing. There was one good thing about having his parents here. His mom loved to cook and bake.

He was cutting a slice when the light in the kitchen turned on. He turned and spotted his dad by the door.

"Damn, boy, you almost gave me a heart attack." He put a hand over his heart.

Quinton's lips twitched. "My bad. What are you doing sneaking down here?"

Willie pointed at the cake. "Same thing you're doing. Your mom is finally asleep, so I figured I'd get another slice of cake."

Quinton slid the cake across the island. His dad grinned as he picked up the cake slicer and cut a piece.

"I'm glad Mom picked up baking recently," Quinton said.

"Your mom always loved to bake. She would try to make you and your sister's birthday cakes. It was the one time she'd splurge at the grocery store and buy real butter."

"I remember her making birthday cakes, when she had the time."

Willie settled on one of the chairs around the island. "She had to work more as you got older and stopped baking as much. She didn't have a lot of time to do what she wanted." He took a bite of cake.

"You both worked hard to provide for us. I'm glad she has the time to bake now."

His dad let out a heavy breath. "Seems like we were always working back then. Trying to pay for your sister's doctor bills and give you both what you needed, but it was never enough."

Quinton squeezed his dad's shoulder. "It was enough. We turned out alright."

Willie chuckled and patted his hand. "You did. All the way to play professional football. We're proud of you."

"I know you are. I couldn't have had a better dad."

A shadow flashed across his father's face, before he shook his head and grinned. "Sure you wouldn't have wanted someone richer?"

"I'm sure. Richer doesn't mean better. Just look at Khris's dad."

His father scowled. "That man is a bastard."

"So is his son. I saw him tonight. At the bar."

"How long is he in town for?"

"Just until the end of the week." The magazine crew was scheduled to leave on Sunday. Khris couldn't get out of his town fast enough.

Willie nodded and looked satisfied with that answer. "Good."

Quinton thought about leaving it at that, but he couldn't hold back the emotions still boiling inside him. "He apologized for what he did. Said he was jealous of me and didn't know how to react. Why in the hell would he be jealous of me?"

Willie looked down at his cake and pinched off a piece. "People find all kinds of reasons."

"I know that, but he said he found out something and didn't know how to deal with it."

His dad looked up quick, eyes narrowed. "What did he find out?"

Quinton shrugged. "The hell if I know. Whatever he found out has nothing to do with me and it damn sure didn't give him a reason to take out his problems on me."

Willie studied him for a second before his shoulders relaxed, and he nodded. "That entire family is full of assholes. His dad is just as bad as he is. Just stay away from them and out of their bullshit."

"You don't have to worry about me getting involved with him or their bullshit," Quinton agreed. "Once he's gone, I'll never have to see him again. Even if I come visit you and Mom back home, I can easily avoid his family. They don't run in our circles."

Willie grunted. "They sure as hell tried when you made it to the NFL. Acting like their kid hadn't almost ruined your career. I still can't believe that."

"Neither can I." Quinton remembered his dad calling and saying Mr. Simmons congratulated them when Quinton was drafted and invited them to dinner as if they hadn't treated them like they were nothing before that.

"You know, me and your mom were thinking about moving."

Quinton cocked his head. This was the first he'd heard of this. "Really? I thought you liked it there."

"We did, but now that your grandmother has passed there's nothing to keep us there. Your sister is ready to move, too."

"Where are you thinking of moving?"

"Here, to Peachtree Cove."

Quinton's eyes widened. "You said Peachtree Cove was too small for you. I thought you'd try to go to Atlanta or somewhere else."

His dad shook his head. "That was before we found out about Shania. Now we've got our son and granddaughter here. There are a lot more reasons to move here than anywhere else. Plus, seeing you work with that high school team, I can tell you're really becoming a part of this community. We never had that back home. It's nice to come here and see how much people respect you."

The people of Peachtree Cove did respect Quinton. At first, they'd respected him because he was a former professional ball player who was in charge of their beloved football team. Now they respected him because of the work he'd done and his involvement in the school. That respect had been earned just like he'd earned everything else in life. The respect had flowed over to his parents when they'd come to the football game or been out in town. He was proud about being able to give them that. Money was one thing, but respect was something else.

"You all really would move here?" He liked the idea of having his parents and sister closer. He had friends here, but there was nothing like having family around. He'd promised himself to never go back home after he graduated. He tried to visit when he could, but he'd missed having his family around him.

"We would move here," his dad continued. "Shania is great. We've only got a few years before she'll be graduating high school and heading off to college or something. Then we'll see where life leads us, but we don't want to miss out on anything. You'd be okay if we moved here?"

Quinton grinned and held up his fist. "I'm okay with that. You just can't stay here in my house."

His dad laughed and bumped his fist against Quinton's. "Are we cramping your style?" He winked.

"I don't have a style to cramp, but I am used to living alone. Not used to coming out of my room naked and finding my mom in the hallway." His mom had laughed and shooed him away. Quinton had been mortified.

Willie's deep laugh echoed in the kitchen. "Your mom knows what parts you got, but I understand. A man likes to have his space. We'll have to find someplace with room for Shania to visit. You know your mom is ready to spoil her?"

"Mom doesn't need to spoil Shania."

"She wants to. She didn't get the chance to spoil you and your sister growing up. I think now she wants to make up for it. She wanted to get her those shoes she likes."

Quinton shook his head. "She really doesn't need to buy Shania gifts."

"Why not? She's our grandbaby." Willie spoke as if that was all the excuse they needed.

"Dad, this isn't a normal situation. Halle and I just found out about me being her biological dad. We're still trying to figure out how to make this situation work. You all need to give us some time before you just take over."

His dad waved off his words. "Just because you didn't put the baby up in her yourself doesn't mean that she's not our grand-daughter. Doesn't mean we can't treat her like a granddaughter. If you ask me, you're being too lenient with Halle. Letting her call all the shots. She's your kid, too."

"I know, but Halle's done this alone for nearly fourteen years. It's going to take some time to get used to having me involved in her life."

"Yeah, and Shania still sought you out because she wanted a dad." He pointed a finger at Quinton. "Not some guy to hang around and follow her mom's orders. She's your kid. Start acting like it."

"I'm trying to respect Halle."

"By letting her tell you what to do? You're a good guy and

you wanted kids one day. Now you've got one. Be that girl's dad and not just her coach. Let us be her grandparents. Halle will be okay."

His dad stood, now finished with his slice of cake. "Now I'm going to bed. You get some sleep and think about what I said."

Twenty-Seven

HALLE HURRIED INTO THE KITCHEN. SHE HOPPED ON one foot as she got her shoe on and reached for the coffeemaker with the other hand. She skidded to a halt just as she reached the counter, narrowly avoiding banging her bent knee. She grabbed a mug from the rack next to the machine and poured coffee into it.

She hated when she ran late. She was usually good at getting up early and being at the school before the first students and teachers arrived, but she'd overslept today. Hitting her snooze button multiple times. That was what happened when she stayed up later than usual, video chatting with Quinton. They hadn't had the chance to be alone since that day in his place, but he'd found a way to make up for not being able to see each other.

They'd started off talking about mundane things. He'd seemed like he'd just wanted to get lost in conversation, and she'd been more than willing to help get his mind off whatever had bothered him. They'd talked about their day at school and their plans for the next. The progress the town was making and what they wanted to do that weekend with Shania. When they'd exhausted all safe topics, they'd finally had to admit that they both were eager for a repeat of their stolen moment. An admission that nudged the conversation into dirty talk. They'd talked in detail about the specific activities they wanted to repeat, which escalated into self-pleasuring demonstrations while the other watched.

Halle's face heated and her nipples hardened with the memory. She couldn't believe she'd done that. Not that she would take it back for a second. The memory of Quinton's big hands squeezing and gliding up and down his length and then hearing his ragged breaths as he released, drove her over the edge. Knowing he watched her, that he was fixated on seeing what brought her pleasure and then his low whispered encouragement followed with a promise of "I'm going to touch you just like that the next time we're together," had almost made her climax again.

That memory would bring a smile to her face for the rest of the day. She'd woken up with smile on her face. A smile that faded the second she'd realized she hadn't set her alarm the night before and that she was going to be late.

The sound of Shania's alarm clock chimed through the quiet of the house. Halle pulled out a packet of hot chocolate and prepared a mug for Shania. A few minutes later her daughter came shuffling into the kitchen wearing her dark green bathrobe and a purple satin scarf over her hair.

Halle held out the hot chocolate. "I've got you."

"Thank you," Shania mumbled. "You're just getting coffee?"

"I woke up late. I'm going to be late for work."

Shania's eyes lit up. "Does that mean you can take me to school?"

Halle cut her eyes at Shania while she sipped her coffee. "Taking you to school will make me later."

Shania appeared unfazed. "You're the principal and the boss. And since you're already late, you might as well take me."

"If you're ready in the next ten minutes I'll drop you off at school. Prepare to be early."

Shania's eyes widened. "Twenty minutes."

"Fifteen," Halle countered.

Shania gave her a thumbs-up. "I'll be ready."

Twenty minutes later Halle tapped her foot by the front door. She checked her watch and called, "Shania, come on, girl, before I let you go ahead and take the bus."

"Here I come!" Shania ran from the back of the house, book bag in tow. She stopped in front of Halle and spread her arms. "Check out the fit. Maximum drip, right?"

Halle laughed then took in her daughter's outfit. When her eyes landed on the shoes on her feet her smile faded. "Where did you get those shoes?"

Shania's face brightened. "I was hoping you noticed. Grandma got them for me."

Halle blinked. "Grandma?"

"Yeah, Grandma Laura. I told her that I like them and then she got them for me. She dropped them off after practice yesterday."

"Why didn't you tell me?" Even more important: why hadn't Quinton told her? He'd jacked off with her but hadn't thought to mention that his mom had bought her daughter shoes?

"I wasn't thinking about it. I had practice and then you were busy on the phone getting stuff ready for the Business Guild meeting. I just thought I'd see if you noticed. I'm telling you now."

"She shouldn't be buying you gifts."

"Why not? She's my grandmother."

"Because." She hesitated as her mind scrambled for a reason

other than Halle didn't like it. That she felt uncomfortable accepting gifts from Quinton's parents. That she was going to get Shania the same shoes for Christmas and Laura had swept in and stolen her thunder. "She just shouldn't. She's not a normal grandmother."

Shania gave her a *you can't be serious* expression. "Just because you and Coach Q didn't…you know, doesn't mean she's not my grandma. Plus, she wants to do nice stuff for me."

"It's not her right to do that."

"It is her right. Why can't you just be happy for me? I found my dad and my grandparents. You got to have grandparents. Why can't I?"

Guilt tried to stifle Halle's justification, but she refused to let it. She was right in this. She didn't mind Laura and Willie getting to know Shania, but she didn't want them to believe she needed to be showered with gifts. She'd tried hard to teach Shania that she had to earn the things she wanted. She couldn't have them come in and undermine that. "What did I tell you about accepting gifts?"

Shania scoffed and looked toward the sky. "Mom, this is my grandmother. She's not some guy trying to take advantage of me or someone who's going to think I owe them something. She's just being nice. You just don't like that it's not just you anymore."

Halle sucked in a breath. "What's that supposed to mean?"

"Just that you liked being the only person in my life. You got to dictate everything and be the only influence. Now I've got a dad and grandparents and you don't want anyone else to do anything for me."

"That's not true and you know it. You don't know your grandparents' income situation. If buying those shoes hurts them financially."

"Coach Q has money," Shania said, sounding a little less confident.

"He played professionally, but his parents didn't. He's now teaching high school math and coaching football. You don't know how much money any of them have. Those shoes cost two hundred dollars. Give them back."

Shania sighed. "Mom."

Halle held up a hand. "Don't *mom* me. Give them back."

Shania crossed her arms. "I'll ride the bus."

"The hell you will. I'm late because I waited on you. Now get in the car and be happy that I'm dropping you off."

Shania huffed but headed out the door. Halle pressed a finger to her temple and took a deep breath. She just had to get through the day and then she'd deal with Quinton and his parents and the expensive shoes. She was not about to stand aside and let them undercut everything she'd taught her daughter. Shania was not a spoiled kid, and just because she suddenly had grandparents didn't mean she was about to become one.

That afternoon, Halle left Shania at home doing homework and went to return the shoes to Quinton's parents. Her daughter had pouted but hadn't repeated her earlier comments about Halle overreacting. Halle supposed her lecture about not knowing her grandparents' financial situation had stuck. Honestly, Halle didn't know if they were still struggling financially. She doubted that they were. Quinton had played professionally, and he'd mentioned once that he'd taken care of his parents once he'd gone pro. But that didn't mean they could spend indiscriminately on Shania.

She rang the doorbell and took a deep breath as she waited. She hoped they understood what she was saying and didn't get upset about her returning the gift.

Quinton came to the door a few seconds after she rang the bell. He looked as if he'd recently showered and changed after football practice. The smell of body wash hovered around him, and he was dressed in joggers and a T-shirt.

He smiled when he saw her. "What are you doing here?"

He looked so happy to see her. She thought about their late-night pillow talk. His excited, choppy breaths. How she'd imagined it was his hands touching her as their eyes locked virtually.

Halle cleared her throat and broke eye contact. She came here for a reason. She needed to stick to it. "I came by to return something." When he frowned, she held up the shoebox.

His frown deepened. "Nikes?"

"The Nikes your parents bought Shania."

Confusion clouded his face. "What Nikes?"

Halle opened the box so he could see the pair of black and red shoes. "These Nikes. They bought them for her."

Frustration crept across his features. "When?"

"I don't know when, but they gave them to her yesterday."

"Shit, I told them not to buy her anything. I'm sorry, Halle. I didn't know about this."

She searched his face for any signs of deceit. "Really?"

He raised a brow and lowered his voice. "Do you think I would have gone through last night and not said anything?"

Heat crept up her neck and across her cheeks. She shifted as the memories flickered through her mind again. "I'd hope you wouldn't do that and not tell me."

He stepped outside. His fingers laced with hers and he pulled her close. "I wouldn't have let things go so far last night if I'd known. I promised that I would check in with you when it came to Shania and that's what I meant."

The righteous indignation that had driven her there melted against the heat in his gaze. "I just had to be sure." She tried to make her voice firm, while her heart raced.

"Trust me. I meant it when I said that I was here to support you. Not make things harder."

"I know she really wanted these shoes, but I don't want your parents to think they have to buy her gifts. Or for her to expect them every time she sees them."

"They want to spoil her. My dad said that the other night. I told them to take things slow. That you're still getting used to this."

Her brows rose. "Aren't you still getting used to this?"

He nodded. "I am."

"Why aren't you upset that they stepped over a boundary already?"

He lifted a shoulder. "I've known my parents all my life. One thing I can safely say is that they're going to do what they want and they're stubborn. I'm afraid that even though we tell them not to buy Shania anything that they're still going to try."

She tried to pull back. "She doesn't need gifts."

Quinton held on and didn't let her step back. His eyes stared back into hers. "She may not need a gift, but that doesn't mean that my parents won't want to show her some type of affection. They're happy. She's happy to have them. They never got the chance to give me and my sister the things we wanted. Now they're making up for it with Shania."

Halle understood that, but it didn't change how she felt. "I don't want to spoil her."

"Neither do I, but can you at least try to understand where my parents are coming from? They finally have a child they can afford to do stuff for. I'll talk to them and ask them not to do anything extravagant."

Halle shook the shoebox in her other hand. "Two-hundred-dollar sneakers is extravagant."

"When I was a kid, it was. Now it's not." He spoke easily.

She narrowed her eyes. A suspicion that her claim of his parents being unable to afford expensive gifts was about to be proven wrong. "They have more money now?"

"They have the money I gave them and the investments that they've made. I meant it when I said going pro meant I helped them out. I never wanted anyone in my family to struggle.

Don't worry. Two-hundred-dollar sneakers isn't going to break my parents' bank account."

"But I can't afford two-hundred-dollar sneakers like that. I'm a principal. I have to save up for big gifts. These were going to be her Christmas gift."

Her world shifted again. She'd fooled herself into thinking that just because Quinton taught school that he was on the same level as her financially. She'd been wrong. "Are you rich?"

"Do you care if I'm rich?" His voice was calm but he watched her warily.

"Yeah. I need to know what kind of life you plan to give Shania. Are you going to spoil her?"

He shook his head. "I'm not trying to spoil her, but..."

This time when she pulled back he let her pull away. "But what?"

"But I'm not going to let her struggle unnecessarily."

Halle clutched the shoebox with both hands. "What does that mean?"

"It means I'll help her pay for college, so she doesn't have student loans. When she's ready for prom, I'll rent a limo for her and her friends. When she's ready to buy a house, I'll help with the down payment."

Halle frowned, all things she wanted to do and had scrimped and saved to try to be able to do. "You can do all that?"

"I can. Is it a problem that I can do that?"

"I can't do all that," she blurted out. Quinton and his family could give Shania everything Halle had wanted to give her. But they could do it easily. Once again she felt control slipping.

"Do you think Shania will care about that? She loves and respects you, Halle. I don't plan to rent out Disney World for a graduation party or buy her expensive gifts just because. I want her to be responsible and know how to take care of herself."

"That's what I want for her."

"I know. I just want her to feel secure. Growing up, I was

always worried about money. How the bills would get paid and what would my parents be able to afford. I took on a lot of responsibility to keep them safe. I don't want her to worry about me."

"After my parents died, I struggled," Halle admitted. "They didn't have a will. I had to figure everything out. I want her to feel secure."

He reached for her, and she didn't resist when he pulled her in close. "We want the same thing. I promise. No big gifts without talking to you."

"What's a big gift? Two hundred dollars isn't big?"

"Again, I didn't know about the shoes. What limit do you want to set?"

She sighed and thought about it. Did she really want to give Quinton and his parents trouble if they bought Shania a pair of shoes? What was a good limit to check in before spending? She'd never had to navigate co-parenting before. Now she was supposed to have an answer to a question she didn't know she'd ever be asked.

"I don't know, but I like that we want the same thing for Shania," she said honestly.

He leaned in and brushed his lips across hers. "You don't have to know today. Right now, I'll talk to my parents about the shoes. Okay?"

She wanted to kiss him again. To lean into him and finally accept that she had a partner in this. "I still feel…"

"Feel what?"

She searched for the right words. "Like I'm disrespecting your parents and hurting Shania."

"I'll talk to them. They'll understand."

She looked at the shoebox in her hands. "Maybe I should let her have the shoes."

"Let me talk to them first. The shoes aren't going anywhere. We can give them back to her."

She met Quinton's gaze. Saw the understanding and support reflected back. He'd respected her feelings but also made her understand his side. This was compromise, partnership, and she liked it. "Why are you so understanding with me?"

"Because I like you."

Her heart flipped. So many emotions filled her. She'd never thought she would want to lean on anyone else, or that someone would be on her side in this the way Quinton was for such a simple reason. "That's not the reason why."

He leaned forward, his voice serious. "That is the reason. I like you, Halle. I like you a lot."

Halle didn't know how she'd gotten here. How her life had been turned on its head so quickly, but she wasn't going to fight this anymore. "I like you, too."

He smiled as if she'd given him a present. Quinton leaned in and kissed her quickly. "That's enough for now. We'll figure out how to make this work and become a family."

She took a shaky breath. The realization both unsettling and comforting. "We are a family, aren't we?"

He nodded. "Yes, we are."

Twenty-Eight

BECAUSE HE HAD NO GOOD REASON TO GET OUT OF IT, Quinton attended the special Business Guild luncheon on Sunday afternoon. The point of the meeting was to give Khris and his crew from *Travel Magazine* one grand goodbye after they finished their official review on Friday. Quinton could have skipped the entire thing, but the school district asked him to be there. That and Halle had agreed to back him up if Khris tried to get slick.

The memory of that offer had made him smile. He liked her being willing to defend him, even if he didn't need it. He'd made his thoughts clear to Khris earlier that week. He and Halle didn't arrive together. The town gossips had moved on from the startling discovery of him being Shania's dad once the magazine reps had come to town, but arriving together would get things started again now that there wasn't a need to put their best foot forward.

The farewell luncheon was at Tracey's Get Fresh Inn. It was a sunny day with mild weather that was perfect to enjoy the grounds and the nearby pond. Picnic tables were set up on the lawn where she hosted weddings. Her cook, Shirley, had brought in all the help to prepare a Southern Sunday dinner complete with fried chicken, mac and cheese, cornbread and all the fixin's.

He walked onto the lawn and immediately spotted Brian on the edge of the crowd. He made his way to his friend.

"I didn't expect to see you here," Quinton said.

Brian clapped hands with Quinton before looking back at the gathering crowd. "Tracey is loaning out some of the shrubs from my nursery for the event. I want to make sure everything looks good."

"You're caught up in the best-small-town thing, too, huh?" Quinton asked.

Brian gave a lopsided grin and shrugged. "Hey, if my nursery even gets a mention in this article, I'll take it. I've got some people from Augusta coming here to buy from me, but if I can get people from other areas to visit my nursery, too, I'm not going to complain."

"I hear that. Tracey loans from you a lot?"

Brian nodded then frowned. "For her big events. I gave her a deal, but she talked me down even more. That woman is stubborn as hell."

Quinton chuckled. "You've got to be stubborn sometimes to start your own business. You know that."

He shook his head. "Yeah, but she's stubborn about the wrong things." His scowl deepened before he nodded toward the crowd. "Her husband is here."

Quinton looked in the direction Brian indicated. He recognized the guy from around town but didn't know Bernard well. "I don't ever see him a lot."

"Because he's always running around in Augusta. That guy is trifling as hell."

Quinton looked at Brian. "That's Tracey's problem. Not yours."

Brian sighed and nodded. "I know. Still, I knew Tracey in high school. I don't like seeing him treat her like that."

"Still, not your place. Don't get involved in other people's relationships. Never ends well."

"You right. Don't mean I have to like the mutherfucker."

Quinton chuckled. "I agree with that." His eyes scanned the crowd and landed on Halle. Damn, she looked good in a dark orange sweater dress that clung to her curves. All he wanted to do was peel the damn thing off her and get lost in her body.

"I'm going to ignore what you just said and get all up in your relationship. What's really going on with you and Halle?"

Quinton blinked and looked back at his friend. "Huh?"

Brian shook his head. "That *huh* and look on your face tells me all I need to know. You hit."

"None of your business," Quinton said firmly. He and Halle had made headway in their relationship. They were able to talk through most of their disagreements, but he wasn't ready to let a lot of people in on what he was building with her.

Brain nodded. "You hit." He raised a hand when Quinton glared. "You know me. I'm not going to tell no one your business. I guess you made up your mind to go for it."

"I did." No need to deny that much. Brian knew how he felt about Halle. "I think she's coming closer to making up her mind. She's worried about Shania. I am, too. Do you really think she'll be upset if we get together?"

Brain shrugged. "The hell if I know. I'm not an expert on teenage girls by any means. I'd think she'd want her parents together, but kids these days are different. Either way, you'll figure it out."

"We've got to." Because Quinton didn't have any plans to let her go.

They made their way from the edge of the crowd and joined the others settling in around the tables. The mayor and her sister, Mattie, sat next to Dr. Watts and Cheryl Green from the booster club. He was going to avoid that table. No need to hang out with co-workers outside of work. Bookshop owners Patricia and Van sat with Jackson Bowman, who'd opened an art gallery on Main Street, and Carolyn Jones, who owned Sweet Treats bakery. He waved at Joanne Wilson and her boyfriend Khalil, Tracey's younger brother. All in all, most of the business owners in the town were there, including Robin Baker, the owner/editor of the *Peachtree Cove Gazette*. He was sure she'd find a way to find some scandal in what had been an otherwise good week with the editors in town.

Quinton met Khris's gaze and didn't feel the rolling sickness in his stomach anymore. He'd said what he needed to say. Doing that had allowed him finally to close the door on that connection. Khris was an asshole who'd tried to ruin his life, but he hadn't succeeded. Quinton's life was doing just fine. He wouldn't give Khris another thought once this day ended.

The luncheon started and Quinton slid into a chair next to Halle before someone else could snag it. He didn't care if others noticed his eagerness to be next to her. He wasn't ashamed, and if anyone asked then he'd say it was so they could talk about Shania.

The mayor stood and waved her hands for everyone to quiet down. "Before we get started," Miriam said, "I just want to thank everyone for joining us today for this farewell luncheon with our guests from *Travel Magazine*. We appreciate you considering Peachtree Cove as one of the best small towns. No matter what your choice is, I hope you walk away feeling our sincere hospitality and gratitude to have any recognition of our town. Turning Peachtree Cove around wasn't just an effort on my part, but of many of the people you see sitting around this table. Our citizens are what makes us great, and as your mayor, please know that I appreciate everything that you all do for Peachtree Cove."

A round of applause came from the crowd. The pastor of Mount Grove A.M.E. church stood to give the blessing. Once everyone started eating and conversation flowed, Quinton leaned into Halle.

"Can I see you tonight?"

Halle glanced at him from the corner of her eye. "See me to what?"

He suppressed a grin before saying in a low voice that wouldn't carry, "I'd like to see you doing what you did the other night on the phone."

She glanced around before straightening her shoulders. "Oh really?" She used her principal's voice, but he noticed the twist of her full lips.

"Wouldn't you like to get an up-close and personal view of my talents as well?"

She turned and met his eye. "I think I'd like that."

His stomach clenched as desire rushed to his groin. This woman did wild things to him. "So, can I see you tonight?"

"Luckily, Shania is at her cousin's house. They plan to have a sleepover and then go to school tomorrow."

"A sleepover on a Sunday?"

She nodded and sighed. "She's still upset about the sneakers. I'd rather her hang out at Kayla's where I know what she's up to than watch her sulk around the house."

"We can give her back the sneakers," Quinton said.

"Not while she's in the middle of a pity party. She understands why I took them. She just wants to be upset. She can get the shoes at Christmas like I planned."

Quinton leaned back. "You still want to wait until Christmas?"

She nodded. "I do."

"I'm sorry my parents got them before you could."

She shook her head and looked away. "We talked about it. It's no big deal."

He had a feeling it was a big deal. He understood even more so why she was so upset about the gift. "You're still calling the shots on this. We're not trying to take over."

"I know that." She gave him a reassuring smile. "It's just going to take a while for the independent side of me to accept that I have help with Shania."

"You're accepting our help?"

She lifted her glass of tea. "Maybe just a little."

The small admission made his chest swell. He'd hoped she wouldn't pull back after admitting they were becoming a family and she hadn't. He hadn't been this happy in a long damn time.

Someone across the table called his name and asked about his thoughts on the upcoming game with Peach Ridge High. Quinton suppressed his frustration with once again being asked about the non-division school. He'd much rather focus on the fact that they were four and one in their division versus the petty rivalry. But Quinton pasted on a smile and joined the conversation.

The luncheon ended after another round of speeches and thanks from the various members of the Business Guild. Khris stood and thanked the town for the hospitality the town had shown to him and his colleagues. Quinton slid his shades on to hide his eye roll. There was nothing slightly appreciative or humble about Khris.

He leaned to Halle after the back patting and congratulations were done. "Your place at six or seven?"

Her eyes met his and the eagerness there made him want to pull her in and kiss her regardless of who watched. "Six and don't be late."

"Oh believe me, I won't." He quickly got up and tried to escape. Several people stopped him for conversation, but finally Quinton made it to the front of the bed-and-breakfast.

"Quinton! Hold up."

Quinton turned at the sound of his name then immediately wished he'd kept going. "I thought we were done, Khris."

Khris jogged the last few steps toward him. "I know you don't want to talk to me."

"No, I don't."

Khris's fake smile was gone, and a serious expression covered his face. "But we need to."

"There's nothing left for us to say."

Khris lifted a brow. "Talk to your parents and get the whole story."

That stopped Quinton. He was glad his shades might hide some of the surprise he felt. "What whole story?"

Khris's smirk returned, but even though he typically looked self-satisfied whenever he'd given Quinton that smirk as a kid, today he looked like he was annoyed to have to deal with this. "Talk to them, then call me."

"What the hell is that supposed to mean?"

Khris took a few steps back. "I'll wait for your call." He turned and hurried back to the crowd breaking up.

Quinton frowned, watching him. Annoyed that he was once again playing games. There was no story to tell. Khris was an asshole who'd tormented him his entire childhood. No way was he going to fall for his games now.

He walked toward the line of cars where he'd parked his truck. Noticed a couple and stopped in his tracks. "What the hell?"

"What the fuck!" Tracey's voice came from the porch.

Quinton looked at Tracey's husband wrapped up in the arms of another woman. Quinton pulled off his glasses. He couldn't be sure, but he'd swear that was Monique, the woman who worked the desk at the inn. Tracey ran off the porch toward her husband and employee before the thought finished taking shape. Her arms rose and fire in her eyes. Bernard pushed the woman behind him, grabbed Tracey's flying fists before she could hit either of them. Quinton closed his eyes and cursed. So much for a successful Best Small Town farewell luncheon.

Twenty-Nine

HALLE DROVE ONTO HER STREET RIGHT BEFORE EIGHT
that evening. After the chaos at the luncheon, she and Imani
had spent the afternoon trying to console their friend. Tracey
had been angry, that was evident from the way she'd tried to
claw Bernard's eyes out the moment she'd seen him kissing
her employee. After the anger had died down, the pain had
taken its place. No amount of wine or ice cream was going to
heal the hurt of being betrayed, so Imani and Halle did the
best they could to try to just let their friend have room to vent
her feelings.

Bernard came back home around seven thirty and said he
and Tracey needed to talk. Halle and Imani had offered to stay
and help her kick him out if that was what she wanted. Tracey
insisted that she was ready to talk, so they'd left.

Now, as Halle approached her house, she sent up a silent
prayer for Tracey. No matter how much her friend had already

assumed that Bernard was cheating on her, it wasn't the same as actually finding out. And in such a brazen way. How could they be so bold as to kiss each other, no matter how brief, at a popular event at Tracey's place of business? She hadn't disliked Bernard, but she hadn't been a big fan of his either. To know that he would do this to Tracey made her want to turn around and ram her car into the back of his.

Sighing, she pulled into her driveway. Her cell phone rang shortly after she got in the house. Quinton's number and she remembered she'd asked him to be at her place at six.

She answered the call. "I'm sorry, I forgot about six."

"Don't even bother to apologize," he said in a strong, supportive voice. "I know you were taking care of your friend. I just want to check and see if you were okay."

She sighed. "I've been better. Do you still feel like coming over?"

"You still want to see me?" he asked, surprised.

She wanted nothing more than to be comforted and have someone with her right now. "Yes. It's been a rough day. I could use a hug."

"I'm on my way."

The call ended and Halle smiled. She took a shower and changed out of the blazer and slacks she'd worn to the luncheon into gray loungewear. She'd just made herself a cup of tea when the doorbell rang. She left the tea on the kitchen counter and ran to the front door. Quinton engulfed her in a strong hug as soon as she let him in.

"Thank you," she whispered against his chest.

He squeezed her tight. "What did I tell you?"

She smiled and pressed her ear against his chest. The sound of his heartbeat steady and calming. "That you've got me."

"Even if it's just to give you a hug."

She pulled back and looked up into his handsome face. "Come on in. You got here quick."

"I was downtown," he said. "At A Couple of Beers."

"Sit on the couch. Let me get my tea. You want anything?"

"Just you."

She grinned from ear to ear and hurried to get her tea. A few minutes later she was settled on the couch next to him. "Was everyone in the bar talking about what happened?"

He shook his head. "Not everyone. Most people can't believe Bernard was so dumb. Everyone except Brian."

She frowned. "Why wasn't he surprised?"

"Before the lunch Brian wasn't happy to see Bernard there. He said he never liked him and that he treated Tracey wrong."

"Did he know Bernard was cheating?" she asked incredulously. How could he know and not say anything?

Quinton let out a breath and rubbed her knee as if trying to calm her down. "I think he may have. He didn't really say anything specific, but I think he knew Bernard was doing Tracey wrong."

"Why didn't he say anything?"

"He said he tried to warn her once, but she told him to mind his business."

Halle sighed and sipped her tea. "I'm not surprised. Tracey and Brian would often argue in high school. She hated when people got into her business or talked about her family. If he had said something, then she would have pushed him away."

He squeezed her knee. "Are you okay?"

"I'm good. Worried about Tracey."

His gaze became serious. "Will we be okay?"

She raised a brow. "Are you sleeping with someone else?"

Quinton scowled and shook his head. "Hell no, but I just have to ask. All this made me realize I don't know much about the guys you dated before other than Gregory. You ever been cheated on?"

She frowned and considered. "Not that I know of. Remember, I got pregnant through artificial insemination. I haven't spent a lot of time in long-term relationships."

"Why not? I can't believe it was due to lack of opportunity."

She grinned and sipped her tea before answering. "At first, it was grief after my parents. Then I became a parent. I didn't want to bring anyone into Shania's life if they weren't going to be here long-term. Then I got used to just doing things on my own. I didn't worry about a relationship, and I preached to Shania that it was important to be able to handle things on your own. All I wanted was to make sure Shania had a stable life." She raised her brow. "What about you? Ever been cheated on?"

He nodded. "Once."

Her eyes widened. "Who?"

"This girl in college," he said easily. As if the hurt of that long-ago betrayal had long since faded. "It was around the time I donated. She found out my parents were about to be kicked out and that my draft chances were slim. I caught her giving head to one of my teammates with better draft chances."

She sat up and put the mug on the coffee table with a heavy thud. "No."

He nodded slowly. "Yes. That guy was drafted in the second round. They got married. Had two kids before he caught her with another teammate."

"Damn, I'm sorry." Sorry for Quinton, but not for the teammate.

"I'm not. I liked her, but after that, I was done. I donated, saved my parents' place and was drafted at the end of the last round. Mr. Irrelevant. That's what they call the person who gets my pick. But despite all of that, my life turned out okay, and I honestly don't miss her."

She was glad he'd moved on from that. "Obviously you didn't stay irrelevant for long. You were dating some model when you first moved here, right?"

He nodded. "We'd been dating for a few years. When I retired, she understood, but she thought I would move to New York or Atlanta to be an anchor for a sports network. When I told her that wasn't what I wanted, that I wanted to coach high school, she said she'd stick with me. But it didn't work out." Again, he spoke easily, no lingering resentment or pain.

"Why not?"

"She lives in New York. I live in Peachtree Cove. We grew apart and she knew the story of what happened with my girl-friend in college. She said she'd rather break up with me than cheat. So, we broke up."

"I'm sorry." Again, for Quinton but not for that ex-girlfriend. They'd let a good man go. Halle wasn't about to make the same mistake.

He reached over and brushed a hand across her cheek. "Don't be sorry. If it had worked out with either of them, I wouldn't be here with you."

"Well, when you say it that way, I guess it's good."

"I think everything worked out the way it was supposed to work out. Besides, when I first saw you at the school district meeting, I knew that I was going to be breaking up with her."

Halle's eyes widened. She stuttered for a second before blurting out the only thought in her head. "You're lying."

"No, I'm not," he said with a straight face.

She pressed a hand to her chest. "You didn't talk to me."

"Because I was in a relationship, but I knew I was interested. When we broke up, I planned to approach you, but then I over-heard your athlete comment. So, I kept my interest to myself."

Halle blinked several times. Her brain still processing that Quinton had a crush on her while she'd easily dismissed him like a dummy. "You've really liked me for that long?"

He entwined their fingers and nodded. "Yes, Halle, I've been into you from the moment I saw you. Which is why I was patient while you realized Gregory wasn't the one for you, and I'm patient while we figure out what to tell Shania about us because, Halle, if I have my way we're going to keep this going for a while."

The words were simple, nowhere near as explicit or erotic as what he'd said the other night on the phone, but they heated her body just as much if not more. Desire cut through her exhaustion and stress with almost painful precision. She squeezed her thighs together to try to take the edge off.

She leaned forward and brushed her lips across his. Quinton was as straightforward as usual. His large hand cupped the back of her head and deepened the kiss. They made love right there on the couch like they had the first time. Quick and fast as if each moment was stolen and precious. But afterward, when they were both breathless and tangled, Quinton carried her to her bedroom, and they cuddled beneath the sheets. Quinton's hands ran lazily over her stomach and trailed down to the dampness between her thighs. Halle smiled and opened her legs.

"Stay the night," she whispered. It was the first time she'd had a man in her bed. In all the years she'd dated, she'd either gone to their place or a hotel. Rarely had they come to her place and never had she brought a man into her bedroom or asked him to stay over. Her home was her safe place. A place where she didn't want anyone to have access to her or Shania without permission. Tonight, she couldn't imagine sending Quinton away.

His body stilled. Worry and embarrassment made her heart stutter and her cheeks flame. Was she expecting too much? He leaned in and kissed her ear. "You want me to stay the night?" The hand that lazily played between her thighs became more active, his finger slipping between her folds to push in deep.

Halle gasped, her back arching on the mattress. "Yes."

"Good, because that's exactly what I want to do."

Thirty

HALLE WAS GOING TO BE LATE, AND SHE DIDN'T CARE.
She grinned as she buttoned up her dark red dress shirt and watched Quinton in the mirror behind her slide on his joggers. She liked watching him get dressed in the morning. Liked the way he placed his hands on her back, hip or thigh as he'd passed her in the bathroom where they'd showered and gotten ready for the day. Liked the way he pulled her back to his front and kissed the side of her neck after they'd showered. Was this what it was like to have someone who cared about you living with you? She could understand the appeal. She'd always believed she didn't need this in her life. That she was fine without a partner, and while she had been fine and she had been happy, she also couldn't deny that this was nice, too.

Quinton slipped on his shirt and looked up. He caught her watching in the mirror and grinned. "Quit looking at me like that."

Halle finished buttoning her blouse and tucked it into the dark gray pants of her suit. "Like what?"

"Like you want me to come over there and do some things to you."

"Who says I don't want you to do that?"

He grinned; his eyes flashed with desire and the same happiness she felt deep inside her gut. "You know, we're both going to be late. I've got to go home and change."

"You're right," she said, using her principal voice. "We shouldn't get one more in before we go to work."

Desire flashed again in his dark eyes. He crossed the room and slipped an arm around her waist. "You know what? I can be late."

Halle laughed and turned in his arms. More than ready not to follow the rules for once in her life. The sound of the front door opening made her freeze.

"Mom?" Shania asked. "Why is Coach Q's truck in the yard?"

Halle's eyes widened. Her stomach dropped to her feet. "Shit."

"Damn," he said at the same time.

She pushed him away, but it was too little too late. "What are we going to do?"

Quinton took a slow breath. "Go out there and tell her," he said in a steady voice.

"It's Monday," she hissed.

He cocked his head to the side. "Would Tuesday be better?"

She cut her eyes at him. "Of course this would happen on a Monday." She hurried to go out the door. She crossed the threshold just as Shania came into the hall.

"Mom?" Shania said, a frown on her face. Her eyes darted behind Halle and her frown deepened. "Coach?"

"What are you doing here?" Halle asked in a too bright voice. "I thought you were going straight to school?"

Shania looked back at Halle. "I live here. Mom, what's going on? Are you two…" The words trailed off as the frown on Shania's face went to horror. "Eww…please tell me you're not."

"Shania, girl, come on. I need to get you to school," Kayla's voice came before she appeared in the hall. When she spotted everyone, her eyes widened. "Halle, Coach Q… Damn, girl! I didn't know."

Halle glared at her cousin. Who'd probably come into the house just to find out why Quinton's car was in the yard, too.

She pointed to Kayla. "Not right now." She looked at her daughter. "Shania, let's talk."

Shania's face hardened and she shook her head. "You know what? Let's not. I don't need my headphones today." She turned to Kayla. "Let's go." She pushed passed Kayla and went toward the door.

Kayla shot Halle an apologetic look. "Next time give me a heads-up and I won't bring her by the house." She turned to follow Shania.

Halle moved to go down the hall, but Quinton stopped her with a hand on her arm. "Give her a minute."

"What? I need to talk to her."

Quinton held fast when she tried to jerk away. "Do you really think she wants to talk about this rationally right now?" he asked gently.

Halle would make her talk. Make her understand. This couldn't be ignored. "I don't care. I can't let her go to school like this." She jerked on her arm and he let her go.

Quinton's long stride followed her down the hall. "Halle, she's with your cousin. She'll be in school at a safe place. I'll talk to her today."

Halle spun on him. "It's not your job to talk to her."

He didn't flinch or look away. "She's my daughter, too."

Halle sucked in a breath. The words a reminder that she couldn't fix this on her own even if she wanted to. She crossed her arms and tapped her foot. "Don't do that."

"Do what? Remind you that she's just as mad at me as she is with you? That she's going to want to know that I'm not just playing around with her mom and that I won't hurt you?"

Halle frowned. "Do you think she'll believe that?"

"You said yourself you never brought guys around. Gregory was the closest and even then, she wasn't okay with you two. Let me talk to her."

She held up a hand. "I should handle this."

Quinton placed his palm against hers, then wrapped his fingers around hers. He stepped closer, his eyes just as worried, but also calm and steady. "Let's handle this together. You aren't alone in this parenting thing anymore."

Halle stared back. Frustration warred with relief. She wasn't in this alone. She should be happy about that. And she was, but still felt like the last bit of control she had on her life had slipped away.

Shania did a great job avoiding Quinton at school. Every time he saw her in the hall, she'd disappear in the crowd. When he tried to talk to her during the lunch period she huddled with a group of friends and rushed out of the lunchroom. She even found a way to avoid him during football practice. She stayed with the special teams coach, avoided eye contact and kept to the opposite side of the field from him.

He admired her ability to give him the cold shoulder so completely. But he was still the coach and her father. Something he hadn't pressed before. He wasn't about to let her go home without speaking a word to him.

"Shania." He called her name after practice. His voice crisp and to the point.

She stopped talking, cringed and looked his way. "Yes, Coach?"

"Come to my office after you get the rest of the equipment put up."

"But my mom will be waiting."

He lowered his aviator shades and met her eyes. "My office."

Shania sighed. "Yes, Coach."

Quinton slid his shades back up and nodded. He headed back to the school. Zachariah jogged up to him. "Everything alright?"

Quinton kept walking. "Why do you ask?"

"Well, Kayla told me about what happened this morning."

Quinton stopped in his tracks. He didn't have to worry about the Peachtree Cove gossips; Halle's family was going to spread the news faster than anyone else. He turned to Zachariah and said with steel in his voice, "We're not talking about that."

Zachariah held up his hands. "I'm just checking to make sure all is good. I mean, we're practically family now."

Quinton rolled his eyes behind his shades. He was inheriting all of Halle's cousins and their boyfriends. "Everything is good."

"So, you and Halle?"

Quinton shook his head and turned to walk away. "Mind your business."

Zachariah took the hint and stayed behind. Quinton kept going until he got back to his office. He really hoped Kayla kept what she found out between herself and Zachariah. The last thing they needed was for everyone in the town to start talking about him and Halle getting together. He was happy to be with her. Happier than he ever would have expected and didn't want to hide that they were together, but the gossip would splash back on Shania. He didn't want that.

Ten minutes later, Shania knocked on his office door. Her arms crossed and lips pinched as she looked everywhere but at him. Quinton hated that she'd avoided him. He was used to being on the end of a teenager's anger or frustration. He was a coach and teacher, so of course some kids had an automatic problem with him. But having it from Shania hit different. He didn't want to hurt her. He only wanted to protect her.

"Have a seat, Shania," he said, pointing to the chair across from his desk.

Shania let out a sigh but sat. "You don't have to do this."

"Do what? You're a mind reader now?"

She slouched in the chair. Her arms remained crossed, and she avoided looking at him. When she didn't speak, he continued talking.

"About this morning…"

Shania held up a hand. "Spare me the details."

"I have no intention of giving you any details. But what I do plan to tell you is that I like your mom and that has nothing to do with you."

She cut her eyes at him. "Yes, it does. You never would have bothered her if it wasn't for me."

"That's not true. Are you saying the only thing your mom has going for her is the fact that she's your mother? That I wouldn't have been interested in her for any other reason?"

Shania sat up straight and glared back. "My mom has been happy by herself."

"Does that mean you want her alone for the rest of her life?" He kept his voice calm compared to the angst in hers.

"No, but I don't want her to think she has to be with someone just for my sake. She was into Gregory and that didn't work out. Now we find out you're my dad and suddenly she thinks she should be with you? I don't want her to do that."

Quinton folded his arms on his desk and leaned forward. "Do you really think your mom isn't smart enough to pick a guy for herself? That even if she didn't like me, she'd just throw herself at me for your sake? Especially after you told her you didn't want us together?"

Shania pouted for several seconds as she considered his question. Finally, she looked at him with worry in her gaze. "I don't want her getting hurt. She does everything for me. I want her to date for herself."

Some of the tension eased out of Quinton. Her walls were down, and she was finally ready to hear him out. "Shania, I'm here to tell you that your mom doesn't do anything she doesn't want to do."

"Then how come she likes you so much after she liked Gregory?"

"Gregory wasn't the right guy for her."

"And you are?" she shot back with a raised brow.

He knew that just as sure as he knew he could coach this team to their first division title this year. "I'd like to be. Not just because I'm your dad, but because I liked your mom from the moment I first saw her when I moved to town."

Shania absorbed that information before asking warily, "Why didn't you say anything before?"

"I'm a patient man. Which is why I'll be patient with you, too. You don't have to trust everything I'm saying today. Time will tell. But please trust that neither of us would have gone with this if we didn't really think there was something there to go after. We don't want to hurt you, Shania. We love you."

Shania's eyes widened. "You love me, too?"

He nodded; the realization that he did brought a smile to his face. "I do. You're my daughter. I'd do anything to protect you."

"Do you love my mom, too?"

Quinton considered her words. He loved Halle's stubborn independence. Loved the way she would do anything for Shania and her friends. Loved how she looked at him. The sound of her voice.

"I love a lot of things about your mom."

"But do you love her? Gregory didn't. He just wanted to fit into her life. He never did, but you do. If you love her then that's okay."

"I think your mom should be the first person to hear my feelings." Because the realization that he had fallen in love with Halle had his world spinning. He wanted to believe it was too soon, that he was still in the throes of infatuation, or that this was the precursor to love, but he knew that wasn't the truth.

Shania grinned and sat back in her chair. "You love her. I can see it."

Quinton sat up straight and frowned. "How do you know that?"

"Because everyone gets a goofy look on their faces when they fall in love. You look goofy."

Quinton grunted and scowled. "Teenagers."

Shania laughed off his comment. "Can I go to your place and see Grandma and Grandpa? Mom won't mind."

Quinton blinked, surprised that she would want to spend time with his parents instead of going home, but thrilled that she believed what he said. "First, you need ask your mom if it's okay. And, you need to talk to your mom about what happened today. You stormed out today without talking to her. You shouldn't do that."

Shania lowered her eyes and bit the corner of her lip. "I know. I was just upset."

"Even when you're upset you need to talk to us. Storming off and ignoring a problem doesn't make it go away. Understand?"

Sighing, she straightened her shoulders and met his gaze. "I understand. So, I'll say this. I still don't understand how you two got together, but you're right about Mom. I'll wait and see what happens. I just don't want my mom to get hurt."

"Neither do I, Shania. Believe me when I say, you and your mom are two of the most important people in my life right now. I don't want to hurt either of you."

Thirty-One

HALLE WAS STILL UPSET ABOUT SHANIA RUSHING OUT of the house that morning when she got the text from Shania asking if she could go to Quinton's place after practice. They must have talked. Had they made up? If so, would Shania be as forgiving with Halle?

Instead of demanding that Shania come straight home and talk to her, she'd agreed to let her go visit her grandparents. Maybe Quinton had been right to let her calm down before they talked. Halle was used to facing everything head-on instead of letting it simmer and get worse. Her tendency to push did make Shania clam up. She hated to admit it, but this co-parenting thing might work if she and Quinton could tag team on dealing with Shania's problems.

Her cell phone rang as she neared Quinton's house. She quickly answered when she saw Imani's number. "Hey, everything good?"

Imani sighed. "Yeah, it's good. Work was hectic. Did you get a chance to talk to Tracey?"

Halle cringed. She was a horrible friend. "No, I was only able to text. She said she was okay, but I still want to check on her later today. What time are you done?"

"I'll be finished here around seven. I can shower and meet you over there."

"That's fine. I'm picking Shania up from Quinton's now. Call me when you're leaving your place."

"Oh, you're letting Quinton take her home." Humor entered Imani's voice. "Look at you letting go of some of the reins."

"I'm not that bad," Halle said.

Imani laughed. "You're not that good at sharing responsibility either."

Halle rolled her eyes. "You may be right about that. But I'm learning. It's not bad to have a little help with Shania. I think we're figuring this out. Especially after today."

"What happened today?"

Halle pulled up into Quinton's driveway. Well, at least she had proof Kayla hadn't put the word out to all their cousins. "I'll tell you when I see you later. I just got to Quinton's place."

"I can't wait to hear this. Okay, talk with you soon."

"Talk with you soon."

She hung up and got out of the car. She could only imagine Imani's expression when she told her about Shania catching her with Quinton. She'd rather save that conversation for an in-person discussion.

She rang the bell and Shania came to the door. She had a smile on her face that slowly melted away to a look of unease when she met Halle's eyes. Halle took a breath and clasped her hands in front of her.

"Are you still not talking to me?"

Shania lowered her head then looked up at Halle from beneath her lashes. "I'm sorry I ran out like that."

Halle raised a brow. Surprised by the contrite nature of her daughter's voice. She expected her to be upset. "You are?"

Shania nodded. "I thought you were only with Coach Q because of me."

Halle stepped forward and lifted her daughter's chin. "Why would you think that?"

"You were with Gregory, and I know you liked him, but I was worried you were trying to make him a part of the family because I kept asking about my dad. I don't want you to be into Coach Q just for me."

Shania's unease and worry made sense. Halle had liked Gregory and thought he was the right guy for her. The strong feelings Quinton sparked in her had even taken her by surprise. The realization that Shania would be upset and confused about all the changes in her life softened her tone. "Did I want things to work out with Gregory, yes. I did like him and I was interested, but my life changed. Dramatically, and it became clear that we weren't going to work out. But, I promise you, that I am not seeing Quinton just because he's your dad."

"But you kind of are. If I hadn't found out, you would have stayed with Gregory. You two wouldn't have gotten together."

"Maybe we wouldn't have gotten together. Maybe things with me and Gregory wouldn't have worked out and I would have given Quinton a chance later. Maybe both of us would have gone our separate ways and never dated. We don't know what would have happened if you hadn't discovered he was your father. That doesn't mean I shouldn't try to get to know him because we were put together under these circumstances."

Halle opened her arms. Shania stepped closer and accepted the hug. "This is all new and confusing and going to take some time to work out. But I promise you we're going to be okay. No matter what happens."

"Coach Q is a nice guy," Shania said when they broke apart. "He's also turning out to be an okay father. I guess it won't be so bad if you two got together. But can we wait to tell everyone you're officially a couple?"

"Why do you want to wait?"

"The kids at school aren't saying much because they don't want Coach Q to get on them, but they still talk."

Halle frowned. "Are they saying things to you?"

She shrugged. "Not everyone, but Octavius's girlfriend is trying to keep it going. She's just jealous because she thinks that he likes me."

"Does he?"

Shania rolled her eyes. "Yeah, but I don't like him like that. So, she wants to make it weird. Most kids don't care. I don't want to give her anything else to add. Can you two just keep it quiet until after football season? Maybe after Christmas break?"

Halle didn't mind waiting. The longer they kept the town out of their business, the easier it would be for them to get used to their new family dynamics. "I'll talk to Quinton." She wasn't going to agree to something that included him without talking about it first.

"Don't make a big deal about Octavius's girlfriend when you talk to him, okay? I can handle her. She wants me to react and I'm not giving her the satisfaction."

"I'll tell him that we want to be sure before we add more gossip for the town to feed off. That work?"

Shania grinned and nodded. "That works."

They went inside where Quinton sat on the couch watching television. He saw them and raised a brow. "Everyone good?"

Shania beamed. "All good. You two can date, but please, keep the kissing and stuff to a minimum around me."

"That's not a problem," Halle said.

"And use condoms. I'm not ready for a baby brother or sister."

Halle's eyes widened and her jaw nearly touched the floor. "Shania!"

Her daughter held up a hand. "What? You'd tell me the same thing if I was dating someone."

Quinton shook his head. "I think we can all agree that we're not ready to add another person to the mix."

Shania sighed. "Good." Her cell phone rang. She pulled it out of her pocket. "It's Grandma." She answered the call. "Hello? Now? Okay?" She looked at them. "Grandma is coming back from the store. She asked me to help her get something out of the car."

They watched as she turned and ran out of the house. Quinton came over and wrapped an arm around her waist. "You okay?"

"Sometimes it takes three days to get Shania out of a mood. How did you do it in one day?"

"I was honest with her. I told her that I'm serious about you. And I reminded her that her mom is pretty smart and wouldn't be with me just for her. She's a rational kid. She understood."

Shania was a straightforward kid. She shouldn't be surprised that Quinton realized the best way to deal with Shania was to be straight up and honest. He didn't raise his voice or fly off the handle. He was as calm and rational off the football field as he was intense and pushing on the field. And he'd been right to suggest they all cool down instead of talking in the heat of the moment.

"Thank you for talking to her. It's hard for me to get used to having someone to help with this, but it's kind of nice."

"Get used to it. We'll figure out how to make this a true partnership."

"You want to figure this out with me?"

He leaned down and kissed her. "Don't ask dumb questions you already know the answer to."

Halle grinned and kissed him back. The sound of a shriek came from the front of the house. They froze and broke apart. The shriek came again, and they ran outside. They stopped on the porch where Shania jumped up and down next to her grandparents. The shriek coming over and over. Quinton's parents laughed and clapped. Shania turned to them and pointed at the bright red car in the yard.

"They bought me a car! Can you believe it!"

A car. They'd bought Shania a freaking car! What in the world was she supposed to do with that? Hadn't they clarified all of this after the shoes? Why would they go against her and Quinton's wishes and get Shania a damn car?

The questions rolled through Halle's head as she made her way to meet Imani at Tracey's place. She had not handled the car surprise well. She'd immediately insisted that Shania couldn't accept. Quinton's parents had tried to make her feel guilty and Shania had cried. Shania never cried. Quinton had seemed just as shocked as she was. Thank goodness for that. She wouldn't have been able to trust him if she'd known he'd been involved.

She and Shania left in a hurry after that. All the goodwill they'd built up after the day they'd had was thrown out the window with one impulsive move. They argued on the way home about keeping the gift or sending it back. When they'd arrived at their house, Halle had let Shania storm off to her room to let off steam. She needed to cool off herself before having that conversation again. She'd forgotten about her promise to check on Tracey with Imani until she'd gotten the text from Imani saying she was leaving her place.

So Halle opted to try letting Shania cool down before talking and headed off to be a good friend. No matter how much she felt like her life was out of control, Tracey's had to be more so.

She and Imani arrived at Tracey's place at the same time. Bernard's car wasn't in the yard, but Tracey's Fresh Place Inn van was parked in the driveway.

"What's wrong with you?" Imani asked after they hugged.

Halle rolled her eyes but waved off her friend's words. "I'll tell you later. Let's check on Tracey first."

Imani eyed her then nodded. "You're not going to keep this to yourself, are you? You will tell us if you need anything?"

"I'll tell you. I promise."

They went to the door and rang the bell. No one answered, so they rang again. Halle knocked on the door. "Tracey, it's us. If you don't answer, I'll use my key." They knocked again.

A few seconds later, the lock clicked and Tracey answered. She was still wearing the outfit she'd had on the day before. Her braids hung loose around her face, and dark circles framed her eyes.

Imani and Halle immediately rushed forward and hugged her. Tracey let out a shaky laugh. "I'm okay. You don't have to squeeze the life out of me."

They pulled back. Imani studied her friend. "You don't look okay."

"Or smell okay," Halle said, raising a brow. "You smell like wine."

"I needed a lot of wine after Bernard left," Tracey said blithely. Her natural defense mechanism. This was bad.

Imani pointed toward the stairs. "Go shower and then we'll talk. You'll feel better after a shower."

Tracey didn't argue. She just turned and followed instructions. Halle and Imani exchanged glances before getting to work cleaning up the bottles of wine and empty ice cream tubs littering Tracey's kitchen. When Tracey came back to them freshly showered, her braids in a ponytail and in a pair of sweats, they handed her a cup of tea.

Tracey frowned at the mug. "Tea? I need something stronger than this."

Imani shook her head. "Doctor's orders. You're drinking tea for now."

Tracey sighed and sank onto her sofa. "Wait until you hear this and then we'll talk about what I do and don't need."

They settled on either side of her. Halle placed a hand on Tracey's knee. "What happened?"

Tracey stared straight ahead. "They've been seeing each other for a year. It started off as just sex, according to him. One time they hooked up and he said they never would again, but of course that was a lie. All the visits to help his cousin were nothing but a front for him to meet up with her in Augusta. Same for her, all her sick days or family emergencies were him. He said they fell in love three months ago."

Halle scoffed. Her hand balled into a fist. A fist she wished she could put in Bernard's face. "I can't believe this."

"He's such an asshole," Imani said.

Tracey's lips lifted in a sad half smile. "That's not all. She's pregnant. She told him at the luncheon and that's why they were kissing." A tear slipped down Tracey's cheek. "They're keeping it. He's going to *be there for his kid*." She said the last part with a sneer.

Halle sucked in a breath. "No, Tracey. How could he?"

Tracey looked at Halle with sad, angry eyes. "I wanted to have a kid. I asked him about having a baby. He said the time wasn't right. That he wasn't ready for kids. That kids would hold us back with me starting a new business. That fucking asshole said that shit to me just last week. And now he's ready to be a fucking dad?"

Tracey jerked up the mug and Halle quickly put a hand on her friend's arm. "Let's not throw the mug."

Imani nodded. "Especially since that is expensive-ass tea and Bernard isn't across the room to hit in the face."

The three of them let out a shaky laugh. Tracey sighed and sipped her tea. "Thank you. I'd only have to clean it up."

After a few quiet breaths, Imani asked softly, "What are you going to do?"

"What can I do? I'm not fighting for a man who cheated on me and got someone else pregnant. If she wants his trifling ass she can have him."

Halle ran a hand over her friend's back. "What do you need us to do?"

Tracey shook her head. "What you're doing now. Be here." Tracey groaned and pressed a hand to her forehead. "This is going to suck. Everyone in this town is going to know. They're going to talk about nothing but this."

"But this isn't on you. This is all on Bernard and Monique. You're the wronged person."

"Do you think the old gossips will care?" Tracey said bitterly. "They'll talk about me and my family. They always said Bernard was too good for me. That I was the hood chick he was giving a come up."

"Forget that," Halle said seriously. "He is not too good for you. Just look at what he did. He's the worst for you and anyone who blames this on you will have the Get Fresh Crew to deal with."

Imani nodded. "I'm ready to go off on anyone that has anything to say about you. And you know my mom, Cyril and his dad will do the same. You won't have to face this alone, Tracey."

Tracey gave them a grateful smile. Another tear spilled down her cheek and she hastily wiped it away. "Fuck Bernard. He's not worth my tears." She shook her head. "I don't want to talk about him anymore. Not tonight. Tell me something good."

"I got to eat lunch today," Imani said brightly. "Sit down and eat and everything."

Tracey laughed. "That is good." She looked at Halle. "What about you? No fights at the school?"

Halle sighed. "Shania caught me and Quinton kissing this morning, and this afternoon his parents bought her a car. So, my day's been interesting."

Imani sputtered. "What!"

Tracey's grin widened. "You must have lost it."

"I didn't," Halle said, lifting her chin. Her friends eyed her and she sighed. "I did. Quinton calmed her down when it came to us being together. She just wants us to keep it quiet for a while. The car thing. That's not going to settle for a while."

Tracey shook her head. "In-laws."

"They aren't my in-laws," Halle shot back.

"Maybe not now, but if you and Quinton stay together, they will be. Girl, nip this in the bud now. Bernard's parents were always in our business. Telling him that I was too busy and filling his head with nonsense. Get them together before things get out of hand."

Thirty-Two

"WHAT WERE YOU THINKING, BUYING HER A CAR?"
Quinton said as soon as he was back inside with his parents.

His mom raised her chin defiantly. "She's going for her learner's permit in a few weeks. She'll need transportation."

"She has transportation. Her mom has a car. *I* have a car. She doesn't need her own car." Quinton didn't raise his voice, but frustration sharpened his tone to a razor's edge.

"Don't talk to your mom like that," his dad jumped in. "Is this because of Halle? What did I tell you? Don't let her control you and how you treat your daughter."

"Dad, did you hear anything I said the other night? Halle and I are Shania's parents. *We're* responsible for figuring out what's best for her and what she needs. You two can't come here and undermine everything we say."

Dawn came down the hall. She gave the three of them a worried look. "What's going on? Why are you all arguing?"

Quinton turned to her. "They bought Shania a car."

Dawn's jaw dropped. "No, they didn't." She came farther into the room until her chair was next to Quinton. "Mom, Dad, why did you do that?"

"It was a good deal," his dad said stubbornly. "The girl will need a car. Let us do this for her."

Dawn shook her head. Disappointment clear in her eyes. "You saw how Halle felt about the shoes. Why would you think she'd be okay with a car?"

Laura crossed her arms. "She should have at least talked to us about the car. There's no reason for her to get so upset. I thought she was supposed to be calm and in control."

Quinton stared at his parents. Could they really not understand this? "You completely went against her wishes," he said. "Who's going to remain calm after all of that? You're going to have to take back the car."

"I'm not taking back the car," his mom said. "Me and your dad got it for her, and she can have it."

Quinton ran a hand over his face. He tried to remain calm, but they were pushing him to lose his temper. "Why are you being so stubborn? I don't get it. You never used to splurge like this. I know you wanted grandkids, but you've got to realize this is doing too much. You can't just buy Shania expensive gifts."

"Let us do for her what we couldn't do for you," his dad said.

Quinton pinched the bridge of his nose and sighed. "I didn't want cars when I was a kid. I didn't care about material stuff. All I wanted was for you to support me and back me up. That was it. Just to listen and help. That's all Shania wants and needs right now."

"We did that," his mom said. "We can do this now, too."

Quinton dropped his hand. "No, you didn't. You worked and you provided but you didn't listen. Not then and not now." Irritation and anger that they'd completely dismissed him kept him going. They'd been like this when he was younger. Just pushed what he said aside. "When I told you that Khris was bullying me, you didn't do a damn thing until it escalated to him breaking my leg. Maybe if you would have listened then things wouldn't have gone so far."

His sister grabbed his hand. "Quinton, don't go there."

He snatched his hand back. "Why not? They didn't listen then and they're not listening now. They just ignore issues until they become bigger. I won't let you do that with Shania."

His mom pointed at him. "We did listen to you. There wasn't much we could do back then."

He tilted his head to the side. If she was going there then he would, too. "Oh really? Is that the other side of the story you don't want to tell me?"

His dad scowled. "What story?"

"The story Khris told me to come and ask you about," Quinton said. He'd forgotten all about Khris's parting shot at the luncheon with everything else that happened. He wasn't even going to bring it up to his parents, but today with them being so clueless again, Khris's words popped back up. Khris said they knew why he'd treated Quinton the way he had. Had they known and let him suffer? Dismissing his pain like they pushed aside his words now?

"He said to ask you the other side of the story and then I'll be ready to talk to him. So, what is it? What was the reason you couldn't do anything back then that was so big you can justify buying Shania a car today?"

His mom threw up her hands. "I'm not listening to this." She turned to go into the kitchen.

"Don't walk away from this, Mom."

His dad didn't follow. "Just tell the boy," Willie said in a tired voice.

Laura spun toward her husband. "What are you talking about?"

"You might as well tell him. Khris is going to keep on pushing. Better hear it from us than him."

Quinton frowned. The fight from earlier pushed away by the shock of his dad's words. "Wait, he's telling the truth?"

Dawn's hold on his hand tightened. "Mom, Dad, what's going on?"

"Some things are better left unsaid," his mom said.

"It's too late for that now," Quinton countered. "If you know the reason why he's been bothering me then you might as well tell me. Otherwise, do you really think he's going to quit? He never quit back then, and he won't quit now. So, tell me the truth."

His parents exchanged glances. His dad looked away first. His mom's eyes became sad, and she looked at Quinton. "Khris is your half-brother."

When Halle got the text from Quinton asking if he could come talk with her later, she'd considered asking him to wait until the next day. She hadn't reacted to his parents' gift in the best way. She didn't feel like having another debate with him about how they messed up but meant well. But she didn't want to push him off. If they were going to co-parent and be in a relationship, then they would be best served talking out their situation rather than ignoring the issues.

He texted when he arrived and asked her to meet him outside. She was surprised, but went out after checking on Shania, who was asleep in bed. She hadn't been interested in talking to Halle since she was still mad about having to give the car back.

Halle went outside onto the porch. Quinton was already out there; he sat on the stoop and leaned against the stair rail. His head and shoulders drooped. She'd never seen him slouching. He was always confident, his back always straight and ready to tackle whatever came his way.

She quickly sat next to him on the top step. "What's wrong?"

He lifted his head. He didn't look at her but stared out over her front yard, not appearing to focus on anything out there. "My dad."

She raised her brows and waited. When he didn't say any more, she leaned forward to try to catch his eye. "What about your dad?"

"My dad is…not my dad?" His pitch rose at the end of the sentence, making it into a question and confusing her.

"What do you mean?"

He looked at her, hurt, confusion and shock on his face. He looked lost. Lost and vulnerable. Something she'd never thought she'd see when it came to Quinton, who was always steady. Always so self-assured.

"He's not my dad. I was talking to my parents about the car. They weren't listening. They never listen, they just do what they want or ignore things and hope they get better. I told them that. How they didn't listen to me about Khris bullying me. That they ignored it until it was too late, and my leg was broken and my football career nearly ended. Then I remembered something Khris said the day of the luncheon." The words came out of him in a rush. He took a breath, scowled and spoke again in a ragged voice. *"Ask your parents to tell you the truth then come talk to me.* That's what he said. I thought he was bullshitting because that's what he always does. I didn't think any more about it and wasn't going to ask them anything. But today, Khris's words came back. I asked them what's the real story and that's what they told me."

"That your dad isn't your dad?" The shock she felt mirrored his stunned expression.

He shook his head. "He's not my father. Khris's dad is my biological father."

Halle gasped. She reached out and placed her hand on his arm. Tension radiated through his body. "What? How?"

"My mom and Khris's dad dated secretly. She didn't know he

was also dating Khris's mom at the same time. When they both got pregnant, that's when she found out she was just the one he was seeing for fun. He married Khris's mom and denied being my dad. Apparently, it was about to be a scandal, but my mom also knew my dad…knew Willie. He liked her, he agreed to be there for her. They got married because of me to avoid my mom's family and the church from turning their back on her."

"Would her family have done that?" As soon as she asked she knew the answer. It was the reason she'd kept Shania's origins a secret.

He nodded. "My maternal grandfather was a preacher and the definition of conservative. He was going to kick her out of the family and the church, but my dad married her. She only married him to save face."

"Your mom seems to really love your dad."

"Does she? Are they really in love with each other? Or are they just together because of what happened with me?" He rubbed his temple. "I understand what Shania was saying now. The idea of being the only reason for your parents to be together. To wonder if they'd be better off if you didn't exist."

She tightened her hand on his arm. "No, don't say that. They would not be better off. The reasons why it happened or how you got here are one thing, but your parents care about you."

"It explains so much now. Why my dad always let my mom take the lead. Why he seemed to be more invested in my sister. She's actually his daughter. Why Khris's dad treated me, my mom and my dad like we were shit." Bitterness filled his voice.

Helplessness filled Halle. She could see the doubt in his eyes. The questioning of everything that made him who he was. The second-guessing. Each emotion tore her heart out.

She placed a hand on his cheek and forced him to look at her. "Quinton, stop it. Stop it right now."

"But he's not—"

"Your biological father. Your biological father sounds like a horrible person. You could have turned out just like Khris if he had claimed you. The fact that he didn't claim you already shows what kind of character he has. Instead, you were raised by a man who loved your mom. A man who loved you. Even I can see that he's proud of you and cares about you. Khris told you this to get exactly this type of reaction. For you to doubt and question everything. For you to doubt who you are. Would you want Shania to do that?"

He frowned, his eyes focusing on hers. "No. Of course not."

"Then you can't do that. She's struggled after finding out you were her dad. She didn't want what we learned to force you and I to be together. She could have questioned everything, too, but we showed her that she was going to be okay. You're going to be okay, too."

"How do you know that I'm going to be okay?"

"Because I've gotten to know you. You're steady, controlled and you look at everything from all angles. You aren't ruled by emotions and knee-jerk reactions. I know this is hard and you're allowed to feel everything you're feeling, but don't doubt who you are. Take a day or two to process and then talk to your parents. Ask all your questions."

"What if I don't want to know the answers?"

She wished she could tell him not to ask the questions with answers that might hurt him, but she couldn't. If he didn't ask, the not knowing would eat away at him, or worse, he'd make up his own mind about the answer and that could hurt more than the truth.

"Not knowing and guessing will only make things worse. Figure out what you really feel and what you really need to know, then ask the questions."

"Do you think I should call Khris?"

"Do you want to call him?"

He sighed and lifted a shoulder. "I don't know."

"You don't need the answer to that right now. Figure things

out with your parents first then worry about if and when you'll call Khris. You're not required to build a relationship with him just because you share a father."

He sighed and then chuckled. He wrapped an arm around her shoulder and pulled her against his side. "Thank you."

"For listening?"

"That and not pushing me to have an answer today. I just needed to get it out. I didn't want to go to Cyril's bar and risk being overheard."

"That's what I'm here for. Not just a girlfriend for great sex."

He laughed and she was thrilled that he sounded happy for a moment. That the desolation was gone from his voice. "That's good to know. I'm glad I subscribed to the listening and supportive girlfriend plan versus the just great sex plan."

She leaned back and looked at him through narrowed eyes. "Are you saying my plan doesn't come with great sex?"

"Never that." He pulled her in and kissed her slowly. "You're everything I could have asked for and more."

Thirty-Three

QUINTON SAT IN HIS OFFICE STARING AT HIS CELL phone on his desk. He took a long breath and thought about what he was doing. He hadn't talked any more to his parents about their revelation. They were still at his place; he ate breakfast with them, came home after football practice for dinner, then worked on grading tests and homework before going to bed and starting over. They didn't push him to talk either. That was how they were in his family. Nosey and intrusive as hell until it was something heavy. Even his sister was giving him space to process, which he appreciated. He needed to process everything they'd said.

That and he needed answers. Answers to something that bothered him almost more than discovering the truth about his dad.

With a sigh, he picked up his cell phone with one hand and the business card with Khris's number with the other. He dialed the number before he would change his mind again.

He answered on the third ring. "Khris speaking."

"It's Quinton."

There was a moment of silence before Khris spoke. "You got the entire story?"

"My mom told me that you're my half brother." He didn't bother beating around the bush. He wanted to get to the point of this discussion as soon as possible.

"I am."

"And you knew that when we were in school?"

"I found out in middle school."

"How? Did your dad tell you?"

"Our dad—"

"Your dad," Quinton cut in. He didn't care what DNA said; that man was not his father.

Khris hesitated a second before continuing. "My dad got drunk one night. I was telling him that you were trying out for the middle school team. That you were good. He got mad. Told me I was better. Then told me that I had to always be better than my bastard of a brother. I didn't really believe you were my brother. But the more he pushed me to be better than you, and he said it a few more times, the more I realized you really were his kid."

"He made you hate me?" Quinton asked. Confused and frustrated to know that a grown man was ultimately responsible for Quinton's teenage trauma.

"He made me resent everything about you. You didn't have what I had. Your family struggled. But you thrived. People liked me because my dad paid for their respect. People liked you because they respected you. The resentment he put in me turned into something else. It turned into my own hate."

"Why are you telling me this now?" Quinton asked.

"Because, when the Best Small Town application came by, and I saw that you were the football coach, I finally asked my dad if it was true. He said it was. Then he laughed about you falling from glory to become a coach of some rural football program. I wanted to see you. You're nothing like what he said. You're still getting respect. You've turned that damn team around. Hell, you even have a daughter who's kicking ass on the football field. I remembered how much I hated you just for existing. How he wanted me to hate you."

"Hate me enough to break my leg."

"Yeah…that was really fucked up on my part." Regret filled Khris's voice.

"Why did you do it?"

"Because he beat up on me the night before," Khris answered bluntly. "You were going to get recruited, I wasn't. I took it out on you. I was wrong for that."

"Yes, you were."

A pause before Khris answered. "I know we won't ever be brothers. Not for real, but I also didn't want to continue pretending like I didn't know. I wanted you to know."

"Why? So I'll second-guess my upbringing and my dad?"

"Nah, your dad loves you." Khris answered as if that thought never crossed his mind. "You don't know it, but he came to my dad after I broke your leg. I don't know what happened in that room, but I've never seen my dad that shaken before. He didn't say a word about you for the rest of the year or through college."

"My dad came to your dad?"

"He did. You got the better dad, Quinton. Never forget that."

When Quinton got home that night, he was surprised to find Willie sitting in the kitchen eating a piece of cake. He'd deliberately stayed out later than normal, hoping to avoid his parents and any awkward conversation.

"What are you doing up?" Quinton asked.

"Waiting on you. Shouldn't you be home early? You've got an important game coming up this weekend."

Quinton waved off his dad's words. "I'll be fine. I'm going up to bed."

"Quinton, wait."

Quinton stopped at the door of the kitchen and sighed. He turned, lifted his chin and faced his dad. "Sir?"

"You can't ignore me forever."

"I'm not ignoring you." He just didn't know what to say right now.

"Then what do you call it?"

"Processing."

His dad scowled. "What the hell is processing?"

Quinton hated it, but he wanted to smile at the ornery look on Willie's face. "What do you want me to call it? Trying to get my anger and frustration under control so that I don't say something to you or Mom that I might regret later."

His dad waved his hand as if urging him to come back. "Go ahead and say it. No need to hold back."

"I'm going to bed."

"Just say it, Quinton," Willie said firmly. "Don't be afraid. I'm a grown man. I can handle whatever it is you want to say."

Quinton eyed his dad and then crossed his arms. "I should have known. You all lied to me for years."

Willie flinched but didn't look away. "We did what we thought was best."

"Best for who? Was it better for me to hear this shit from Khris? From the guy who made my life hell for years?"

His dad's shoulders slumped. "I didn't think his dad would ever admit it."

"That doesn't make it better." Quinton turned to leave. The anger at them keeping this from him for so long bubbling like acid in his midsection.

"I didn't want you to leave."

Quinton turned around. "What?"

Willie glanced away before dragging his gaze back. "I

thought that if you knew he was your dad, you'd wish you had something better."

Quinton came back into the kitchen. "Why would I do that?" He never would have chosen Mr. Simmons over Willie.

"Because kids don't always appreciate what they have. I heard you one day wishing that we had something better to eat. You mumbled something about betting Khris had better for dinner."

"When did I say that?"

"It was so long ago you probably don't even remember, but you said it. That hit me like a knife through the heart. I loved you from the moment you were born. I never once thought of you as anything other than my child, but that day, I worried that if you knew the truth, you'd turn your back on me and try to be more like him. That man didn't want you then. He would have made your life a living hell or worse, used you to get back at your mom and play with your emotions."

"I never would have chosen him over you. Do you think I didn't see how much you sacrificed for me and Dawn? *You're* my dad. Always have been and always will be. You should have trusted me with the truth."

Willie's chin wobbled before he nodded stiffly. "Maybe I should have."

"No maybe." They were silent for a second when Quinton scoffed and shook his head.

"What?"

"I called Khris today. To see if he knew. Which of course he did. He admitted that was why he treated me the way he did. Said his dad was horrible to him and planted the hate he felt for me."

Willie let out a heavy breath. "I believe it. That man was horrible."

"Khris admitted the same. He said I had the better father. The thing is, he didn't have to tell me that. I already know I have the better father. I knew back then that you were the better man. I just wish you would have told me."

"What are you going to do now that you do know?"

He shook his head. "Nothing. I'm not trying to build a relationship with anyone over there. You're my dad." He was angry and upset they'd lied, but he knew that with every part of his being.

His dad let out a relieved sigh. "Thank you."

Quinton held up a hand. "But it's going to take me a minute to get over the fact that you and Mom lied to me. For so long. I need you to respect that."

Willie nodded. "We will."

"And respect what I'm trying to do with my own family. You've got to take the car back. Let me and Halle figure out the best things for Shania."

"But—"

"No buts. You tried to do what you thought was best for me back then and it backfired. Trust me to know what's best for me now."

His dad met his eyes and after a few seconds he nodded. "I trust you, son."

Thirty-Four

HALLE COULDN'T BELIEVE IT. SHE WATCHED AS THEIR quarterback threw the ball toward Octavius, but the Peach Ridge defensive player had him covered. Peachtree Cove was down by one point, and if Peach Ridge somehow got this interception, they would win. Her eyes jumped to the timer on the board. One minute to go. She sucked in a breath with the rest of the crowd. Then, out of nowhere, Shania cut across the field and caught the ball. The Peachtree Cove fans cheered.

Laura jumped to her feet. "She got it!" Laura called.

Willie was on his feet as well. "That's my grandbaby!"

Halle joined the rest of the fans on the Peachtree Cove side who'd jumped up and beamed with pride. Then cringed as the defensive player Shania had cut off tackled her to the ground. The ball remained in Shania's hands. The referee blew the whistle. Shania jumped up and the rest of the team ran over to her, clapping and cheering.

"That's it," Dawn said. "If we score, that's the ballgame."

"We've still got a little over a minute left," Halle said.

Dawn waved the Peachtree Cove flag in her hand. "They'll make it."

Sure enough, Peachtree Cove scored just as the timer went off. Cheers erupted as for the first time in seven years, Peachtree Cove finally beat their across-the-river rival, Peach Ridge, South Carolina. Halle slapped hands and cheered with the rest of the fans. This was a long time coming. She watched with pride as her daughter was slapped on the back and raised onto the shoulders of her teammates.

Halle couldn't help but smile. They'd started the football season with people doubting her ability, but she'd proven them wrong. Quinton hadn't given her special treatment, nor treated her as if she wouldn't be able to keep up. Shania had wanted to prove not just to the team but to herself that she could make it on the team, and she'd done just that.

"I'm so proud of her," Willie said.

Halle nodded. "So am I. Let's walk out of the stadium and get ready to greet them."

They made their way toward the exit but were stopped constantly along the way. Many of the same people who'd questioned her letting Shania play were now praising her for doing such a great job. Halle let them take back their words and give her daughter the praise she deserved.

"The people in this town are really proud of her," Laura said with pride when they'd finally made it out of the stadium and got a moment alone.

"They are now, which is good enough for me."

"I'm glad we'll be living here so we can watch her play every year."

Halle gave them a double take. "You're moving to Peachtree Cove?"

Laura gave her a hesitant look before nodding. "We just

made the decision. We mentioned maybe moving to Quinton, but…with everything that's happened, he probably forgot to mention it."

Halle didn't doubt that. Between Tracey's troubles, their buying the car and the revelation about Quinton's dad, they hadn't had time to talk about much else. She was glad Quinton had talked things out with his dad and Khris. It was going to take a lot of time for them to work out the pain of withholding the information, but she was happy knowing Quinton was now speaking to his parents and they were mending fences.

"No, he didn't mention it." She tried to sound neutral but wasn't sure if her disappointment was hidden. She liked his parents, but she wasn't sure how her and Quinton's relationship would progress if they kept meddling in their lives or going against their wishes when it came to Shania. Halle wanted time for their family to grow into each other; she worried his parents would force them all together.

Laura stepped forward. "I know you're worried."

Halle shook her head. "No, I'm not."

Dawn snorted. "I would be. My parents are not easy to live with."

Laura cut her eyes at Dawn before looking back at Halle. "Even though she's rude, Dawn is right. I know we overstepped our bounds with Shania. We were so happy to finally have a grandchild that we just wanted to do whatever we could for her."

Willie stepped closer to Laura. "We weren't able to do things for Quinton or Dawn. We've been doing for her what we couldn't do for him. But we realize that you're the parents."

Laura nodded. "I wouldn't take anyone stepping in and giving what I thought was charity to Quinton or Dawn when they were younger. I'd forgotten how I was like that. Until I saw how upset you both were with the car. We didn't think it through. I'm sorry, we're sorry. We'll respect your wishes and try not to interfere anymore."

Willie gave her a pleading look. "We don't want to drive you and Quinton away."

Halle relaxed, the trepidation from before easing a bit. "I reacted a little harshly with the car. I lost my parents young, and I'm not used to having grandparents intervene with Shania. I'll also try to be more understanding in the future." She held up a hand. "But still, no expensive gifts without talking to us first. Please?"

Laura smiled and pressed a hand to her heart. "I can promise that. And, Halle, I know we can never replace your parents, but we'd like it if one day you'll consider us as your family. If you think you can."

Dawn bumped Halle's side. "It would be cool to call you sister."

Halle couldn't speak. Words left her brain as the thought of them wanting to view her as their daughter swept over her. Though she'd started to accept that Quinton's family would embrace Shania, she hadn't considered them also embracing her. She really wasn't alone in this anymore. Shania not only had a support system that wasn't just Halle and her cousins, but Halle would also have their love and support. And she was okay with that. More than okay. "I'd like that very much."

"Well, Coach, when I'm wrong I say I'm wrong," Clyde Tucker said after the game.

"Wrong about what?" Quinton played dumb but he knew what Clyde was talking about. The rest of the team had already cheered and celebrated their victory over Peach Ridge. Everyone also acknowledged Shania was one of the stars of today's game. Her catch had kept them from losing. Quinton couldn't have been prouder. Though he didn't play favorites, he couldn't deny that tonight she was his favorite person on that team.

"About Shania," Clyde said slowly. "I didn't believe in her, but you've proven me wrong."

Quinton shook his head. "I didn't prove you wrong, she did. All I did was encourage her, like I asked you to do."

Clyde patted his chest. "You're right. My bad."

There was no reason for Quinton to hold a grudge. Clyde was a decent coach and a part of this team. As long as he admitted his mistake, Quinton was willing to move forward. "Just keep working with her. Today's win was good, but the season isn't over. Playoffs will start soon. Let's focus on winning those games."

Clyde laughed. "Alright, but you know as much as I do that this is the real playoff game. Congratulations, Coach." He patted Quinton on the back.

Quinton gave him a small smile even though he wanted to grin. As much as he played down this game, he was happy as hell to beat Peach Ridge! "Thanks, but we both know this was a team effort."

They headed out of the locker room toward the parking lot. He wouldn't be surprised to find the parking lot still full of Peachtree Cove residents celebrating the win and congratulating the kids on finally beating their rival.

What he didn't expect to find right on the edge of the parking lot was one of the cheerleaders in a shouting match with Shania. Octavius's girlfriend. Quinton cursed and hurried over as a crowd began to form. One glance and he summed up the situation. Octavius tried to hold back his girlfriend, who yelled at Shania. Shania stood there, arms crossed and disdain on her face.

Quinton immediately moved over to Shania's side. "Hey, hey, hey, what's going on over here?"

The girl stopped yelling and Octavius let her go, but she didn't stop glaring. "Tell your daughter not to be messing with my man."

Octavius sucked his teeth. "We're teammates. Why are you acting like this? We were just talking."

She pointed an accusing finger at Shania. "She wasn't just talking. A girl playing football. All she's trying to do is get with some guy. She's probably giving head to everyone on the team." A gasp went through the crowd.

Quinton's anger rose and he glared. Shania jumped forward as if to attack, but he held her back. He stepped in front of her and crossed his arms. "Repeat what you just said."

The bravado in the girl's face wavered and she leaned back. "It's not right."

"Before you start rumors about a player on my team, one who happens to be my daughter, I need you to think about what you're doing and the consequences."

A man pushed through the crowd. He moved Octavius aside and stood next to the girl. "What's going on? Are you threatening my daughter?"

Quinton looked at him. "I'm not making any threats toward your child. But your child did try to assault my child. Not only that, she's starting rumors and throwing insults. You better handle her before she's reported and suspended from school."

The man's chest puffed up. "My daughter isn't going to be suspended."

Jeremiah rushed forward. "Now, now, everyone calm down. It was just a misunderstanding."

Quinton turned to Jeremiah. Now wasn't the time for the principal to search for a compromise. "No misunderstanding." Quinton pointed to the kids with cameras recording everything. "We've got tons of video evidence right here. I want a thorough investigation on what happened and a promise that it won't happen again." He glared at the girl's father. "Understand me?"

The man wrapped an arm around his daughter. "They're just kids playing around."

Quinton slowly pulled off his aviators so the man could see his eyes and know he was dead serious. "Playing around until someone gets hurt for real." He looked at Jeremiah. "Deal with it. Or you'll be looking for another football coach." He turned to Shania. "Let's go."

She nodded and slid her hand in his. Quinton gave it a squeeze and led her from the crowd.

"Thank you," she said when they were several steps away.

"Has she said stuff like that before?"

Shania shrugged. "It's just girl drama."

"No, it's not just girl drama. It's wrong. Why didn't you tell us?"

"I was trying to handle it," Shania said defensively. "Besides, everyone knows she's just jealous."

"Never let people walk all over you. If they think they can get away with it, they'll keep going."

"I know. I just didn't want you or Mom to feel guilty about people teasing me."

He stopped walking and looked her in the eye. "We're adults. Our job is to protect you. Not the other way around. Understand me?"

Her eyes watered, but she blinked quickly and smiled. "I understand... Dad."

Quinton's world shifted on its axis. He *was* a dad. And he would protect her for the rest of his life. His own eyes burned, and his throat felt thick. Unable to speak, he nodded, squeezed her hand again and headed toward their family waiting near the exit.

Thirty-Five

EVEN THOUGH QUINTON AND SHANIA TOLD HALLE what happened after the game, and Quinton said he handled everything, she still felt the need to go to the high school during her lunch break and talk with Jeremiah herself. She wanted to make sure they were going to deal with the girl in question.

She was checked into the front desk and quickly led to the principal's office. Jeremiah came around his desk and shook her hand. "Halle, thank you for coming by."

"I wish it was for a better reason," she said in what Shania called her "principal's" voice. This wasn't a social call. "I want to talk about what happened after the game the other day."

"I was going to call you about that. Have a seat." He pointed to the chair in front of his desk.

Halle sat and Jeremiah sat in the one next to her instead of going around his desk. His face was serious. "Coach Q came to me first thing this morning. After calling me on Sunday to ensure that the school was going to investigate."

Halle leaned back. "He called you yesterday?" He'd reassured her yesterday that he would handle things, but hadn't mentioned calling Jeremiah.

"He did. First thing in the morning. He actually didn't have to worry. After the game, other parents and kids came forward with complaints about her. Apparently, she's been spreading rumors and bullying other girls in the school. We pulled her and her parents in this morning and showed the evidence of what she'd been doing. There was a lot. Her actions resulted in an automatic suspension and she'll have a hearing in front of the school board to determine if there needs to be any additional punishment."

Halle blinked. "You've already handled it."

"Like I said, we were going to call you and update you as well. I've already informed Coach Q."

"That was quick." Halle was impressed. She'd normally tell Jeremiah that if she wasn't so shocked.

"We like to deal with these things quickly."

"Or, were you worried about losing your head football coach?"

He didn't bother to deny. "That played a small part. But Coach Q has always been our anti-bullying champion. He heads up the anti-bullying committee at the school. Even if Shania wasn't his daughter, he would have had the same response."

She was not surprised to hear that. Just further confirmation that Quinton was an amazing person. "Is he in class?"

"I think this is his free period. I can have the ladies at the front desk check and see."

"If you don't mind."

Quinton was free and Halle was able to go to his classroom. Quinton sat behind his desk, eating a sandwich and watching something on his cell phone.

Halle knocked on his door. "Am I interrupting?"

He smiled and paused the video on his screen. "Not at all. Just watching ESPN on demand. Let me guess what brings you here," he teased.

She was glad that he didn't seem upset that she checked herself. He had to know her personality by now. "I came to check on the progress of the investigation, only to find out it's already handled."

He stood and came around his desk. He sat on the edge and Halle moved closer. "I urged Jeremiah to get on it quickly." He frowned. "I should have told you. I'm sorry."

She shook her head. "Actually, I'm good. You don't have to apologize for being a caring parent and coach."

"This was more of a parent move than coaching. Seeing that girl go after Shania like that. I never felt so protective in my life."

"I understand. I would fight a bear to protect her."

He nodded. "Same."

She took a step forward. Quinton shifted his position so that she could stand between his spread legs. Halle placed her hand on his shoulder. "But now I don't have to fight the bear alone. You'll be there to fight it with me."

He placed his hands on her hips. His gaze intent and serious. "I will. Are you okay with that?"

"More than okay. Quinton, you're my family now. I like having you in my life. I'm glad you turned out to be Shania's father."

He squeezed her hips and pulled her closer. "So am I. Shania is amazing. I couldn't have asked for a better kid." He smiled sheepishly. "She called me Dad the other day."

Halle chuckled. "I noticed she switched. I thought it would be weird, but strangely, it's perfect."

His smile faded and he looked her in the eye. "I love you, Halle. You and Shania. I know it's early and we've got a lot to work out, but you're my family now. I want to continue to build a family with you."

Her heart stopped then beat again at a hundred beats per minute. Her hands tightened on his shoulders. "I think I love you, too."

He raised a brow. "Think?"

She chuckled and then grinned. "I do love you, Quinton. Is this weird? Are we moving too fast?" Because she didn't feel like it, but she had to know that he felt the same. That he was ready to take this wild ride.

"Fast in love doesn't mean it's bad. Besides, we've got the rest of our lives to figure out what this love will look like. We're going to bump heads, we're going to go through ups and downs. We may not be a perfect family, but dammit, Halle. We are a family. Which makes it perfect to me."

Tears burned her eyes. Love and happiness she hadn't felt in years covering her like the warmest of blankets. "I've been alone for so long."

He pulled her into his embrace and whispered in her ear. "You're not alone anymore."

★ ★ ★ ★ ★

Please turn the page for a sneak peek at the next book in Synithia Williams's charming and witty Peachtree Cove series, available soon!

Enjoy this excerpt from Tracey and Brian's book!

One

TRACEY THOMPSON REALLY WANTED TO HIT SOME-
thing. If only she could pin a picture of her soon-to-be ex-
husband's face to the punching bag hanging in her brother's
garage and let herself go. He was the reason her life was in
shambles right now. He was the reason she'd had to hire a new
desk clerk for her bed-and-breakfast, the Fresh Place Inn, instead of continuing with the perfectly capable and mostly reliable front desk attendant who'd worked for her before. Too
bad the reason she was only "mostly" reliable was because of
that teeny, little slip of getting pregnant by Tracey's husband.
So rather than have someone who could actually do the job at
her side, Tracey had to tap into her very limited reserve of patience to make sure that Jessica, the new, unreliable and completely unmotivated desk attendant, didn't enter the wrong key
for the nice couple waiting to check in.

Tracey tried not to be a micromanaging, demanding boss.

She'd been very optimistic when she'd shown Jessica what needed to be done on her first day three months ago. She'd held on to that optimism when, two weeks later, Jessica said she had no idea what she'd done with the checklist that outlined everything she needed to do for guest registration and check-in. She'd even held onto her optimism three weeks after that when Jessica spilled her cappuccino on the keyboard for the fifth time, asking for another replacement keyboard before mentioning she needed another copy of the checklist because she "must have left it somewhere." Despite Jessica's tendency to forget everything she was taught and her inability to keep beverages in a cup, she was a body behind the counter and Tracey needed someone—anyone—to help her manage registrations.

Which was why she was once again trying to be patient as she watched Jessica ignore the newly printed checklist right next to her at the front desk and apologize halfheartedly to the waiting guests, claiming that "she was still new" and "hadn't been trained on the system yet."

Tracey took a long breath and clenched her teeth. She could go rescue Jessica, but she was pretty sure that's exactly what Jessica wanted. The instructions she needed tended to "magically disappear" whenever Tracey was around, and she'd call Tracey to help her figure things out.

Yep, Tracey really wanted to hit her soon-to-be ex-husband in the face. It was all his fault. She wouldn't be dealing with Jessica if Bernard had kept his dick in his pants instead of sharing it with her previous employee, Monique. Worst of all, Monique had been perfect. She'd implemented the new booking system to make online registrations easier. She'd been courteous and friendly with all the guests. She'd been Tracey's right hand at the inn from the day she'd opened the door.

If only she hadn't also been screwing Tracey's husband on a regular basis.

A hand patted her shoulder. The familiar scent of butter and cinnamon wafted over Tracey before she was pulled into a side hug. Shirley Cooke, the woman responsible for all the meals at the Fresh Place Inn, and Tracey's left hand when Monique had been her right.

"Stop scowling," Shirley said in her warm slow drawl. She was shorter than Tracey and older by a decade. Her pecan brown skin was lined around the eyes and mouth from her frequent smiles.

Tracey sighed and forcibly relaxed her face. "I'm not scowling."

"Yes, you are. What's wrong now?"

Tracey had watched Jessica fumble with the guests from around the corner of the hall that led to the kitchen. She motioned in that direction with her head. "Jessica."

Shirley rolled her eyes. "She's still struggling?"

"Yes."

"Does she have the checklist?"

Tracey nodded. "She does, and she hasn't picked it up once. I'm going to have to go help her."

Tracey moved but Shirley's arm around her shoulder tightened. "No, you don't. If you go help that girl, she'll never learn."

Jessica was far from being a girl. She was six years younger than Tracey's thirty-five. Maybe she would have been more patient if Jessica was nineteen instead of twenty-nine. At least then she could blame some of her laziness on youth.

"She hasn't learned in three months."

"If you have to do her work, then what do you need her for?" Shirley's question was rhetorical and often repeated.

"I need her because reservations are up now that Peachtree Cove got the Best Small Town designation. We're full almost every week, not to mention the reservations for weddings and birthday parties. I can't afford to let her go."

Shirley grunted before shaking her head. "That's just what you're telling yourself. You can find someone else."

"I don't have the time to look."

"So you're going to work yourself to the bone by managing this place *and* doing Jessica's job. While you're at it, can you come and cook for me?" Tracey cut her eyes at Shirley, who just cut them back before grinning. "What? You don't want to also handle the food?"

"First of all, you don't want me in your kitchen. I'll mess everything up. Second, I'll deal with Jessica. I just need to get through wedding season."

Shirley let Tracey go and threw up her hands. "Wedding season is a long time. Go on. Go help the girl. I saw another car pull up so it might be the other guests for the carriage house."

Tracey placed a hand to her chest and took a long, calming breath. "This is a good problem. This is a good problem." She chanted to herself.

Shirley patted her back. "It is. We'll figure it out. Don't worry."

"Thanks, Shirley," Tracey said before going into the reception area to help Jessica.

She didn't know what she would have done if she didn't have Shirley there. Shirley had kept things together while Tracey's personal life imploded. She'd made breakfast, lunch and dinner for the guests on time and to perfection. She was always there when Tracey needed her and ran her kitchen like a five-star general. Without Shirley reminding Tracey every day that she couldn't just give up her dream because her husband and employee were assholes, Tracey might have closed the inn. She still wondered how she'd gotten there. How she'd actually opened a bed-and-breakfast and was somehow keeping it going. Not many people had expected much of Tracey, including her parents. A part of her was still waiting for things to go wrong.

Her failed marriage was strike one. Strike two and three had to be coming.

She slid up next to Jessica. "Is everything okay here?" Tracey asked sweetly.

Jessica sighed and turned to Tracey with a relieved smile. "Ms. Thompson, thank goodness you're here. I can't figure out how to pull up their reservation."

Tracey kept the smile on her face despite the strong urge to roll her eyes. She looked at the guests, a married couple who'd thankfully remained congenial while Jessica fumbled their reservation. "Sorry for the wait. We'll get you checked right in." She reached for the checklist right next to the iPad with the reservation app.

Tracey pointed to the first step in the checklist. "First let's input their last name here."

Jessica nodded and watched Tracey with wide, clueless brown eyes. Tracey's smile slipped. Jessica wasn't clueless. The woman had graduated from the University of Georgia with a hospitality degree. Tracey had given her the job after someone in the Peachtree Cove Business Guild mentioned their friend's brilliant daughter had just graduated and needed a place to work and recommended her to Tracey. Tracey, struggling after losing Monique in such an embarrassing way, had interviewed Jessica without bothering to check her references and hired her on the spot. A mistake she wouldn't repeat. No, Jessica wasn't clueless. She was brilliant. She could teach a class on how to feign ignorance, and play the damsel in distress, so others would do your work. Tracey knew what Jessica was up to, but, again, she needed someone there and some help was better than no help.

Sighing, Tracey turned back to the couple. "Last name, please."

"Davis," the man said.

Nodding, Tracey input their name and proceeded to quickly pull up their reservation. Jessica pretended to watch, but when the second couple came in, she gave up pretense and moved aside to start scrolling through her phone. Tracey got both couples registered, gave them the keys to their room and then walked them around the inn to explain where the rooms were, when food was served and how their access to the grounds worked. Thirty minutes later, she went back to the reception area to go through the checklist once again with Jessica, except she was nowhere to be found.

Instead, a man leaned against the reception desk. Tracey would recognize his profile anywhere and she cursed.

"Shit, Brian, my bad." She rushed over to the desk.

Brian Nelson straightened and turned to face her. His face was a mask of boredom. His usual expression, as if everything in the world was so far beneath his interest. He was tall, with dark brown skin, piercing black eyes, and curly hair cut into the sharpest fade she'd ever seen. In short, Brian was a pretty boy. Or at least that's how she'd always viewed him in high school. When he'd moved back to Peachtree Cove and opened a nursery, of all things, she'd been surprised he would bother getting his hands dirty.

"You doing Jessica's job again?" he asked in a deep lazy drawl.

Tracey narrowed her eyes. "You minding my business again?" She hated it when he pointed out the obvious. Something he tended to do often and only with her.

Brian tapped the watch on his wrist. Not the expensive ones he wore when he got pretty boy fine and she'd see him at the bar or out with a woman—he was always with some new woman—but an older watch with a worn leather strap. It matched the worn jeans that sagged just enough to make him look interesting, dirty Henley shirt that clung to his broad shoulders, and muddy Timberland boots. He must have come from moving shrubs for another job.

"It's my business when you keep me waiting." He spoke in his "you should know this already" tone.

Tracey also hated that tone. It unnerved her and made her feel like he was judging. So, she did what she always did when Brian Nelson judged her: she pretended as if she didn't care.

"Whatever." She waved a hand. "Did you bring what I need?"

He raised a brow. "I'm here to go over the plans for the wedding so *you* can tell me what you need. Have you picked anything yet?"

Tracey was speechless. Then she cursed and slapped her palm to her forehead. "Damn, my bad. I forgot to give you that."

Between Jessica, the lack of help, and navigating her upcoming divorce she was forgetting to do a lot of things. She wouldn't focus on that now. She would get her life together, but first, she needed to make sure the wedding this weekend went perfectly. She needed shrubs from Brian's nursery to make that happen.

She lightly slapped his arm. "Come on out back and let me show you the setup."

Two

TRACEY LED BRIAN OUT TO THE YARD ON THE SIDE of the bed-and-breakfast where she hosted outdoor weddings and other events. She walked quickly, but Brian had no problem keeping up with her. She wished he would linger behind and take his time. She hated being caught off her game and she hated it even more when Brian caught her off her game. Maybe because Brian Nelson had been catching Tracey off her game since she was in high school.

She hadn't liked him back then. The good-looking, popular boy that all the girls in school had a crush on. Herself included, but she'd known that Brian wouldn't look twice at her. He was raised by well-brought-up parents, lived in a nice house on the good side of town, was a star in both basketball and wrestling, and had a new girlfriend every quarter. She, on the other hand, was the girl brought up in the Section 8 apartments in town, with the alcoholic father and a mother who cheated on him constantly. Tracey's smart mouth constantly got her into trouble at school and the only guys who were interested in her were the ones who thought she was just as easy as her mom.

Every time she was in the principal's office for going off on someone for talking about her family, Brian was also there getting praised. Whenever she stumbled over her own two feet marching in JROTC, Brian was there doing a perfect about-face in a freshly pressed uniform. And when she'd accepted Cornell Murphy's invitation to the JROTC ball senior year because she'd foolishly believed he liked her…only for him to try and shove his hand up her dress in the hallway, Brian was the one who'd witnessed that embarrassing moment and the one that followed when she'd punched Cornell in the stomach so hard he'd thrown up on Tracey's new shoes. Then, when they were adults, he'd been the first person to notice Bernard, her soon-to-be ex-husband, was cheating.

Yep, most of her embarrassing moments in high school were witnessed by Brian and he'd continued to witness them when he'd moved back to Peachtree Cove as an adult. Which meant it was par for the course that he would be there just as she ran back into the inn, frustrated and flustered from doing Jessica's job.

"Where's the fire?"

Tracey stopped and spun to face him. "What?"

He gave her the same bland *I'm bored with this* look that he always wore. Except this time a raised brow accompanied it. He pointed to her feet. "You're damn near running. I thought maybe something was on fire."

Tracey narrowed her eyes. "Hardy har har. You're so damn funny," she said in a flat voice.

"Why are you upset? It's your own fault."

"What's my own fault?"

He pointed to the back of the inn. Jessica was on her phone at the back corner. "You should have fired her two months ago."

"I need help right now. You, of all people, should know how busy things are."

"If you're doing her job, is it really help?"

Tracey crossed her arms over her chest. "You were in the kitchen with Shirley, weren't you?"

Brian shrugged his shoulders. "Doesn't matter where I was. My point still stands. Jessica isn't doing her job. Even I know that. You're running around here like a chicken with its head cut off doing her work and yours. Get rid of her and hire a real manager."

Tracey took a deep breath. She was not going to curse out Brian. She was not going to kick him off her property. She needed his help, even if she didn't want his very obvious and completely unsolicited advice.

After she'd calmed herself, she asked in an even tone, "Do I tell you how to run your nursery? No. So worry about that and not about my inn."

"Then don't keep me waiting next time," he shot back easily.

Tracey shook her head and smirked. "You'll wait because I'm your biggest customer. Now hush up and listen."

Brian grunted, but the corner of his mouth lifted. Despite him having a front-row seat to the "All things embarrassing about Tracey's life" show, Brian also refused to let her sharp tongue cut him. Which was why she couldn't quite go from being consistently annoyed with him to straight up disliking him. Brian witnessed her shame, made the occasional offer of advice she didn't want or need, and then moved on. That she appreciated. Other people took joy in reveling in the messed-up stuff in her life. He never did.

"What's the layout?" he asked.

Tracey looked around the yard and envisioned it with the white chairs set up for a small wedding. "The usual. A small wedding. The happy couple will be in the gazebo." She pointed to the wooden gazebo at the far end of the yard. "There will be about fifty guests. The colors are red and yellow, so I need flowers or shrubs to go with that."

Brian frowned as he considered the yard. Tracey let him do what he did. The side yard for the Fresh Place Inn was cute and quaint, but it wasn't very decorative. Tracey used Brian's nursery to provide the extra pizazz needed for events. He brought in shrubs and flowers of various colors and sizes to provide natural decoration. Tracey paid him for the temporary use, and then he hauled them away after the wedding was complete.

"I can bring in some gold zebra and maybe some admiration barberry. We can put those around the gazebo."

Tracey nodded. "I don't know what you're saying, but I trust your judgment. Do it."

Brain turned to her with a quizzical look. "You're not going to hand select the flowers this time?"

She shook her head. "I don't have time. The wedding is this weekend."

His head fell to the side and his eyes widened. "Saturday?"

"Yeah."

"Tracey," he sighed, looked heavenward, then shook his head. "It's Monday, Tracey. You know I need more time to get the plants in."

"I know, but this slipped through the cracks. I thought I'd already booked the shrubs with you, but I didn't."

"What if I can't do it by Saturday?"

Her heart jumped damn near out of her chest. If he couldn't then the cute side yard she'd promised the bride would not be possible. The bride would leave a horrible review. Others would pile on and then the inn would fail. Probably not immediately, but if she kept this up it would.

She clasped her hands together as if praying and held them out to Brian. "If anyone can do it by then it's you. Please, Brian, do this for me." She may not be as easy as her mom, or half as desirable, but she did know that if she batted her eyes and pleaded her pitiful look sometimes worked on Brian.

Brian rubbed his temple. "How did this slip through? You used to be better organized than this."

"I used to have a good person working next to me, but now I don't. So, this is what happens."

He dropped his hand and his eyes met hers. "Don't do that."

"Do what? Bring up why I had to hire Jessica and let important things like booking the flowers for a wedding at my inn slip through the crack? Why not?"

"You need to let that shit go," he said easily. As if getting over betrayal and heartbreak was something a person could just wake up one morning and say, "Yeah, that sucked, but I'm over it now."

"Well, I can't. You, more than anyone, should also know why I'm struggling here."

His eyes narrowed. "Don't go there."

"Too late. I'm already there. I've set up a chair and got comfortable." She took a few steps closer until there was only a few inches separating them. "So, because you know why I'm floundering. With the increased bookings and popularity of Peachtree Cove, you should know that I really need you to do me a solid and get the shrubs here for the wedding on Saturday."

Brian glowered down at her. Hands on his hips and nostrils flared. She had to fight not to smile back at his frustration. She loved frustrating Brian, mostly because his observations frustrated her. He was also cute when he was upset. She liked watching the cool, playboy, down-for-whatever façade disappear when she pushed his buttons. And, again, he was cute when he was upset. Teenage Tracey liked to come out and play and remind her of the old crush she used to have on him.

"What time is the wedding?" he asked through gritted teeth.

She didn't bother to hold back her smile. "Two in the afternoon."

His eyes narrowed more but he asked, "What time do you need them set up?"

Her cheeks hurt from the grin on her face. "Can you get it set up by eleven?"

He pointed at her. Tracey grabbed his finger and shook it. "Thank you, Brian. You're a life saver. And, I'll pay you ten percent extra."

He sighed and jerked back on his finger. Tracey let him go. "Get rid of Jessica, get your schedule under control, and don't do this again."

She nodded. "I'll get it worked out."

"I'm for real, Tracey. You can't keep going like this. Losing Monique the way you did was messed up, but don't ruin your life trying to prove that you can keep doing this by yourself."

The smile fell off Tracey's face. In the blink of an eye, he'd reminded her why he stayed on her annoying person list. "Quit minding my business."

He pointed around the yard. "This last-minute thing makes it my business." He reached over and tweaked her chin before turning and walking away. Full-on swag with his ridiculously long legs and broad shoulders. Damn him!

Tracey gave his back the finger. He looked over his shoulder at the same time and caught it. Then, in Brian Nelson fashion, he grinned, turned away and kept on walking.

Don't miss the next book in Synithia Williams's
Peachtree Cove series, available soon!